ENCORE FOR MURDER

AN AMY ROWLINGS MYSTERY

T. A. BELSHAW

For Sue
Best Wishes

SPELLBOUND BOOKS

07/25

This book is dedicated to the memory of Carole Ann Ford, a wonderful lady who was a great support to authors in many online book clubs and groups over the years. Carole was a good friend and an avid collector of my books and merchandise. I will miss her.

CHAPTER ONE

The high winds that had battered the north Kent town of Spinton for over a week finally eased off, leaving the streets covered with a carpet of autumn leaves and many buildings missing roof tiles. Trees had fallen, partially blocking the busy Gillingham road. In the centre of the town, the famous, ancient, horse chestnut tree that sat behind the boundary fence at the back of the town hall, had survived after losing two thick branches and spreading its spikey conkers across the parkland it had called home for over two hundred and fifty years.

Alfie Graham, a man in his late forties who had worked in the council's parks department for most of his working life, grunted as he let go of his end of the huge two-man crosscut saw and motioned to his workmate, to do the same.

'Take five minutes, Dan,' he said as he stretched and looked over the carcass of the old beech that had given up its battle with the deadly winds over the weekend and come crashing down across the Gillingham road, narrowly missing a truck carrying newly conscripted troops heading towards their training camp in southern Kent.

'I doubt German bombers could have caused much more

damage,' he said as he wiped his brow before bending to pull his thermos from his knapsack. After drinking almost half of the remaining tepid tea in one long gulp, he replaced the cap and pushed the flask back into his pack.

'We don't know how much damage they can do yet. We've not seen hide nor hair of them since war was declared,' his colleague replied. 'When they do come, I think we'll know about it. I reckon it'll be buildings we'll be clearing then, not trees.'

'Aye, maybe you're right,' Alfie replied, placing his hand on the long saw. 'Come on, let's get this bugger shifted or our brave young lads will never get trained to shoot straight.'

In Spinton itself, little had changed since the declaration of war on the third of September. Apart from the sight of a few military vehicles and the huddles of young men with their families on the station platform, life went on pretty much as normal.

The only major change young Amy Rowlings had noticed working at a factory nicknamed The Mill, a building that dated back to the cotton industry in the late eighteenth century, was that the factory had taken on government contracts and instead of producing women's clothing they were now turning out heavy serge uniforms for the military.

Amy was a bright, flaxen-haired twenty-one-year-old who had worked at The Mill since leaving school with a distinction in her national school certificate. Amy was a collector of American records, supplied by her uncle, who ran his own importation business. She was also an avid reader, especially of her literary heroine, Agatha Christie. Amy devoured her books, particularly the ones starring her fictional hero, Hercules Poirot.

Over the past year, she had assisted Inspector Bodkin of the Spinton police in no less than five of his murder inquiries. The police hierarchy had been so impressed with her input during the investigations that they issued her with an identity card with the words, Police accredited, printed on it. To get the recognition Amy had set up her own private investigation agency, ARIA (Amy Rowlings Investigations Agency) although time constraints meant she had never taken on a single case outside of the ones she had been invited to take part in by the untidy, thirty-year-old, ruggedly handsome Inspector Bodkin. The pair had become involved in a deepening personal relationship over the year and were now considered an 'item' by Amy's family and her best friend, twenty-one-year-old Alice Mollison, a single mother and farm owner who lived just down the lane from Amy. They had been best friends since childhood. Alice had taken on the responsibility of running the farm following the death of her father the year before.

Amy's own father had recently been promoted to the position of production manager when the factory he worked at in nearby Gillingham had switched to making parts for the newly developed Spitfire aircraft that the government was desperate to get into production. To Amy's absolute delight, the company had insisted that the Rowling's household should be connected to the telephone network. Amy had been begging her father to have a phone installed since Alice had hers put in at the end of nineteen thirty-eight. Although they lived on the same lane and the dwellings were a mere five hundred yards apart, Amy had dreamed of being able to speak to Alice any time she felt like it.

Amy spent every Saturday morning perusing the rails at her favourite clothing store, Brigdens. The shop sold high-quality second-hand garments, some of which had only been worn once or twice. Although Amy dreamt of one day buying a couple of the dresses featured on the mannequins that were dotted around the store, in reality she could only afford to buy the items with a loose seam or some other minor imperfection that had been placed on two sales rails at the bottom end of the shop. Amy had a wardrobe full of dresses, tops, and skirts that she had come across on the rails. She was usually found hanging around the front of the shop when Sharon, the assistant, who had become a good friend of Amy's over the years, opened the double doors at nine AM on Saturday mornings.

On the morning of Friday the 27th October 1939, Amy stamped her timecard in the machine in the loading bay of The Mill and walked through to the changing rooms, where she found the rest of her machinist friends and acquaintances tying up their flower patterned pinafores and headscarves, before taking their place at their machines. Amy wiggled her fingers at her best friend Carol and smiled at one or two of the other women as she took off her coat and hung it on a peg before bending to fish out her own pinny and headscarf that she had fashioned into a turban. She sighed as she heard the whiny tone of the factory's head gossip monger, Big Nose Beryl, as she began to pronounce on the hot news she had picked up the previous evening.

'I was told last night that Dom Fieldman is trying to help his son avoid the call up. I heard from a very good source that he's sending him over to stay with relatives in Ireland so he can dodge conscription. He's twenty-two now, so the registration papers ought to be falling on their doormat this week.'

Amy tied off her apron behind her neck and shook her head sadly as she replied to her colleague. Beryl, despite her nickname, didn't have a particularly big nose, she just couldn't resist sticking it into other people's business.

'Beryl. Do you ever have anything nice to say about anyone?'

Beryl gave Amy one of her looks and tapped the side of her nose. 'It's from a good source. Someone very close to the Fieldman's.' She looked around the room with a look of disgust on her face. 'He can't be allowed to get away with it. Our sons will have to go and fight for the country. Why not his?'

'You don't have any sons, Beryl,' Amy said.

'I was speaking fig leaf tea,' Beryl retorted.

'FIGURATIVELY,' Amy replied.

If Beryl was embarrassed by the correction she didn't show it. 'He has Germans in his family tree, doesn't he? The surname gives him away. It ends in man... loads of German names end in that.'

Amy sighed again. 'Surnames ending with man can come from a lot of different sources,' she argued. 'They aren't just common in Germany. What about Freeman? That's Old English for someone not tied to the land as a serf. What about Bergman? That came over with the Vikings, so it's Scandinavian. There are lots of examples; it doesn't mean someone came from Germany.'

'Bergman is still foreign,' Beryl sniffed. 'Anyway, if he does have German relations it explains things, doesn't it?'

Beryl looked around for support but found none, except her best friend and fellow gossip, Mabel, who nodded her head sagely.

'You're right, Beryl,' she said. 'It doesn't look good, does it?'

Amy pulled on her homemade turban and tucked a few loose strands of hair up inside.

'So, the fact that Dom's son, Benny, works at Mollison Farm and, as a farmworker, will be exempt from the call up along with miners, policemen and munitions workers AMONGST OTHERS, doesn't count?'

Beryl shook her head vigorously. 'It shouldn't matter. If he's old enough, he should face the German guns like the rest of the brave young men of the town. He shouldn't hide behind that excuse.' She paused for a moment, then looked directly at Amy.

'That policeman of yours will dodge the draft then... that's very convenient, I must say. No wonder you're sticking up for Benny blooming Fieldman.'

Amy shook her head again. 'That's a different argument altogether, Beryl. A few seconds ago, his dad was sending him off to Ireland to stop him having to kill his German cousins.'

'He'll be on the next boat. You wait and see.'

'I won't have to wait long to find out, Beryl. He works at Mollison Farm, so that means he works for my best friend Alice. I'll give her a call from the phone box at lunchtime and ask if he's turned up for work today, if you like?'

Just before lunch, Amy cut the thread and hauled the last serge jacket of the morning across her machine and dropped it into the finished garment bin. A few seconds later, the hooter sounded and she stood up, stretched, then made her way along the aisle that separated the lines of machines. After waiting for Carol to finish her final pair of battledress trousers, the two friends walked towards the canteen to get their lunch. As they passed the inspection room where the garments were checked before being shipped out to their various destinations, Amy heard her name being called out and after telling Carol she'd catch up with her in the canteen, she stepped through the open doors and made her way along a line of steel inspection tables to where her workmate, Julia, was waiting wearing a big smile on her face. Amy grinned back.

'Did he ask you, Julia? I can see he has by the look on your face. Oh my dear, I'm so happy for you.'

Julia pulled her hand from behind her back and wiggled her fingers in front of Amy's eyes to show off her engagement ring.

'He asked my dad last night. He wants us to marry before he gets his registration papers. He's twenty-three, so Mr Chamberlain will be sending it out to him soon. He only just missed the latest one. Unfortunately, he's not in a reserved occupation like your Mr Bodkin or Benny Fieldman.'

Military registration had been made compulsory for all men not in reserved occupations from the ages of twenty-one to twenty-two on the 17th of October. Amy was sure that the next call up would be for men aged twenty-three and above and that it would be announced soon. She looked at Julia with an expression of sadness on her face.

'Oh, Julia, I'm so sorry. I didn't even think about that. Poor Raymond... and poor you.'

Julia sighed. 'Oh, he's quite excited by the idea... the war that is, not our engagement... though I might be doing him an injustice there. He really wants to get married quickly so we get a bit of time together before he has to go. He's nipping around to the register office in his lunch break today to see if he can book a date. I asked if he'd rather not just stay engaged until he comes back, but he said if we get married before he goes, I'll get what's called a separation allowance from the government and he can have part of his wages paid to me. I won't get that as his fiancée. He said if I can afford to live on my wages from The Mill, I should be able to put the rest away every week and depending how long the war lasts, there could be a tidy sum waiting when he gets home. Enough to get us started with the deposit on a house, even.'

'He seems to have it all worked out,' Amy said with a sad smile. She leaned towards Julia and kissed her on the cheek. 'Congratulations, my dear. I hope I'll get an invitation to the wedding.'

'It depends on what date he can get. He thinks a lot of couples might do the same thing so the wedding might take place midweek when all of our friends are at work. We'll have a bit of knees up in the Bell or the Old Bull the weekend after, though, so you'll be invited to that.'

'I'll look forward to it. I'm so happy for you.' Amy gave Julia a hug, then turned away towards the door. As she walked, she looked over her shoulder towards Julia, who was looking at her engagement ring with a sad look on her face. Turning back to face the door, she tripped over a pair of battledress trousers that had fallen from the tall pile to her right. Grabbing at thin air, she fell to the ground with her right arm held out in an attempt to break her fall. As she hit the floor, she shrieked as the weight of her body forced her wrist into an unnatural angle. Rolling onto her back, she pulled her hand towards her midriff and cradled it in her left hand.

'Amy, are you all right?' Julia shouted as she hurried towards her.

Amy winced as she sat up, using her left hand for support.

'I think I've broken my wrist,' she said, as tears of pain flowed down her face.

'Wait there,' Julia said. 'Don't move, Amy, I'll get Harold Swarkestone, the first aid man from the canteen.'

Amy nodded through her tears as she looked down at her already swelling right hand. She kicked out at the pair of battledress trousers that had caused her to fall. 'How am I going to manage now?' she whispered.

CHAPTER TWO

'It looks to be a bad sprain, Amy. I'm pretty certain it isn't broken because you can bend it.' Harold, the factory first aid officer, was a machine mechanic who stepped up if one of the workers sustained an injury. He finished wrapping the bandage around Amy's wrist before snipping it with his scissors and tying off the bandage. 'You can go to the Royal Free for a second opinion if you like.'

She winced as Harold formed a sling and tied it off behind her neck. 'Sorry, Amy, but it needs to be supported properly.'

'I'll trust your judgment, Harold,' Amy said with a weak smile. 'For a while there, I honestly thought I'd broken it.'

'I saw plenty of broken wrists back in the Great War,' he replied. 'I was a medical orderly in the trenches. I know a sprain from a break.'

'I bet you saw a lot worse, too,' Amy said with a weak smile. Harold helped her up from the chair and packed away the spare bandages and strips of plasters into a white metal box with a red cross on the lid.

'I try not to think about it too much,' Harold said. He was a tall, stringy man with tufts of wispy hair lying across an increasingly balding pate. He groaned as he straightened his thin frame. 'Are you sure you don't want to go to the Free hospital? I can ask if Mrs Handsley will allow someone to go with you on the bus.'

Amy shook her head. 'I'll be fine, Harold, thank you, but I'd better go up to the office to let her know what's happened and to see if she can put me on light duties for a while. I can't afford to be off work without wages.'

'There isn't any light work since we started on the uniforms, Amy,' Harold replied. 'But don't you work two days a week at her dress shop in town? There might be some extra days up there for you.'

'I have to help women in and out of their clothes at the London Connection,' Amy said, grimacing again as she walked alongside Harold towards the door. 'I doubt I can do that with my arm in a sling.' She looked down at it. 'How long do you think I'll have to keep wearing it?'

'It depends how bad the sprain is, Amy, but I'd say at least a fortnight. When you take it off, your wrist will be weak for a time, even bandaged up.'

Amy sighed, thanked Harold again for looking after her, then made her way across the shop floor to the two sets of stairs that led up to the mezzanine, where the offices were situated.

Georgina Handsley was a tweed-clad woman with a body the shape of a cottage loaf. She was around sixty years old with steel-grey hair tied back in a severe, Victorian style bun which stretched the skin on her face, pulling her eyebrows up, giving her the appearance of being continually surprised.

'Oh dear, Amy, what have you been up to?' she said as Amy pulled open the door to the office.

'I tripped over a pair of soldier's trousers, believe it or not,' Amy replied, looking forlornly at the sling.

Georgina's expression turned to one of mock shock. 'I'd keep that to yourself if I were you,' she said, before smiling.

'Oh dear,' Amy said, blushing. 'I'd better find a new way of saying that.'

Georgina pulled a chair from under the desk and held the back of it until Amy had sat down. Then she walked around the desk and settled into her own chair.

'I take it you've come to inform me you're going to be away from your machine for a while?'

Amy shrugged, then yelped in pain. 'I was hoping you could find me something to do. I can't afford to be off work with no wages.'

Georgina pursed her lips as she thought. 'I don't have anything on the shop floor, Amy.' She sighed. 'We're going to miss your output. You know how highly we regard the quality and speed of your work.'

'That's very kind of you. So there's nothing at all I can do?'

'It's all heavy duty work these days, Amy. You can't possibly use your machine and the garments are too heavy even for you to be given a job checking uniforms before they go out for delivery.' She narrowed her eyes as she had an idea. 'Can you write left-handed?' she asked. 'We might be able to find something for you in the office.'

'I'm sorry, I can't. I'm totally right-handed. The left one is only there to pick things up or help guide garments through the machine.' Amy lifted her left hand and looked at it. 'I can't even think of anything I could do in the London Connection shop if I can't pick items from the stock rail for the customers or help them dress.'

'No, I can't either, Amy. It looks like we're stuck.' Georgina gave her a sad smile. 'How bad is it? Did Harold have any idea?'

'Not bad enough to need the hospital,' Amy replied. 'But he said it would be at least a fortnight before I could take the sling off. Even then, it will be very weak.'

'That's a shame. So it could be a month or more before you're back?'

Amy's face dropped as she took in the consequences of her situation.

'I'll get back as soon as I can. If you put me on shirts, vests and underpants instead of the battledresses, it might help to strengthen up my wrist. If so, it might only be three or four weeks.'

'I think we'll be able to manage that,' Georgina replied. 'We could do with someone more experienced in that department, but until then I'm afraid I don't have anything suitable.'

Amy got to her feet. 'Ah well, I suppose I'll have to raid my Post Office account. I was saving up.'

'You'll be entitled to employee injury compensation, Amy. We can't give you your full wage and bonus, but you'll get something.' Georgina walked to the filing cabinet and pulled out a file. She studied it for a few moments, then pulled an accounts book out of a drawer and studied that for a while. 'You'll get pretty much half pay and a bit of a lump sum, so it's not the end of the world.'

Amy let out an enormous sigh of relief. 'Thanks so much, Mrs Handsley. I haven't heard of that. I've never been off work before.'

'The government insists we have a scheme,' Georgina said, getting to her feet and placing the accounts book on her desk before looking at her watch. 'Now, I've got to go. I've an important meeting with the material suppliers.' She walked around the desk and put her hand gently on Amy's left arm. 'Heal swiftly, Amy. I hope to see you back at your machine soon. Just drop in on Friday lunchtimes to pick up your pay packet and give us an update on your injury.'

Mrs Rowlings was a fair-haired woman with hints of the grey showing through. She was a kind-hearted person who didn't have a bad word to say about anyone. Her figure was wholesome rather than trim. The sort of body that you would look forward to receiving a hug from.

'Oh, Amy, what have you done?'

Mrs Rowlings rushed to help Amy hang up the coat that Carol had draped across her shoulders before she left the factory.

'It's alright, Mum,' Amy assured her. 'It's only a sprain. It looks worse than it is.'

'Oh dear. Have you been to the hospital?'

'No, Mum, Harold, the first aid man, fixed me up. He knows what he's doing. He was a medical orderly in the Great War.'

'Are you sure you wouldn't like a doctor to see it, our Amy? I'll get the bus with you if you like.'

'I'm fine, Mum, honestly. I just need to rest it up for a few weeks.'

'A few weeks? That's good. I think you could do with a rest. You work so hard.'

Amy smiled softly and gave her mother a peck on the cheek. 'It's not all bad news. Mrs Handley says I'll get a few pounds in compensation once the incident has been investigated and I'll be on half pay while I'm off. They have some sort of employee insurance.'

'That *is* good news. It's very kind of her.' Amy's mum stood aside to let her walk into the living room first.

'Can I get you anything? I think I've got an aspirin or two left. I'll get some more when I go to the chemist.'

'That would be nice, Mum, thank you. I'd love a cup of tea. I missed lunch because of the accident. And don't worry about getting more aspirin in. I'll pick some up when I go into town in the morning.'

'Are you sure you'll be up to it?'

'I'll be fine, Mum. I'm going to Brigdens as normal, then I'm meeting Bodkin for lunch at the Sunshine Café.'

'You just take it easy, our Amy. Don't go overdoing it.'

'We were going to go on a trip into the country tomorrow in Bodkin's car.' Her face fell suddenly. 'I was supposed to be driving. That's something else I won't be able to do for a few weeks.'

Mrs Rowlings patted her daughter on the arm and walked through to the kitchen to make the tea. 'Did you bring your sandwiches home or should I make you a round? I've got some nice beef paste.'

'I've got the sandwiches in my bag, thanks, Mum.' She got up from the table, but before she could get to the door, her mother came rushing in. 'I'll get your bag, dear. I'll get your work stuff out, too. It can go in the wash tomorrow.'

Ten minutes later, whilst sipping at her steaming cup of tea, Amy found herself wishing once again that they were on the telephone network.

'Have the GPO said when they're going to install the telephone yet, Mum? I was hoping it would be in by now, seeing as Dad has started his new manager's job.'

'I haven't heard anything, Amy. It could be the New Year before they install it. There's a long waiting list, what with the war and everything.'

'I'll nip up to the phone box a bit later on then,' Amy said. 'I'd better give Bodkin a ring to let him know I can't drive tomorrow.' Amy thought for a moment. 'No, scratch that. I think I'll take a slow walk down to the farm and call him from Alice's phone. She'll want to know how I came by my injury.'

'You just be careful walking down that lane.'

'It's my wrist that's injured, Mum, not my ankle. I'll be fine.' She picked up her cup again and blew into it before taking a long sip. 'I wonder what Bodkin's up to.'

Alice had just that minute put the kettle on when Amy pushed the door open and stepped into the farm's kitchen. After forgetting she was wearing the sling for a moment, she performed a half turn and pushed the door shut with her left hand.

'It's me,' she said.

'You must have smelled the teapot,' Alice said, spooning three heaped spoonfuls of tea into the big brown pot. She looked up with a fond smile, then her face changed. 'My goodness, Amy, what happened?'

'I tripped over a pair of soldier's trousers.'

Alice stifled a giggle, then gave up trying and let it escape.

'Don't let Bodkin hear you say that,' she said with a snort.

'I was a bit embarrassed when I said that to Mrs Handsley, but I think it sounds quite funny now.'

'Quite? It's hilariously funny.' Alice poured boiling water into the pot and carried it across to her enormous, well-scrubbed oak table. After placing it on the cork mat, she looked across towards her best friend and shared a grimace as she watched Amy pull out a chair to sit down. 'Does it hurt awfully?'

'Only when I laugh,' Amy said as she slid onto the chair and used the lower half of her body to shuffle it forwards so that her knees were under the table.

'Are you going to be off work with it?'

'For a few weeks, then I might get some lighter garments to

work on while my wrist strengthens.' She nodded towards the teapot. 'I'm parched,' she said.

'Give it a minute to brew, or it will be like cat's piddle,' Alice replied. 'What are you going to do for money? Have you informed Brigdens yet? They might well end up going bust if you don't have any money to spend.'

'As it happens, I'm going to be looked after by some workers' insurance scheme. I won't have as much to live on, but it'll be enough to see me through for a few weeks.' She suddenly let out an exclamation. 'HA! Just think, when I go back I'm going to get my hands all over some soldier's underpants.'

Alice laughed as she reached for the teapot. 'I wouldn't tell Bodkin about that, either.'

When they had finished their tea, Amy asked Alice if she could use her phone to call Bodkin's office number. Alice opened the living room door for her and went back to the kitchen table as Amy walked through and picked up the phone. After dialling, she only had to wait a few moments before Bodkin's voice was heard.

'Spinton police, Inspector Bodkin speaking.' There was a pause and then he said, 'this better be important, Smedley.'

'It's not Smedley, it's me,' Amy said.

'Then it's important enough,' Bodkin replied. Amy could picture the smile appearing on his rugged, stubble chinned face. 'What can I do for you?'

'I'm just ringing to let you know that I won't be able to drive us to the country tomorrow. I had a bit of an accident at work and now my right arm is in a sling.'

'Have you been to the hospital? I can give you a lift. I've got to go out shortly, but it's not an urgent matter and I can pick you up on the way.'

'You're a sweetheart, Bodkin, but I'm fine. It's only a sprained wrist. I just need to go easy on it for a few weeks.'

'A few weeks? Blimey! How will you get on at work?'

'I'm off on half pay. I'll survive on that. I'm more worried about being bored out of my mind, just sitting around doing nothing.' She paused for a moment. 'I don't suppose you have the odd juicy murder or two I could help solve?'

'I don't have a single one at the moment, sorry.'

Amy sighed. 'Ah well, I suppose we should look on the bright side. Someone's walking around who might not have been. What are you working on? Anything interesting?'

'I've got a pig rustler to find and a couple of other bits and bobs that came across my desk this morning.'

'A pig rustler? That would be quite a difficult thing to rustle, wouldn't it? I've heard of cow and sheep rustling but never pigs.'

'I thought that. I'm going over to have a look at the scene of the crime. Tom Piper left the gate to the pigsty on the floor when he rammed it with some vehicle or other. It must have been a truck or a van... you wouldn't get a pig onto the passenger seat of your car in a hurry.'

'Tom Piper? You know who did the deed then?'

'Tom, Tom the piper's son, stole a pig and away he run, as in the children's rhyme. It's the nickname I've given him.'

'Tom wasn't called Tom Piper. No one knows his surname. All we know is he was a piper's son,' Amy said.

'Spoilsport,' Bodkin replied.

Amy giggled. 'Oh, call him Tom Piper if you like Bodkin. I'm only teasing. It's a good nickname, really.' She paused for a few seconds before continuing. 'What were the other things that came across your desk? Surely there's something to get your teeth into?'

'Pig rustling is a very serious offence,' Bodkin replied. 'I have to look into it myself. Chief Inspector Laws gave me the case. He knows the farmer involved. It's Jeremy Anderson's farm, the big one on the outskirts of town. He's always hobnobbing with the mayor and the local bigwigs. That sort of thing impresses Chief Inspector Laws, as you know.'

Amy sighed. She and Laws didn't always get on too well. He was a stern faced man who lived in fear of his wife, so took out his frustrations on anyone who came within range. On at least three occasions, it had been Amy. If it hadn't been for the patronage of Chief Superintendent Grayson, she wouldn't have been allowed within a mile of the police station.

'I'd better let you get your investigation going then, Bodkin. Laws is relying on you to bring home the bacon.'

Bodkin groaned, then laughed. 'I gave Farmer Anderson a call earlier. He's at the tailor this afternoon. Getting a new suit to wear at some posh do with the mayor and the alderman. How come I never get invited to these functions?'

'They've probably seen you wearing your wrinkly old trousers, Bodkin,' Amy replied quickly. 'Have you got that stain out of the front yet? It makes you look like you've had an accident.'

'I'm wearing my other suit at the moment,' Bodkin replied. 'I put the trousers in at the dry cleaners this morning.' He paused. 'He wasn't too hopeful.'

'Okay, it's time we dropped into Stan's Second Hand Emporium again. He might have a suit on the seconds rail that will fit.'

'I don't need another suit,' Bodkin complained. 'I've got two.'

'We'll just have to agree to disagree about that,' Amy replied. 'If you've got time in the morning, I can meet you at the Sunshine Café and we can nip into Stan's.' She continued quickly to stifle Bodkin's protestations. 'If the dry cleaners aren't hopeful about those trousers, then neither am I.'

Amy was silent as she heard another voice in the background. Then she heard Bodkin say loudly, 'WHAT!' followed by, 'That can't be right.' A couple of minutes later, he came back on the line. 'Sorry Amy, but I've got to run. There's been a development.'

'Is it Tom Piper? Has he made a pig of himself?' Amy asked.

'I've no idea, I've just been informed that there's a man's body lying in the alley at the side of the Dragon pub. From the report, he's definitely been murdered.'

'Oh dear,' Amy said. 'I feel guilty now. It's like I was asking for it to happen.'

'It's a strange one,' Bodkin replied. 'More than strange actually... more like impossible.'

'Why? What do you mean?'

'We already know the man's identity from the contents of his pockets. The problem is... this man is already dead. I investigated his murder in Gillingham three years ago.'

CHAPTER THREE

'That looks painful,' Bodkin said, nodding at the sling as he stepped into Amy's hallway. He closed the front door behind him and smiled as Amy leaned forward to give him a peck on the cheek. 'How did the accident happen, anyway? You didn't say on the phone.'

'I tripped over a pair of soldier's trousers,' Amy replied.

'Was he wearing them at the time?' Bodkin asked.

Amy shook her head as she laughed. 'I knew you'd have some funny remark.'

She led him into the living room where her mother had just stepped through from the kitchen.

'Good evening, Mr Bodkin, please, take a seat.' She waved her hand towards the table.

Bodkin pulled out a chair and sat down. 'Good evening, Mrs Rowlings, I hope you are well.'

Amy's mum nodded and smiled fondly at the policeman before returning to the kitchen to pick up the tea tray she had been preparing.

'Can I get you anything to eat, Mr Bodkin?' she asked as she placed the tray on the table in front of him.

'I'm okay, thanks, Mrs R,' Bodkin replied.

Amy studied him. He looked tired, but that was nothing new. Bodkin barely took any time off work and she knew when he walked the short distance home from the police station to his apartment in Bluecoat House, he would take case files with him that he would read long into the night.

'Have you eaten anything at all today, Bodkin?'

'I, erm, I had a sandwich this morning in the canteen.'

'Then I bet you didn't finish it. The food in there is disgusting.'

'I got called away, so I only worked up to a level of utter distaste. I didn't reach the heights of disgust.'

'He hasn't eaten, Mum,' Amy shouted into the kitchen.

Mrs Rowlings' head appeared around the edge of the open door. 'Right, you can have some of the stew I cooked for James. He'll never eat all that.'

'Is he working overtime again?' Bodkin asked.

Mrs Rowlings sighed. 'He is. It's almost every night since trial production started on those aircraft parts.' She looked at Amy with a sad look on her face, then turned back to Bodkin. 'The government wants those Spotfire parts as soon as possible and poor James is the one that has to make sure they get them.'

'It's a huge responsibility,' Bodkin said, biting his tongue, trying not to correct her. 'But the extra money must be nice. All that overtime.'

'He doesn't get a penny more for his efforts,' Amy cut in. 'He's hardly ever away from the place, but they don't pay anything extra. He's salaried now, so he gets the same money every week, regardless of how many hours he puts in.'

'That's a shame. He deserves to be paid more.'

'So do you, Bodkin. I bet you don't record all the extra hours you put in either.'

Bodkin looked at his hands, then intertwined his fingers.

'I'd feel guilty just sitting around when there are villains waiting to be nicked.'

'You could spend more with me,' Amy replied with a grin.

'I'm sure Mr Bodkin knows what he's doing, Amy,' Mrs Rowlings said as she placed a bowl of steaming stew and a thick heel of bread in front of the policeman.

Bodkin smiled his thanks, picked up his spoon and got stuck in.

Mrs Rowlings stood back and eyed Bodkin critically. 'Eat up, you could do with putting some meat on those bones. I'm sure you've lost weight since you last ate with us.' She turned towards the kitchen, then looked back over her shoulder. 'There's apple pie and custard for afters. Amy's had hers, but I'm sure she can find room for a bit more.'

Amy stuck her good thumb up, then rubbed her tummy and smacked her lips. 'I've got a tiny space that needs filling.' She turned her attention to Bodkin. 'Are we going up to the Old Bull later?'

Bodkin nodded, then attacked the stew again with relish. 'Do you watch your mum when she's cooking so you can pick up a few tips? She's a superb cook.'

'She is,' Amy replied with a frown, 'but no, I don't watch her and I don't ask for cookery tips, Bodkin. If, when, we ever do get married, you'll be fed a diet of bread and dripping... that's when it's my turn to cook, of course. You can rustle up anything you like when it's your turn.' She grinned at him as he looked up, wide eyed from his plate. 'Speaking of rustling up, is there any news on Tom Piper?'

'I'm going over to the farm first thing in the morning, just to have a look at things. I've got Ferris ringing around the meat wholesalers and the abattoir to see if anyone has been trying to sell them a job lot of pork, or even a live pig.'

Ferris was the latest recruit to the CID team. He had previously worked in uniform at the Spinton police station. He was an excellent jazz singer and was paid to sing once a month at the posh Milton Hotel. He spent most of his Saturday nights with Bodkin, Amy and Alice at the Roxy picture house.

'So, Laws isn't going to let you off with that one, then. I thought he might with the new murder case you've been handed.'

'Chief Inspector Laws won't allow anyone else to handle the case,' Bodkin said between mouthfuls. 'I could do without it, to be honest. I've got to see Chief Superintendent Grayson at some stage tomorrow to try to explain how a man can be murdered twice.'

'I was going to ask you about that, Bodkin. How can it possibly happen?'

Bodkin nodded towards the kitchen door, then held a finger to his lips. 'We'll talk about it up at the Old Bull, Amy. I don't want to upset your mum with all the gory details.'

'Laws can't possibly think that pig rustling is as important as murder, surely, Bodkin. Mr Grayson will take you off that case if he has any sense.' She laughed suddenly. 'Hey! Maybe Tom Piper doesn't exist. Maybe he's just a "pigment" of Law's imagination.'

Bodkin lowered his head over his empty bowl as he groaned. Then he suddenly burst into laughter. 'I can't wait to tell Ferris that one.'

The Old Bull snug was as busy as it usually was on a Friday night. The clientele was largely female. Single women who worked at The Mill with Amy stood gossiping with their married counterparts as they sipped their gin and tonics while their men got drunk in the public bar on the other side of the counter. The husbands were seldom seen in the snug, only appearing now and then to ask their wives for a half crown from their purses to see them through, after handing the contents of their pockets over the bar, long before the time bell sounded.

The night had become chilly, so Amy and Bodkin sat on opposite sides of a small, round top table a few feet away from the fire that crackled, popped and hissed in the seventeenth century fireplace. Amy and Bodkin were both non-smokers, and the air was heavy with cigarette smoke. Amy picked up a beer mat and wafted it in front of her face in an attempt to clear the air a little. 'One day, some clever landlord will open a lounge for non-smokers only, and I think he'll make a fortune out of it.'

Across the room, standing near the bar, Big Nose Beryl nodded knowingly to her band of cronies, then winked as she pointed out Bodkin to them. 'That Amy Rowlings will be sticking her nose into things that don't concern her, that's for sure. He's a copper, you know? I bet he's given her a good grilling more than once, if you catch my drift.'

Bodkin took a long sip of his pint and held it in his mouth for a few seconds to savour it. 'Ah, that's hit the spot.'

Amy took a dainty sip of her port and lemon, then set the glass back on the table. 'Never mind the beer, Bodkin. I've been dying for you to tell me all about the man that's been murdered twice. He hasn't been, obviously, but why the confusion?'

Bodkin looked around to make sure they couldn't be overheard before he replied in a low voice.

'His name is Lonnie Firth, and he grew up in Maidstone. That's where he first came to the attention of the police. Oh, nothing serious. He was a bit of a lad but no worse than many of his peers.' Bodkin took another sip from his drink, then continued. 'He moved up to Gillingham when his father died. His mother took the kids to live with her sister, who was married to a local hoodlum. He soon had Lonnie doing bits and pieces for him. Climbing into places he shouldn't have been climbing into, reporting back on well-to-do drunks coming out of the local pubs so they could be robbed on the way home. That sort of thing. He left school at twelve and started work as a bookies runner. Carrying betting slips between punters and the back street bookmakers. Off course betting is illegal. After a couple of years, he got in with Reggie Tumbler and his gang. They were into much heavier stuff than Lonnie had been used to, but he learned quickly and soon became one of Reggie's loyal henchmen. By the time he was eighteen, he was collecting protection money from local businessmen and by the time he was twenty-one, he was Reggie's right-hand man. Not a lot went on in Gillingham without Lonnie, and therefore Reggie knowing about it. Pubs and clubs were targeted from the opening night. If a landlord or owner refused to go along with the racket, their premises were set alight or ransacked by a drunken mob sent by Lonnie. At twenty-three, he had his own little side business and no one ever wanted to get on the wrong side of him. By the time he was twenty-five, he was semi-independent, and that's when he bit off a little more than he could chew.'

Amy leaned forward in her seat, her hands clasped together, eager to hear more. 'He sounds a right Jimmy Cagney type character.'

'Oh, he wasn't quite in the gangster league, but the people who came after him were.' Bodkin picked up his pint, but just stared into it instead of drinking. 'I don't know the entire story, but he tried to get too big too quickly and managed to upset some proper gangsters from London, when he demanded a cut from a high-stakes gambling school, outside of what was deemed to be "his area". He was sent a first and final warning from the London gang, but the message never reached him, and Lonnie and his cronies broke into the hotel room where the card school was in session. They walked away with over a thousand pounds. Sadly for Lonnie, revenge arrived swiftly and his body was found lying in an abandoned warehouse a few days later. His face was so badly beaten, he was pretty much unrecognisable. There was nothing on his person to identify him. In the end, we only got to know who the victim was when his mother came to the mortuary to identify his body. She pointed out a tattoo of a grinning skull on his right shoulder that he'd had done when he was sixteen.'

'So, it could have been anyone, really?' Amy said.

'I was open-minded about it at first, but when we saw the state his mother was in at the funeral, we were pretty convinced we had the right man. No one has seen hide nor hair of him ever since and he wasn't the sort to hide his light under a bushel. If there was money to be made somewhere in town, Lonnie wouldn't have been able to resist taking a share of it.'

'He didn't have a twin brother, did he? That might explain it.'

'He has a brother, but not a twin. His name is Brian, and he's about a year or so younger than Lonnie. He's a similar sort to his brother, but he's not as smart. I Interviewed him as part of the investigation. There's a sister too. Erma, her name is. You wouldn't want to get on the wrong side of her, either.'

'And there were no missing persons at the time, young men of about his age and build?'

'Not that we knew of, from Gillingham, at least. As I said, his mother's behaviour at the funeral and later on when she would come to the station to berate us for not finding his killer, made us pretty sure it was Lonnie that had been murdered.' Bodkin finally took a drink from his raised glass. 'Scotland Yard got in touch with us a short while later. They'd been given a few snippets from a snout, an informer, who told them that the Best Brother's gang had been behind the murder. The informant told them he had been killed for leading the raid on the gambling club.'

Amy finished her port and lemon and put the empty glass on the table. Bodkin picked it up, got to his feet, and headed for the bar. When he returned with fresh drinks, Amy had had time to think about what she had heard.

'It's stating the obvious that it wasn't Lonnie's body that was found but knowing that doesn't explain why he's been bumped off again. Unless the Best Brothers finally realised they'd bludgeoned the wrong man to death and had found out where the real Lonnie was living.' Amy took a sip of her port and lemon, then held the glass just above the table. 'What was he doing here? I can understand him not wanting to be seen in Gillingham after all that happened, but Spinton is only a few miles away from there. He could easily have been spotted and news of him reported back to the Bests.'

'The Best Brothers were killed in a shootout in the East End, eighteen months ago. The rest of the gang, or at least the leading figures, were rounded up by the police. They're all doing long sentences in jail now. An annoying little tiddler like Lonnie wouldn't have lived long in their memories. I don't think his death has anything to do with them. It could have a lot to do with his old boss, Reggie Tumbler and his cohorts, though. I mean, he wouldn't be best pleased if he found out that, far from being dead and buried, Lonnie was back in the area trying to pick up where he left off.'

Amy looked across the table towards the policeman, her eyes shining. 'Ooh, Bodkin, it's all very Edward G. Robinson, isn't it? How exciting.'

'I'm hoping it doesn't get too exciting,' Bodkin replied, reaching for his pint. 'As I found out when I was investigating that first murder, these people don't care who gets hurt. We're going to have to tread very carefully with this case.'

'So, I'm going to be allowed to help? Oh, Bodkin, thank you so much. I can't wait to get started.'

'I'm not sure about that, Amy. Because of who is involved, I'm going to have to square it with Chief Superintendent Grayson. You can't get too close to Reggie Tumbler and co. They might not be up there with the real Cagney types, but I can't take the risk that they'll come after you. How would I explain that to your mum and dad? I'd never forgive myself if anything happened to you.'

Amy studied him seriously. 'I understand, Bodkin, I know you're trying to keep me safe, but I can still help in the background, can't I? I can still help question the family members. They will be the first people we talk to. Who knows? We might never have to question the hoods at all. The answer to the riddle might lay a lot closer to home.'

Bodkin smiled as he nodded. 'I think the boss will go along with that. I'll try to persuade him.'

'Good,' Amy replied, 'because I've got a long three or four weeks ahead and I'm going to need something interesting to fill the hours.'

CHAPTER FOUR

At nine the next morning, Sharon, the shop assistant, found Amy waiting on the pavement as she unlocked the front door of Brigdens Fashion Store. The shop sold cut price, designer labelled items, good quality factory overruns and slight seconds. Many of the second hand items had only ever been worn once or twice. There was also a pair of sales rails at the back of the store, where garments with slight faults could be purchased at a bargain price. Amy, as a machinist, had little trouble repairing the items she often bought for as little as five to ten shillings.

'What on earth have you been up to?' Sharon asked as she held the heavy glass door ajar to allow Amy to enter.

'I fell over at work.' Amy looked eagerly towards the back of the store where the sales rails were situated. 'Anything new in?' she asked as she stepped into the shop.

Sharon let go of the door and followed Amy across the floor. 'It's all very similar to what we had in last week, Amy.' She thought for a moment. 'There's a nice, single pleat, A-Line skirt on the back rail if you fancy doing a bit of work on it. You'll probably need to take the waist in by an inch or two and the hem needs a bit of attention, but it's a lovely skirt.'

Amy hurried past the line of mannequins showing off a few of the more expensive dresses the store offered and made her way to the back rail.

'It's at the far end,' Sharon said. 'Hang on, I'll get it for you.' She pulled the hanger holding the charcoal grey skirt from the rail, held it under her chin and fanned it out so that Amy could see the full letter A shape that gave the design its name.

'Ooh, that's lovely, Sharon. What waist size is it?'

Sharon checked. 'Twenty-eight. As I said, you'll have to take it in an inch or two, but it won't affect the flow of the skirt. It should flare nicely down to just below your knee.' She held the garment out towards Amy, who put down her bag and held the skirt at waist level, before turning to view herself in the half mirror.

'I love those pleats. It hangs perfectly,' she said, holding it up to look at the price tag. 'Ten shillings... I wonder if Eileen would knock a couple of bob off, seeing as that hem needs fixing.'

'Good luck with that,' Sharon laughed. 'I don't think she's in a haggling sort of mood this morning.' She nodded across to the till where Eileen, the manageress, was working on a sales ledger. 'Oh, I meant to add, there's a lovely cream single-breasted jacket on the other rail there. It's fifteen shillings, but it would go beautifully with that skirt.'

Amy winced as she pushed her slinged arm towards Sharon. 'A jacket is no good to me while I have to wear this thing. Thanks for the tip though. I'll take a chance and see if it's been reduced a bit further when the sling comes off.'

She winked at Sharon, then walked across to the till where she laid the skirt out on the counter.

'Can you do me a deal on this, Eileen?' she asked as the manageress looked up.

'I doubt it, Amy. There's an identical one on the mannequin in the window and it's going for one pound, five shillings.'

'Ah, but that one doesn't have a torn hem,' Amy said. 'And I'll have to take the waist in an inch and a half. The side seam might need a little work too.'

'Spare me,' Eileen said, exasperated. 'This isn't a barter stall in the marketplace, Amy. I have to make a profit or I'll be out of a job.'

'I think eight shillings would be a fairer price,' Amy said, pointing out the damage to the hem.

'It's ten, Amy. I can't drop the price any further. I paid se... never mind. I can't drop the price for you this time.' She flicked her head towards the stockroom at the back. 'Unless, of course, you can help me out by running your experienced eye over a few of the items that came in this morning. One or two need a tuck or a stitch before I can put them on display and I don't have time to do the work myself.'

Amy looked down at her injured arm. 'Sorry, Eileen, I can't, not for a while anyway. It's going to be a few weeks before I can get onto a machine again and it might be a bit longer before I can hand stitch anything. It's only a sprain, but it's a pain.'

'How long do you think? I can keep them back for a week or two. They're Spring fashions, anyway.'

'I'll be happy to sort them out for you when I can, Eileen.' Amy smiled her best smile and looked down at the counter where the skirt lay. 'Eight shillings?'

Eileen shook her head as she sighed. 'You'll be the ruin of me, Amy Rowlings.'

. . .

Amy left the store carrying her new purchase in a gaily coloured Brigdens bag and made the short walk to the Post Office where she deposited five shillings into her savings account. From there she walked around to the Sunshine Café where she found Bodkin sitting in a window seat waiting for her. He stood up and smiled at her as she walked in. Amy smiled back before calling to Ruth on the counter. 'Coffee please, Ruth... oh, and could I have a slice of that fruit cake too? Thank you.'

She turned to face Bodkin, who had pulled out a seat for her at the table. He was just a tad over six feet tall with a mop of unruly dark hair which fell untidily across his forehead. Bodkin's hair was pretty much uncontrollable. He would look like he needed a good haircut even as he walked out of the barber's shop. He was wearing a navy suit with a badly creased jacket and a white shirt that looked like it hadn't seen an iron in months. His red tie had egg stains on it. His trousers were, as usual, bunched up around the top of his shoes, which had what appeared to be clumps of mud stuck to the uppers. Amy had cut two inches off the length of those trousers and used her mother's sewing machine to make a new hem. They had fit him perfectly. The length was so good, in fact, that they could have been made to measure at the town's only tailor's shop, but somehow, they had managed to resume their former bunched up appearance within an hour of the alteration. Amy had begun to wonder if the trousers were possessed by some untidy demon.

'Thank you,' she said as she took the proffered seat. The policeman waited until she was comfortable before sitting down himself.

'Have you been here long?' she asked.

Bodkin picked up his still steaming coffee and took a sip. 'I'm on my second cup,' he said. 'I've been here about twenty minutes. I almost came into Brigdens to find you, but I figured you'd be busy looking through the sales rails.' He nodded to the bag that Amy had placed carefully on the seat next to her. 'Your journey wasn't wasted, then?'

'You know me, Bodkin. I seldom come out of Brigdens without blowing a good portion of my wages.'

'You'll have to be a bit more careful with money for a while,' he replied. 'Hey! Maybe I could buy you something while you're in penury. I'd like that.'

Amy reached across and patted the back of Bodkin's right hand with her left. 'You're such a sweet man, Bodkin, and it's very kind of you, but I don't want you to go wasting your money on me.' She hesitated for a moment. 'Not when you could be spending it on a new pair of trousers for yourself.' She sniffed the air and pulled a face as Ruth carried her coffee and cake over to their table. 'What's that horrible pong?' She sniffed again. 'My goodness, it smells like Alice's farmyard.'

Bodkin lifted his foot to examine his shoe. He pulled a face when he saw the lumps of farmyard detritus that was clinging to it. 'Do you know, I thought I smelled something in the car? I...'

'Good God, what's that dreadful smell?' Ruth exclaimed as she put her tray down on the table. She looked down at Bodkin's shoe as he lowered his foot to the floor. 'Don't put it back down there. I'm going to have to get the mop and disinfectant on that mess.'

Bodkin slipped both shoes off and held them away from the table. 'Do you have anywhere I can clean them?' he asked.

'Follow me. There's a tap in the yard, out back. You can clean them there. I've got an old scrubbing brush you can borrow.' She led Bodkin across the café floor, passing customers, pulling faces and holding noses as he went.

By the time he returned, some five minutes later, Amy had almost finished her coffee and Ruth was busy making her a second cup. 'Would you like another cup, Mr Bodkin?' she asked, looking suspiciously at his dripping wet shoes as he passed by. 'The other one will be cold by now.'

Bodkin nodded and hurried back to his table, where he found Amy looking doubtfully at her slice of fruit cake.

'That smell put me off,' she said, pushing the plate away.

'They're clean now,' Bodkin said, raising his foot to show her. 'But I've got sopping wet socks. I had to stand in a puddle while I washed the shoes. I'll have soggy feet all afternoon now.'

Amy put the palm of her hand to her brow. Suddenly, she began to laugh. 'Oh, Bodkin, I sometimes wonder if you ever properly grew up.'

Bodkin sniffed the air, then, satisfied that he had removed all of the offending material from his shoes, he took the cup of fresh coffee from Ruth and sipped at it. 'Just call me Peter Pan,' he said.

Amy waited for Ruth to go back to the counter before she spoke again.

'Speaking of fictional characters. What did old Farmer Anderson have to say about Tom Piper?'

'He seemed more interested in Alice than his stolen pig, to be honest,' Bodkin replied.

'Alice? What has she got to do with anything?'

'I think he quite fancies her,' Bodkin replied. 'He never shut up about her. I only got the barest of details about the theft. He did show me the flattened five-bar gate. The tyre marks in the mud were still there. It was definitely a van of some type. The tracks weren't wide enough to have come from a lorry.' He took a longer sip from his cup. 'He does want the pig back, though.'

'Never mind the pig. What did he say about Alice? He's fifty-five if he's a day. Alice was only twenty-one last month.'

'He said...' Bodkin looked at the ceiling as he gathered his thoughts... '"You know that Mollison woman don't you, Inspector? The young dark-haired filly who owns the farm at the bottom of Long Lane? You hang out with that friend of hers, the Rowlings girl, don't you?" I told him I did, then he patted me on the shoulder and asked me if I'd ask you to put a word in for him with Alice. "It makes sense," he said. "I've got four hundred acres here and the bottom fields back onto her land. She's got a hundred acres so... well, our union makes perfect sense to me."'

Amy's jaw dropped. 'Oh, my goodness.'

'You haven't heard the best yet,' Bodkin said. 'He went on to say how much he admired her. He said, she's a handsome young thing. She's got a rump like Hortense, my prize winning Shorthorn.'

Amy's mouth gaped open. 'Oh, Bodkin, that's priceless. I can't wait to tell Alice. She'll be so flattered.'

Bodkin shook his head as he continued. 'He reckons that as she's already produced one child, she must be considered prime breeding stock. He asked me if I had her telephone number. He wants to take her out on a date.'

Amy began to giggle. 'Hahaha. Oh, Bodkin, can you imagine? He probably wants to show her how fresh the hay is in his loose box.'

Bodkin blew out his cheeks. 'I think that's pretty much the plan. The randy old goat.'

Amy finally stopped laughing. 'He's one of the young farmers that attend the ball every year. Alice and I went once. There wasn't a single person under fifty. Goodness knows what the old farmers look like.'

She composed herself and looked around the café to see if the other customers had noticed her fit of laughter. Satisfied that she was no longer the centre of attention, she returned to the conversation.

'So, you didn't learn much about Tom Piper? What did Laws have to say? Have you been to see him yet?'

Bodkin nodded. 'I saw him when I got back this morning. He seems to think I should have had the case sewn up by now.'

'You're kidding me.'

'I only wish I was. He told me I should make it my priority. When I mentioned the murder of Lonnie Firth, he just shrugged and said the death of a local hood should be way down on my list. He said if I'd done my job properly the first time around, we wouldn't have to re-investigate the case.'

Amy pulled a face. 'Oh, I despise that man.'

'I did mention the fact that he was the officer in charge of the case. I was only there to make up the numbers initially, but I was left holding the reigns when he moved up here from Gillingham.'

'What did he say to that?'

'He said that if he'd have remained in charge, there would have been a different outcome and we'd have learned the true identity of both victim and murderer.'

'Oh... that stupid... I'd better not say what I'm thinking out loud,' Amy replied.

'I told him that Chief Superintendent Grayson had called me in for a briefing today and he suddenly changed his tune. He said I suppose murder does take priority, but don't leave the stolen pig case collecting cobwebs. I want a quick resolution on that. Mrs Laws is hoping we'll get an invitation to the Mayor's next dinner party. Old Farmer Anderson is on the guest list, so I can do him and, by association, me, a favour if we get a quick result.'

'I wonder how Old Man Anderson will describe Shirley McKenzie, the mayor's wife's rump?' Amy said.

'I'm sure he'll have some creature on his farm to compare it with,' Bodkin replied.

Amy laughed.

'Speaking about the murder. Has anything else come up this morning that I should know about?' Amy picked up her cup and, hiding a smile, looked over it at Bodkin.

'We've had one or two snippets,' Bodkin said. He looked up at the clock on the wall, then got to his feet. 'I'd better be off, Amy. I've got to prepare for my meeting with Grayson. I need to have a quick look through the case files of the original murder just to refresh my memory. I bet Laws has been riffling through them while I've been away. He'll want to make sure he isn't tarnished with the same brush as me.'

'Are you in the car, or did you walk up from the station?' Amy asked.

'I walked. I needed to clear my head.'

'Good. Then I'll walk you back down the hill and get the bus home from there,' Amy said.

The new police station had been built on the corner of Middle Street and the main Gillingham road. When they reached the entrance to the car park at the side, the pair stopped and faced each other. Carefully avoiding putting any sort of pressure on Amy's injured arm, Bodkin leaned down and kissed her on the lips. 'What's on at the Roxy tonight? I've been so tied up with pig rustling I forgot to check.'

'It's very apt, actually,' Amy replied. 'It's a comedy starring Will Hay. It's called, Ask A Policeman.'

Bodkin grinned. 'I'll look forward to that. I'll tell Ferris when I get inside. I assume Alice is coming?'

'Yes, she'll be there,' Amy said. 'Providing she can get over the shock of her rear end being compared to a heifer.'

As the pair laughed together, a black Hillman saloon pulled

up and the driver wound his window down. A few seconds later, Chief Superintendent Grayson's face appeared.

'Ah, Bodkin, there you are. I was hoping to catch a word.' He smiled as he recognised Amy. 'What an absolute delight. How are you, Miss Rowlings?'

Amy smiled back. She liked Grayson. He was a forward thinking man who could see how women could find a place in the modern police force. Sadly, the hierarchy down in Maidstone could not.

Grayson checked his watch. 'I've got a meeting with Chief Inspector Laws in a few minutes, Bodkin, then I'm on the phone for God knows how long with a colleague in Rochester. Do you think you could make yourself available at around two-thirty to go over the details of this very strange murder case?'

'Of course, sir,' Bodkin replied. 'I'd like to talk to you about how we might involve Amy... I mean, Miss Rowlings, in the case. As you can see, she's sustained an injury, which means she'll be off work for a while. On the bright side, it means she will have plenty of time to help us with the inquiry should we need her input.'

Grayson put the car into gear and he pulled his head back inside. 'Of course, Bodkin. Bring her along. I'll see you in your office. Two-thirty, sharp.'

CHAPTER FIVE

Amy caught the bus home and spent the next hour chatting to her mother as Mrs Rowlings, herself a capable machinist, restitched the ragged hem of Amy's new skirt.

At five past two, just as she stepped outside to catch the bus back to Middle Street, Bodkin pulled up in his black Morris 10. 'I had a few minutes spare before the meeting so I thought I'd come and pick you up,' he said.

When Amy had made herself comfortable in the passenger seat, he turned the car around and headed back to the police station.

'Are you all prepped for the meeting?' she asked.

'Pretty much,' Bodkin replied, 'but I had to ask Trixie to get the files from Laws' office. He's been going through them since I saw him this morning.'

'How is the blonde bimbo?' Amy asked. She and Trixie had got off on the wrong foot and had never managed to hop back onto the right one. The more they saw of each other, the worse their relationship became.

'Now, now,' Bodkin said. Trixie lived in the flat below in his apartment block and worked as a secretary at the police station. Amy claimed that Trixie was the spitting image of Mae West and she could do a very presentable impersonation of her.

'Now, nothing,' Amy almost spat. 'I sincerely hope she doesn't feel the need to come into your office while I'm there, Bodkin.'

'I can't really stop her if she has a reason to come in, Amy. She does work at the station, after all.'

'Stick a note on your door, Bodkin. It ought to read, No Bimbos, or Bimbos Keep Out. Something so simple, even she can understand.'

Bodkin sighed and turned into the police station car park. 'I wish you two would just ignore each other.'

'How can you ignore breasts like that, Bodkin? They're in the room two minutes before the rest of her.' Amy climbed out of the car, slammed the door shut with more force than she had meant to, and followed Bodkin into the building.

As they reached Bodkin's office door, Detective Constable Ferris called out to her from the office on the other side of the corridor. He was a handsome, fair-haired young man, twenty-three years old. He was almost a polar opposite of Bodkin in appearance. He was smartly dressed in a newly pressed, dark grey suit with a crisp white shirt and an unstained tie. He made up the foursome on their Saturday night trips to the Roxy cinema. Alice liked him a lot, but although they were pretty much the same age, there was no romantic involvement between them. Alice preferred a more mature type of man. Ferris had recently started a relationship with Sal, Bodkin's sister, who lived in Dover and could only make it up to Spinton every other week. Ferris had a beautiful baritone voice and performed at the Milton Hotel, singing along with a jazz band in the cocktail lounge once a month. He was always looking to add bits of comedy to his routine. When he spotted Amy, he ducked into a crouch and slipped easily into a poor impression of the comedy legend, Groucho Marx.

'I've had a wonderful evening, but this wasn't it,' he drawled as he performed the famous Groucho walk.

'Very good,' Amy said.

'Do you really think so? I was going to put it in the act, near the end, just as I'm saying goodnight to the audience.'

'I'd work on it a bit more before you use it,' Amy advised.

Ferris sighed. 'That bad, eh?'

'I've seen better,' Amy admitted. Turning away, she walked into Bodkin's office, where she found him already sitting in his chair behind his desk. Hung on a green painted radiator at the side of him was a pair of soggy-looking grey socks.

'Ferris was just showing me his Groucho,' Amy said.

'I've seen it,' Bodkin replied. 'He showed me in the toilets earlier.'

Amy raised her eyebrows but said nothing.

'I'm trying to get him to use my joke,' Bodkin said as he straightened up a pile of green coloured files that were leaning at a very precarious angle.

'Your joke? Have I heard it?'

'I don't think so,' Bodkin said. 'Would you like to?'

'If I must,' Amy said.

'Right.' Bodkin stood up. 'Okay, the first man says to his mate, I saw a fox on the way to work this morning. His mate replies, Really! How do you know it was on its way to work?'

Amy blew out her cheeks. 'I think I prefer Groucho.'

'It could do with polishing up a bit,' Bodkin replied, as he sat down again.

Chief Superintendent Grayson was a tall, broad-shouldered man with an angular face and a friendly smile. His thinning grey hair was cut slightly longer than was the fashion, in a failed attempt to cover up some of the bare patches of skin. He marched into Bodkin's office in almost military fashion with his peaked cap tucked under his arm.

'Don't get up, my dear,' he said to Amy as both she and Bodkin began to get to their feet. He smiled at her, then nodded a greeting before turning to his inspector. 'Now then, Bodkin, what's all this about some chap being murdered twice? What's his name... Laurie, something?'

'Lonnie, Sir. Lonnie Firth.'

'That's the fellow.' Grayson pulled a chair away from the wall and sat down next to Amy. He placed his cap on Bodkin's desk and crossed his long legs. 'There has obviously been some mistake in identifying the man in the past. Are we sure we know who he is this time around?'

'Yes, Sir. The victim had identification on his person.'

'But so did the other chap... or have I got that wrong?'

'The "other chap" was identified by his mother, Sir. She recognized the tattoo on his shoulder.'

'Hmmm, I suppose a mother ought to know her own son. Why the confusion then? Does this fellow have an identical tattoo?'

'He doesn't have a tattoo at all, sir. There was a driving licence issued under the name Grant Huckerby, but that was probably stolen or issued fraudulently. He also had a photograph in his inside pocket, featuring himself, his mother, brother, and sister. It had writing on the back that read, Mum, me, Lonnie and Brian. Clacton, 1932. He is in that photograph, sir. I believe it was his sister, Erma, who wrote on the back of it and if she's listed them in order, then Lonnie is the taller of the two, the first male on the left.'

'Hmm, so who was the chap found with no face in that warehouse three years ago?'

'We don't know yet, sir. That's obviously one of the first things I'll be looking into.'

'His mother identified him, you say? Do you think it was an honest mistake or are we going to find there is a lot more to it?'

'With hindsight, I think she played her part in saving her son's life, sir. By identifying the faceless body as her son, she not only gave the London gang a reason to believe they'd killed the man they were looking for, she also gave him the chance to start a new life.'

'Hmm. Where can we find her? She obviously has some of the answers.'

'From what I learned from the Gillingham police when I rang them earlier, the whole lot of them left town a few months after Lonnie's funeral. They believed the family had moved out of the county. They had queries from the Nottingham police regarding Brian, Lonnie's brother, who had been getting up to mischief in their patch, but that was back in thirty-seven, only a year after Lonnie... allegedly died. They haven't heard anything since. There's no record of him being imprisoned, so he's either kept his nose clean since then, or he's living some place that hasn't yet connected him with Kent.'

Bodkin spent the next twenty minutes telling Grayson everything he knew about Lonnie, his criminal past, and his gang related connections. When he had finished relating it all, the chief superintendent sat quietly for a few moments.

'I've heard of this Tumbler fellow Bodkin. He was active around the Maidstone area when I was working down there. I was an inspector at the time and although I never got to lock him up, I was involved in investigations in which he was the prime suspect, though we never managed to get a charge to stick. I followed his career with interest when I moved to Gillingham, but I've heard nothing about him since I moved up here.' He paused. 'He must be fifty-five... sixty now. Possibly older. Is he really still up to no good? You'd think he'd leave it to the younger men. Wouldn't you?'

'Some men find it hard to give up their careers, Sir. I'd like to question him at some stage. He'll know something about the earlier killing. He may not have been involved directly, but nothing went on in Gillingham without him knowing about it.'

Grayson nodded. 'Yes, I agree. He must be questioned but keep Miss Rowlings well away from him. There's no reason for him to even know of her existence. As for the family, that's a different matter.' He looked sideways at Amy and smiled warmly. 'You, young lady, have the knack of being able to see through people as they attempt to tell us a pack of lies. You are particularly impressive in reading the body language of women when they are being questioned. I have seen the reports that Bodkin wrote up after some of our trickiest murder investigations and you feature heavily in them.' Grayson pursed his lips, then went on. 'I'm so sorry you suffered your injury, my dear, but your employer's loss is our gain. If you really think you have the time to help us with this investigation, I'd be truly grateful. If you'd like to, you can assist Bodkin with his inquiries. I'd like you to sit in when the family is questioned. If we can find out where they are living now, of course. It may entail travelling to a different part of the country, but we'll cover any expenses you may incur. I particularly want you to be present when the mother and sister are questioned.' Grayson got to his feet and picked up his cap from the desk. 'Right, Bodkin, get to it. You can have Ferris, and if you need a uniformed officer, take Smedley. If you find the team isn't big enough, I'll try to find you extra officers, but they will only be uniform. I can't spare another member of the CID. We need someone to look after the run-of-the-mill crimes the town is blighted with every day.'

'Like the pig rustling case, sir?'

'The what?'

'The pig rustling case, sir,' Bodkin repeated. 'Someone stole a pig from Anderson's Farm and Chief Inspector Laws asked me to look into it.'

'Did he, by Jove?'

'I did, sir. I thought Bodkin's talents might be put to use on that case. We need a speedy resolution.'

Grayson spun around on his heel as his chief inspector walked into the office. 'We do?'

'I asked Bodkin to make it a priority, sir. It's a delicate thing, local politics and all that.'

'It's the theft of a pig, Laws, local politics or not.'

'Regardless of the crime, I'd like to get it resolved sooner rather than later, Sir. I can spare a few hours here and there to help Bodkin with this murder case. We both worked on the initial murder, so I already know a lot of the background.' Laws put his finger into his over tight collar and separated it from his bulging, sweaty neck.

'Righto, Laws, but it's Bodkin's case. It's very kind of you to offer to help, but don't forget you have to get your report about staffing levels and expenditure projections to HQ before the end of the month.'

'It's well in hand, Sir. I'll follow up a few things on Bodkin's case when I can. I'm sure I'll be able to help out.'

'Capital,' Grayson replied. 'Right, now I'd better get on.' He turned to Amy and bowed his head. 'It was a pleasure to meet you again, my dear. I hope that injury of yours heals quickly. Good luck with the investigation.' He slipped his hat onto his head and marched out of the room.

When Grayson had gone, Laws took half a dozen steps forward and came to a halt a few feet away from Bodkin's desk. He shot a glance at Amy and forced a smile.

'I see you're still getting yourself involved in police business, Miss Rowlings.'

Amy gave him a half smile. 'Mr Grayson asked me to help, seeing as I've got some time on my hands,' she said.

'Mr Grayson has a title, and I'd prefer that you use it,' Laws said sternly. He turned his attention to Bodkin. 'How did you get on with the pig thing? Do you have any suspects yet?'

'There is one, Sir, goes by the name of Tom Piper. I don't have any leads as yet, but I'm asking around after him.'

Amy began to laugh, then quickly turned the sound into a cough. Holding up her good hand to her mouth, she cleared her throat and shot a glance at Bodkin.

'Piper, eh? Is he from outside the area? Have you been in touch with the abattoir and the meat wholesalers? If there's nothing in Spinton, try Gillingham. There's a few of them down there.' He stared hard at the inspector. 'Good God, man, I shouldn't have to tell you how to do your job.'

'No, Sir, you shouldn't, but it's in hand. Ferris has been making a few telephone calls. I'll check in with him in a few minutes.'

'Make sure you do, Bodkin,' Laws said sternly. 'And have a strong word with him, will you? When I walked past his office just now, he was crouched over, muttering something about having a good night out.' He turned towards the door, but immediately turned around again. Lifting his arm, he waved a beige coloured file in the air. 'This might help you with the original murder case. I pulled it out of the evidence room earlier.' He held the file out towards Bodkin. 'Well? Come on, man, I'm not your secretary.'

Bodkin stepped out from behind his desk and took a few paces forward. Laws' eyes dropped to his bare feet. 'What in God's name...?'

'My socks got wet, sir,' Bodkin said. 'I stepped into some pig slurry and had to run a hose over my shoes.'

'Well, find some clean ones, Bodkin. You're supposed to be conducting a murder inquiry, not going for a paddle in the sea.'

Bodkin wriggled his toes and reached out to take the file from Laws. 'What's in it, sir?'

'It's my report about the first murder in Gillingham, Bodkin. I've added a few details to it today. It needed a bit of an update. Hopefully, you'll learn something from it.'

Laws handed the file to Bodkin, then with a curt nod to Amy, he turned and walked slowly out of the room.

CHAPTER SIX

When Laws had gone, Bodkin went back to his desk and turned over his socks on the radiator.

'I want to wear these tonight,' he said, stroking the paisley pattern. 'One good thing came out of having to hose my shoes down. My socks got a free wash.'

Amy sighed. 'You know, sometimes I can't tell if you're joking or not.'

Bodkin looked puzzled. 'Why would I be jok...?' His words were cut off when there was a tap on the door and Trixie, the blonde bombshell secretary, stepped into the room carrying two cups of steaming tea.

'Detective Constable Ferris asked me to drop these in for you.'

Amy's eyes narrowed as Trixie did her wriggle bottom bimbo walk across the office. She was wearing a pure white dress that seemed to fit like a second skin across her hips. The buttons down the front of her chest looked as though they might give way under the strain at any moment.

Although Amy was nearer, she passed the first cup to Bodkin, then taking a sideways glance at Amy, she put her cup on the desk. ‘Three sugars, just as you like it,’ she looked back at the policeman, gave him a broad smile as she placed one hand on her hip and jutted it out to the side. ‘Yours has no sugar, Inspector.’ She put a finger to her lips and giggled. ‘Oops, did I get that the wrong way around? Ah well, she could do with putting a pound or two on. She looks so... thin.’

Bodkin’s face dropped. He knew what was coming.

‘I don’t take sugar in tea, thank you,’ Amy said coldly. She stood up and ran her hands over her own hips. ‘That’s why I’m so slender. It goes straight to the hips, does sugar.’ She looked Trixie slowly up and down, then held out her hand towards the tea on the desk. ‘You have it, dear; you probably won’t notice the extra ounces.’

Trixie scowled, then she screwed up her face as she desperately tried to think up an insult. ‘Men prefer curves,’ she said eventually. She turned away towards the door, then stopped, stuck out her bottom and looked back over her shoulder. ‘And you don’t have any,’ she said as a parting shot.

Amy waited until she reached the door. As Trixie walked through into the corridor, she put her finger into the side of her mouth and made a pop noise. ‘Ooh, you managed to squeeze through,’ she said. ‘Well Done!’

Bodkin rested his elbow on the desk and put his palm to his brow, then he shook his head as he blew out his cheeks. ‘You can cut the air with a knife when you two are in the same room,’ he said.

‘She could do with having a few slices of bacon cut off her rump,’ she said. ‘I wonder what Farmer Anderson would compare her with... his missing pig, probably.’ She got to her feet, put a finger to her lips and struck an identical pose to the one that Trixie had just done. ‘Oops!’ she said. ‘She reminds me of a blonde Betty Boop.’

'Very good,' Bodkin said. 'You should join Ferris on stage next time he's on. Your impressions are much better than his.'

Bodkin took a sip of his tea and pulled a face. 'No sugar, this is yours,' he said, passing the cup over the desk and picking up the sugared one. 'Now, where were we before Spinton's answer to Mae West interrupted us?'

'You were going to tell me what was in the file that Laws handed you,' Amy said.

Bodkin picked up the file and opened it. After scanning it for a few moments, he passed it across the desk to Amy. 'He's written an addendum, absolving himself of all responsibility for the mess the first murder case turned into. He claims all the important decisions affecting the case were made *after* he left for Spinton, even though initially the case was investigated under his instructions.'

Amy read the added sheet, then sat back in her chair and tossed the file onto the table.

'He's blaming you for all the mistakes, Bodkin. Not in so many words... he doesn't mention you by name, but he keeps referring to decisions made by the investigating sergeant.'

Bodkin shrugged. 'He's redacted the original report, too. He's blacked out certain paragraphs that mention him personally and any section that points to him having handed out instructions to the investigating team.'

'That's awful, Bodkin. Will he get away with doing that?'

'There'll be a copy of the original file at HQ and maybe one in Gillingham. I'm down there on Monday. If there is, and if I can get to it before he does, I'll make a copy. I could do with knowing everything that happened in that case, not Laws' revised version of events... Actually, now I think about it, I'll get them to send it up to us; it will save me a trip.'

Bodkin picked up the phone and dialled a number. A few seconds later, he was talking to the officer in charge of the evidence room. After carefully passing on the case file reference number, he asked him to have it transferred to Spinton as soon as possible.

'It'll be here on Monday morning.' Bodkin grinned to himself as he placed the handset on the cradle.

'He was really pushing it with Grayson over the pig theft, wasn't he? You could tell Grayson thought he'd be better off leaving it with the uniformed officers.'

Bodkin nodded. 'He... or should I say, she... his wife, is desperate to improve her social standing. She seems to think a Chief Inspector is on a par with a Chief Constable in society terms.'

'I wonder if Tom Piper has managed to sell it yet. The money might be in his piggy bank already.'

Bodkin snorted. 'HA! Laws did look a little disgruntled.'

Amy clapped. 'You're getting better at this, Bodkin.' She finished her tea and put the cup back on the desk. 'What are you up to this afternoon?'

'I'm going to nip up to the Dragon to have a word with the landlord. Ferris told me he wasn't available when he was at the murder scene yesterday and the pub was closed by the time I got there. I'd like to ask him, and any of his regulars who might be about, if anyone can remember seeing Lonnie Firth in the pub the night before. It's a right den of iniquity, as you know, so it's not beyond the bounds of possibility that his killer was drinking there too.'

'You mean it could be just a local thing? A pub argument that got out of hand?'

'It's a possibility,' Bodkin replied. 'I'd like to know what Lonnie was doing in Spinton and if he's been living here, or if it was just a flying visit?'

He rubbed his hands together eagerly. 'I love it when I get

something meaty to get my teeth into.' He looked across the desk at her. 'What are you going to be doing?'

'I have to somehow take a bath... it won't be easy with this sling on.' She lifted her arm slightly. 'Mum will help me get in and out.' She thought for a moment, her eyes drifting to the ceiling. 'I wonder if Dad has a bit of waterproof material I could wrap around the bandage while I have a soak. He's got all sorts of things in his shed that he's put aside in case he ever needs it.'

'What time are you planning to bathe?'

'I usually get in about four-thirty. Why do you ask? You're not offering to come and scrub my back, are you?'

Bodkin grinned. 'Only if I'm invited.'

'In your dreams, Bodkin.' Amy laughed.

Bodkin feigned disappointment. 'I was going to invite you along to the Dragon. That's why I was asking.' He looked at his watch. 'It's three-fifteen now. That gives us an hour before you jump into the tub.' He got to his feet, then, realising he was still barefooted, he reached for his socks. 'They're still a bit damp,' he said, giving them a sniff, 'but they'll have to do.'

The Dragon was a yellowish brown, London brick pub that had been built amongst the rows of tiny, terraced houses during Spinton's industrial expansion in the mid-Victorian era. Situated between the slum dwellings of Ebeneezer and Nelson Street, the pub was pretty much a second home for many of the miners, foundry workers, and various ne'er-do-wells who plied their nefarious trades in the surrounding area. The installation of modern pull handle beer pumps aside, the only improvement the pub had undergone over the years was the installation of what was now a dirty, much used dart board that hung in the main bar.

At the side of the pub, a wide alley ran between the two

streets. Used by the drays to deliver beer to the establishment, it was also a useful thoroughfare for anyone wanting to get from the bottom end of the two up, two down housing estate to the railway station that was only a hundred yards from the pub. The front door of the alehouse was on Station Street, but there was a side door leading into the back room of the hostelry from the alleyway.

Amy held her nose as the pair stood by the side entrance while Bodkin crouched down to study the cobbled floor, marked with the words Body Found Here.

'Is there a lavatory in the pub or do the regulars prefer to urinate in public?' Amy asked with a grimace.

'It's ripe, isn't it?' Bodkin replied as he surveyed the surrounding area. Satisfied that Ferris and the uniformed officers hadn't missed anything, he stood up, shuddered when the sudden movement caused the air to shift, and pushed open the door.

'Why can't we use the front door, Bodkin?' Amy asked.

'I want to surprise whoever's in there, Amy. If we go in the front, as soon as I'm recognised, there'll be a stampede for the side door. This way, when we walk into the main bar, most of the riffraff will have their backs to us.' Bodkin held the much painted, peeling plank door open to let Amy go in first, then, pinching his nose to keep out the worst of the smell, he followed her in.

The back room was small, with just half a dozen empty tables littered about. There was no bar, and the room had two other doors leading from it. One, to the right, had the word toilet, hand painted on it. The artist had obviously been in a hurry whilst slapping paint on the door because the drips ran most of the way down to the sill at the bottom.

The door to the taproom was open and Amy could hear the muffled voices of the clientele getting clearer as she walked towards it. She stopped on the threshold and took a quick look over her shoulder to make sure Bodkin was close by before she stepped through the doorway.

As soon as she entered the bar, the conversation stopped abruptly, then a chorus of catcalls, wolf whistles and offers to give her the best time of her life rang out. They ceased as soon as Bodkin's broad frame appeared behind her.

'Christ, it's the law!' One dirty faced man called out. He got to his feet, almost knocking the unsteady oblong table over in his haste, and headed for the door.

'It's a waste of time running, Herbert Norris. I know where you live,' Bodkin called over the hubbub.

Norris stopped dead. Thought about it for a moment, then returned to his stool where he picked up his glass and downed what was left of his pint.

'Gimme another one, Caleb.' He waved his glass in the air, then walked the short distance to the bar and put it down on the counter. Caleb, the landlord, picked it up and slipped it under the dark mild hand pump before pulling hard twice on the lever. Placing the frothy brew on the counter, his eyes never leaving Bodkin, he muttered. 'Another one for the slate?'

Norris nodded quickly. 'I'll, erm, I'll pay a bit off it when I come in tonight, Caleb. I haven't picked my wages up from the colliery yet.'

Caleb wiped his hands on his dirty apron and narrowed his eyes at Bodkin. 'Coppers aren't welcome here, Inspector, as you well know.' He pointed at Amy. 'And whatever it is you want here. It won't concern her. Get her out now. Women and pubs don't mix, they always cause trouble.'

'She's old enough to be in here,' Bodkin said. 'And she's not breaking the law as she is accompanied.'

Caleb snarled. 'She's been in here on her own in the past. She almost got what she deserved, too.'

Bodkin gave Amy a quizzical look.

'The Reverend Villiers case,' Amy hissed. 'I was looking for my dad's friend, Joe Proudfoot, to ask him something important.'

Bodkin turned his attention back to the landlord. 'I've got a few questions for you, Caleb.'

Caleb picked up a cloth that was even dirtier than his apron and proceeded to polish a glass with it. 'I have nothing to say to you, Mr Policeman so, sling your 'ook and take her with you.'

Bodkin pulled out a seat from under a rickety table and motioned for the landlord to sit down on it. 'I'd order a drink, Caleb, but I don't want to spend the next twenty-four hours throwing my guts up.' He crooked his finger and beckoned the landlord to join him. 'We can chat here or in the back room. It's up to you.'

'And I told you. I have nothing to say to you.'

Bodkin tipped his head to the side as he looked at the publican. 'Suit yourself, Caleb, but you can count on a visit from the weights and measures department before the day is out. Oh, and you might find that a few of my colleagues will start using this place as their local. He looked around at the dingy pub with its flaking paint, peeling wallpaper and beer stained floor. Then again, I might just put in a report to the magistrate to check how valid your licence is.'

Caleb scowled and nodded towards the door leading to the back room. 'In there,' he said.

The barman threw his cloth onto the counter, then glared at the dozen or so drinkers. 'Keep away from this side of the bar,' he growled. 'No bloody freebies. Touch my pumps and you're barred for life.' He lifted the bar hatch and stepped into the room before turning and lowering the wooden flap. 'I'll hear if anyone lifts it,' he warned.

Bodkin led Amy through to the back room and pulled a

chair from under the table for her to sit on, then he pulled one out for himself.

'It's nice here, isn't it?' he said to Amy as Caleb walked down the single step from the bar. 'It has an almost Parisian ambience.'

'Who needs an ambulance?' Caleb asked with a puzzled frown on his brow.

'You will if you don't start cooperating,' Bodkin replied. He reached out with his foot under the table and kicked at a chair. 'Sit!' he ordered.

Caleb sighed and did as he was instructed. 'What is it you want, Sergeant Bodkin?' he asked, almost meekly.

'It's Inspector Bodkin, Caleb. I've been promoted since the last time our paths crossed. I can have you locked up without asking permission now.' He grinned evilly at the landlord. 'So, just remember that when you answer my questions.'

'If it's about that man in the alley, I know bugger all about it.'

'I'm not saying you did it, Caleb. You're not the sort to bludgeon a man on the back of the head. Poisoning's more your style.'

'Very funny,' Caleb replied. He looked over his shoulder towards the door. 'Hurry up with it, then. That lot will have drained the porter barrel by the time I get back.'

'The man in the alley's name is Lonnie Firth,' Bodkin said. 'Did you know him?'

'No.'

'Was he in the pub last night?'

Caleb looked towards the door again and lowered his voice. 'He might have been.'

'So he was. Did you serve him? How long was he here? Who was he with?' Bodkin rapped out the series of questions like a sergeant major running in a new recruit.

'He was... what was the question again? I didn't get all that.'

'I'm just trying to speed things along a bit, Caleb, so you can get back to your scummy customers.'

'Okay. He came in around nine-thirty and stayed until closing time. He came in alone, but another stranger came in at about ten. They sat together until chucking out time.'

'What time did you chuck 'em out, Caleb? Please don't insult me by telling me it was half past ten. I know you have a lock in every night.'

'It was before midnight. Possibly half-past eleven. There were only a couple of punters left and I'd had a long day, what with the drayman coming and everything. My bed was calling and Angie from Ebeneezer Street had come over to keep me warm.'

Amy tried not to pull a face as she looked at the flabby figure of Caleb Rumbelow sitting opposite in his filthy apron. Sweat was running down his face as he suffered the grilling from Bodkin. His body odour wafted across the table towards her. She wondered what Angie got out of the deal. She hoped it was worth it.

'Did they argue at all, or did it seem like they were good friends?'

'They seemed to get on all right.' Caleb thought for a moment. 'The other chap wasn't from around these parts, though. He had a funny accent.'

'Funny as to what? Foreign, the north of England... Scottish...?'

'I dunno. They all sound the same to me. He wasn't forrin, but he definitely wasn't from round 'ere.'

Bodkin sighed. 'You haven't travelled much in your time, have you, Caleb?'

'Furthest I've been is Gillingham,' the landlord replied.

'What did he look like? Was there anything unusual about him?'

'He was tall, he had a big 'ooter, and a moustache. One of those silly thin things over his top lip.'

'Hair colour… Age?'

'He didn't have a lot of hair, to be honest. It was cropped very short. I don't mean he was bald. As for age… he was probably in his late twenties, early thirties.'

'Was he well dressed? Did he look like he had money?'

'He had a suit on. Nothing peculiar about that. Even the miners wear a suit on a Saturday night.'

'Did he look like he had money?'

'Oh, he had money all right; he tried to change a fiver. Like I'd have change for a fiver.'

'So how did he pay for the drinks then?'

'The feller who was killed bought them. He had a few ten bob notes. I could manage those.'

Bodkin scratched at the stubble on his chin. 'So, they left together at eleven-thirty and they hadn't had a row. Were they drunk?'

'They'd had a few, yes.'

'Could they walk out or did they stagger a bit?'

'They looked like they could hold their beer. They walked pretty straight.'

'Who was still in the pub when they left?'

'Herbert Norris was still here. He was supposed to be on nights at the pit, but he fancied a night off. He was going to meet his missus when she finished her shift. Oh, and Seamus McTaggart was here, but he was asleep in the corner. I had to wake him up to chuck him out.'

'Did they leave soon after Lonnie Firth and the stranger?'

'Five minutes, more or less. Herbert helped Seamus out of the door.'

Amy leaned forward in her chair, then, after catching another whiff of Caleb, hurriedly leaned back again. 'You said Herbert was waiting for his wife to come off shift. She must work very odd hours to be clocking off at that time.'

Caleb suddenly burst into a fit of laughter, which left him coughing and spluttering as he tried to answer. 'Clocking off... that's a good one... she's not on a time clock, dearie, she's on the game.'

Amy blushed as Bodkin came to her rescue.

'Who left just *before* Firth and his drinking buddy?'

'Abel Sculley and Arthur Bradfield left about a quarter past. They had to be up at five for the early shift at the foundry.'

Bodkin nodded to himself. 'And there were no other strangers in the bar? No one in the back room here?'

'No one uses this room as a rule.'

'So there wasn't a card school in operation?'

Caleb choked. 'I don't allow card schools. There's no gambling for money going on 'ere.'

Bodkin tutted. 'Caleb. You not only allow a card school to flourish. You allow young lads to run bets to the bookie from here, too.'

'That's not true,' Caleb almost choked. 'Who's been spreading malarky gossip?'

'The word you're looking for is malicious,' Bodkin replied. 'And it's common knowledge in Spinton, Caleb. We just turn a blind eye to it because it's too much hassle to fill in all the reports. I can look into it if you really want me to, though.'

Caleb shook his head swiftly and got to his feet. 'Look, I've got to get back in there or I'll have no ale left to open up with tonight.'

Bodkin nodded. 'All right, you can go. I'll be back when I know a bit more about this affair. Tell Norris he's next up for the audition.'

Caleb looked puzzled. 'Audition, what audition?'

'The best liar in Spinton contest,' Bodkin said. 'Off you go.'

The landlord nodded slowly and turned back towards the bar. As he took the step, Amy called out to him.

'One more thing before you go. Where can we find this, Angie?'

Caleb stopped dead. 'Why would you want to speak to her?'

Amy shrugged. 'Because she's your alibi. No one else knows what you got up to after Norris and Seamus left. For all we know, the victim might have come back in... or you might have followed them out.'

CHAPTER SEVEN

Herbert Norris was a wiry man of around five feet seven inches, with a head of greasy, slicked back hair, a short stubby nose and a mouth that looked as if it had been drawn on with a kid's crayon. His face was grimy, as though he had just finished his shift at the pit. He wore a ragged suit jacket that had once been navy, over a filthy vest. So dirty were his trousers, it was difficult to guess what colour they had once been. His boots looked relatively new, and he limped as he walked towards them as though they were pinching him. When he opened his mouth to speak, he showed off a surprisingly full set of nicotine-stained teeth.

'I'm not happy about this,' he said as he came to a halt near the table where Amy and Bodkin were sitting.

'Oh, I'm so sorry. Are we putting you out?' Bodkin asked sarcastically.

Herbert picked up the tone in Bodkin's voice and decided to be more amenable. 'I just mean I've got to go to work later. I'm on nights.'

'You look like you just clocked off, Herbert.'

'I didn't have time to wash properly, I just had a cat lick.'

Bodkin raised his hand and pointed to Herbert's grimy face. 'You missed a bit.'

'I'm a busy man, Mr Bodkin. Is there a reason you want to talk to me?'

'Were you on the night shift last night, Herbert?'

Herbert smelled a trap and gave an honest answer. 'I was supposed to be, but I had a toothache so I dropped off sick.'

'But you came in here, Herbert.'

'For medicinal reasons, the beer dulls the ache.'

'Ah, of course,' Bodkin said. 'On a side note, Herbert. Do you *ever* wash or change your clothes?'

'I have a bath in the tin tub in front of the fire on a Saturday night before I go out,' Herbert replied. 'The missus fills it for me from the copper boiler. I always let her go first. She has to, or she'd come out dirtier than she went in.' Herbert gave a throaty chuckle.

'She'd need to be clean, wouldn't she, Herbert? She wouldn't get much custom if she was as dirty as you.'

'What do you mean... custom?'

'Let's be kind and call them clients,' Bodkin said. 'Your wife is a prostitute, Herbert.'

Norris shrugged. 'So what? There's no law against it, is there?'

Bodkin's eyebrows shot up. 'There are lots of laws against it, Mr Norris. Lots and lots.'

Herbert looked at his boots. He lifted one foot and winced. 'They're new,' he said.

Bodkin leaned across and took a look. 'Very nice, Herbert. Where did you get those? Did they fall off the back of a lorry?'

'I got them on the market, as it happens, not that it's any business of yours.'

'You're quite right, it isn't any of my business. Unless, of course, the market trader was selling stolen goods. Then it would be... but as it is, I really don't care where you got your boots. I want to know about what you got up to with Seamus last night when you walked out of here.'

Norris looked nonplussed. 'I didn't get up to anything with Seamus. I helped him up the hill towards Station Road and left him to find his own way home. I walked down to the station to meet the missus after work.'

'Had she had a busy night?' Bodkin asked and got a look from Amy.

'Same as usual. She doesn't make much, she's not really a looker, and she's getting on a bit. Still, what she makes helps keep the wolves from the door.'

'Indeed.' Bodkin said. He scratched at the stubble on his chin as he thought.

'Do you remember seeing Lonnie Firth in here last night?'

'Who?' Herbert looked puzzled.

'The man who was bumped off outside that door.' Bodkin half turned and pointed.

'I knew nothing about that until I walked in this afternoon.'

'Let's put it a different way. Did you see two strangers in the bar last night? They left a few minutes before you and Seamus.'

'Oh, the bloke who was waving his money about. The one with the Nottingham accent. Yeah, I remember seeing him. He was with... ah...now I get it... he was with the bloke that was murdered, wasn't he?' He frowned. 'So how come you're asking me questions and not this other feller? He was the one that walked out with him, after all.'

'We don't know who he is, Mr Norris, that's why. Any help you can give that will reveal his identity will be warmly welcomed.'

'I don't know much about him at all,' Norris said. 'I saw him in the bar. He was flashing money about. The berk asked me if I had change for a fiver. I've never seen a bloody fiver, let alone had change for one.'

'Tell me about him. What can you remember?'

'Tall, close cropped hair. Nice suit... he looked as if he'd just got out of jail, to be honest. No one has their hair cut like that unless they've been in the nick. It's the lice, you know. They have to cut it short or they breed like flies.'

Amy suddenly felt a desperate need to scratch her head.

'You think he'd just got out of jail, then?'

'I can't say for sure, Mr Bodkin, but no one asks for their hair to be cut that short at the barbers.'

'What about the other man? Did anything unusual occur between them? Did they have an argument?'

Norris thought for a few moments. 'No, nothing like that. The one that got topped bought the other chap's beer for him all night. He couldn't get anyone to change his fiver.'

'When you left, Herbert... now consider. Did you see either of them outside the pub?'

'No, there was no... hang on. Yeah, one of them at least was hanging around. He was having a pi...' Herbert cut his sentence short when he remembered Amy was sitting at the table. 'He was peeing up the wall.'

'Who was?' Bodkin leaned forward eagerly. 'Which one?'

'Not the money-man. The other one.'

Amy cleared her throat to let Bodkin know she wanted to ask a question. He gave her a quick nod, then looked back at Norris to see his response.

'Earlier, you said you thought the money-man was from Nottingham. What made you think that?'

'Because he called everyone, Duck. That's how they talk up there. It's a greeting they use. "Ay up me Duck." I used to work with someone from Notts when I first started at the pit.'

'Is there anything else you can tell us, Mr Norris? You have been remarkably helpful, I have to say.'

Herbert shook his head, then looked over his shoulder to make sure he couldn't be overheard. 'Please don't say that to anyone else, Mr Bodkin. I've got a reputation to keep up. Being helpful to the police won't help it.'

CHAPTER EIGHT

'That's a bit of good luck, the stranger being from Nottingham, Bodkin.' Amy took his arm as they walked to the car which he had parked at the top of the alley. 'He'll stand out like a sore thumb down here.'

'There can't be too many people walking around calling people duck,' he agreed. 'Most men around here only mention the unfortunate creatures when they want to shoot them.'

'The question I want to know the answer to is, did this Nottingham chap come to Spinton to meet up with Lonnie Firth, or did Lonnie come here to meet him?'

'Maybe they were both already here,' Bodkin said. He looked down the length of Ebeneezer Street towards Victoria Street, the most notorious road in the town. 'If they've been holed up down there, it's no wonder no one knew Lonnie was living here. Even the police will only go in if they're mob handed. Someone could hide away for years if they wanted to.' Bodkin checked his watch. 'I'd better get you home or you'll never get that bath.'

Amy pulled a face. 'I'm really looking forward to it after sitting so close to those two in the Dragon. Have they never heard of soap?'

. . .

At six on the dot, Amy opened the front door to find Alice standing on the porch. She looked Amy up and down before stepping into the hall. 'That skirt is new, isn't it? Oh, Amy I love it... and it goes so well with that cream blouse.'

'Thank you, dear heart,' Amy said as she closed the door. 'I got the skirt from Brigdens this morning. I've had the blouse a while now.'

'You'll need your big coat tonight if you can wear it with your sling. It's getting decidedly chilly out there.'

'You'd better take yours off for a while or you won't feel the benefit when we go out again,' Amy said as she gave her best friend a peck on the cheek. 'Hang it up and come through. Dad got home early tonight. He'll be pleased to see you.'

Mr Rowlings was sitting in his favourite chair at the back of the living room, reading his evening paper. He looked up as Amy led Alice into the room.

'Good evening, young lady,' he said cheerfully. 'You look absolutely delightful, as usual.'

Alice was wearing a green dress with a wrap over front, and black Oxford shoes. Her dark chestnut hair was held in place with two red Bakelite clips.

'Flattery will get you everywhere, Mr Rowlings,' she replied. Alice had never called Amy's parents by their given names in all the years she had known them.

Mrs Rowlings came in from the kitchen with a tea towel in her hands. 'I thought I recognised that voice.' She smiled warmly at Alice. 'How are you, my dear? Thank you so much for the extra rashers of bacon. We can have it twice this week now and James can have a bacon sandwich for his supper tonight. You really do spoil us.'

'You're always welcome,' Alice said. 'Although we might

have to cut back a little, now the war's on. I had a letter from the ministry during the week. They said that we farmers will have to account for every ounce of meat we produce as imports are likely to be affected by the war. I was talking to Graham Stacks at the wholesaler today. He said he's had a top secret letter from the government. They're looking into rationing food in the New Year.'

'Top secret, eh?' Mr Rowlings chuckled. 'That Graham Stacks couldn't keep a secret if his life depended on it. Everyone in town will know about it by Monday.'

'Don't worry about your bacon supplies,' Alice said. 'I've got an arrangement with Percy Cutts at the abattoir. He's quite creative in the way he weighs a pig carcass. We'll still get our extra slices of bacon. Though the amount of pork and lamb chops we've enjoyed over the years might reduce a bit.'

Mrs Rowlings patted Alice on the arm. 'Don't go short yourself on our account, dear. We'll be grateful for anything you can let us have.'

'I'll build another pen,' Alice replied, 'and get in a few more sows. Hector and Horace, my prize boars, will love me for it.'

'While we're on the subject of pigs,' Amy said. 'Jeremy Anderson has had one of his prize porkers rustled, so keep an eye on yours, Alice. Bodkin's after the thief. He's nicknamed him Tom Piper after the kid's nursery rhyme. If Tom finds a buyer for it, he might start thinking about nicking another one.'

'I heard about that at the wholesaler's this morning,' Alice replied. 'There's a notice on the wall asking anyone with information to contact the police.' She grinned at Amy. 'That rustled pig could be rissoles by now.'

Amy laughed. 'Genius! Bodkin will love that one.' She took hold of Alice's arm and whispered. 'Speaking of Jeremy Anderson. I have news and a message to impart. Let's go up to my room. I'll tell you all about it.'

'A message from Old Man Anderson?' Alice followed Amy out into the hall. 'I'm intrigued.'

'He compared me to *WHAT!'* Alice turned sideways on, tugged the flare of her dress tight across her backside and looked at her reflection in Amy's half-length mirror. '*A HEIFFER!* My bum's not that big, surely.'

'You have a perfectly proportioned bottom,' Amy said soothingly. 'Ignore him. His brain is addled. He's lived on his own for so long, he's forgotten how to talk to women.'

'I could compare him to my big fat boars, Hector and Horace,' Alice said, taking one last lingering look in the mirror. 'Pass that message on.'

'I'd better not,' Amy replied. 'He might take it as a compliment.'

Alice laughed. 'True. I don't want him knocking on my back door carrying a bunch of thistles instead of roses.' She looked down at Amy's dressing table. 'Do you think I can borrow a splodge of lipstick? I couldn't make my mind up which one went with the green dress when I was getting ready.'

'Of course, dear heart,' Amy replied. 'Splodge away. I got a new one this week. It's from Max Factor.' Amy pointed out the lipstick. 'It's called Ruby. I got that one, and another called Flame. I saw them in a mail order advertisement in Mum's Woman magazine. I thought I'd better stock up before this blooming war spoils everything for us.'

Alice picked up the lipstick and applied a thick coating, then she smacked her lips and blotted them using a Kleenex paper tissue. After pursing them twice, she smacked them again and placed the lipstick back on the dressing table.

'Ooh, that's gorgeous,' Amy said. 'I was wary of using that

one, so I stuck to my usual Vermillion, but it looks wonderful on you.' She stood back and whistled. 'Look out, men of Spinton. Alice is on the loose.'

'It does look nice, doesn't it?' Alice said, taking another look in the magnifying mirror. 'The green dress really sets it off.'

'The green dress and your beautiful chestnut locks,' Amy said. 'You can use it whenever you like, Alice. I honestly can't see me wearing it too often. It's a bit... vibrant for my skin tone.'

'Amy, Mr Bodkin's here,' Amy's mum shouted up the stairs.

'Coming, Mum,' Amy shouted back. When both women had taken a last look in the mirror, they left the bedroom and walked slowly down the stairs. They found Bodkin waiting in the living room, chatting to Mr Rowlings.

'So, which case is the most important, Mr Bodkin?' James Rowlings held up his evening paper. 'The murder at the top of page one, or the pig rustling escapade that is mentioned at the bottom of the page? Your Chief Inspector Laws has been interviewed about both. He seems uncertain.'

'Bodkin's working on both cases, Dad,' Amy said. She got on her tiptoes and gave the policeman a peck on the cheek. 'Have you developed webbed feet yet?' she asked.

Mrs Rowlings gave Amy a strange look, then went back to studying the knitting pattern she'd got free with her Woman's Own magazine.

'I decided to change my socks in the end,' Bodkin replied. 'They had a bit of an odour when they'd dried out.'

'Spare me the details,' Amy said, pulling a face. 'I thought we were meeting you at the bus stop in town.'

'It's raining,' Bodkin said. 'So, I thought I'd pick you up. I'll park up at Bluecoat House, and we can use Cow Lane as a shortcut to the Roxy.'

'That's very thoughtful of you, Mr Bodkin,' Elizabeth Rowlings said. She patted her hair into place as she looked up at him from her seat on the sofa.

'What are you going to knit?' Bodkin said, nodding to the pattern.

'New socks for you,' Amy said. 'And you need them by the sounds of it.'

'What's all this talk about socks?' Amy's mum asked. 'I'm not knitting socks. It's a pullover for James. He says it gets a bit nippy in his new office.' She looked at her husband proudly. 'Imagine. My James in his own office.'

Amy crouched down and gave her mother a hug and a kiss on the cheek. 'He deserves it, Mum.' Getting to her feet, she kissed her father and followed Alice and Bodkin out of the room.

'Was there any news when you got back to the station earlier, Bodkin?' Amy asked as the inspector slipped into the driver's seat. She adjusted the heavy wool coat that hung around her shoulders like a cloak and turned her face towards him.

'Regarding the murder or the pig?' Bodkin asked.

'Either, or,' Amy replied. 'I gave Alice the message from Farmer Anderson, by the way.' She looked over her shoulder into the back seat where Alice was sitting.

'I was flattered, but I don't think I'm ready for a new relationship just yet,' Alice said.

'It's your decision,' Bodkin said. 'But you don't get offers like that every day.' He turned to Amy. 'Regarding the pig... nothing. But I got a bit of news from Ferris about the Firths. It appears that his mother wrote to her former neighbour in Gillingham only a month ago. She gave Mrs Robertson a Spinton address to reply to.'

'How did Ferris get to find out about that?' Amy asked.

'Gillingham police came up trumps. Ferris asked them to check with the ex-neighbours to see if anyone had heard from the family since they moved. This old lady had. She's been looking after a largish box for them and Mrs Firth told them she'd like to pick it up.'

'And has she?'

'Yes, she drove down about a month ago with her son, Brian. She picked up the box and left without stopping for as much as a cup of tea.'

'Ooh, we're on their trail, Bodkin. Did Mrs Robertson pass on the address? Whereabouts in Spinton are they living?'

'Victoria Street. Right in the middle of the den of iniquity, in the heart of the old Victorian estate. I was only talking about it earlier.'

Amy clapped her hands excitedly. 'When are we going to drop in on her?'

'We are not,' Bodkin replied. 'That place isn't safe for decent folk to visit.'

'But you want to question her, surely, Bodkin?'

'Oh, I do, and I will. But there's no need to go into Hell's Kitchen to find her. She'll want to see her son's body. Any mother would. She'll also have to make funeral arrangements, whether for a service up here or down in Gillingham. One way or another, she's going to have to get in touch with the authorities. I'll just sit back until she does. The body is still at the morgue following the postmortem, and they'll let us know as soon as she asks to see him.'

'Oh, of course she'll want to see her son's body. Good thinking, Bodkin.'

Bodkin tapped his head, then pointed towards his feet. 'Up here for thinking, down there for dancing.'

'You've said that a few times now,' Amy replied, 'and I still have no idea what it means. You don't do enough of the dancing, that's for sure.'

~

They didn't have to wait long to hear more about Mrs Firth. As Bodkin, Amy and Alice walked across the street from Cow Lane to the Roxy, they found an excited Constable Ferris waiting for them.

'I've got news,' he said eagerly as soon as Bodkin placed a foot on the pavement. 'Mrs Firth is going to see her son's body tomorrow, Sir. She wanted to go in tonight, but Dr Allinson at the morgue put her off, knowing that we want to speak to her urgently. She's going in at one o'clock.'

CHAPTER NINE

Hetty Firth was a good looking, well-proportioned woman with mid-grey short, shoulder length hair that was flecked with white. Her heavily pencilled eyebrows had been plucked and shaped to form a dramatic curve on the outer corners. Her eyes were ice blue and piercing. She would have looked even more attractive were it not for the deeply furrowed brow and a down turned mouth that made her look permanently peeved. She was dressed in a heavy, black, calf-length skirt and a black satin, lace trimmed blouse that buttoned up her neck, giving her a severe, Edwardian look.

Bodkin watched her sit down on the bench outside the mortuary where the body of her son was laid out on the embalming table. Dr Allinson's assistant, Elias Storer, had done such a good a job on Lonnie Firth, that he looked as if he had just climbed onto it to take a nap.

Dr Allinson himself sat at a desk in the corner making what he called an 'idiot's guide' of the postmortem report for the policeman, although Bodkin already knew the reason for Firth's death. He had been struck on the back of the head with something heavy. A leather covered, lead cosh perhaps.

As Bodkin stepped away from the short, double curtains that were pulled across the glass window at the top of the door, Amy took his place and looked through the chink in the middle of the curtain to get a look at Hetty, herself. She stepped back quickly as the slight movement of the curtains alerted the victim's mother.

'Right,' Bodkin said as he took hold of the door handle. 'Let's get this over with. It's going to be a bit like déjà vu. We've been here before.'

'Oh, sweet Jesus, don't tell me they've left you in charge of the investigation,' Hetty snapped as Bodkin emerged from the mortuary.

Amy followed behind the broad policeman and stood by the green painted corridor wall as she watched Hetty glare at Bodkin.

'I'm—'

'Don't you dare tell me you're sorry for my loss... Buttkiss...is it? I've heard it all before.'

'It's Bodkin,' the policeman said, unflustered by Mrs Firth's greeting. 'And I am sorry. No parent should have to go through this.'

'Twice!' Mrs Firth snapped. 'I've had to go through it twice, and all because of your bungling.'

'I'd like to talk to you about that,' Bodkin replied patiently. 'But that can wait until you've spent a bit of time with your son.'

Hetty looked at him through narrowed eyes. 'Are you sure it's him this time?'

'I'm certain,' Bodkin answered. 'There was a family photo in his pocket. It can't be anyone else.'

Mrs Firth showed the first sign of emotion as her bottom lip twitched. She got to her feet, smoothed her skirt and, as if just noticing Amy for the first time, gave her a puzzled look.

'Who's this?' she demanded to know.

'I'm Amy Rowlings,' Amy said before Bodkin could introduce her. 'I'm so sorry for your loss.'

Hetty looked at her suspiciously. 'I'm sure you are, but what are you doing here? That's what I'd like to know. This is an extremely personal moment. It isn't an occasion for all and sundry to witness.'

'Miss Rowlings helps the police on some of our investigations,' Bodkin said. 'She's here because in these situations, it sometimes helps to have another woman to talk to.'

'Is that what you think this is, *a situation*?' Hetty growled. 'I don't need comfort and sympathy from the likes of her,' she said. 'My daughter Erma is outside. She'll provide all the comfort I need.'

'Doesn't she want to go in with you?' Amy asked.

Hetty screwed up her face as she glared at Amy. 'Don't you think she'd be here if she did?' She turned away and gave Bodkin the same look. 'She can't face it, so she's having a ciggie in the car park while I go in.'

'I'd like to speak to her too, if that's all right,' Bodkin said. 'It doesn't have to be today. She can come down to the station in the week.'

'She's going no bloody where near a police station and nor am I,' Hetty said vehemently. 'We've got a reputation to uphold, you know.'

Bodkin turned away and sighed. Then, after opening the mortuary door, he stood aside to let Mrs Firth enter. He followed her to the side of the embalming table and waited as Elias, the mortuary assistant, pulled the sheet back to allow Hetty to see Lonnie's face.

Hetty's own face crumpled, and she burst into a fit of

sobbing that soon developed into a howl. 'Oh my boy, my darling boy, what have they done to you?'

Bodkin, Amy, Dr Allinson, and Elias left the room at that point to allow Hettie to have a few minutes alone with her son.

Ten minutes later, Bodkin led Hetty Firth into a small room that had been set aside for relatives of the deceased to recover after seeing their loved one.

'Again, Mrs Firth, I'm so sorry for your loss.'

'What do you care? He's just another name in a case file for you.'

'I care a great deal,' Bodkin replied. 'I'd much rather be locking Lonnie in a cell than looking at him lying on that table, Mrs Firth, and that's the truth.'

Hetty sniffed, then blew into her hanky. 'Where's my Erma? I want my Erma.'

'I'll get her for you,' Bodkin said as he opened the door and stepped into the corridor.

When she was alone with Hetty, Amy sat down in an armchair on the other side of a small oblong table. 'Can I get you anything, Mrs Firth? I think there's someone who can make you a cup of tea if you'd like one.'

'You can stick your tea where the sun doesn't shine,' Hetty sobbed as she buried her face in her hanky again.

Amy smoothed down her skirt and sat quietly as Hetty snuffled.

'Have you lived up here long, Mrs Firth?' she asked after a full two minutes of silence.

'What's it to you?' Hetty spat.

'I'm just trying to make conversation until Inspector Bodkin gets back with Erma,' she replied.

'Well, I don't want to talk. What are you anyway, one of those counsellors?'

'I'm not a qualified counsellor, but there's someone at my church who helps the bereaved if you'd like me to get in touch with him for you.'

'I'd like you to shut up,' Hetty said. 'My Lonnie is lying on a cold slab in there. He's all alone.'

'He's with God now,' Amy said. 'He's not alone anymore.'

'Pah! Spare me,' Hetty said, as she began to snuffle again. After a few seconds, she looked up over her handkerchief towards Amy. 'Do you really think he's with God...? I mean, if sin counts against you, he did a lot of sinning.'

'God will forgive him, Mrs Firth.' Amy reached across and took Hetty's hand. 'He forgives us all.'

Hetty blinked through watery eyes. 'You aren't going to try to get me to pray, are you?'

'No. If my dad was here, he would. I'm a believer, but I'm not as religious as he is. I'm not one for praying outside of church.'

Hetty suddenly grabbed Amy's hand with both of hers. 'I've never been sure, but I hope he's with God. The alternative is scary. You give me hope that I'll see him again one day.'

'You can count on it,' Amy said.

Just then the door opened and Erma, Hetty's only daughter, walked in, followed by Bodkin.

Erma plonked herself down in the seat next to her mother and looked across at Amy. 'Nice skirt,' she said. 'The blouse isn't bad either.'

Amy was wearing the same pleated skirt and cream blouse she had worn the night before. 'Thank you,' she replied with a smile.

'Where did you get it? I reckon that would suit me too.'

'Brigdens,' Amy said as Bodkin took the armchair next to her. 'It's just off High Street.'

'Ah, I know it,' Erma said with a nod. 'Isn't it a bit pricey in there?'

'Not really, not for what you get for your money. It's all decent quality.'

Amy smiled again as she looked across the low table towards Erma. She was a fresh-faced young woman in her early twenties with full lips, blue eyes and eyebrows pencilled in the same style as her mother. Her dark brown, wavy hair was thick and hung down to her shoulders. She had a trim figure with shapely legs that she crossed elegantly before reaching into the pocket of her powder blue jacket to retrieve her cigarettes and a silver Ronson lighter.

'Anyone mind?' she asked, sticking a Craven A in her mouth and lighting it before anyone could reply. She twisted in her seat to face her mother. 'What are you doing holding hands with her? Have you gone all soft or something?'

'I was just reassuring her that Lonnie will be with God now,' Amy said with a soft smile.

Erma's mouth sagged open. She looked at her mother with wide eyes. 'Religion... you were discussing...? Oh my God, that's priceless.' She continued to laugh as she turned to Amy. 'You're wasting your time there, love. She believes in Santa more than she believes in God.'

Hetty glared at her daughter and mouthed something that Amy didn't quite catch.

Bodkin leaned forward in his chair as he studied the two women. 'Your mother told us you didn't want to see your brother, Miss Firth. Are you sure you wouldn't like to spend a little time with him? I can arrange it.'

'It's ghoulish,' Erma replied. 'He's not really there, is he? It's just the shell of the person who used to be in there.'

'Even so...'

'No thank you,' Erma said firmly. 'I'll remember him how he was.' She paused. 'We didn't get on that well, anyway.'

'Why was that, Miss Firth?'

'Oh, call me Erma. Miss Firth indeed. No one ever calls me Miss Firth.' She looked over the table at Amy's feet. 'I like your shoes, too. Did you get those from Brigdens?'

'No. Though I do have a couple of pairs from there.' She lifted up a foot and wriggled it. 'I got these from Stead and Simpson.'

'Really? They look quite posh.' She looked Amy up and down again. 'I do like that skirt.'

Bodkin took a deep breath. 'Is that it for the fashion chat?'

Erma took a deep pull on her cigarette and blew the smoke across the table towards Bodkin. 'You could do with some fashion advice,' she said. 'That suit looks like it's been slept in for a week.' She gave Amy a quick glance, then turned her head back towards Bodkin. 'Is he your bloke? He's a bit of all right, isn't he? I wouldn't say no.' She paused as she looked him up and down again. 'He'd have to get rid of that suit, though.'

Amy bit her cheek to stop herself from laughing. She found that she liked the young woman immensely.

Bodkin was unfazed. 'I asked you what did you mean when you said you didn't get on with your brother, Miss... Erma?'

Erma leaned forwards and flicked ash from the end of her cigarette into the glass ashtray on the table. 'We had different interests. I like clothes, music, kissing men. He liked hitting or choking them until they gave him what he wanted.' She flicked her eyes towards her mother, who was giving her a disapproving look. 'Oh, it's true, Mum, you know it as well as I do. He was nothing more than a thug. He had no redeeming qualities at all.'

Erma stubbed out her cigarette, causing sparks to rise into the air. 'Can you get a drink in here?'

'I can ask if they can rustle up a pot of tea?' Amy said. 'The Salvation Army comes here most days to sit with the bereaved.'

Erma snorted. 'I said, a drink. You'd think they would have a cocktail bar in here, just to help people come to terms with their loss.' She shrugged. 'Ah well, I'll wait until I get home. Mum's still got half a case of the gin that Lonnie dropped off a few weeks ago.'

'You won't miss your brother, then?' Bodkin asked, trying to get the conversation back on track.

'I didn't see much of him, to be honest, and I didn't miss him when he was away. He used to go for months at a time.' She sighed and smiled to herself. 'Life was so much easier then.'

'How do you mean, easier?' Amy asked.

'We didn't have to put up with Mason bloody Lark for a start, and as for that Tumbler bloke...'

'Lark?' Bodkin tipped his head to the side as he asked the question.

'Yep. Lark, as in, sod this for a,' Erma replied. 'His sister is okay in small doses. She works behind the bar in a club in Gillingham. Mason was one of Lonnie's recruits.' She shuddered at the memory. 'More arms than an octopus.'

'Who else did he used to hang around with? Recently, I mean.' Bodkin leaned forward in his chair.

'Vincent Jury. He was another one who thought he could just touch you whenever he felt like it. Then there's that Mervin Challenger.' Erma pursed her lips and blew out. 'He's a cold fish, that one. He's not from around here, originally. He's from up north. Short cropped hair. Talks funny. Has a face even a mother would slap.'

'Up north. You mean Nottingham?' Amy asked.

'Yeah, I think that's where he's from.' Erma forced a thin

smile and narrowed her eyes as she did a quick impression of him. 'Ay up me duck. He talks like that.'

'Do you know where we might find this... Bodkin pulled out his notebook and jotted down a few words... Mervin Challenger?'

Erma shook her head. 'He's new to the scene. I don't know a lot about him apart from the fact that he thinks he has the right to grab hold of any woman he takes a fancy to.'

Bodkin made a note. 'What about Vincent Jury?'

Erma shrugged again. 'Dunno. He comes and goes. He never stayed with us. He only ever paid fleeting visits. Never even stopped for a cuppa or a drop of Lonnie's knocked off gin.'

'When was the last time you saw him?' Bodkin asked.

'Thursday evening. He came around to see Lonnie, but he wasn't in. Brian... that's my brother, went off with him. He knew where Lonnie was.'

Bodkin nodded as he jotted down more notes. 'And what about the rest of Lonnie's motley crew? Do they live around here?'

'They're all based in Gillingham, but they came up to see Lonnie if he was here.'

'Anyone else deserve a mention?' Bodkin asked.

'Just shut it, Erma,' Hetty snapped. 'You've told them more than enough already. Be careful. Word will get around that you're a snitch. You don't want Reggie Tumbler and his mob coming up here looking for you.'

'At least it would liven things up,' Erma replied as she reached for another cigarette.

Bodkin turned his attention to Hetty. 'Do you see much of Reggie Tumbler, Mrs Firth?'

'I've seen him on and off over the years,' she replied.

'Recently?'

'A few weeks ago. He was in the Bell with Lonnie, discussing something or other. I was in with Erma.'

'Did they argue?'

Hetty shrugged and didn't reply.

'I take it you really do want me to find out who killed your son, Mrs Firth?' Bodkin said.

'Of course I bloody do and if it turns out to be that vile swine, Reggie Tumbler, he'd better watch out.' She glared across the table. 'He doesn't scare me.' She sniffed, then straightened up in the chair.

'If he was behind it, we'll get him,' Bodkin replied.

'I don't mean to sound offensive, but you don't exactly fill me with confidence,' Hetty said sarcastically. 'I mean. Look what a balls up you made of it last time.'

'Last time,' Bodkin mused. 'Ah, you mean the time when your son hadn't actually been murdered?'

'That's irreverent.'

'Irrelevant,' Bodkin corrected.

Hetty snarled at the policemen. 'Oh, you're so sharp, aren't you? You ought to be careful, you might cut yourself.'

Bodkin scratched his stubbly chin. 'It's happened more than once.'

'Sharp as you might be, I still don't have any confidence in you, not after what happened before.'

Bodkin gave her his best smile. 'I was getting around to that, Hetty... do you mind if I call you, Hetty?'

'Call me Henry if you like. It won't make me think any better of you.'

Bodkin grinned. 'Let's go back three years, then, Henry. You identified the body and swore that it was your son. Do you remember that? You can't really accuse me of being useless for failing to find his killer when he wasn't even dead.'

Hetty's lips became a thin line. 'No one would have recognised that body. There was nothing left of his face. It could have been anybody.'

'Anybody, indeed. Any body to stand in for your son. Do you have any idea who that unfortunate young man was? Did he work for Lonnie or Reggie?'

Hettie shook her head. 'Like I said, I—'

Bodkin scratched the stubble on his chin again. 'It was a mess; I have to admit. Someone did a proper job on him, but you still identified him as Lonnie. Wasn't it from the skull tattoo he had on his right shoulder?'

'Yes.'

'A tattoo he'd had done in Margate when he was sixteen?'

'Yes.'

Bodkin scratched his head and gave her a confused look. 'But the body lying through there doesn't have a tattoo on his shoulder... nor anywhere else on his body, for that matter.'

Hetty and her daughter exchanged glances.

'He's got you done up like a kipper,' Erma said with a grin.

CHAPTER TEN

'I need the lavatory,' Hetty said, getting suddenly to her feet. 'It's all this talk of tea.'

'I'll show you where it is,' Bodkin said, getting up from his seat. He winked at Amy, then walked to the door and opened it. 'You two can have a chat about skirts.'

After Hetty and Bodkin had gone, Erma stubbed out her cigarette and again studied Amy's shoes. 'I really like those. Do you think I could try them on?'

'Of course,' Amy said, slipping them off her feet.

Erma took off her black and brown, two-tone saddle shoes and pulled on Amy's black Oxfords. 'Hey, we're the same size,' she said. She looked at her feet as she walked around the room. 'Stead and Simpson. I'll check them out tomorrow.' She lifted a foot and looked down at it, twisting her ankle to get a side view. 'How did you break your arm?'

'It's not broken, it's just a bad sprain. I fell over something at work.'

'Work? What do you do? I wouldn't mind a little job. I might have to get one now that we can't rely on Lonnie to keep us in the manner to which we have become accustomed.'

'Lonnie looked after you, did he? That's nice... I don't mean the way he got his money was nice, but at least he looked after his family.'

'Looked after is pushing it. He used to drop rolls of banknotes off for Mum to hide away. She used to take a bit for herself as a commission.'

'Oh, I see,' Amy replied as Erma began to walk around again.

'These are really comfy. Have you got many pairs of shoes at home?'

'I've got six pairs, and my winter boots.'

'Six pairs,' Erma said, looking down at her feet again. 'I've got two, those...' she pointed to the saddle shoes, 'and a pair of clunky lace up ankle boots. I need something different.' She looked at Amy hopefully. 'Do you think I could come around to your house and try some of your dresses on? We're about the same size.' She did a model walk across the back of the room, swinging her hips. 'Maybe we could go shopping together. Would that be possible? I'd really value your opinion on what suits me and what doesn't. I'm never quite sure, and you have such good taste.'

'I only buy from the sales rails at Brigdens,' Amy replied. 'I can't afford the expensive stuff.'

'I've got a fiver put away. Mum slipped it off Lonnie's stash roll on my birthday, but because I don't really know what suits me, I haven't spent it.'

'Has your mum still got Lonnie's money?' Amy asked.

Erma sat down, slipped off the shoes and handed them back to Amy. 'I'm not sure... I wouldn't tell you, anyway. The police might want it back... ill-gotten gains and all that, and we need something to live on for now.'

'I can show you around Brigdens. You should be able to build up a nice wardrobe for five pounds. Most of the clothes I buy are around ten shillings, though I'll sometimes go up to fifteen for something special.' She crossed her legs and smoothed down the pleated skirt. 'I work part time at The London Connection. Have you seen that shop? They don't do second-hand clothes or seconds, but it's good value if you want to buy something that's in fashion now.'

Erma closed her eyes and smiled to herself. 'I can see me in something sparkly for a night out at that posh Milton Hotel.' She opened her eyes again and looked into Amy's. 'Have you ever been in there?'

Amy nodded. 'A few times. They do a lovely Pimm's and you get ice with it as well as the fruit. It's very expensive though. My friend Constable Ferris sings there once a month. He's so good they pay him to do it. He needs to work on his impressions, though.'

Erma leaned forward and lowered her voice. 'I'll see if Mum still has a few quid stashed away in her undies drawer. We could go out one Saturday.'

'I'm booked up most Saturday nights. I go to the cinema with my best friend Alice, Ferris and Bodkin. We always go into the Milton if Ferris is singing. You're welcome to tag along if you're sure you won't feel like gooseberry.'

'This Ferris chap... is he very handsome?'

'He's very handsome, and he has a wonderful voice, but I'm afraid he's spoken for.'

'Your friend, Alice?'

'No, Alice likes someone a little older. Ferris is seeing Bodkin's sister, Sal. She lives down in Dover and can only get up here every other week. You'd like her. She's nice.'

'I don't fancy hanging around like a lost lamb,' Erma said. 'You said Ferris is a policeman. Are there any single, handsome coppers down at the station? That would really set the cat amongst the pigeons at home.'

'There are a few,' Amy said. 'I'll talk to Bodkin. He knows everything about everybody down there. Meanwhile, don't go stealing from your mum. She'll need every penny now she doesn't have Lonnie's money to look after.' She paused. 'How do you think she'll get on without him? I mean, I don't know her at all, but she doesn't seem the type to look for a job in a factory.'

'Mum...WORK! Oh, that's the funniest thing I've heard today. I might get a job. I'd like to be independent of her, but she'll never work. She thinks it's beneath her now.' She took out another cigarette and lit it. 'She used to work before Dad died, but when we moved up to Gillingham, her sister looked after us. Lonnie and Brian did a bit of work for Uncle Jed to pay our way. Uncle Jed wanted me and Mum to work on the streets. Auntie Cath had done a bit of that when he wasn't swindling enough out of people to keep us all going. Mum put her foot down and flatly refused. She said she'd move us all back to Maidstone and Jed needed the lads to do a lot of his dirty work as the police were watching him. They used to run for the bookies and pick out likely drunks as they left the pubs. Uncle Jed and his brother would rob them on the way home.'

Amy sighed. 'I'm so glad you didn't get roped into that business, Erma. It's no life for a young girl.'

'I was only twelve when he asked me to do it. I had no idea what he was talking about. I said I didn't want to walk the streets at night because I was scared of the dark and I was at school in the daytime.' Her face became sad as she thought about it. 'He was a dirty swine. He tried to get me and my best friend Anna into bed one night when Mum was out with Aunty Cath. Anna hit him on the head with the brass bedpan. I told Mum, and she got a knife to his throat when he was sleeping. He never tried it again.'

'What a horrible man,' Amy replied. 'Is he still living in Gillingham?'

'He was found floating in the canal one Sunday morning when I was thirteen. There were rumours that he'd got on the wrong side of Reggie Tumbler, but nothing was ever proved. My life got a lot easier after that. I wasn't asked to do anything a young girl shouldn't do. Reggie is a decent bloke, despite his reputation. He wouldn't have anything to do with prostitution. I'm not exactly sure why, but I heard Mum and Aunty Cath talking one night and I sort of got the gist of it. You see, Reggie's dad was a wife beater who forced his wife to go on the game to fund his drink and gambling habits. When Reggie was old enough and strong enough to be able to do something about it, he hit his dad with a piece of iron hidden in a sock. He was never the same after that. The attack left him brain damaged. He couldn't even eat properly and had to be spoon fed. Aunty Cath told Mum he ended up in an institution and Reggie did five years in prison.'

'What a life,' Amy said with a sigh.

'Reggie hated seeing women get hurt. When he was older and had a bit of money behind him, he started donating to a charity to help street girls, and woe betide anyone who worked for him if he discovered they'd treated a woman badly. He put his mum and sisters up in a fancy flat. They wanted for nothing. He was ruthless with men, though. You only ever got to make one mistake with Reggie. Make the same mistake twice and you paid for it.'

'So, Lonnie and Brian went to work for him after your uncle died.'

Erma nodded. 'It wasn't like being in Fagin's gang in Oliver Twist, but they did have to get their hands dirty on a regular basis. Reggie paid them well, but he insisted that half of what they earned went to Mum. They weren't too happy, but they couldn't do anything about it. Reggie paid her the money direct. He stopped it from their wages, like tax.'

'I don't know what to make of this Reggie Tumbler,' Amy said. 'Is he living up here now?'

'No, he lives in Gillingham. We don't see him much at all. Lonnie was doing bits and bobs for him still, but he had his own little crime empire that he was trying to expand.'

'What happens to that little crime empire now?'

'Oh, Brian will probably try to step up. He'll make a mess of it, though. He isn't as tough and nowhere near as smart as Lonnie. He tries to make out he's a hard man, but he isn't, really. Not hard enough for that game, anyway. He'll need someone to help enforce the rules. My guess is, he'll ask Reggie to help out. It will mean giving up more than half of the money the gang makes from protection, bookies running and the robberies they take part in, but at least he'll be safe. No one around here will dare take him on if he has Reggie's backing.'

Erma was quiet for a time, then she suddenly smiled at Amy. 'Do you think you could get me a job at your dress shop?'

'I can ask,' Amy said. 'They need someone temporary while I'm off. I don't work there all the time, though. I'm a machinist at The Mill. Do you know it? It's the big garment factory on the other side of Spinton.'

'I've heard of it. I'm not trained on sewing machines, though.' She tipped her head as she looked at Amy. 'You don't look like a machinist. You look like you work in an office... not a stuffy one, like a solicitor's or an estate agent, but something exciting, like a fashion magazine.'

'I wish,' Amy replied. 'I quite like both my jobs as it happens.' She laughed. 'And as far as I'm aware, there aren't any fashion magazines based in Spinton. We're lucky to have a couple of decent shops. It's a bit of a backwater when it comes to fashion.'

'Well, you should move to London then. Hey! I could come with you. We can get a flat together and hit the fleshpots.'

'I'm happy enough here,' Amy replied. 'It's where I grew up. Everything I know is here. My family, Bod... I mean, I know it's not Monte Carlo, but it suits me.'

'You should set your sights higher,' Erma said seriously. 'Ah well, never mind. I suppose I can stick it here now that I've found someone I can relate to.' She reached across the table for Amy's good hand. 'Please say you'll be my friend.'

Before Amy could reply, the door opened, and Bodkin stuck his head into the room. 'It's time to go, Amy. Bring Coco Chanel with you. Her mother has slipped the leash. Hurry now. The car's outside. She can't have got far.'

CHAPTER
ELEVEN

'Where are you living?' Bodkin asked Erma as she clambered into the back of the Morris.

'Victoria Street, number forty-six, but I don't think she'll have gone there.'

'I hope not. I'd need a van load of coppers with me if we ventured too far up that street.' He looked over his shoulder. 'Where will she have gone then? The pub?'

'Not when she's got all that free gin at home,' Erma replied. She thought for a moment. 'I reckon she'll head for Lonnie's place.'

'Where's that? Is it close by?' Bodkin asked.

'He was looking after a small flat in an apartment block down by the river. It's owned by Reggie Tumbler.'

'Looking after it?'

'House sitting,' Erma replied. 'Mum wanted us all to move in because anything would be better than that rat infested dump we're living in at the moment, but it wasn't feasible. It only has one bedroom. He said he'd find us something better, but he never did.'

'How long have you been on Victoria Street?'

'About three months. We moved around the Gillingham area before that. A month here, two there. I got sick to death of moving house, but we didn't have enough money to stay anywhere for more than a few weeks, and we couldn't risk anyone finding us and tracing Lonnie. He moved around the country. He spent some time in Scotland, a few months in Liverpool, then Nottingham, but he dropped in to see us every so often. I'd like to say he was missing us, but I think he came by more to make sure his protection racket and other schemes were still paying their dividends. He used to drop us a fistful of cash, then clear off again. It was never enough for us to live comfortably on, hence moving around so much. I lost count of how many moonlight flits we did.'

'Who looked after the... I hate to use this word... business when Lonnie was away? And what did he do himself when he was in Liverpool or Nottingham?' Bodkin asked.

Erma shrugged. 'I have no idea what Lonnie was up to when he wasn't here. Brian was supposed to look after things but he got into a mess when he tried to muscle in on some of Christopher Dagger's territory. His daughter, Bessie, is running the show for him while he does a three-year stretch for embezzlement. She's a harder nut than her dad, Inspector. She's not much older than me, but she rules her little realm with a rod of iron. I wouldn't like to cross her, that's for sure.'

'And Brian got on the wrong side or her.'

'With knobs on. It took a long meeting with Reggie to sort matters out. Even then, Brian had to hand over a large amount of cash. Lonnie was furious when he found out.'

'Did he do anything about it?'

Erma let out a sharp laugh. 'Oh yes. But then he thought he was the new Al Capone.'

Bodkin stretched his neck to see if he could spot Hetty

amongst a small crowd of women walking along High Street. Disappointed, he took a quick look into the back of the car.

'What did he do?'

'He knocked over one of the Dagger's back street bookmakers as he was counting the takings. He got away with over three hundred quid.'

'I bet that got Bessie's back up.'

'You'd think so, but we didn't get to hear of anything. Nothing happened to Lonnie, at least. He was with us for ten days.'

'How long ago was this, Erma?'

'A couple of months. Not long.'

'What about Brian? Were threats ever made against him over the matter?'

'Not that I know of. I'm sure Mum would have heard if there had been. Brian would have come to her, begging for help.'

'Or he might have gone to Reggie Tumbler again,' Bodkin said.

'It's possible, but no, I don't think so. Brian was extremely concerned when the robbery happened, but after a day or so, it seemed to be business as usual. Lonnie didn't clear off again, either. That's when he moved into Reggie's flat. Mum and I had come up to Spinton to get away from it all, just in case.'

'Speaking of cases. What was in the box that your mum picked up from your old neighbours in Gillingham a few weeks ago?'

'I honestly don't know. I assumed it was a few of her things that we didn't have room to fit in the van when we did yet another moonlight flit.'

'Where is it now?'

Erma shrugged. 'I never saw it. She didn't bring it into the house on Victoria Street, that's for sure.'

'Where does Brian live, Erma?' Amy asked.

'He's got a house in Gillingham. Just a rented place. Nothing special. He shares it with Mason Lark's sister, Birdie. I think they're an item now.'

'Birdie Lark? Is that her real name?' Bodkin asked.

'No, her first name is Dora, but everyone's called her Birdie since she was a kid. She works in a club in Gillingham. It's one of Reggie's, I believe.'

Bodkin craned his neck again to look at a gaggle of women walking along Middle Street.

Erma noticed him check the group. 'I wouldn't bother if I were you, Inspector. She's far too lazy to walk. She'll have hailed a cab or got on a bus if there's one going in that direction.'

'You don't think much of Hetty, do you?' Bodkin said as he moved up into third gear and accelerated along Middle Street.

'She's my mother. There's not a lot else to say about her. I know she had it rough for a long time and I feel sorry for her, but to be honest, Mr Bodkin, I can't wait to get a job and a place of my own. I can't wait to be rid of the lot of them.' She tapped Bodkin on the shoulder. 'I tried to get your girlfriend to go to London with me and set up a new life there, but she couldn't bear to leave you behind.' She smiled to herself. 'That's so romantic. Have you asked her to marry you yet? I'd hurry if I were you. There'll be a queue of men waiting in line.'

Bodkin slowed, then pulled up outside of the police station. Leaving the engine running, he rushed through the front door and came out a couple of minutes later carrying a small bunch of keys. Getting back into the driver's seat, he waved them at Amy before slipping them into his jacket pocket. 'They're from Lonnie's evidence bag,' he said. 'I reckon one of them will fit the front door of his little hideaway flat.'

Bodkin pulled up to the junction with the main Gillingham Road, then took a right and drove for just over a mile until he came to a sign advertising three, as yet, unsold apartments in the two blocks of flats that had been finished the previous year. Bodkin and Amy had visited them once before, to question a young PA about the murder of one of her clients. As he pulled into the drive leading to the flats, a black cab from the Spinton Taxi Company pulled out.

'I wonder why Reggie chose to buy one of these,' Bodkin said as he pulled up on the forecourt outside the twin blocks. He got out of the car and stared up at the yellow brick, four-storey buildings. 'Did he buy one with a river view or one out of the way at the back overlooking the cement works?'

'It's on the top floor at the back, so it has a beautiful view of the cement works and as a bonus you can see the iron foundry too,' Erma said as she climbed out of the car. 'It's tiny, but you can get to it from a fire escape staircase. No one would know anyone was living there if you didn't want them to.'

Bodkin searched the bunch of keys in an attempt to find one that fitted the lock of the sturdy-looking, white-painted front door. Frustrated at being unable to find one, he slipped the keys back into his pocket and set off for the rear of the block.

The fire escape was made of iron and zigzagged its way up the back wall of the building, giving emergency access to all floors. Grumpily climbing the series of stairs, the policeman looked through the crescent moon shaped glass that was built into the top of the door on each floor, into the narrow corridors that separated the flats. When he got to the top level, he blew out his cheeks and reached for the keys again.

'Top floor flats are a young man's domain,' he puffed as he tried the first key in the lock. It didn't fit. The fourth one he tried did, however, and he pushed the door open and stepped into the duck egg blue painted corridor. 'What's the flat number?'

'Seven,' Erma said as she came to a halt behind Bodkin.

'Shall we be polite and knock or should we just...' This time he found the key at the first attempt and after turning it in the lock, he pushed it open and stepped into the apartment's kitchen, where he found Hetty Firth drinking from the neck of a bottle of Johnny Walker Black Label whisky.

'Fancy meeting you here,' he said.

Hetty choked as she looked wide eyed at the three interlopers. 'Couldn't you at least knock?'

'We thought we'd surprise you,' Bodkin said, giving her his best smile. 'Have you got a key for the front door? We had to use the tradesman's entrance.'

Hetty took another glug from the whisky bottle, wiped her mouth on the back of her hand, then put it down heavily on the short counter. 'I don't know what it is you're looking for,' she said eventually. 'But it's probably gone. Someone got here before you... and me. They've left a right mess behind.'

Bodkin looked around the tiny but tidy kitchen before his eyes fell on the open door that led to the lounge. Even from this viewpoint, he could see some of the objects that had been left scattered across the floor of the living room. Holding up one hand to warn everyone to stay where they were, he stepped through the doorway and looked around.

The place had been ransacked. The room served as both bedroom and living quarters. There was a single bed on the far wall that had been stripped of its sheets and blankets. The mattress was doubled over on the bedsprings so that you could see the wooden floor beneath. The drawers belonging to the highboy dresser had been pulled out and their contents tipped into untidy piles on the floor. The single wardrobe door was hanging open and Lonnie's clothes had been unceremoniously thrown out. Even the small rectangular dining table had been tipped onto its side. In the tiny bathroom that led off the lounge, towels and the contents of a small wall cabinet were strewn across the white-tiled floor.

Lying near the table was a highly polished wooden box which had had its small padlock forced open and three dresses, a single brightly coloured curtain, and several sheets of paper, had been tipped out.

Bodkin knelt down and picked up one of the sheets. It was a receipt for a two-piece suit. Another receipt was for a month's rent on a property in Nottingham, while a third one gave details of the purchase of a leather-covered, lead nightstick and a four-inch switchblade knife.

There was also a handgun licence in the name of Michael Standish, but there was no sign of the weapon.

'Was there a gun in here when you picked it up from Gillingham, Hetty?' Bodkin asked.

Hetty shrugged. 'No idea. I was just asked to pick it up.'

'So, you were unaware that three of your dresses were inside? I assume, judging from the style, they are yours.' He looked up at Hetty. 'I can't see Erma going within a mile of them.'

Hetty glared at the policeman but said nothing.

Bodkin picked up the curtain and held it up. Stained onto the brightly coloured floral pattern was a dirty black mark. Bodkin sniffed it. 'Gun oil, if I'm not mistaken.' He dropped the curtain into the box and straightened up before turning to face Mrs Firth. 'So, Hetty, I'll ask again, was there a gun inside this box?'

'I honestly don't know and I wasn't looking for that, anyway. I was more concerned about the blue bag with two thousand pounds in it.'

CHAPTER TWELVE

Bodkin whistled.

'Two thousand pounds? Where on earth did he get two thousand pounds?'

Hetty shook her head. 'I do not know. He said it was his nest egg.'

Bodkin's eyes widened. 'And you left it with your neighbours? That was risky, wasn't it? What if they'd opened the box to have a sneaky peek? They could have been in Monte Carlo by now.'

'They wouldn't have dared. They were terrified of Lonnie and the people he hung around with.'

'Another question that springs to mind is, why didn't you grab some of it before the padlock was snapped on?'

'It was already snapped on. I was warned not to touch it. He said trouble might find me if I did. Anyway, there was only one key and Lonnie had it.'

'So that was it. You just left two thousand pounds sitting in a box in a neighbour's house in Gillingham while you live in a slum in Spinton. Forgive me, but I can't see that. Why didn't you force the padlock and put a new one on? They only cost a few shillings.'

'Because padlocks come with two keys,' Hetty replied. 'Lonnie had one, but I don't know who had the other. I could have really dropped myself in it if I'd changed the padlock. I didn't want Reggie Tumbler's mob coming after me.'

'So you think it was Reggie's money that Lonnie was looking after? Couldn't it have been someone else's, maybe money Lonnie had stolen from his rivals? We know he took three hundred from the Dagger family.'

'He didn't say. He just said I was to look after the box and to keep my hands off the contents.'

Bodkin sat down on the bed frame and looked towards Amy. 'Do you have a question or two?'

Amy nodded. 'I've got a few thoughts.' She turned to Hetty. 'How did you know there was money in the box?'

'He told me. He said that he, and someone else, knew exactly how much was in there, so I mustn't do what I usually did with his money and skim a few pounds off the top for myself. He knew I always did. He kept empathising that.'

'Emphasising,' Amy said, then went on. 'I still don't understand why you left the box with the neighbours, knowing what was inside. I mean, as Bodkin said, it was really taking a big risk. Especially as it contained a gun. If their curiosity had got the better of them and they had opened it, the Robertsons might have gone to the police.' She pointed to the box. 'It's not that big, is it? Surely you could have found room for it in the van when you moved.'

Hetty smiled a thin smile. 'There was never any danger of them opening the box. You didn't see the way they acted when Lonnie was about. They almost tugged their forelocks, they were so afraid of him. As for leaving it behind. Lonnie warned us that we might be followed, and as it turned out, we were. It took us two trips to get all our stuff out and we were tracked both times. While we were back in Gillingham to pick up the second load, the house on Victoria Street was broken into. A car followed us all the way up here on the second journey, too. We left the back door of the house open on that first night to save anyone the trouble of breaking the lock.'

'Did anyone come in?' Amy asked.

'I don't know. They didn't disturb Erma and me if they did.'

'I'm surprised you had anything left by the next morning,' Bodkin said. 'That lot on Victoria Street would nick the milk from a crying baby given half a chance.'

'They knew better than to try it on with us. They'd been warned off.'

'Who helped you move?' Amy asked. 'You and Erma couldn't have managed it on your own.'

'Brian and the Lark lad.'

'Lark?'

'As in, up with the,' Hetty replied.

'Yes, but did he have a first name?' Amy asked.

'Oh, yeah, Mason... Mason Lark. Erma doesn't like him; says he can't keep his hands to himself.'

'His sister's all right, though.' Erma added.

'Birdie?'

'That's the one,' Hetty said.

'She's Brian's girlfriend, right? So Brian didn't move to Spinton with you. He went back to Gillingham?'

'Yes.'

'Your sons left two women alone in that place?'

'Lonnie dropped in the next morning to see if we were all right.'

'And to check on the whereabouts of his box.'

Hetty nodded. 'He was happy with where we'd left it. He said he was going up north for a few days, but he'd be back soon. He told us that he'd had a word with a few of our new neighbours and that they were going to look out for us. He said it was only a stopgap measure, and he'd have us out of there as soon as he could.'

'And did Brian come over to visit?' Bodkin asked.

Hetty shook her head. 'No, he couldn't tear himself away from Birdie's feather bed.' She sniffed. 'They live in sin, they aren't married.'

'Did Brian know what was in the box?' Bodkin asked.

Hetty pulled a face as she thought. 'I don't think Lonnie ever told him, but I could be wrong. He had to come with me to pick it up from the Robertsons because I can't drive and nor can Erma.'

'And the Larks? Could they have got to know?'

'If Brian knew, he could have told Birdie, but I don't think he'd be that stupid. Mason Lark was just someone Lonnie used as a bit of extra muscle. He wasn't in the privy with him.'

Bodkin scratched his head. 'In the privy with him?'

'I think she means he wasn't privy to Lonnie's business doings,' Amy said.

Bodkin stuck up a thumb. 'Privy... doings... good one.'

'I know what I mean. Stop bloody correcting me,' Hetty said, glaring at Amy.

Erma put her hands over her face as she groaned. 'In the privy,' she said, then she began to laugh.

'Don't you start,' Hetty warned her. 'I've got enough on my plate with Albert Inespine over here.'

Amy bit her cheek and looked out of the window.

'How did you get your keys, Mrs Firth?' Bodkin asked suddenly. 'I've got Lonnie's keys here... the one to the fire escape door, at least. I couldn't find one to fit the main entrance.'

'Lonnie gave them to me. He wanted me to check everything was tickety-boo over here while he was away.'

'Brian didn't have a key then?'

'No.'

'Are you sure of that?'

'As far as I know, he didn't have a set, but then my name's not Claire Voyant, you know.'

'No, I get that,' Bodkin said, struggling to keep a straight face. 'But did he know you had a set?'

'Of course he did. He was there when Lonnie gave them to me.'

'When was that?'

'The day Brian and I brought the box over to this place. Lonnie was waiting when we arrived. He gave me two keys. One for the main entrance and one for the flat. He said he always used the back entrance key so that he wouldn't have to risk bumping into the other residents as he came and went.'

'And it's definitely Reggie Tumbler's flat?' Bodkin asked.

'Yes, though Lonnie said he wasn't sure if he still used it himself.'

'So why keep it? Why go to all the expense if you're not even going to rent it out?'

'Maybe he used it in the same way Lonnie did. Coming in and out of the back door. Reggie might have stashed money away, or something he wouldn't want anyone to know about,' Amy said.

Bodkin frowned. 'That's a possibility, but he's got access to more than enough properties in Gillingham. He's got his clubs, pubs, back street bookie's houses.' He got to his feet and stretched his back. 'I'll check with the council to see whose name is on the rates bill.'

Hetty picked up the three dresses from the floor and folded them over the crook of her arm. 'I'll have to press these now.' She sniffed the air. 'I hope the stink of that gun oil comes out with the hot iron or I'll have to wash them and I don't fancy the chances of them still being on the line the next morning.'

Bodkin put the curtain back into the box, then closed the lid and picked it up. 'I'll get this dusted for prints and I think we'd better get forensics in to check over the whole flat to see if we can get an idea of who else has been in here. We've got Reggie's prints on file down in Gillingham and I know we'll have Lonnie's.' He turned towards Hetty. 'Has Brian ever been arrested for anything serious?'

'He's been questioned a few times but never arrested, as far as I know,' Erma said. 'You can take my fingerprints if you want.'

'You're getting too familiar with the police, Erma,' Hetty said. 'Just remember which family you belong to.'

'As if I could forget,' Erma whispered to herself.

'We'll need your prints too, Mrs Firth,' Bodkin said. 'And I'd like that set of keys, please. We'll have to get a couple of uniformed officers over to question the other residents and I don't think the forensic team will be too happy if I tell them they've got to cart all their equipment up the fire escape to get in.'

After locking up the flat, Bodkin followed the women down the stairs to the third floor, where he found a white-haired man standing outside flat five. 'Are you buying flat seven?' he asked Bodkin.

The inspector shook his head. 'I'm a policeman,' be replied. 'I'm involved in a murder inquiry.'

'Murder, eh,' the old man said. 'Was someone killed in the flat?'

'No,' Bodkin replied. 'But we'd like any information you can give us about the person who was living there, or anyone who has visited recently.'

'Only recently? People have been coming and going for a couple of years now. There was a young woman living in there initially. Then it was empty for about a year. I heard someone moving about for a few days, a month or so back, but over the last week there have been a few people visiting. It sounded like there was a herd of elephants trampling about on Friday night. Then a man and a woman came flying down the stairs. He was carrying a blue bag. She was laughing like a maniac.'

'Can you describe them?' Bodkin asked.

'Of course I can. My old knees might be playing up, but there's nothing wrong with my eyes.'

Bodkin waited patiently.

'Oh, sorry, you want the description. Well, he was in his mid to late twenties, brown hair, needing a cut. He was wearing dark trousers, a checked shirt, and a striped pullover under a brown jacket. Oh, he had a brown hat on. She was a pretty girl with short fair hair, she was dressed more like a bloke than a woman... she had trousers on, at least.' He thought for a moment. 'She had a beauty spot on her chin, but the thing I remember most was the language. I've never heard anything like it coming from a woman. What the... I won't use the word... are you looking at you old ....? Well, you get the gist of it.'

Bodkin put the box down and pulled out his notebook and pen. After jotting down a few notes, he took the old man's details, then put the notebook away and picked up the box again. 'I'll send someone around to take a full statement tomorrow, Mr Neilson. Thank you for the information you provided. You've been very helpful.'

As they walked down the stairs to the second floor, Erma suddenly stopped and waited for Bodkin to catch up. 'I know who the old man saw,' she said quietly. 'It was Brian and his girlfriend, Birdie.'

CHAPTER THIRTEEN

After begging Amy to allow her to pay a visit to look through her record collection and wardrobe, Erma, along with Hetty, got out of Bodkin's car at the bottom of Victoria Street. After watching them walk up the hill towards their dingy terraced home, Bodkin drove Amy back to her parent's cottage on Long Lane.

'Do you fancy a couple in the Old Bull tonight seeing as you haven't got to go to work tomorrow?' he asked as they stood with their arms around each other at her front gate.

'I'd like to, Bodkin, but Dad's home and I've hardly seen him in weeks. You're welcome to come around if you feel a bit left out.'

Bodkin laughed. 'I'll leave you to your lovely family, Amy. I'll spend the evening writing up some notes about today's events, then have a think about what it all means to the investigation. I'm updating Laws and Grayson tomorrow morning, then, in the afternoon, I'm planning to take a trip to Gillingham to see if I can catch up with Brian Firth and his silver tongued girlfriend, Birdie.' He kissed Amy on the forehead. 'I'd be delighted if you could find time to accompany me.'

'Just try to stop me,' Amy said, looking up into Bodkin's face. 'Erma's coming around at about eleven, don't forget.'

'You really like her, don't you.'

'She's lovely, so different from her mother. She needs a clean break from that family. If I can help her do that, I will.'

'She loves you too, that's pretty obvious,' Bodkin replied. He thought for a moment. 'Actually, it might make sense if we took her with us. She knows them both very well and she might be able to help us track them down if they aren't at home.'

Amy smiled. 'She'll love feeling part of the investigation. She's a bright young woman. I'm sure she'll be able to help us a lot. She knows everyone we might need to speak to down there.' She yawned suddenly, then, after putting her hand to her mouth, she kissed Bodkin on the lips. 'It's been such a long day. I'd better get in or I won't have time to talk to Dad before I fall asleep on the sofa.'

Amy spent a happy evening chatting and laughing along with her parents as they listened to the Ovaltineys Concert Party on Radio Luxembourg. The radio show that was actually made for children was a regular feature of the Rowlings' Sunday evening ritual. Afterwards they would sit and chat while Mr Rowlings enjoyed a glass or two of Scotch and Mrs Rowlings knitted. Amy usually sat with an unread book on her lap as she joined in with the conversation. As she predicted, by nine o'clock she was leaning back on the sofa, fast asleep, with her injured wrist resting on a cushion. Her mother woke her at ten and handed over a mug of hot, milky Ovaltine which she sipped whilst listening to the latest news on the radio.

At ten-thirty, she kissed her parents, wished them a good night and went up to bed.

The next morning, at eleven on the dot, Amy answered a repeated knock on the front door to find Erma standing on the porch. 'It's me!' she declared, leaning forward to give Amy a hug. She followed her into the living room, where she was introduced to Mrs Rowlings. Not long afterwards, she was handed a cup of tea and offered a Huntley and Palmer's ginger nut from a colourful biscuit tin.

After they had finished their tea, Amy led her upstairs to her bedroom where Erma put her hand over her wide open mouth as she spotted the highly polished radiogram that sat against the wall opposite Amy's bed.

'Oh, my Go... I mean goodness. Sorry, Amy, I didn't mean to take God's name in vain, but that is beautiful. Does it sound as good as it looks?'

'Better,' Amy said, opening the box that contained her prized record collection. 'It sounds as though you're sitting in the room as the artist sings to you. What do you fancy? There's all sorts in here.'

'Do you have any Bing Crosby? I adore Bing Crosby. I have this recurring dream where our eyes meet as we look across a crowded room and we end up getting married. I know it's silly, but it's my favourite dream.'

Amy sorted through her records and pulled out one in a paper sleeve. 'How about this one? It's about six years old now, but I only got my copy earlier this year. My uncle Maurice imports sheet music and records and I get first choice of his new stock.' She put the record on the turntable, twisted a switch to make it spin, then turned the volume knob up slightly from its usual position. Crosby's dulcet baritone voice almost oozed out of the ten-inch loudspeaker at the bottom of the cabinet as he sang, The Very Thought Of You.

'Oooh, that sound. You weren't exaggerating. It's terrific.' She swayed her hips to the music. 'Where did you get it? How much was it? I bet it was really expensive. How could you afford it on factory wages? No, don't tell me. That's a private matter.' She closed her eyes as she swayed. 'I'm going to get one, too. I'll start saving up for it.'

'Mines only an ex demonstration model, but it was very expensive. I had to save up for ages to buy it.' Amy replied.

'I *LOVE* this song,' Erma said, holding out her arms towards Amy. 'Can we dance? Please say yes.'

Amy slipped out of her sling and the two young women danced slowly across the carpet.

'Don't let on to my best friend,' Amy said with a laugh. 'Alice thinks she's my only dance partner.'

When Bing had finished crooning, Erma begged her to play it again. After that, she sat on the bed, passing Amy the records she wanted to hear.

After half a dozen records had been played, she turned her attention to Amy's wardrobe, where she pulled out dress after dress to hold in front of herself as she looked into the half-length mirror. When she'd had her fill of clothes, she sat in front of the dressing table and had a good look through Amy's makeup collection.

'When do you think we could go shopping?' she asked. 'I'm so looking forward to it, Amy. I've got nothing at home to compare to your gorgeous dresses. How many do you think I'll get for my five pounds?'

'I usually go on a Saturday morning,' Amy replied. 'Mainly because that's when all the new items are put on the sales rails. You don't have to wait until then, though. I think there are quite a few items on the rails that would suit you. Your skin has a darker tone than mine and your hair is a different shade and style. There was a dress I looked at the other week that they can't sell. It has a tear on the seam at the side. It would only take me twenty minutes to sort that out. There's a skirt with a single front pleat too. I reckon that would suit you down to the ground.'

'You mean you'd fix it for me? Oh, Amy, that's very kind of you. I'll pay you for your time, of course.'

Amy patted her on the arm. 'I'd be happy to do it. There's no need for payment.' She suddenly remembered her injured wrist. 'Oh, I'd forgotten about that. You might have to wait a few weeks to get the repairs done… mind you, I bet Mum would do it. She's a fantastic seamstress.' She smiled at Erma. 'Not everything we buy will need a repair, though. You'll get plenty of things to wear straight off the rail.'

Erma suddenly leapt to her feet. 'Can we go now? There might be someone buying that dress as we sit here talking.' She hurried to the bedroom door. 'Please, Amy.'

Amy shook her head sadly. 'Actually, Erma, Bodkin's picking me up soon. We're going over to Gillingham to see if we can find Brian and Birdie. He wondered if you would like to come with us, seeing as you know where we might find them.'

'Really! Ooh, that sounds exciting! I'm sure I can help.' She grinned, then looked back towards Amy's wardrobe. 'When do you think we can go shopping? Tomorrow perhaps?'

'I'll have to see what Bodkin has planned for me,' Amy replied. 'It's not often we get to spend so much time together and I don't want to miss out on any of the excitement of the investigation.'

'No, of course you don't. I quite understand. He's your lover, after all. You must want to spend as much time with him as you can.'

Amy blushed. 'He's not my lover, Erma. Not yet anyway. We'll have to be married before we get that close.' She turned away to hide her embarrassment. 'We are very close, just not that close.'

'I do envy you,' Erma said wistfully. 'He's so handsome. Not like Bing Crosby or Clarke Gable, but a little more rugged.' She sighed. 'I wish I had a boyfriend like that. He'd have to wear smarter clothes, though.'

'There's someone perfect for you. You just haven't met him yet,' Amy said reassuringly. 'Besides which, you're only young. You should be looking to have a bit of fun before you get tied down. Live a little first.'

Erma's face lit up. 'You're right, of course. It's just that... well, I'd like a strong, handsome man to look after me, someone to put his arm around me when I need a cuddle.' Her eyes shone as she imagined the scene. 'You said there were some single men at the police station. That would really put the cat amongst the pigeons in the family. I can just see me turning up to a christening with a copper on my arm.' She laughed. 'I can picture Birdie's face, too.'

'Forgive me for asking this,' Amy said. 'But you really don't seem to be too upset by Lonnie's death. He was your brother, after all.'

'He wasn't a nice man, Amy, and we were never close. He spent all his time hurting people. I didn't like him at all. We've hardly spoken for the last five years. He didn't care about Mum either, he just used her.' She looked down at her hands, then back at Amy. 'Does that sound awful? It probably does, doesn't it? But he used to leave me with those disgusting friends of his. He didn't care what they tried to do to me. As long as they obeyed his orders when he dished them out, he let them do what they liked.'

A tear ran down her cheek. Amy hurried across and hugged her tightly. 'They didn't... hurt you, did they?'

'They came close. I ended up sleeping with a knife under my

pillow. Vincent Jury came into my room drunk on more than one occasion. And that Mason Lark... he used to try it on every time we were alone, sometimes when we weren't. Mum had a word with Lonnie and he said he'd talk to them, but I don't think he ever did. They used to call me frigid. Mason reckoned I must be a lesbian because I kept turning him down.'

'You'd think your older brother would want to look after you,' Amy said. 'What about Brian? Do you feel the same way about him?'

Erma shook her head. 'No, Brian's all right. He got me out of a scrape or two, but as I told you, he's not as tough as he tries to make himself look. Vincent gave him a proper beating once. He was drunk, or on something harder than liquor. There was no reasoning with him. I thought my number was up, but Brian stepped in, bless him, and I managed to get away. I stayed out all night. He'd cleared off by the time I got back the next day, but he'd made a right mess of Brian's face. Brian wouldn't say anything to Lonnie because he was terrified of Vincent, but I told him. Lonnie just laughed and said that Brian needed to toughen up a bit if he wanted to make a name for himself.'

'Poor Brian,' Amy replied.

'He got to hate Lonnie too, in the end.'

Amy shook her head. 'I feel so sorry for you, and your mum, having to put up with all that.'

'Mum's not quite as tough as she looks either, Amy. It's mostly a front, though she does have a lot of people fooled. I'd have left her a long time ago if she was anywhere near as bad as Lonnie.'

Before Amy could reply, she heard her mother's voice calling up the stairs. 'Amy! Bodkin's here, love. Lunch is ready.'

When Amy walked into the living room, she found Bodkin standing by the table, which had already been set for lunch.

'It's only potted meat on the sandwiches. It should have

been shrimp paste, but we've run out.' Mrs Rowlings pulled a concerned face. 'I hope that's all right.'

Amy greeted Bodkin with a peck on the cheek, then after motioning for Erma to take a seat, she sat down herself. When Mrs Rowlings had taken her own seat, Bodkin finally joined them.

He looked hungrily at the mound of potted meat sandwiches that Amy's mum had placed in the middle of the table.

'Get stuck in, Mr Bodkin,' Mrs Rowlings said. 'I bet you haven't eaten today.'

Bodkin reached forward and picked up a handful of the triangle cut sandwiches. 'I didn't have time. I had to be in first thing to meet Chief Inspector Laws.'

'Oh, him!' Amy said with a feeling. 'I bet he asked you about the missing pig before anything else.'

Bodkin chewed quickly and swallowed his food. 'Correct,' he said. 'But this time I had some news for him.'

'About Tom Piper?'

Bodkin nodded. 'There was a report on my desk when I got in. A man tried to sell a live pig to a farmer in Mossmoor over the weekend. The farmer in question didn't want it, but he mentioned the event in the pub on Saturday night and the village constable had dropped in for a pint or two. He'd received a message from us, asking him to keep his eye out as Mossmoor is a farming community.'

'So the pig is still alive? That's strange. He must be having to feed it. I wonder where he's getting the food from... Mind you, they'll eat anything. Just ask Alice. She's an expert in anything remotely piggy.'

Traffic on the Gillingham Road was fairly light until they reached the outskirts of the town where they ran into a tailback caused by a line of slow-moving army trucks.

Erma, sitting in the rear seat of Bodkin's black Morris, waved to the soldiers in the back of the trucks as Bodkin accelerated to pass them. 'I wonder how Lonnie would have fared in the army,' she said aloud. 'Though I think he'd have found a way to dodge the call up.' She waved to another truck load of recruits. 'They won't make a soldier of Brian, either. He's not the warrior type.'

'I don't think the army has a need for the skills Lonnie and Brian possess,' Bodkin said, as he pulled onto the right side of the road to pass another truck. 'Although they could maybe send them over the enemy lines to nick all their guns while they're asleep.'

'Will you be called up, Inspector?' Erma asked.

Before Bodkin could respond, Amy jumped in. 'Bodkin won't have to fight. He's in what they call a reserved occupation. Policemen, farm workers, engineers and miners are all exempt from the call up. Isn't that right, Bodkin?'

Bodkin nodded but said nothing.

'That's lucky,' Erma said. 'There are going to be a lot of lonely women out there in a few months' time. The remaining men will have a field day.' She was silent for a few moments, then went on. 'Speaking of policemen. Amy says you know which ones are available at the police station, Inspector. Could you run me up a list of the good-looking ones?'

Bodkin snorted. 'I've got enough on my plate as it is, young lady. Besides which, I'm no judge of handsomeness. You might need Amy's help with that.'

Erma pursed her lips. 'But you have a good idea which ones I might stand a chance with. It's even better that he wouldn't have to go away to war when it all kicks off properly.'

'They can still enlist if they want to. They aren't forced to sit it out at home.'

'Sit it out? It's not a football match, Bodkin,' Amy replied. 'They could be volunteering to get themselves killed or badly injured, at least.' She turned side on in her seat and looked at Erma in the back. 'There will be some who want to do what they think is the heroic thing.'

'It's a patriotic thing, Amy. They'll want to do their best for King and Country.'

'Oh, I know, Bodkin. I'm not unpatriotic myself, but I've overheard young men in the Old Bull talking about the war as if it was something exciting to do for the weekend. Some of those lads are in for a harsh lesson. They think they're going to be acting out a Douglas Fairbanks Junior role. A lot of them will be crying for their mothers the first time they see real action.'

'That's young men for you. Full of bravado,' Bodkin replied. 'But the vast majority of them will do their best, fighting for their country, even if they do cry for their mothers occasionally.'

'Well, that told me,' Amy said with a short laugh. 'And you're right, Bodkin, of course you are. I just meant that some of them will have to grow up very quickly.'

Bodkin turned his face towards her, smiled, and then looked back to the road. 'Welcome to Gillingham,' he said, reading the signpost. 'Now, where do we go from here?'

They found St. Lawrence Street at the back of the Priestfield football ground, the home of Gillingham FC. It was a narrow thoroughfare made up of small, red brick, Victorian terraced houses, in blocks of four with an alleyway between them. Number twenty-six was halfway up on the left-hand side. As they got out of the car, they were treated to the smell of roast pork emanating from the house next door, which had its front sash window lifted despite the cold weather.

'That's very apt, isn't it?' Bodkin said, as Amy joined him on the pavement.

Amy grinned. 'I wonder if it's our pig.'

'I hadn't thought of that, actually,' Bodkin replied. 'I was thinking of Saint Lawrence and how he died.'

Amy narrowed her eyes at him. 'Now, now, Bodkin. Don't go making fun of a Christian Saint.'

'I wasn't going to make fun. He was the comedian, wasn't he? When the Romans were halfway through grilling him alive, didn't he say, "turn me over now, I'm done on this side?"'

'Yes,' Amy replied. 'And your point is?'

'It was the smell of the pork roasting, put together with the name of the street I just found it...' Bodkin stopped mid-sentence when he saw the look Amy was giving him. 'It probably wasn't that funny... Right, let's see if Brian's home.'

Amy gave Erma a wink and a sly smile. 'I got the joke,' she whispered. 'I just like to tease him now and again.'

Bodkin rattled the lion's head door knocker. Thirty seconds later, the door opened and a young woman's face appeared in the opening. 'We don't want any, whatever you're selling,' she growled.

Bodkin stuck his foot in the gap as the woman tried to close the door. Reaching into his pocket, he pulled out his warrant card. 'Police,' he said. 'I'd like to ask you a few questions.'

The woman let go of the door and, spinning on her heel, she shouted into the house. 'Brian, get out, quick, it's the cops.'

CHAPTER FOURTEEN

Bodkin stepped quickly into the front room as he heard the noise of the back door being thrown open. As he attempted to make his way across the room, the woman pulled a chair from under the dining table and let it fall in front of him. Bodkin tripped and fell headlong onto the dingy square of carpet that part covered the plank boarded floor.

Getting quickly to his feet, he climbed over the fallen chair and hurried through to the kitchen, where he saw the back door was hanging open. The policeman stepped through the gap, took two well-worn steps in a single leap and landed on a rough, paved path that led to a small oblong of overgrown garden. He looked right and left before taking the path that ran behind the neighbours' house, and hurried towards the alleyway that split the block in two, but by the time he reached it, there was no one to be seen.

As Bodkin walked back to the house, he found Dora waiting on the top step. She was in her mid-twenties, with reddish brown hair pinned up in rolls. She had an oval-shaped face with green eyes and a slightly turned-up nose that gave her a youthful look. Her lips were full and covered in a deep pink lipstick. On the left side of her chin was a single, dark brown freckle. The softness of her looks, however, was overshadowed by the vitriol that came out of her mouth. She hurled abuse at the policeman as he walked back up the path, and the tirade didn't stop even as he climbed the two steps that led to the kitchen.

'I'm warning you now. If you don't button your lip, you'll be in a cell before you can say Jack Robinson.'

Dora glared at him, but after seeing the angry look on his face, she choked back her words and slammed the door behind him as he stepped into the back room.

'Where has Brian gone, Dora?' he asked as she followed him into the front room.

'How the hell would I know?' she spat. 'And don't call me Dora. You're not my mother. Everyone calls me Birdie.'

Bodkin pulled the front door fully open to find Amy and Erma still standing on the doorstep. Birdie hurled a mouthful of abuse when she recognised her boyfriend's sister.

'We didn't have you down as a nark, Erma.' She shook a fist at her. 'You're a disgrace to the family.'

'My family is a disgrace to the rest of mankind,' Erma spat back, standing her ground.

Bodkin pushed his wide frame between the two women. 'That was your last chance, Birdie. One more mouthful and I'll take you down to the nick. As things are, your neighbours might think you've got a visit from the Baptists, trying to convert you, but they'll know I'm a copper if I drag you out to my car wearing a set of handcuffs.'

Birdie opened her mouth to complain, but then thought better of it. 'What do you want, anyway?' she asked.

'I think we ought to sit down and have a cosy little chat.' Bodkin said calmly.

'Do I have a choice?' she replied with a snarl.

'Yes, as I said, we can do it here or down at the station. It's entirely up to you.'

Birdie rolled her eyes towards the ceiling and muttered something under her breath. Eventually, she turned her face towards Erma and glowered. 'You'd better come in then.'

Bodkin held the door for Amy and Erma, then closed it behind them. 'Shall we sit down? I find that people tend to be a little less aggressive when they are seated.'

'Who's this?' Birdie asked, giving Amy a look.

'This is Miss Rowlings. She's assisting us with the investigation into the murder of Lonnie Firth.'

Birdie's eyes rested on Amy's sling. 'Been in a fight?'

'No, it was an accident. I don't get involved in fights.'

'Sit down then,' Birdie said, pulling out a chair from underneath the table and plonking herself on it.

Bodkin picked up the fallen chair and held the back of it while Amy sat down, then he pulled out a chair for Erma. Finally, he took a seat himself before pulling out his notebook and pen.

'Birdie,' he said with a smile. 'I believe you were in Spinton last Friday evening.'

'I was nowhere near Spinton.'

'Really? We have a witness that says otherwise.' The policeman tapped his notebook with the tip of his pen.

'Your witness is lying. I was at home all night.'

'Alone?'

'No, Brian was with me.'

'Now, that is strange, Miss Lark,' Bodkin replied. 'Because our witness said that Brian was with you at an apartment block down by the river. Flat seven, top floor, to be exact. The witness gave a perfect description of you both.' He pointed to her chin. 'Right down to that beauty spot.'

'That old bast—'

Bodkin shook his head. 'Now, now.'

'He'll get what's coming,' Birdie snarled.

'Making threats against a witness in a murder case. That's another offence.'

Birdie bit her tongue and glowered.

Bodkin sucked on the end of his pen as he watched her. 'Okay, Birdie, we've established where you were on Friday night. What I want to know now is, where is the money you took from Lonnie's box?'

'I don't know what you're talking about. We didn't take any money.'

Bodkin sighed. 'We know there was two thousand pounds in that box, Birdie. We also know that there was a gun. You and Brian took it. You were seen carrying a bag down the stairs. Was the gun in the bag with the money, or did Brian have it in his pocket...? Maybe you had it in yours.'

'I have nothing more to say.'

'How did you find out about the money?' Bodkin asked.

Birdie crossed her arms and stared at the wall.

'We'll find Brian soon, but for now, we're stuck with you.' Bodkin grinned. 'Right, let's get back to it. Where did you get the keys to the apartment?'

Birdie looked at Bodkin, then back to the wall, but said nothing.

'Did you get copies made from Hetty's set, or did she give them to you?'

Silence.

'Maybe someone else gave you a set of keys. Reggie Tumbler perhaps?'

As Tumbler's name was mentioned, a look of alarm flashed across Birdie's face.

'Was the money his?'

Birdie shrugged.

'No reply? Ah well, it doesn't really matter. We'll ask him ourselves.' Bodkin tapped his notebook again. 'He's on my list. We'll be chatting with him soon.' He paused as he looked coldly at her. 'I'll be sure to ask if he gave Brian the keys to the apartment.'

'Don't...' her voice wavered. 'Don't tell him we were at the flat.'

'I don't see how I can keep your names out of it,' Bodkin replied. 'If you won't help us, why should I help you?'

Birdie screwed up her face before she replied. 'All right, ask your stupid questions, but don't expect me to drop anyone in it. I'm not a grass.'

'That's the spirit,' Bodkin replied. 'I'm sure you'll find my questions aren't quite as hostile as Reggie's would be.'

Birdie held up both hands in surrender. 'Okay, let's get on with it.'

CHAPTER
FIFTEEN

'Question one,' Bodkin crossed his legs causing his bunched up trouser legs to ride up a little, but still not enough to show his socks. 'Tell me about your relationship with Lonnie Firth.'

'I didn't have a relationship with him. I have a relationship with his brother.'

'We'll come to bashful Brian in a while,' Bodkin replied. 'For now, I want to know how you got on with Lonnie.'

'I didn't like him much if that's an answer.'

'Why not?'

'He was too full of himself. He thought he was Jimmy Cagney. He ordered everyone about, even if they didn't work for him, he still expected them to do as they were told.'

'Give me an example,' Bodkin said. 'Did he order you about? What did he want from you?'

'Not that...' Birdie replied. 'I wouldn't let him anywhere near me.' She thought for a moment. 'He expected me to make tea and sandwiches for his motley crew whenever he held a gang meeting. Brian told me not to let it get to me, but it always did. Who was he to order me about?'

'He was the boss of the gang your boyfriend belonged to,'

Bodkin replied. 'I'm not saying it was right, but you were sharing in the spoils via Brian, so you can see why he thought you were part of it, too.'

'Spoils, HA! Brian could have made more working for Reggie. In fact, he had to do that when Lonnie was waiting for payment from one of his scams or he had to finance a new project. It wasn't like he paid his brother any more than the rest of them. Brian had the responsibility of nominally being in charge when Lonnie was away on one of his long absences, but he was never rewarded properly for doing the number two job.' She laughed. 'That's what it was too, a number two job, it was shi—'

'We get the idea,' Bodkin interrupted her. 'Was Brian resentful? I mean, like you say, he had the responsibility but got none of the rewards.'

'He hated his brother.'

'Enough to kill him?'

'Don't put bloody words in my mouth.' Birdie glared at Bodkin. 'He wouldn't have done that to him, but he wouldn't have cried if someone else took their revenge.'

'Who do you think killed him?'

'I have no idea. The list of names would be too long to jot them all down in that notebook. You'd have to borrow her sling by the time you finished writing it out.' Birdie shot a glance towards Amy, then she crossed her legs and folded her arms as she concentrated on Bodkin again.

'You must have talked about the murder with Brian. Lonnie was his brother. Who did he think the culprit was?'

'You'll have to ask him. Like I said before. I'm not going to drop names into your collection box.'

'You wouldn't be dropping anyone in it, Birdie. It's hypothetical, isn't it? Just an opinion.' He rubbed the stubble on his chin. 'Do you think Reggie might have been involved, for instance? You're not actually saying he was. It's just an opinion.'

Birdie shrugged.

'What about his gang members? Do you think any of them had a grudge big enough to want to bump him off?'

'I told you. I'm not a grass, but I honestly have no idea who it might have been.'

'Did Lonnie fall out with any gang members recently? Someone who thought he hadn't been paid promptly enough when Lonnie was away on one of his jaunts?'

Birdie shrugged again.

'What about people on the periphery? People who you only saw now and again. Was there anyone new hanging around?'

'You'll get bored before I do,' Birdie said. 'I told you, I'm not a nark. Unlike her.' She nodded towards Erma.

'You're not really helping, are you, Birdie?' Bodkin said. He cleared his throat. 'I could do with a cup of tea. Would you like to make us all one? Or do I sound too much like Lonnie?'

'Make your own tea. There's a half-full caddy out in the kitchen. You know how to boil a kettle, I take it?'

'I do,' Bodkin said, getting to his feet.

'That's more than most men do,' Birdie replied. 'I have mine white with two sugars. You'll find the milk in the top cupboard.'

When Bodkin had gone to put the kettle on, Birdie turned her attention towards Amy.

'Are you and him at it?' she asked.

Amy shook her head. 'No, we're not at it.'

'He's your bloke though, isn't he? I can tell by the looks you give each other.' She tipped her head to the side. 'You're a good-looking girl, but you want to be careful. If you don't give it to him, someone else will. He wouldn't be too bad if he got a suit that fits him and ironed his shirt.' Birdie picked up a pack of cigarettes from the table and lit one with a match. 'I hope you don't do that for him. If he can make tea, he can iron his own shirt.'

'I don't do his ironing,' Amy replied.

'No one does, by the look of it.' Birdie took another long draw on her cigarette and blew smoke across the table towards Erma. 'What does your mum think about your becoming a nark?'

Erma pursed her lips as she looked back at Birdie. 'I don't give a shiny one what she thinks. I gave up caring about that a long time ago.'

Amy heard the sound of cupboard doors closing and cups rattling in the kitchen, so decided to get a few questions of her own in before Bodkin came back.

'I know you said you didn't get on with Lonnie, but how do you get on with the rest of the gang? From what I've heard, there are some pretty despicable characters amongst them.'

'I get on with them just fine. They leave me alone in the main. Apart from asking for more sandwiches or pots of tea, that is.'

'They haven't tried to take advantage of you in any way?'

'They wouldn't bloody dare.'

'You mean Brian would protect you?'

'I mean, they wouldn't bloody dare. I'd cut their balls off and they know it.'

'What about Vincent Jury? Has he ever tried it on?'

Birdie blinked a few times before she answered. 'He doesn't know what he's doing half the time. He's away with the fairies when he gets on the white stuff.'

'You didn't answer the question,' Amy replied.

'The answer is no. Not for a long time, at least. He got the message when I hooked up with Brian. Anyway, even Vincent Jury wouldn't want to get on the wrong side of my brother too often.'

'Mason looks after you, does he?'

'Mason's not the brotherly type. But he has some standards. Anyway, he likes to keep his nose clean in both senses of the phrase.'

'Are Mason and Brian good mates?' Amy asked.

'It depends what you call, good. They get on all right. There's no bad blood.'

'Do you and Brian argue about money? Most couples do at some time or another. Especially when things are tight.'

'We argue about a lot of things, but we get on in the main.'

'Does Mason do any work for Reggie on the side?'

'Bits and bobs. He runs the odd errand.'

'How did Mason get on with Lonnie?'

'Fine. Just like everyone else.'

Amy crossed her legs and smoothed down her skirt before flicking a bit of imaginary ash from it as the sound of footsteps and doors being opened and closed came from upstairs.

Birdie got to her feet and walked to the door leading to the back of the house. 'OI! Don't you need a search warrant to do that?' she shouted. On getting no response, she walked back to her chair and sat down again. 'Isn't there a law against that?' she asked Amy.

Amy shrugged. 'I honestly have no idea.'

Birdie didn't appear to be too concerned. After stubbing out her cigarette in the ashtray, she cocked her head to listen to the sound of Bodkin's feet as they clomped down the stairs.

As the sound of rattling cups replaced the heavy footsteps, Amy continued with her questions. 'What about Lonnie and Reggie? What was their relationship like? They were very close at one time. Did Reggie resent Lonnie going off on his own?'

'You'll have to ask him when you see him,' Birdie replied. 'He'll love you. He likes a pretty face, does Reggie.'

'Did he ever try it on with you?'

'Reggie? Don't be daft. He's a mummy's boy when it comes to that sort of thing. Don't get me wrong. You wouldn't want to get on the wrong side of him, but he wouldn't hurt or try to embarrass a woman.'

'Is he married?' Amy asked.

Birdie almost choked as she laughed. 'No, Reggie isn't married. He doesn't go for women in that way.' She cleared her throat and stopped laughing before adding. 'Don't get me wrong, he doesn't go for men either. He's just not interested in that side of things.'

Before she could ask another question, Bodkin came in with the tea tray. After placing it on the table, he took the lid off the teapot, gave it a stir, then picked up the strainer. 'Add your own milk and sugar,' he said as he poured tea into four cheap looking cups.

When tea had been served, Bodkin sat down, blew into his cup and took a sip before placing it on the table. Picking up his notebook again, he studied it as though refreshing his memory, then looked across at Birdie, who, after trying her tea, was nodding appreciatively at the policeman.

'Are you allowed to search someone's house without a warrant?' she asked.

'I don't need one if I have reasonable grounds to suspect that evidence might be destroyed or moved,' he replied.

'I hope I remembered to make the bed,' Birdie said. She took another sip of her tea. 'This is re—'

'Where's the money?' he asked, cutting her off as she was about to compliment him on his tea making abilities.

'I honestly don't know what you're talking about.'

'Okay, let's play your game for a few moments,' Bodkin said. 'If you didn't take the money from Lonnie's flat last Friday, what did you take?'

'Nothing. There was nothing *to* take. Someone had got to it before us. The place had been trashed, and the box was already open.'

Bodkin picked up his cup but didn't drink from it. 'What was in the box then, Birdie?'

'An old curtain, a few gaudy dresses that I wouldn't be seen dead in.'

'Some papers?'

'Yeah, there was a handful of invoices, but the money had gone.'

'What about the gun?'

Birdie looked confused. 'Gun? There was no gun.'

Amy cleared her throat. Bodkin sipped his tea and waited for her to ask a question.

'Was there anything else in the box apart from the dresses, papers and curtain?'

'Nothing. We had a good rummage through it. There was nothing worth taking.'

'If there was nothing worth taking, what was in the bag that Brian was carrying? And why were you laughing so gleefully? I doubt I'd be laughing like an excited child if I had just been disappointed at having made a wasted trip and going home completely empty-handed.'

Birdie tried to put on an inscrutable look, but her eyes gave her away. 'He wasn't carrying anything.'

Bodkin's own eyes narrowed as he stared hard at the young woman. 'He was carrying a blue bag. We know he was carrying a blue bag and we know that you were skipping down the stairs behind him, acting as though you had just won the football pools. So, I'm going to give you one more chance to answer Amy's question. What was in it the bag?'

'Nothing. There was no bag.'

Bodkin got to his feet. 'Dora Lark, I am arrest—'

'Oh, all right, but I'm saying nothing while she's here.'

Birdie scowled across the table at Erma. 'I'm not having her telling all and sundry about this. I have a reputation to keep up.'

'Do you know, I'm sick to death of hearing about reputations,' Bodkin answered angrily. 'The only reputation you lot have around the town is one of being a thieving, lying, waste of good clean air.' He put his cup down, then slammed on the table with his hand. 'And I say who sits in on interviews in my investigation, not the person answering the questions.' He took a deep breath, then picked up the cup again before speaking in a far quieter manner. 'Now... let's hear the truth.'

Birdie was so taken aback by Bodkin's outburst that she spilled her tea down the front of her dress.

'Okay, we had the gun. We found it in a bag at the bottom of the case, but we didn't find any money. Someone had beaten us to it.'

'Hmm,' Amy said thoughtfully. 'Who do you think took it? Who got to it first, Birdie?'

'I don't bloody know. If I did, I'd tell you.'

'No, you wouldn't,' Bodkin said. 'But go on, have a guess.'

Birdie sighed and gave Erma another one of her looks. 'If I were to make an educated guess. I'd say it was her mother.'

Bodkin raised his eyebrows. 'Really? What makes you say that?'

Birdie scratched her head with her free hand whilst trying to keep the saucer full of tea from spilling. 'She had the keys. She knew the money was there. She lived local. She had plenty of time to get over there after hearing that Lonnie had been killed. I'd say she's a good candidate.'

Erma shook her head fiercely. 'I'm not Mum's biggest fan, but she didn't take that money. When was she supposed to have done it? She was with me on the night Lonnie was killed and she was with me on the Friday night when the place was ransacked. We spent it listening to the radio as we made inroads into her gin stash. She was in no state to go anywhere after that.'

'I was asked for my opinion and I gave it,' Birdie said with a glare.

'Do you think Reggie Tumbler might have sent someone over?' Bodkin asked. 'It could well have been his money, after all.'

'I'm not even going to speculate about that,' Birdie said. Her hands shook as she finally put her cup and saucer on the table.

'Vincent Jury?'

'He wouldn't have known about the money and he didn't have a key.'

'Which brings me back to my earlier question,' Bodkin said smoothly. 'Where did you get your keys from?'

'Brian got copies made at the shoe repair kiosk at the arcade in Spinton,' Birdie said. 'It was the day after he and Hetty had dropped the box off at the flat. Brian took them out of her bag when she was making tea. Then he said he had to run an urgent errand for Lonnie and nipped into town to get them copied. It only took twenty minutes. When he got back to Victoria Street, he slipped the originals into her bag again.'

'Had Brian been to the flat prior to the day he dropped the box off?'

'Yeah, he'd been there to visit Lonnie when he was hiding out.'

'I see,' Bodkin replied. 'Would Brian have mentioned that he had a set of keys for the flat to anyone else?'

'No, why would he?'

'Do you think he was already planning to steal the money when he brought the box up from Gillingham?'

'Possibly... All right, probably.'

'You say Vincent Jury is out of the frame, for stealing the

cash at least, but what about Mason, your brother? Did he know anything about the box's contents?'

'I honestly don't know who Lonnie told about what was inside or where he'd stashed it, but I can't see him telling anyone outside of his family. Why would he?'

'Okay, but who might have suspected he had a large amount of money hidden away?'

'I can't answer that.'

'Let me suggest someone. What about Bessie Dagger? She knew he had a fair bit of cash because he'd just stolen it from her.'

'I'm saying nothing about Bessie. It's more than my life's worth.'

'Who's her main man? Does she have an enforcer?'

Birdie snorted. 'She doesn't need one. She's quite capable of doing things herself.'

'She must have a lieutenant, though, someone to help with the daily chores.'

'Ellis Hawke,' Erma said suddenly. 'He's her bloke. They're the perfect couple. He's as vicious as she is.'

'Nark!' Bridie said. She turned quickly to Bodkin. 'Just don't let anyone think I've given you that piece of information. I value my bits and pieces and she's quite likely to want to cut them off.'

Bodkin got to his feet and rubbed his hands together. 'I haven't done with you by a long chalk, Birdie. But time's getting on and I want to have a chat with Bessie and her young man. Where will I find her?

'Ask her,' Birdie said. Pointing directly at Erma. 'She can take the bloody flak. I'm staying out of it.'

As Amy got to her feet, Bodkin walked across the room and opened the front door. 'Oh, tell Brian I want a word when he comes back. He'll find that I'm a much more agreeable person if I don't have to spend my time searching for him.'

Back in the car, Bodkin started up the engine before turning to look into the back where Erma was sitting. 'Where do we find this Bessie Dagger?'

'Coleman Road,' Erma replied. 'It's her dad's house. But there's also a newsagent's shop on Farley Street. She's running the business from there while her dad's inside.'

'You'll have to direct me,' Bodkin said. 'I worked here for a year or two, but I can't remember where that street is.'

Bodkin pulled away and drove around to the front of the Priestfield stadium before turning onto Livingstone Road. 'You're quiet,' he said to Amy as he pulled out to pass a parked van.

'I was just thinking.'

'I thought I heard something clanking,' Bodkin said with a smile. 'What did you make of what our Birdie had to say?'

'You certainly ruffled her feathers,' Amy replied. 'But she's lying about not taking the money. I'm certain of it.'

'I agree,' Bodkin replied, 'but what makes you so sure?'

'The bag. She said they found the gun in it at the bottom of the box, but if that was so why was there gun oil on the curtain? To me, that says that the gun was wrapped up in it. Why would there have been a handy, empty cloth bag just sitting there? I think the money was in the bag. That's what Brian was carrying, and that's why Birdie was chirping away like a love struck blackbird in spring.'

'I like your thinking,' Bodkin replied. 'But we now know that not only has Brian got the money, he's also got himself a gun.'

CHAPTER SIXTEEN

Farley Street was made up of similar houses to the ones found on St Lawrence, only these were in a much worse state of repair. The red brick Victorian terraced houses seemingly all had flaking paint on the doors. A few had had their windows broken and were boarded up with plywood, and sometimes even cardboard. Gutters dripped, a lot of the brickwork was in desperate need of pointing up and a few tiles were missing from a good many of the roofs. From the back of a mid-terraced house came the sound of a dog barking. Its call was immediately answered by an animal further down the road. Having parked at the top of the street, Bodkin climbed out of the car, then leaned back in to have a few words with Amy.

'You'd better stay here, Amy, and you, Erma. I don't know what I'm going to find inside. If Bessie Dagger is running her criminal empire from the shop, there are bound to be a few of her henchmen hanging around. Don't follow me in, even if I'm gone for a while.'

Amy and Erma watched the broad back of the policeman as he walked at a steady pace towards the newsagents. As he approached, a man carrying a folded newspaper and tucking a betting slip into his pocket came out of the front door and stood for a few moments on the cracked, dirty paving stones as he looked up and down the street. Planting his feet firmly on the pavement, he squared up to Bodkin, who was forced to step aside to walk around him. As Bodkin entered the shop, the man pulled the brim of his dark grey trilby down towards his eyes before crossing the street and walking up the slight incline, towards the car.

'Down!' Erma said as she recognized the man. She threw herself onto the rear double seat as Amy slid down in the passenger seat at the front.

'Who is it?' Amy hissed, resisting the urge to sit up straight and take a look.

'Vincent Jury,' Erma hissed back. 'What the hell is he doing here?'

Amy gave it a full two minutes before craning her neck to look over the top of her seat towards the T junction. There being no sign of Jury, she sat up straight, smoothed down her creased dress, then half turned to talk to Erma.

'I thought he worked for Lonnie's gang,' she said.

'So did I,' Erma replied. Her brow furrowed as she thought. 'I wonder what he wants with Bessie.'

'He may think that the Daggers are on top of the pile now that Lonnie's gone. They'll know Brian isn't as strong as his brother.'

Erma shook her head. 'As far as I know, Brian still has Reggie Tumbler behind him. Bessie wouldn't mess with Reggie... unless she's seen an opportunity to get one up on him. If she were able to combine the two gangs, she'd be able to reduce his influence, possibly even take over some of the real money-making schemes.'

'Hmm,' Amy mused. 'Have the Daggers always been rivals to Reggie, then?'

'Bessie's dad, Christopher, lost out to Reggie a good few years ago. There was a turf war, and the Daggers came in runner-up. It's always rankled with Bessie, even though she was only a kid at the time. There was another gang led by a man called, of all things, Aloysius Throgmorton. He was kingmaker in the battle, and in the end he sided with Reggie.'

'What happened to him?' Amy asked. 'I haven't heard his name come up.'

'Oh, he's long gone. He died of Consumption... TB they call it now, I think. His gang was absorbed into Reggie's and he ruled the roost without anyone questioning it after that. The Daggers were always looking for ways to get one up on Reggie, though. They've always had aspirations of taking over, but they've had to be patient.'

'Tell me about Bessie,' Amy said. 'What's she like? Do you know anything about her?'

'Bessie is a very attractive woman, but she has a mean streak, as many suitors have found out. Men can't seem to get it into their heads that being drop dead gorgeous doesn't mean you're soft or pliable. Bessie has movie star looks... I'd die for that hair... but she's got a heart made of solid granite. There's a rumour that she had a man beaten to within an inch of his life because he disagreed with one of her decisions. He'd been living with her for over six months too, or so the story goes.'

'I suppose she has to be strong while her dad's in prison. She can't be seen to be soft on people who get in her way.'

'She was the same before her dad was banged up, Amy. I was told that she takes after her grandmother, who was the matriarch of the family until she got too old to control it all. Christopher stepped up when his father was hanged for treason during the Great War. One story says he was involved in a plot to kill the War Minister, but another says he was caught trying to sell canisters of poison gas to a German. I think the latter story is most likely.'

'Blimey,' Amy said. 'What a family.' She twisted in her seat to look along the road, to see if Bodkin was on his way, but when there was no sign of him, she turned back to Erma.

'How old is Bessie?'

'Twenty five... twenty six, maybe. Not that much older than us.' She craned her neck to see through the windscreen. 'It looks like things are getting interesting. Can Bodkin look after himself in a fight?'

Amy spun around in her seat to see what Erma was pointing at. Five men had formed a small crowd outside the newsagents. They began to hurl insults at Bodkin as he stepped outside to join them on the pavement. If he was concerned by their behaviour, he didn't show it. Instead, he waved his warrant card at them, then with a half-smile on his face, he turned back towards the car.

Amy watched nervously as the policeman walked at a steady pace until he reached the Morris. Only after opening the door of the vehicle did he take a look back down the street. 'Madam was not amused,' he said with a grin as he ducked his head and climbed into the driver's seat.

'Are you all right, Bodkin?' Amy asked. 'We were a bit worried about you there for a moment.'

'They know better than to attack a policeman in broad daylight. Especially when he's involved in a murder investigation. That place would be shut down in less than an hour if they'd had a go at me.'

'They didn't look very friendly, all the same,' Amy said.

'I've arrested plenty of that sort in my time,' Bodkin replied as he started up the car. He gave the crowd of men one last glance, then began to drive slowly down the slight slope towards them. 'Heads down,' he ordered as they got to within thirty yards. 'I don't want them to get a good look at either of you.'

Amy slid down in her seat for a second time as Erma laid herself across the back seat. 'Stay down until I give the word,' Bodkin said as he slowed the car to a crawl and glared at the group of men as he passed. At the bottom of Farley Street, he took a left turn, then another left and drove back towards the town centre. 'You can get up now,' he said as he slipped the Morris into third gear and accelerated along the Gillingham Road towards Spinton.

'You said Madam wasn't amused, Bodkin. What happened in there?'

'Bessie Dagger wasn't expecting a copper to walk into the hub of her criminal enterprise and ask questions about a murder case in front of her punters,' Bodkin replied. 'There were quite a few people trying to put bets on as I announced myself. You should have seen their faces.' The inspector chuckled at the memory. 'She wasn't taking the bets, obviously, but as I wouldn't move from the counter, one of her cronies nipped into the back to tell her I was asking for her.'

'Did she come out?'

'No, she stuck her head around the door to tell me to bugger off. When I refused, she said she was conducting a meeting and that I'd have a long wait. I put one of my cards on the counter and told her that if I hadn't heard from her by five o'clock, I'd be sending the troops in. That message seemed to hit home because suddenly getting their bets on were the last things on the minds of the punters, and they all walked out of the shop. They were the men you saw me arguing with outside. Anyway, when they'd gone, Bessie came out from the back, picked the card up and said she'd be in touch when she had a minute. I told her that I expected her to answer all of my questions and it was going to be a face-to-face meeting, not an interview held over a phone line.'

'I bet that went down well. Erma was telling me she doesn't like to take orders from men.'

'If looks could kill, I'd have been turned into a pillar of salt on the spot,' Bodkin replied. 'But she's not stupid. She knows I wasn't bluffing when I threatened to have the place raided and closed down. She'll find time to talk to me soon.'

'Us, Bodkin. I'd like to be in on that one. She intrigues me.'

'I'll have to think about that, Amy. She's a nasty piece of work. She wouldn't dare have a go at an on duty policeman but I know she wouldn't think twice about roughing up a civilian. I don't really want to risk putting you in danger, especially if word gets to her through the grapevine that you and I are involved romantically.'

'Do you think her tentacles are so long she could get hold of information like that?'

'There are bent coppers in every police station in the country, Amy. Gillingham and Spinton are no different. If she started asking questions about me, my personal life would come up for sure and your name would soon follow.'

Amy sighed. 'I so wanted to meet her. She sounds such an interesting character.'

'Oh, she is. But she's a real life character, not one from a book. No, I'll really have to think long and hard about this one.'

Amy was silent for a moment, then she asked. 'What did you make of her?'

'Oh, she's an attractive woman for sure, but she's as hard as nails. I prefer my women a little softer than that. Her eyes could set fire to cold coal.'

Amy narrowed her eyes as she looked at him. 'Your women? Just how attractive is she?'

Bodkin began to speak, then cleared his throat. He shot her

a quick glance. 'Not a patch on you, of course. There's no comparison.'

'Good answer,' Amy said, hiding a smile.

'Aw, that's so sweet,' Erma said from the back of the car. 'Inspector Bodkin is right about her eyes, though. She can see right through you. She can spot a lie coming from a mile off. She'd make a good detective.'

'No, she wouldn't,' Bodkin replied. 'She'd have the accused, hung, drawn and quartered without the inconvenience of a trial.'

'Be careful if you have to drive down on your own when you meet her, Bodkin. Take Ferris with you, or a couple of uniformed officers at least.'

The policeman smiled at her concerned face. 'I'll be careful,' he said.

Bodkin dropped Erma off at the bottom of Victoria Steet and then drove Amy home. After a few minutes chatting outside her house and agreeing to have a couple of drinks in the Old Bull later, he left to return to the police station.

The Old Bull snug was relatively quiet, with only half a dozen people dotted about the room, sipping at pints or chatting quietly amongst themselves. Bodkin and Amy found a space away from the rest of the drinkers and sat on the bench seats beneath the window. The benches had once been pews at St John's church, but had been bought by the landlord at the time, after the church was refitted following a fire just after the turn of the century.

Amy had the feeling that Bodkin had something to tell her, but he was biding his time, letting the anticipation build up. Eventually, he put down his beer, wiped his mouth on the back of his hand and looked over his shoulder to make sure he couldn't be overheard.

'Oh, come on, Bodkin. I know you've got news. I can see it in your face. Out with it, man.'

Bodkin grinned. 'Bessie Dagger is coming up to be interviewed tomorrow.'

Amy's mouth sagged open. 'Here? In Spinton? Why...? I mean, I fully expected her to demand you drive down there again. She's got her people around her in Gillingham.'

'She doesn't want any of them to know she's talking to the police,' Bodkin replied. 'It's not a good look, and down there it's far too much of a risk. Only her most trusted people know she's coming.'

'But like you said, some policemen would sell that information in a heartbeat. She must know that.'

'Oh, she does. That's why we're meeting somewhere other than the police station.'

'Where are you meeting her?' Amy leaned forward and placed her good hand on the tabletop. 'Not your flat, surely. You don't want them to know where you live.'

'No, not my flat. We're actually going to meet here. At one o'clock. There'll be no one in the snug at that time of day. Stan doesn't usually open it up. There'll be a handful in the bar, but we'll be able to have a quiet chat in here.'

'Oh, I'd love to be here to listen.' Amy looked around the snug. 'But there's nowhere I can hide.'

'You'll already be too close for my liking. You only live a hundred yards away.'

'All right, I do understand why you don't want me to get too close to her. But I want to know what's said, word for word, within five minutes of the meeting ending.'

Bodkin put his hand on hers. 'I've just had a thought. Maybe you and Ferris could be a couple, sitting over by the fire. You wouldn't be able to hear what was being said, but you'd get a good look at her at least and you can tell me what you make of her body language afterwards. You're so good at that.'

'Ooh, exciting. That's a wonderful idea, Bodkin. Who is coming with her?'

'Her bloke, Ellis Hawke, and a driver. The driver was the person who called to make the arrangements. I'm looking forward to meeting him.'

'Why, he's just a driver, isn't he?'

'I don't know what else he does besides driving, but the first thing I noticed when I answered the call was his strong Nottingham accent.'

CHAPTER SEVENTEEN

At ten-thirty, Amy and Bodkin left the pub and walked the hundred or so yards along Long Lane until they reached the white picket gate in front of Amy's cottage. The sky was clear and lit up with more shining diamonds than a thousand jeweller's windows. The temperature had dropped considerably since they had left the cottage to go to the pub a couple of hours earlier. Amy shivered and her warm breath formed a silvery mist as it hit the cold night air. Bodkin opened up his overcoat and pulled her towards him. She put her head on his chest as he wrapped his arms around her. She had taken off the sling in the pub, after resting her arm in some spilt beer on the bar when it had been her turn to get a round in.

As he moved his hands over her upper body, she undid the buttons on her own coat and allowed him to slip them inside. Stretching her neck towards him, their lips brushed before embarking on a deep passionate kiss.

The kiss stalled as they heard the sound of an angry fist hitting a windowpane. Bodkin looked over Amy's shoulder to see her neighbour, the elderly Mrs Dormer, glaring at them as she hammered her hand against the glass.

'Mrs Dormouse has come out of hibernation,' he said.

Amy chuckled at Bodkin's nickname for her eighty-year-old neighbour. 'Perfect timing, as usual, just as it was getting interesting.'

Mrs Dormer reached for the catch, then pushed the six pane window open. Pulling her dressing gown tight at the neck, she wagged the index finger of her free hand at the couple. 'It's too cold for that sort of thing. I can see the hot breath coming out of you.' She tutted. 'You ought to be ashamed of yourself, being a policeman and all.'

'I'm just making sure she doesn't get cold,' Bodkin replied as he gently squeezed Amy's breast.

'She needs to get into bed,' Mrs Dormer said, then, after seeing Bodkin about to reply, she added. 'On her own, of course. You aren't allowed in there until you're married. You should keep your hands to yourself until that day arrives.'

'She'll be going to bed in a few minutes,' Bodkin replied, letting go of her left breast. 'She can't see what I'm doing, surely,' he hissed.

'Maybe she can remember being in a clinch with Mr Dormer when they were courting,' Amy said quietly.

'She must have a bloody good memory,' Bodkin replied, before looking back at the window. 'Get yourself into the warm, Mrs Dormou... Dormer. Amy's going in now.'

Mrs Dormer pulled the window shut, but continued to glare at them as the glass began to fog up.

'She's having steamy thoughts in there,' Bodkin said to Amy as they separated. He clicked the latch on the gate and followed her up the short path to the porch. 'I hope she doesn't mention any of this to your mum and dad.'

'Oh, she definitely drops hints,' Amy replied. 'Mum just tells her we were all young once.'

Bodkin ducked his head, and the pair kissed again, Amy

pushing Bodkin's exploring hand away as he attempted one last crafty feel.

'I'll come over to your flat tomorrow evening if you like, Bodkin. Your hands won't be as cold in there.'

Bodkin grinned. 'Just name a time and I'll come around to pick you up. Shall I rustle something up for dinner?'

Amy almost choked. 'Rustle something up? You're not going to do a Tom Piper, are you? I'll warn Alice to keep an eye on her pigs.'

Bodkin laughed. 'I've got to see Laws again tomorrow about those latest reports from Mossmoor. I was actually thinking of cooking for you myself. I can get something from the market tomorrow.'

Amy shook her head quickly. Bodkin's cooking was notoriously bad. 'No, no, don't put yourself out, Bodkin. Mum's making a cottage pie tomorrow. You're welcome to join us.'

'Mrs Dormouse might think I'm getting my feet too far under the table, so I'd better not,' Bodkin replied. 'Anyway, I have to tidy the flat before you arrive. It's a bit of a mess at the moment.' He gave her another quick kiss. 'I'll bring your new boyfriend Ferris around at about twelve.' He was quiet for a moment. 'I wonder what Bessie's going to have to say for herself.'

When Amy got inside, she put her stained sling to soak in the kitchen sink with a little Dolly Blue bag to give the cloth a whiter, brighter appearance and to stop any yellowing of the material. As her parents were already in bed, she made herself a mug of Ovaltine and carried it into the front room where she picked up a few sheets of paper and a pen, and sat down at the table to write out her initial thoughts about the people she knew were involved in the investigation so far. Her wrist ached as she picked up the pen, but after a while, the pain subsided and she was able to write without too much discomfort.

Hetty Firth

A complicated character who likes her drink above anything else. Her relationship with her daughter seems a little at odds with her general bolshy attitude. Although she is constantly correcting and chastising Erma, verbally, at least, she obviously loves her daughter. Erma says she isn't as tough as she appears on the surface, but so far I've seen little evidence of that. Erma knows her far better than I do, though. She had a set of keys to her son's flat so in theory could have taken the money, but her daughter says she was at home with her on the night Lonnie was murdered, as well as the following night, when the flat was ransacked. Seeing as she knew exactly where the money was, why would she have needed to trash the apartment to find it? She loved her son, that's for certain. She deliberately misidentified the body assumed to be Lonnie three years ago, but did she do that to try to protect him, or, did he threaten her? She put on quite an act when convincing the police that her son was dead. Lonnie was her only source of income and despite the fact that he didn't provide her with enough of it to have a decent standard of living, without his financial input, she would have been in big trouble. I wonder how she'll manage without his contribution.

Erma Firth

A friendly, outgoing girl who I like a lot. She's intelligent and wants to get as far away as possible from what remains of her family and their underworld connections. She made one thing abundantly clear; she didn't like or trust her brother at all, particularly after he refused to protect her from the likes of Vincent Jury and Mason Lark. Erma should be an asset in the investigation, as she knows a lot about the main suspects. I'll have a word with Mrs Handsley when I go to pick up my wages on Friday. She might have an opening for her, even as a trainee machinist. I'll drop into London Connection soon to have a word with them too. She might make a good assistant as she's friendly and cares about fashion. They'll need someone to help out until I get back, at least. She may be too forthright for the customer's sensitivities, though.

Dora 'Birdie' Lark

A tough, forthright young woman who has lived amongst the criminal fraternity for a long time and has a very strong allegiance to them. She was very reluctant to give us information, but that's hardly surprising given the sort of people we're dealing with. She was at Lonnie's flat on the Friday night with Brian but refuses to admit that they took the money. She has admitted they took the gun. She might be telling the truth, but if so, who got there before them and took the money whilst leaving the gun behind? Birdie feels safe in her relationship with Brian. She knows a lot about Reggie Tumbler and the Daggers, so she will obviously have to be careful with the snippets of information she gives us. I wonder how she'll react under pressure from either the members of her own gang or the competing ones. If they did take the money, where would they have stashed it? Did Brian take it with him when he ran? Birdie didn't seem worried, or at least she didn't object too strongly when Bodkin had a look upstairs. It will be interesting to see if her name comes up tomorrow when Bodkin interviews Bessie Dagger.

. . .

Bessie Dagger

I haven't met her yet, so it's difficult to gauge an opinion, but from what Erma said about her and from what little Bodkin learned today she appears to be a formidable woman who definitely rules the roost and takes no nonsense from the men around her. She took to the leadership role like a duck to water when her father was imprisoned, so she had obviously learned her trade well before he was incarcerated. She is a beautiful woman, according to both Erma and Bodkin. I wonder if she'll play on her good looks tomorrow when Bodkin interviews her. I'm so pleased I'm allowed to be there when he does. The poor man still doesn't have a clue when it comes to understanding women. Especially women who know how to use their feminine wiles to get under a man's skin without them realising it's happening.

I'm really looking forward to tomorrow.

Amy put down the pen and flexed her fingers, which had begun to cramp. Rolling the sheets of paper into a scroll, Amy tucked it under her right arm and after carrying her mug through to the kitchen she put it down on the draining board and gave the blue-coloured water in the sink a whisk with her mother's wooden tongs. Then she switched off the light and went up to bed.

CHAPTER EIGHTEEN

Bodkin and Ferris arrived the next morning at eleven-fifty-five. Amy showed them through to the living room and called her mother in from the bathroom where she was washing sheets in the bath.

'You've met Constable Ferris before, haven't you, Mum?'

Mrs Rowlings dried her hands on her flowered pinafore, took hold of Ferris's hand and gently shook it. 'How's the singing coming along, Mr Ferris? Amy tells me you'll be singing at the London Palladium soon.'

Ferris laughed. 'I don't know about the Palladium. I'm just happy singing at the Milton Cocktail Bar at the moment. It's good fun and the extra money comes in handy.'

'Are you still doing it once a month? James... Mr Rowlings said he'd like to take me to hear you sing. Maybe as a Christmas or birthday treat, if he can get the time off, of course.' She lowered her voice to a stage whisper as she looked over her shoulder to make sure no one else had entered the room. 'He's making those Spotfire things, you know, the top secret aeroplanes.' Her hand suddenly flew towards her mouth. 'Oh, dear, I shouldn't have told you that, should I?' She turned to Amy with a look of horror on her face.

Amy smiled and reached out to give her a reassuring pat on the arm. 'It's all right, Mum. Ferris is a policeman, remember? He's not going to send a secret message to Mr Hitler.'

'I should think not,' Mrs Rowlings replied, giving Ferris a look that clearly said, 'and you had better not even think about it.'

'Your husband's secret is in safe hands,' Ferris said, giving Amy's mother his best smile.

Mrs Rowling almost reverted to being a flustered teenager who had just been paid her first compliment. Her cheeks flushed as she looked down towards her hands. Then, lifting them, she fussed with her hair and muttered something about tea.

Bodkin and Amy exchanged glances as Ferris followed her into the kitchen. 'Let me give you a hand, Mrs Rowlings.'

'Oh, do call me Elizabeth,' Mrs Rowlings said as she patted her hair down again before picking up the kettle.

'Ferris leaves another fluttering heart in his wake,' Bodkin said as he sat down next to Amy at the dining table.

Amy shook her head slowly. 'She still falls under the spell of a man's winning smile. It's a good job Dad's got one too.'

Bodkin grinned. 'I was surprised to see the effect that Ferris had on her.'

'You have the same effect when you look into her eyes, Bodkin, haven't you ever noticed? She's a sucker for a good-looking man. It's hilarious. She's like a seventeen-year-old again.'

'I haven't noticed,' Bodkin said. 'Mr Rowl... your dad... is he all right with that?'

Amy erupted into laughter. 'She's not planning on running away with you, Bodkin. She just doesn't get the attention very often. Dad's eyes are usually glued to his newspaper.'

'I'll, erm… I'll try not to hold her eyes for too long in the future. I'll look away, shall I?'

Amy slapped the back of his right hand with her left. 'Don't you dare, you spoilsport.'

Bodkin looked up as Mrs Rowlings came back into the room. 'Have you done something to your hair, Elizabeth? It suits you.'

Mrs Rowlings became flustered again and began to pat it into shape. 'I went to the hairdresser's on Monday, but I had it cut the same way I always do.' She raised her eyebrows twice in quick succession as she looked at Amy. 'Thank you for noticing, though.'

'Bless you,' Amy whispered, giving Bodkin's hand a squeeze. 'Ah, here's the tea.'

Ferris came into the living room, carefully carrying a tea tray, and placed it in the centre of the table. 'Shall I be mother?' he said.

After tea, Mrs Rowlings made her excuses and returned to washing her sheets. When she had left the room, Bodkin got to his feet and clapped his hands. 'Right,' he said. 'We need to get this subterfuge spot on. We can't have Bessie suspecting that you're a copper, Ferris. You two are a pair of lovesick young lovers.' He closed his eyes, then spoke again. 'Friends, I mean. Don't go getting ideas above your station, Ferris. There's acting a part and behaving as though you really are an item.' His eyes narrowed as he looked at his colleague. 'So no canoodling. You get your heads together, but don't try to get too deep into the role.'

Amy put her hand in front of her mouth to suppress a laugh.

'I think Sal would have something to say about that too, Bodkin.' She grinned. (Sal was Bodkin's sister who came up to see Ferris every other weekend.) 'I'm sure Ferris will be the perfect gentleman.' She got to her feet. 'Right, if I'm going on a proper date, I'd better put something nice on. Have another cup of tea, lads. I'll be back down in ten minutes.'

Amy was as good as her word and ten minutes later she came back into the room dressed in a red, flower-patterned wrap over dress which, although she had pinned it at the breast to hold it together, still showed a fair amount of cleavage. Her hair was held off the ears with two deep red Bakelite grips. She had applied the minimum amount of makeup, but her lips were coated with the new Ruby lipstick that Alice had borrowed the weekend before.

'Wow!' Bodkin exclaimed. 'You're going to the Old Bull at lunchtime, not the Ritz, on a Saturday night.'

'I'm wearing this for you, Bodkin,' Amy said. She gave him a peck on the cheek, then rubbed the lip shaped mark off with a paper hanky.

'I'll be concentrating on you more than her,' Bodkin said, looking her up and down.

'Good,' Amy replied. 'That's how it should be. I don't like competition.'

At a quarter to one, Amy and Ferris left the cottage and walked arm in arm along the lane, heads together as if sharing a secret. When they reached the Old Bull, Ferris pushed open the door to the snug and after seeing Amy to a seat at the round table near the unlit fire, he went to the bar and ordered drinks. Beer for himself and a port and lemon for Amy.

'Where's the suspects?' Stan asked, as Ferris looked shocked. 'It's all right, Mr Ferris, the inspector gave me the heads up. I'm sworn to secrecy.'

'Just make sure no one tries to come into this side from the bar,' Ferris replied. 'There will be enough ne'er-do-wells in here already.'

Ferris carried the drinks over to the table and the pair sat nervously, waiting for Bodkin to arrive. At one on the dot, the door to the snug opened and a good-looking man of about thirty years old, wearing a blue pinstriped suit, stepped into the room. He was followed by a beautiful woman with dark red, almost ruby coloured hair, hanging in curls down to her breasts. She was wearing a figure hugging green dress, what looked to be a pair of American sheer nylon stockings and a pair of black, three-inch heels. She tossed her head when she saw Amy and Ferris looking at her, then she walked across the snug to the bench seats by the window where she sat down and crossed her elegant legs. Bessie Dagger had arrived.

CHAPTER NINETEEN

Ellis Hawke strode across the floor of the snug as if he owned it. He was a tall man, around thirty years old and standing a little over six feet, wearing a dark grey trilby hat that made him look even taller. He wore a nicely pressed white shirt and a blue tie under his suit jacket, the trousers of which hung at the perfect length to show off his dark brown brogues. He was a narrow-shouldered man with dark, sleek hair combed back above his ears; he had a long neck and a pointed jaw. His cheekbones were high and his deep-set, hooded eyes made him look as though he had just got over a serious illness. His hands were adorned with a ring on every finger and there was a long, jagged cut on his chin, that looked as if it had only recently had the stitches take out of it.

He took hold of his trousers just above the knee and gave both legs a tug before he sat down. When Bessie took a cigarette out of a silver case and put it into her mouth, he immediately reached into his pocket and produced a Ronson lighter, which he sparked up, producing a yellow/blue flame. Bessie leaned forward slightly and lit the end of her Dunhill. After taking a deep draw, she blew smoke across the table, then leaned back against the bench seat and took a long look at her gold trimmed watch.

'He's got two minutes and then we're gone,' she said, removing a tiny sliver of tobacco from her lip with a red painted fingernail.

Ellis's voice was slightly higher pitched than Amy expected it to be. He licked his lips as he looked towards the bar. 'Are we having a drink or what?'

Bessie replied in a voice that had a warm, velvety, slightly husky tone, as if she had just swallowed a mouthful of whisky. 'Let's see if he turns up first.' She looked at her watch again.

'I was just thinking—'

'Don't think, Ellis, you know you're not very good at it.'

'I know but...'

'Ah, at last, here he is.' Bessie looked towards the door as it opened, and Bodkin stepped into the room. He lifted his grey hat and nodded to the corner where Bessie and Ellis were sitting. Ignoring Amy and Ferris, he aimed his thumb towards the bar. 'Can I get you anything?'

'Does this constitute a bribe?' Bessie said.

'If you like,' Bodkin replied as he beckoned Stan in from the bar side. 'But don't let on or every crook in Spinton will want one.'

'I'll have a scotch, single malt,' Ellis said.

Bodkin snorted. 'In here? You might as well ask for a Strawberry Daiquiri.'

'Whisky and soda,' Bessie said. 'Ice if they have it.'

'The only place that serves ice in Spinton is the Milton Hotel,' Bodkin replied. 'And we might be noticed if we met in there.' He turned to Stan. 'Beer for me, a whisky and soda for the lady and a single malt for the gentleman.'

Stan picked up a bottle of Bells. 'A what?'

'Told you,' Bodkin said, looking over his shoulder at Ellis. 'Shall I try for the Daiquiri?'

'Straight scotch,' Ellis snapped.

Bodkin carried the drinks over to the table and set them down. 'Ooh, that looks nasty,' he said, pointing to Ellis's chin.

'Knife fight,' Ellis muttered, wincing as he touched the wound with his fingertips.

'He fell over drunk and landed on the beer bottle he was holding,' Bessie said with a roll of her eyes.

Ellis looked as if he was about to protest, but after a cold look from Bessie, he bit down on his bottom lip and said nothing.

Bessie slid along the bench seat so that she was in the gap between two small round tables, giving Bodkin the perfect view of her nylon covered legs. She blinked her long lashes slowly, took another deep draw from her Dunhill and blew the smoke towards him. Then, slowly crossing her legs, she took a long look at the policeman.

'I can see you dishing out my orders in the back office on Farley Street.' She looked him up and down again. 'You'd have to smarten yourself up a bit, of course.'

Bodkin grinned. 'Are you offering me a job, Bessie?'

Bessie paused, then shook her head. 'No, thinking about it, I can't see you doing as you are told. I'll stick with him.' She gave a curt nod in the direction of Ellis. 'He knows his place.'

Ellis narrowed his eyes, picked his glass up and stared into it.

Bodkin clapped his hands together and straightened up on his stool. 'Right, shall we get down to brass tacks?'

Bessie held up a beautifully manicured hand. 'Before we begin, are you going to introduce me to your girlfriend?' She looked across the room to where Amy was sitting, trying to look inconspicuous. The redhead wiggled her fingers in greeting. 'Come and join us, Miss Rowlings, or shall I call you Amy?'

Bodkin closed his eyes and grimaced.

'I assume the supposed boyfriend is a copper?' she said, craning her neck to get a good view of Ferris. 'Is he the one that sings or another of your minions?' She was quiet for a moment. 'He's quite dishy, isn't he?'

Bodkin pursed his lips as he thought. Then, realizing there was no way he could deny it, he half turned on his stool and gave Amy a sad smile. 'No Oscar for you this year. Come and join us, Amy.'

'Not the cop,' Ellis growled, five's a crowd.

Bessie gave him another of her cold looks. 'I decide who sits with us and who doesn't.' She paused. 'But he's right for once. We agreed to meet you, Inspector, not any of your colleagues. Dishy as he is, he'll have to go. I'm not going to risk the details of this conversation being gossiped about over a weak cup of tea in the police canteen.' She looked up into Amy's face as she approached the table. 'Wow, she's a beauty. I'm glad I don't have her for competition back home.' She patted the seat next to her. 'Come and sit with me, Amy. I'm sure we've got a lot of things in common. I think we could become very good friends.'

Amy shot Bodkin a glance and after seeing him nod quickly, she eased herself along the bench seat and sat down next to the temporary head of the Dagger crime family.

CHAPTER
TWENTY

'Go have a chat with the driver, Ferris,' Bodkin said as Amy smoothed down her dress. 'He's from Nottingham, isn't he, Bessie?'

Bessie frowned. 'How on earth did you know that? Not that it matters.'

'He's got a lovely accent, me duck,' Bodkin replied. 'He rang me to organize this meeting.'

'So he did,' Bessie said as she held out her hand to flick ash onto the floor. 'You understood him then?'

'Ah did,' Bodkin replied. 'E's gorra rate gud axeunt if ah say so me-sen.'

Bessie dropped the butt of her cigarette on the floor and crushed it under the sole of her stiletto heeled shoe as she applauded him. 'That's very good. It's almost as if he's sitting there, not you.'

Bodkin grinned. 'We aim to please,' he said. The policeman took a sip of his beer and smacked his lips. 'You should try this, Ellis. It'll put 'airs on yer chest.'

Ellis picked up his whisky glass and swished the liquid around. 'I don't understand a word he bloody says.'

Bodkin put his pint down and turned his attention to Bessie, who leaned back and recrossed her legs. 'How long has he worked for you?'

'Who? Robin Hood? About three weeks.'

'And you trust him enough to organize this meeting when there are people who have worked for you for years who could have done it? I mean, driving's no big deal. You must have plenty of men on the books who could do that simple task.' He looked from Bessie to Ellis, then back again.

'Hey! I'm not just some bloody driver,' Ellis spat.

'He does drive me sometimes, Inspector,' Bessie said, flashing a quick look at her boyfriend. 'But when he fell over drunk, he got a bit of concussion, so I'm not trusting him to drive for a few days. Besides which, Mervin has impeccable references.'

'He has a Curriculum Vitae? Blimey!'

'Of a sort,' Bessie replied. She leaned between the tables and patted Bodkin on the thigh. 'You are funny,' she said. Then she winked.

'Where did the bulk of his references come from...? Let me take a wild guess... Nottingham, perhaps?'

Bessie shrugged. 'Amongst other places. He's very highly thought of in that part of the country.'

Bodkin got to his feet and looked out of the window to where Ferris was talking to a broad-shouldered man wearing a nicely fitted light grey suit. He had very short, cropped hair and carried a check patterned cap in his hand.

'He certainly looks like he can handle himself,' Bodkin said. 'What else does he do for you except drive occasionally?'

'He runs the odd errand. He'll step in if something gets a bit out of hand. He is willing to do most things, really.'

'Is he willing to kill for you?'

Bessie's laugh had an almost musical edge to it. 'Inspector, you really are the funniest man. You should join your friend Ferris on the stage. You could form a double act. He sings, you do the jokes.' She leaned forward again and looked closely into Bodkin's eyes. 'I'd come to see you,' she said, her voice slightly deeper than usual.

Amy watched Bodkin's face as Bessie played up to him. She shook her head and whispered, 'Oh, Bodkin,' to herself as he seemed to fall completely under her spell. He smiled as he stared back into the gang leader's eyes.

The spell, if indeed it had ever existed, was broken when the policeman spoke again.

'Did you order Mervin Challenger to kill Lonnie Firth?' he asked.

Bessie's head snapped back as though she'd been slapped.

'No,' she spat. 'Of course not.'

'Of course not,' Bodkin repeated. 'You and Lonnie were the best of friends, after all.'

'We weren't enemies exactly.'

'Even though he robbed one of your bookmakers?'

'Two, actually. We kept the second robbery quiet. One could happen to anyone, two makes you look weak.'

'So, you had every reason to want to see him punished?'

Bessie eyed him cautiously. 'Punishment and murder are two different things.'

'Okay, did you order Mervin to give him a good beating, but it all got out of hand?'

'I didn't order Mervin to do anything to Lonnie.'

'Why not? He'd just made your entire organization look weak and incompetent.'

Bessie reached for her whisky glass. 'I'd like to have done something, believe me. I was livid when I heard about the second robbery, but I was... persuaded to overlook it after receiving recompense from his brother and another benefactor.'

'Reggie Tumbler?'

Bessie took a slow sip of her drink. 'I couldn't possibly say.'

'How much did he steal in the second robbery?'

'A few hundred. Why does it matter? You can't charge him with anything now.'

'I was trying to work out where his money came from. We know Lonnie was in possession of a large amount of cash just before he died.'

'Ah, his nest egg... though it was more of a box than a nest.'

'You knew he had the money? Did you know where he kept it?'

'Word gets around, Inspector.' She stretched, placed her hands behind her head, then leaned forward and reached for her cigarette case. She offered it to Amy, then to Bodkin.

Both shook their heads. 'I don't, thanks,' Bodkin said.

'That's a shame,' Bessie replied. 'I like a man who smokes. There something... sexual, it adds to their manliness somehow.' She raised her eyebrows slightly as she looked across the table at him, her red lips parted slightly. 'Not that you need anything to enhance your... manliness,' she breathed.

Amy suddenly swung her foot and kicked the table leg, making the drinks sitting on the top slosh around in their glasses. Bodkin looked quickly away from Bessie.

'Sorry,' Amy said with a forced laugh. 'I had a bit of cramp in my foot.'

'And there was me thinking the green-eyed monster had struck,' Bessie said, taking a deep draw on her cigarette.

'Hardly,' Amy said, trying to laugh it off. 'I'm not the jealous type.'

'I do like that dress,' Bessie said, twisting to the side to get a good look at Amy. 'I didn't expect to see someone from the sticks wearing anything of that quality. How do you afford it on a machinist's wage?'

Amy took a sip of her port and lemon before she answered. 'I save up.'

Bessie patted Amy's knee. 'Good for you, but if you ever want a proper job, earning decent money, just give me a call.' She turned to Ellis. 'Give her one of my cards. I think we can find a place for her in the club, don't you? I can see her in a little short dress holding a tray of drinks.' She smiled thinly at Amy. 'The money's better and you'd meet a much more mature type of man.' She patted Amy's knee again. 'Wouldn't you like to have a sugar daddy?'

'The father I have is sweet enough, thank you,' Amy said, trying desperately to hold back her anger. 'He's not in jail, either.' She shot Bodkin a glance. He shook his head almost imperceptibly, warning her not to bite.

Bessie flicked her head towards Bodkin. 'I hope he treats you like a daughter. He is a fair bit older than you.'

Now it was Amy's turn to give Bodkin a warning look. The policeman took note and after intertwining his fingers, he cracked his knuckles, then lifted his head and gave Bessie his best smile. 'Enough of the sweet talk. Let's get back to the murder, shall we?' His eyes became narrower as he gave her a stern look.

'I've already told you; I don't have the slightest idea about who killed Lonnie Firth.'

'And I've already made it clear that I don't believe a word of that. Even if you didn't give the order yourself, you've got a good idea who did.'

Bessie got to her feet and picked up her cigarette case. Reaching to the side, she grabbed her bag. 'I'm a busy woman, Inspector. I don't have time for this nonsense.'

'Sit down, Bessie,' Bodkin said smoothly. 'We won't be that much longer, I promise.' He held out a hand towards her seat.

To Amy's astonishment, Bessie meekly did as she had been asked.

'What are you gaping at?' she said, giving Amy a look.

Biting back the urge to use the line she usually reserved for Trixie, *'I don't know. The label has fallen off,'* Amy forced a smile and finished her port and lemon in one long gulp.

'That's better. We're all friends again,' Bodkin said with a grin. 'Now, let's get back to Mervin. I've heard from a reliable source that he's a bit of a hands-on man. Has he ever had his hands on you, Bessie?'

'He bloody well hasn't,' Ellis exploded. 'No one has. They know what they'll get if they ever did.'

Bessie reached across and patted Ellis's hand. 'Now, now,' she said before turning back to face Bodkin. 'He doesn't know everything. We women have to have some little secrets.' She leaned towards Bodkin again and lowered her voice. 'We like it when men pick up the scent.'

Bodkin turned to look at Ellis. His face was a mask of pent up rage. He twisted his hands together as though he was wringing a chicken's neck. The inspector transferred his glance to Bessie again.

'You can discuss that little bombshell in the privacy of your car,' he said, as he picked up his beer again. Swilling it around to make a bit more froth, he took a long sip, then put the glass back on the table. 'You see, what I don't get...' he said as he rubbed at the dark stubble on his chin... 'is where Reggie Tumbler sits in all this. Was he the one who made up the shortfall after Brian couldn't come up with the full amount that had been stolen?'

Bessie shrugged.

'Okay, it obviously was. Did you take much persuading? I mean, Lonnie had taken what? Five or six hundred pounds of your hard earned money. He was due for a bit more than a slap on the wrist, wasn't he?'

Bessie sucked air in through her teeth. 'I went to see Dad to get his thoughts.'

'And he advised you to forget the slight? That doesn't sound like the Christopher Dagger I've read so much about in the police reports.'

'He wanted me to teach him a big lesson,' Bessie said, reaching for her whisky. 'Can we have another one of these?'

'Of course,' Bodkin replied, holding his hand out. 'But it's your round. I can't afford to buy drinks all day, not on a copper's wage.'

Bessie looked at Ellis and flicked her head towards the bar. 'Get them in,' she ordered.

Ellis looked back at her belligerently.

'Hurry up, I'm dying of thirst here. I know your pride's been hurt, but it's been hurt before and I'm pretty sure it will be hurt again before too long. Now...' she leaned forward and pointed toward the bar. 'GET THE DRINKS IN!'

Ellis's face dropped as he patted his trouser pockets. 'I don't have any money left. I used the last of it when we filled up with petrol.'

Bessie sighed, reached for her bag and pulled out a silver purse. Snapping it open, she took out a pound note and handed it to Ellis. 'I want the change,' she said as though she was giving a child instructions.

As Ellis stood at the bar, Bodkin finished his pint and wiped his mouth with the back of his hand. 'You were saying?'

'Dad wanted me to come down hard on Lonnie. He said he was, what was the term he used... syphoning off the urine, that was it. He hardly ever swore. He always found some inventive way of saying what he meant without cursing.' She chuckled throatily. 'I'm not blessed with the same restraint. I'm more like my gran.'

'So, why didn't you teach Lonnie a lesson? As your father instructed.'

'He didn't. I managed to talk him around. It took a while and a big tip for the prison officer who left us alone in the visiting room for three hours.'

'How did you persuade him?' Bodkin asked.

'I told you that Reggie Tumbler had been in touch. Well, he had given us quite a sum by way of compensation. He told me he had a lot of irons in the fire and that he needed some of Lonnie's contacts in London to enable them to catch light. He promised that he would keep him in check in the future if we forgot about his recent indiscretions. I told him to put the word out that he had managed to talk us around and that if Lonnie even thought about doing anything like it again, he'd get his just desserts. We needed that from him. We couldn't have every man and his dog thinking we'd become a soft touch.'

Bodkin nodded to Ellis as he put a pint in front of him and a whisky and soda on the table in front of Bessie. Then he went back to the bar and returned with a port and lemon for Amy and two double whiskies for himself. Holding out his hand, he dropped the change into Bessie's still open bag. 'Cheers,' he said grumpily.

'Are the Daggers and Reggie's mob forming a closer relationship then?' Bodkin asked, lifting his pint and nodding towards Ellis.

'Not bloody likely. We're still in competition. It was a one off gesture, that's all.'

'Are you looking to take over Lonnie's gang? Now he's out of the way?' Amy asked.

Bessie looked at her as though she'd only just realized she was there. 'What's it to you? He's the one asking the questions.'

'Amy has a very insightful mind,' Bodkin replied. 'She often sees something I've forgotten or haven't thought to ask.'

'If a word of what is said here ever gets out. I'll know who to come after,' Bessie said, giving Amy a hard stare.

'If you threaten her again, you'll be answering the rest of my questions from a police cell,' Bodkin stormed. 'And I'll make sure the whole of Gillingham knows what I know.'

Ellis, who had already finished one of the double whiskies and half-finished the other, got to his feet. 'I think you've given them enough. Come on, Bessie, let's get out of here. I told you that you can never trust a copper.'

Bessie picked up her drink, took a sip, and leaned back in her seat. She pointed to the stool that Ellis had just got up from. 'Sit,' she spat. 'I decide when it's time to go.'

Ellis dropped back onto his stool. 'I can't believe you're stupid enough to—'

'SHUT IT!' Bessie yelled so loudly that Stan came into the snug side from the bar.

'Shhh, I've got customers in there. They'll hear you,' he hissed.

'Answer the question, please, Bessie,' Bodkin said.

'All right, it's no secret. I've let it be known that the former members of Lonnie's gang would be welcome to join us if they so wished.'

'Is that why Vincent Jury was at the shop yesterday?' Amy asked.

'She doesn't miss a trick, this one, does she?' Bessie said.

'What about Brian Firth? Has he been invited to join too? What sort of position could you offer him?'

'He can clean up the dog shit at the back of the shop,' Ellis sniggered and tossed the rest of his whisky down his throat. Getting to his feet, he held out his hand to Bessie. 'One for the road?'

'I wouldn't let him have any more if I were you,' Bodkin said, looking from Ellis to Bessie. 'He's going to have to drive you home. I'm taking Little John in for questioning.' Bodkin stood up to look out of the window again, but Ferris and Challenger were nowhere to be seen.

'But I've got con... cushions,' Ellis whined.

Bodkin sat down again with a puzzled look on his face. 'I'm sure you'll be fine. It's only a twelve-mile ride.' He waved a hand towards Amy as he looked at Bessie. 'Could you answer her question now?'

'The answer to that is no. He's used to being near the top of the tree, but he'd be just another pawn in our outfit. He's not intelligent enough anyway, and he's as meek as a kitten. If he tried to order our lot about, they'd chase him back home to mummy.'

'Speaking of mummy,' Amy said. 'How well do you know Hetty?'

'We've met. We didn't get on. We never will now, I don't suppose.'

'Have you spoken to her recently?'

'Since Lonnie died, you mean? No.'

'You didn't get in touch to pass on your condolences?'

'I don't have any condolences to pass on.'

'What about Erma?'

'What about Erma?' Bessie tipped her head as she turned to face Amy.

'Do you get on with her?'

Bessie moved her head from side to side. 'She's okay. She's a hell of a lot smarter than her remaining brother, that's for sure.'

'Have you spoken to her recently?'

'Nope,' Bessie looked at Ellis, then back to Amy.

'Birdie Lark? Do you speak to her?'

Bessie shook her head. 'I don't have any time for that foul-mouthed slut.'

'Slut? That's a strong term. Why do you call her that?'

'Because, Miss prim and proper, she'll hop into bed with anyone who might chuck a shilling her way or buy her a gin or two.' She opened her eyes wide. 'Are you shocked? I know you met her yesterday. I thought you were supposed to be the smart one. Surely you could see her for what she is.'

Amy and Bodkin exchanged glances, then Bodkin said. 'I've only got a few more questions for you. The first is. Did you break into Reggie Tumbler's flat last Friday looking for Lonnie's loot?'

'No.'

'Did you send anyone to break into the flat?'

Bessie shook her head. 'Nope.'

'Did you know how much money Lonnie had stashed there?'

'Yes.'

'And you weren't temped to take it, knowing he was dead?'

Bessie sighed. 'No, it was Reggie's money, anyway.'

'Reggie's money? Was Lonnie looking after it for him? I'd have thought Reggie had plenty of places he could stash money away. He owns half the clubs and pubs in Gillingham, as well as a swathe of houses.'

'You still don't get it, do you, Inspector? That money was tainted. Lonnie wasn't looking after it for Reggie. He'd stolen it from him.'

'Now we're finally getting to the truth,' Bodkin said. He was thoughtful for a moment before he said. 'I've only got two more questions, then you can go back to work... or whatever it is you do down there. Firstly, what can you tell me about the money? Have you any idea where it came from? It can't all have come from his betting shops.'

'It was all in five-pound notes,' Bessie said. 'I know that much.'

'Someone's going to stand out a mile trying to pass those on,' Amy said thoughtfully.

'What are your thoughts on where it came from originally?' Bodkin asked.

'Reggie was... and still is, involved in all sorts of stuff,' Bessie said. 'It could have come from anywhere.'

'And an educated guess would be?'

'Oh, I don't know. Have a look into one or two of those secure warehouse raids last year. There was one at Croydon Airport where... well, you're the investigator. I'll leave it to you to work out.'

Bodkin nodded. Something was whirring away in the back of his brain.

'What was the final question?' Bessie asked. She ran her hand through her curls.

'Oh, yes, the other question was, do you have any idea who died when the London mob came up to kill Lonnie three years ago? They left his face in such a state it was impossible to put a name to the poor bloke.'

'That was before my time in charge. I didn't get to know everything that was happening back then. I was fed snippets, but I never got the full story about that. Again, I'd look at Reggie Tumbler. Lonnie was his man and he would have done anything to protect him, even going so far as to find a... what to the Germans call a lookalike... Doppelgänger?'

'I'd like you to let me know if you hear of anyone trying to cash a lot of five-pound notes around the Gillingham area,' Bodkin said.

Bessie laughed her melodic laugh. 'Inspector. You've had all the information you're ever going to get out of me.'

Bodkin got to his feet and held out a hand towards Bessie.

She stood, ran her hands seductively down her hips, then grabbed a handful of her long locks and threw them over her shoulder before pushing out her breasts towards him.

Amy watched the performance through narrowing eyes. She turned to leave as Bodkin smiled again at the gang boss.

'Thank you for being so candid, Miss Dagger. You've been very helpful.'

'I'd like to say it was a pleasure, but sadly, I can't.' Bessie picked up her whisky glass and drained it. 'I really do hope that you're a man of your word, Inspector. You'll leave us alone to get on with our business now?'

'Unless I find anything that ties you or one of yours into Lonnie's murder, then I will leave you in peace. Rest assured, I won't pass on anything I've heard today to the Gillingham police, nor will I ask them to investigate your activities.' Bodkin paused. 'But, if I find out that you or your crew had anything to do with the murder of Lonnie Firth, or the murder of the mystery man, I'll come down on you like twenty tons of bricks.' He smiled warmly and stood back to allow Bessie to walk through the gap between the tables.

Outside, Amy was surprised when Bessie stepped forward with her arms outstretched. Giving Amy a big hug and a kiss on the cheek, she said, 'It was lovely to meet you, my dear. If you change your mind about working in my club, just give me a call.' She pulled away, smiling, then moved back in until her mouth was next to Amy's ear. 'If you so much as mention my name in passing in this God forsaken rathole, I'll know about it, so keep your mouth shut. I know everything there is to know about you, Amy Rowlings. I know where you go on a Saturday night. I know where you shop for clothes, I know where you work... both jobs... and most important of all, I know where you live. I can have you found and silenced any time I want, so...' She pulled her head away. 'Let's both keep what we know about each other to ourselves. If you keep your nose out of my business. I'll keep my boys away from you.'

Bessie turned away and wriggled her way towards her blue Austin Seven Ruby.

'Have a safe trip,' Bodkin said as Ellis opened the passenger side door for his boss.

Bessie turned and blew Bodkin a kiss, then giving Amy one last look, she put her finger to her lips, then turned and got demurely into the car.

CHAPTER
TWENTY-ONE

'Where the heck is Ferris?' Bodkin asked as he looked up and down the Gillingham Road. Narrowing his eyes and shielding them against the glare of the late October sun, he looked across to the telephone box at the end of Long Lane to see if his colleague was making a call. He wasn't.

'Maybe they've gone for a walk?' Amy said, looking around herself.

The answer to the puzzle came when they heard Ferris's voice behind them. Turning quickly, Amy saw the Detective Constable standing on the wide step of the pub. Next to him was a man with close cropped hair wearing a suit that even Bodkin would struggle to look untidy in.

Mervin Challenger was a man of around five feet ten. He was broad shouldered with a thick neck and a strong, square jaw. His eyes were blue and bright. His hair was cropped back to a mere quarter of an inch in length. The short cut showed off his large ears, which sat tight to his skull. His fingers were thick and had poorly applied letters tattooed on them. His knuckles and the back of his hands were bruised. He wasn't an attractive man in the normal sense, but with his broad shoulders, strong facial features, and piercing eyes, Amy was sure he would never be short of female admirers.

'It seems we've been to the same places in Nottinghamshire, sir,' Ferris said by way of explaining his absence. 'The castle, Lord Byron's old gaff at Newstead Abbey and Wollaton Hall. There's a natural history museum and a deer park there and—'

'Spare me the tourist guide speech, Ferris,' Bodkin said with a sigh. 'Have you two been drinking?'

'It was a bit nippy outside, sir, so I thought we may as well have a pint while we chatted. We've been in the bar.'

'And how many pints have you had?' Bodkin asked.

'Three, sir. It's a tasty drop in there today. The Fremlins Best Mild is particularly good.'

'I had the cheap bitter,' Mervin Challenger added. 'It was decent enough but not as nice as the Shippo's I drink at home.'

'Shippo's?' Bodkin looked puzzled.

'Shipstones Ales, it's a Nottingham brewery. You should try it if you get the chance. Gives your guts a proper clean out does Shippo's.'

Bodkin visibly shuddered. 'I'll pass, thanks.' The policeman turned his attention to Ferris. 'Did you actually get to ask him any relevant questions in between catching up on the Nottingham tourist scene?'

'Erm, we... time seemed to fly, sir.'

Bodkin sighed again. 'Right,' he pointed to the snug. 'In there, I'll ask a few questions myself, though I warn you, Mr Challenger, I have no interest at all in Nottingham Castle or Woollytown Hall.'

'Wollaton,' Mervin corrected him, then turned around and pushed open the door to the snug. 'It was built in the time of Queen Elizabeth the first, you know. It has a five hundred acre park and—'

'Get them in, Ferris,' Bodkin ordered. 'But yours will be a

bottle of pop. You've had enough beer for one day. We don't want you falling asleep on your desk, do we?'

Ferris's face dropped as he waved to get Stan's attention.

'Look on the bright side, Ferris,' Bodkin said as he led Mervin over to the seats in the corner. The empty glasses hadn't yet been cleared. 'I'll be playing catch up. I've only had two.'

The inspector waved his hand towards the bench seats. 'Take a pew,' he said.

'Ha! Very good,' Amy said as she smoothed her dress behind her before sitting down. She looked at a puzzled-looking Challenger, who clearly hadn't got the joke. 'These benches were once pews in St John's church,' she explained.

'Really?' Challenger sat down and grinned at Amy. 'I'd better watch my language then.'

'Your accent doesn't sound as broad as I've heard it does,' Amy said. 'I can understand everything you say.'

'I'm trying hard not to slip into it,' Mervin replied. 'I doubt you'd understand anything I was saying if I started using words like me'sen, mardy or mashin.'

Amy leaned forward. 'Wow, fabulous, I love local words. What do they mean?'

'Me-sen is myself, mardy mean, being in a sulky mood and mashin is making the tea.'

Amy clapped. 'Mardy... I love it.'

'You could also have kaylied, which means extremely drunk, which me and my mate Ferris over there would've been if we'd stayed in the bar much longer. Or then there's nesh, which describes someone who doesn't like cold weather, and guzgog, which is a gooseberry.'

'Oh, I wish I had my notebook with me. I love collecting words,' Amy said. She looked across the table at Bodkin. 'I've never seen you kaylied,' she said, then she burst into a fit of laughter. 'What a fabulous word.'

Bodkin rolled his eyes heavenward, then nodded to Ferris as he put two pints of bitter on the table. 'Yours is coming,' he said to Amy as he turned back towards the bar.

'Is this Fremlins bitter?' Mervin asked as he sniffed at the pint before taking a tentative sip.

'Yes,' Ferris called. 'But it's the Best Bitter, not the stuff you were drinking in the bar.'

'It's a nice drop that,' Mervin said, putting his glass back onto the table.

'If we've finished with the beer quality assessment, the discussion on the Nottingham dialect and the recommended tourist traps, I'm hoping to get around to asking you a few questions regarding the murder of Lonnie Firth,' Bodkin said, looking at them each in turn.

'Ask away. I've got nowt to hide,' Mervin replied.

'How long have you worked for Bessie Dagger?'

'About three weeks.'

'And how long have you been in the area?'

'About three weeks.'

'Did you come down here specifically to work for Bessie or did you have other business?'

'I was... how shall we put it... taking a holiday break?'

'You mean things were getting a little too warm for you in Nottingham?'

Mervin nodded.

'With the police or the criminal fraternity?'

Challenger smiled and shrugged. 'I've never been more popular with the cops, so I decided to get away for a bit.'

'What do you do up there, Mervin?'

'A bit of this, a bit of the other. Mostly the other.'

'So, you came down here looking for work?'

Mervin nodded.

'What type of work? I mean, there are lots of coal mines in

Nottingham, there's a big ironworks close by, there's plenty of farm work up there. What are you good at? Were you looking for a job in the pit?'

'Nope.' Mervin picked up his beer. 'Been there, done that. There are easier ways to make a living.'

'Indeed,' Bodkin said. He picked up his own pint and took a long sip as he thought. 'How did you get to hear about the Dagger family gang?'

'I already knew about the family. The people I work for in Nottingham have links with them.'

'What about Reggie Tumbler? Do they have links with him, too?'

Mervin shook his head. 'No, Reggie and the Thom...' He cut himself short. 'Ooh, you nearly had me there... Let's just say they were in competition for the same business opportunities.'

'So, how did it work with Bessie? Did you bring your credentials down with you and slap them on her desk, or did she know you were coming?'

'No, she wasn't aware I was in the area until I dropped by the shop one day.'

'And she gave you a job as a driver. Lucky you.'

Mervin nodded. 'It suits me... for now, at least.'

'The money can't be that good,' Bodkin said. 'I mean, you're a bit of a name up north by the sounds of it. I'd have thought you'd be looking for something a little better paid.'

'I'm on a bit more than a basic wage, Inspector.'

'For driving Bessie about now and then? There must be more to your job than that.'

'I do a bit of everything,' Mervin replied.

'You're the odd job man!' Bodkin exclaimed. 'Was bumping off Lonnie Firth one of your odd jobs?'

'I... no... It wasn't.'

'Were you just about to say you've never heard of Lonnie Firth?'

Mervin picked up his beer again as Bodkin reached down and scratched at an itch inside his sock. 'Amy?'

'Where did you meet Lonnie for the first time, Mr Challenger?' she asked.

'I met him in Nottingham. He was having a holiday away from Spinton. For pretty much the same reason as I'm down here,' he said.

'Did you work together up there?'

'Not on a formal basis.'

'How did you meet then?'

'I was asked to have a quiet word with him. He was... how shall I say... getting on the nerves of people he shouldn't have been bothering.'

'The Thompson gang?'

Mervin raised his eyebrows. 'You've heard of them?'

Amy shook her head. 'No, but you let it slip in one of your previous answers. It was either going to be Thompson, Tomkins or Thomas. I took a guess at Thompson.'

'You're good at guessing,' Mervin said, leaning back on the bench seat. 'Mind if I smoke?' he asked, reaching into his pocket and pulling out a tobacco tin. After opening the lid, he took out a hand-rolled cigarette. 'I got pretty good at rolling these in the nick,' he said.

'As a matter of interest, what were you in for?' Amy asked.

'I ended up in a bit of a ruck with a few members of a rival gang. The judge called it GBH, but I was just trying to sort out a bit of a misunderstanding.'

'What sort of misunderstanding?'

'He ran a local bar. I was led to understand that he owed us money. He didn't think he did.'

'Protection money?'

'There are some nasty people out there, Miss...?'

'Just call me Amy,' Amy said, not wishing to publicise her name any further. He could find out who she was just by asking Bessie, but just in case he didn't, or hadn't, she decided to keep things as informal as possible.

'People can get hurt if they make a bad business decision,' Mervin said. 'The bar owner in question was looking for a cheaper deal elsewhere. I was there to persuade him he was better off where he was.'

'How long did you get?' Bodkin asked.

'Two years with good behaviour.'

'Is that where you got the haircut?'

Mervin nodded and stroked his spikey head. 'Lice are rife in there. I was going to grow it out, maybe get a short back and sides, but I got used to it. Low maintenance, you see.'

'Back to Lonnie,' Amy said. 'What had he done to upset your boss?'

'Bosses, there are three of them.' Mervin lit his roll-up with an Orlik Carlton lighter, monogrammed with the letters DC, and blew smoke across the table.

'Nice lighter,' Bodkin remarked.

'It was a gift.' Challenger dropped it back into his pocket.

As Mervin hadn't answered her question, Amy repeated it.

'He'd robbed one of our bookies.'

'He's good at that,' Amy replied. 'He seems to have made a career of it. Did this *chat* involve violence?'

'It might have. But I liked him. We had similar interests, it turned out.'

'What were they, Mr Challenger?'

'Call me Mervin... or Spike... I got that nickname inside. I quite like it.'

'All right, Mervin. What interests did you share with Lonnie?'

'We both liked money for a start.'

'So you were willing to get into trouble with the Thompsons by joining forces with Lonnie?'

'No. I gave him the warning I was asked to give, but the Thompsons aren't the only firm that runs its own gambling sideline. We knocked over a few of those.' He laughed suddenly. 'I'm mentioning no names. I don't want Inspector Bodkin here to arrest me and send me back home in the back of a Black Moria.'

'I have no professional interest in what you got up to in Nottingham, Mervin, but I'm very interested in what you get up to down here. It's my patch, you see.'

'Did the Thompsons find out you were working with Lonnie? Didn't they want their cut? Was that why you had to leave your hometown?' Amy picked up her drink and took a mouthful.

'The Thompsons weren't bothered about the extracurricular work I was putting in. They just wanted the money back that Lonnie had stolen.'

'That's a big word,' Bodkin put in. 'Who taught you that?'

Mervin laughed. 'The older Thompson brother was a clever man. He liked to use big words. It made him look superior.'

'Did they get the money back?' Amy asked.

'Sort of. Lonnie did a job for them. It involved a guy up in Glasgow.'

'What sort of job?'

'I've no idea. But he must've done it properly because when he came home, they weren't asking for their money back.'

'Did you work with Lonnie for very long?' Amy took another sip of her port and lemon, then put the glass back on the table. As she continued to ask questions, Ferris slipped away and made for the bar. When he came back, he put a pint down and looked away from Bodkin's glare.

'Only a few weeks. He wasn't there all the time. He used to nip back down here every so often.'

'Why did you follow him down here, Mervin? Who were you hiding from? Are you sure it wasn't the Thompsons?'

'They'd hardly have given me a glowing reference if it had been,' Challenger replied. 'No, I was "advised" to make myself scarce for a while because a couple of rival gang members were asking questions regarding my whereabouts.'

Bodkin drained his pint and, to the disappointment of his colleague, picked up Ferris's fresh one. 'I see. So, you came down here and began your new career as a part time chauffeur?'

'I keep telling you. I do other things too.'

'Yes, but you don't elaborate on what those other things are. That's the problem,' Bodkin said, taking a long pull on the pint. After wiping his mouth on the back of his hand, he turned to Ferris. 'This is nicer than the one you bought me. I must've got the bottom of the barrel.' He grinned and took another pull on the beer. 'Carry on, Amy.'

Amy clasped her hands on her lap and thought for a few moments before speaking again. 'You seem to have left everything behind, Mervin. Do you have a house up there, a flat? Don't you need to keep paying the rent? What about family? Are your mum and dad still living there? What about siblings?'

'Mum died of the flu in nineteen-nineteen,' he replied. 'I was put in an orphanage for a while, but then the authorities said they were going to ship me over to Australia on the next boat, so I did a runner. I was out on my own for a bit, but then one freezing cold night, when I was desperate, I knocked on the door of the old lady who used to live over the road from my mother. She took me in, even arranged for me to go to school for a couple of years. I used to do bits and bobs for the Thompson family in my spare time so I could help her with the bills. That's how I got into the game.'

'You don't have any other family, then?' Amy asked.

Mervin dropped his cigarette end on the floor and put it out with his shoe. Then he looked down at his hands. 'Not any more,' he said.

'I'm sorry to hear that, Mervin. Who else did you lose?'

'I had a brother, but he was sent to a different orphanage. The unfeeling bastards split us up.'

'How old were you when you were separated?'

'I was about ten, he was seven.' Mervin reached for his beer glass. 'Look, I don't want to talk about it, all right?' He took a long gulp and almost slammed the glass back on the table.

'I'm sorry to have caused you distress,' Amy said. 'I won't bring the subject up again.'

Mervin nodded. 'It's not your fault. It gets to me, that's all.'

'I understand,' Amy replied. She reached across and patted his arm with her left hand. 'I think Inspector Bodkin wants to ask you some questions now.'

Mervin turned towards Bodkin and grinned. 'Anyone would think she was the copper.'

'I was biding my time, Mervin.' He lifted the beer and waved the glass towards Ferris. 'And enjoying this excellent pint.'

'I could do with another one,' Challenger said, draining the dregs from the bottom of his glass.

'Ferris. Do the honours,' Bodkin said, pulling out his wallet and handing the constable a ten shilling note. 'Amy?'

'Not for me, I'll doze off on the sofa if I have any more.'

'That's just a pint for me and a pint for Mr Challenger, then Ferris... oh, get one for yourself, man. I can't bear to see that sulking bottom lip sticking out for a moment longer.' He winked at Ferris, then turned back to Mervin. 'Why did you meet up with Lonnie in the Dragon last Thursday night?'

The question seemed to catch Mervin off guard. 'I, er... We had a bit of business to discuss.'

'Had you met him before that night... down here, I mean. Forget Nottingham for the moment.'

'I'd bumped into him, yes. He said he'd got a couple of jobs planned and wanted to know if I'd like to be in on them.'

'Which jobs would these be, Mervin? More raids on the Dagger family business?'

Mervin shook his head. 'No, and I'm not going to incriminate myself by going into detail about them. As you just said, Inspector. This is your patch.'

'You're not as daft as you look, are you, Mervin?' Bodkin said with a short smile.

'I'm not as daft as you look, either,' Challenger replied.

'Touché.' Bodkin took a fresh pint from Ferris and handed it to Mervin. 'Here's your prize. You can win a coconut if you get the answer to the next question right.'

'Okay, fire away.'

'Were you working for the Daggers when you "bumped" into Lonnie again?'

'No, it was just before I met Bessie.'

'Just before?'

'A day or two.'

'Hmm,' Bodkin mused. 'So, on the Thursday night at the Dragon. Did you know by then that he had robbed the Daggers and they weren't too happy about it?'

'I had been told, yes.'

'Are you saying they had forgiven him?'

Mervin laughed. 'Bessie doesn't forgive anyone. I learned that very quickly. But, in his case, they had apparently been persuaded to let it lie for now.'

'Persuaded by Reggie Tumbler?'

Mervin shrugged. 'I think it's common knowledge.'

'Where did you get the handful of fivers you were flashing about in the pub?'

'I'm not admitting to having any of those, either.'

'We know you had them, Mervin, and we know you were flashing them about, trying to get one of them changed. I think you got them from Lonnie. He had a bag full. Why did he give them to you? What had you done to earn it?'

Mervin scratched behind his ear as he looked across the table at Bodkin. 'Lonnie gave me the money to make sure I didn't take on Tumbler's contract. Reggie had asked me to kill him.'

CHAPTER TWENTY-TWO

'Hang on a minute,' Bodkin said quickly. 'I thought you said you didn't work for Reggie Tumbler?'

'I didn't, but a message was passed on to me. And before you ask, I'm not saying who it was from.'

'Why would Reggie Tumbler want to have his apprentice killed?' Amy asked.

'He stole a couple of grand from him,' Mervin said.

'And that would mean that you had stolen from him too, seeing as Lonnie gave you a wad of fivers. How much was in the wad, by the way?'

'He made a down payment of a hundred quid?'

'A down payment?' Bodkin whistled. 'How much was the total bill for letting him off?'

'Two hundred and fifty. He was going to give me the rest over the weekend. He also offered me another five hundred if I'd take out Reggie.'

Bodkin's mouth gaped. 'And... and did you accept the offer?'

'That's why we were meeting in the Dragon. To see if I fancied taking the job on... or organising the hit, at least.'

'How did you leave it?'

'There was no way I was getting involved in that mad scheme, but I hadn't told Lonnie. I said I needed more time.'

'When did Lonnie give you the money?'

'In the Dragon. He had it in his pocket.'

'Didn't you think about drawing attention to yourself by waving five-pound notes in the air?' Amy asked.

'In a pub like that? They're all crooks and vagabonds. No one was going to run to the cops with the information, and I doubt any of Reggie's men drink in there.' He reached for his beer, took a long gulp, then pulled out his tobacco tin again.

'What time did you leave, Mervin?'

'Late. It was well after closing time. Eleven-thirty, maybe a bit later.'

'You can't remember?'

'I'd had a few.'

'But you wear a watch?' Bodkin said. 'Didn't that give you a clue?'

'It had stopped. I must have forgotten to wind it.'

'You left with Lonnie, yes?'

'Yes, I can remember that much.'

'Was anyone hanging around when you came out?'

'Not that I remember.'

'Did anyone come out of the pub when you were outside?'

'Not that I remember... hold on. A couple of drunks came out as I was walking away.'

'Which way did you walk?'

'Down the hill. I turned left and ended up on some run down housing estate. It reminded me of home, to be honest. Victorian terraces that could only be improved by demolition, narrow cobbled streets, no street lights.'

'If you went left, how do you know about the two drunks? We know who they are. They went the other way,' Bodkin said.

'I heard them. They were singing some Irish thing... Molly

Malone, is it? The Irish bloke could sing but the other bugger... I've heard animals being slaughtered that are more in tune.'

'Where was Lonnie while the choir was in full flow?'

'I don't know... he was having a piss up the wall when I left him.'

'Where did you stay?'

'I had a room in the Railway Hotel on Station Street. I found my way to it, eventually.'

'What time did you get there?'

'It probably took me about ten, possibly fifteen minutes, so it would have been before midnight.'

'Did you see anyone? Were there any night staff working?'

Mervin shook his head. 'I didn't go into the foyer. My room was on the ground floor at the back. I had breakfast the next morning, though. Someone might remember that if you check.'

'I'll be checking. Count on it,' Bodkin said.

Melvin smiled and killed his cigarette stub with his shoe.

'You didn't hear anything else, as you were walking down the alley? A fight, for instance?'

'Sorry. But you wouldn't have heard a banshee screaming over the racket those guys were making.'

'Are you sure you didn't double back when the two drunks had gone? Are you sure you didn't whack Lonnie on the bonce with a lump of lead in a sock? Are you sure you didn't take a few more of those fivers off him when he was lying on the floor?'

'I walked through the slum houses, took a few wrong turns, and then found my way to the Railway Hotel,' Mervin replied calmly.

'Did you see anyone on the way? Anyone on Station Road?' Amy asked.

'No one. It was late.'

'No one was hanging around?' Bodkin was incredulous. 'No one?'

'I can't remember seeing anyone.'

'What about the prostitutes? You could see them down at the station from the hotel.'

'I can't remember seeing any. I might have taken one to my bed if I had.' He gave Amy a lecherous look.

'They hang around outside the hotel too,' Bodkin said.

'They must've all been busy then,' Mervin replied.

'What about the singing Irishman?' Amy asked,

'He went the other way when he came out of the pub,' Mervin said.

'But he would have come out on Station Road,' Amy said. 'He was drunk. He was walking sideways and backwards as much as forwards.'

'Didn't see him,' Melvin said, holding Amy's look.

'His name is Seamus McTaggart.'

'I don't care what his name was, him and the other bloke, the ferrety looking one, must have gone the other way when they got to the top of the alley.'

'They didn't,' Amy said. 'Herbert Norris went left to pick up his wife from the station, and Seamus went right. He lives down near Victoria Street. The state he was in it would have taken him a good fifteen to twenty minutes to get home. You would have passed him for sure.'

'Maybe he went down an alleyway for a piss,' Mervin replied. Amy flashed a look towards Bodkin and raised her eyebrows slightly when she noticed a flicker of concern cross Mervin's face.

Bodkin finished his drink and motioned for Ferris to do the same. 'Well, it's been nice chatting, Mervin, but we can't sit around here all day. There's policing to be done.' He got to his feet. 'How are you getting back to Gillingham? I forgot all about that when I sent your passengers home.'

'I'll get the train,' he replied.

'Right. Well, give my colleague your address before you go,' Bodkin said. 'And please hang around. I haven't finished with you yet. No scuttling back to Nottingham... me duck.'

As Amy and Bodkin crossed the road to walk towards the Rowlings' cottage, Ferris made for the telephone kiosk. 'I'll give the station a ring, sir. Just to see if anyone has missed us.'

Outside Amy's house, Bodkin unlocked the car, then he stood with her by the gate as he laid out his plans for the rest of the day. 'I'm going back to the station to make a few notes while all this is fresh in my memory,' he said. 'I'd really appreciate it if you could write your thoughts down as well.'

'I started to make notes last night as it happens,' Amy replied. 'So I'll add to them when I go in.' She put her hand on Bodkin's chest. 'There's a lot to think about now, isn't there?'

Bodkin nodded. 'Well done back there, by the way. I think you really had him rattled, and you certainly got under Bessie's skin.'

'She was looking daggers at me,' Amy said.

Bodkin laughed. 'I've been waiting for that joke to come up. I was wary of using it myself.'

Amy grinned. 'When do you want to catch up to compare notes?'

'Are you still coming over tonight? I don't want to tidy up for nothing.'

'I'd forgotten all about that. I'll get the bus over after dinner. I ought to be there about seven.'

'I could pick you up.'

'And rush all that lovely tidying up?' Amy got to her tiptoes and kissed him on the lips. 'I'll get the bus. You get the duster going.'

Before Bodkin could respond, they heard Ferris shouting as he hurtled down the lane towards them. 'It's... Bessie Dagger and her bloke... sir.... They've been involved in a car crash. He's dead, and she's in hospital. She's in a bad way.'

CHAPTER TWENTY-THREE

Bodkin's face crumpled. 'Jesus Christ, I told him to drive and he might have had concussion.'

'Don't blame yourself, sir,' Ferris replied. 'It was nothing to do with concussion. He didn't collapse behind the wheel. A witness said their car was forced off the road.'

'Thank God for that,' Bodkin said, then, realising Amy was still standing next to him, he apologised. 'Sorry, Amy. I shouldn't have let that lot out.'

'You're forgiven,' Amy replied, patting Bodkin on the arm.

'I'd better get to the station to see what's happened,' he said as he lowered his head to kiss Amy goodbye.

'Are we still on for tonight?' she asked. 'Never mind the tidying up. You've got enough on your plate.' Amy smiled softly.

'I'll be there and the place will be tidy...ish, what is tidy anyway?' He walked around the front of the car crossing Ferris on the way. 'It would be a massive help if you could jot down your thoughts on our questioning today. I won't have time now and I'm liable to forget the odd important detail.'

'Consider it done,' Amy replied. 'The sling is coming off this afternoon. I should be able to write for a bit longer than I did the other night without my hand cramping up.'

'Don't push it too far, Amy,' Bodkin said.

'My wrist or the pen?' Amy said with a smile. 'I never had me down as a pen pusher. I'm a factory girl at heart.'

When Amy got back inside, she found her mother in the kitchen running the sheets that she had been soaking in the bath, through the wooden rollers of the mangle. Sweat dripped down her forehead beneath the flowered turban she had made from a headscarf. The front of her pinafore was drenched, and there was a pool of water on the floor next to the galvanised bucket that had been put in place to catch most of the runoff.

'Let me give you a hand with that, Mum,' Amy said, taking off her sling and dropping it on the oak kitchen table.

'Not likely,' Mrs Rowlings replied. 'You're supposed to be resting that wrist, our Amy. These wet sheets are heavy.'

'I can't sit and watch you struggle like that,' Amy said, taking a step towards her mother.

Mrs Rowlings snorted. 'I do it every week, dear. It looks a lot harder work than it actually is.'

'The sheets are a bit lighter when they've been through the rollers, so I'll take that end,' Amy said. 'Come on, Mum, we'll have it done in no time if I help.' Amy positioned herself so she was ready to receive the sheet as it came through the rollers. Grabbing it with her left hand, she held out her right arm and fed it over the crook of her elbow, allowing it to fall onto the floor in a surprisingly neat fold.

When the second sheet had been fed through, Mrs Rowlings picked them up, put them into a laundry basket and placed it near the back door. 'I'll hang them out soon. It doesn't look like rain.'

'No, but it's cold, Mum. You might be better off hanging them across the bath. If you leave them out, they'll look like they're made of solid ice by the morning.'

During the summer, Mr Rowlings had fixed two washing lines across the bathroom at a high level. It had saved his wife from having to run clothes through the mangle again after hanging them out prior to a summer storm. He did occasionally complain that he couldn't find his way to the lavatory when there were sheets or curtains hanging on them, though.

'I'll put the kettle on, shall I?' Amy said, picking it up and filling it with water. 'That mangling is thirsty work. You sit yourself down and I'll bring the tea in. You look like you could do with a breather.'

'Thank you, dear,' Mrs Rowlings said as Amy emptied the teapot into the sink. 'I was halfway through a short story in my Woman magazine. I'll have time to finish it off now.'

'What's it about?' Amy asked.

Mrs Rowlings furrowed her brow. 'It's rather gripping. You see, there is this poverty-stricken artist who meets a rich young woman at the gallery one afternoon and he is so struck by her beauty, that he offers to paint her, but her mother doesn't like the idea, and her father gets hold of the wrong end of the stick completely. Between you and me, Amy, I reckon he thinks Pablo means to paint her, (Mrs Rowlings' voice dropped to a whisper) *naked!*'

'Naughty Pablo,' Amy said with a grin. 'I hope there's a happy ending.'

'So do I, dear, but it's not looking like it at the moment. Rosetta's father has gone to get his flintlock.'

'POOR PABLO!' Amy said, turning her face away. 'Let me know how it all works out, Mum. Now, get yourself sat down.'

Amy poured the tea, then left her mother to find out what fate had in store for Pablo and Rosetta, and carried her mug through to the front room, where she put her tea on a cork table mat before walking over to the sideboard and pulling out a few sheets of paper. After picking up her father's vacuum fill, Shaeffer Balance, black and gold fountain pen that she had bought him for his birthday a couple of years previously, she returned to the table, unscrewed the top, then, after looking up towards the ceiling for a moment, she began to write.

Latest Thoughts.

Some early notes. I'll write out a full report when we've interviewed all the people who might have had something to do with Lonnie's death.

Ellis Hawke

He isn't my cup of tea at all, but if he has died in the car crash, then I'm truly sorry for both him and his family. There has been no confirmation as yet, so I'll just write about him as I saw it. He'll never get to read it whichever way things turn out, but I can't bring myself to speak ill of the dead.

Ellis obviously isn't happy with the way Bessie orders him about. You could see that he was on the verge of snapping back an angry reply, but he somehow managed to keep himself under control. I wonder what his attitude is when they're alone together. I can't honestly see Bessie acting any differently, but I have a feeling that Ellis may have had a little more to say for himself.

Ellis wants to be the top man, or at least thinks he deserves a share at the apex of the hierarchy. Maybe he thinks he could wear her down over time? I don't fancy his chances. It seems to me that he's merely a trophy or an ornament to be shown off in public. Men do it all the time with young women, so it's only fair that women should do it too. I really don't like the way she puts him down all the time, though. I know she runs the gang with a rod of iron, but surely her partner should be treated a little differently. Did he have anything to do with Lonnie's death? I can't see him being the one to land the fatal blow, but he might have given the order on Bessie's instruction.

Bessie Dagger

I almost described her as a vamp, but I think that would be doing her an injustice. She's so much more than that. Bessie has been schooled by her father and it shows. She is a beautiful woman and there are hundreds of men out there who would run over hot coals to stand a chance of getting close to her. She's nobody's fool. Bessie isn't the sort to let a mere man influence her decisions. She is definitely a daddy's girl, there's no two ways about that, but anyone who thinks there's a soft heart hiding underneath that granite shell had better think again. Anyone who so much as attempts to undermine her authority will regret it instantly. I don't envy any man that Bessie decides to allow into her life. Her smile is warm and welcoming on first impression, but it never reaches her eyes.

Initially, I thought she seemed friendly enough. She definitely tried to use her feminine wiles on Bodkin, but as usual with him, her efforts were wasted. Bodkin doesn't have a clue, bless him. He never picks up a woman's signals and despite me explaining about female body language to him on a number of occasions, the poor man never quite gets it. Whether the messages are taken in subconsciously, I can't be sure, but it never stops him from asking the next difficult question. Bessie could be in Hollywood alongside Alice's lookalike Rita Hayworth and Jean Harlow, so good was her performance in front of Bodkin. It's such a shame it was wasted. I did catch him looking at her, dreamy eyed, once, but that might have been an act of his own. You never know with him.

As for what we leaned. She didn't tell us the whole truth, but then we weren't really expecting her to. She answered most of the questions without really telling us a lot. What I found most interesting was when she was trying to ease Reggie Tumbler into the conversation. She obviously wanted to put him front and centre in the Lonnie Firth murder inquiry. I know Bodkin would have noticed that. I'll see what he has to say about it tonight.

Is Bessie capable of murder? Possibly, but she's more likely to have ordered the killing rather than take part in it herself. Mervin came onto the scene at the perfect time. I wonder if it is just a coincidence.

Mervin Challenger

Rugged, lean and mean. It's not hard to see why some women might find Mervin Challenger an interesting man. I think, as his name suggests, he would be something of a challenge and there are quite a lot of women out there who might want to take it on. I'm not one of them. Whilst superficially engaging, Mervin doesn't say anything that hints at what is really going on inside his head. His responses seem immediate, but I think the way he reacts to questions is well practiced. He seemed to be answering quite candidly without actually giving anything away. Mervin is never going to incriminate himself. I was intrigued by his relationship with Lonnie Firth. On the face of it, they got on well. They had similar interests and were of a similar age and background. I wonder what Lonnie was sent to Scotland to do and I also wonder if Mervin played a bigger part in it than he's letting on? I'm not disputing the fact that they first met in Nottingham, but I think it's rather too much of a coincidence that they arrived in Spinton within a few days of each other. Then, of course, there is the money. He has admitted that Lonnie gave him a hundred pounds, ostensively to save his own life. He then stated that Lonnie offered him extra money to kill Reggie Tumbler. I don't know if we can believe that. Lonnie might have been paying him for playing a part in a bookmaker's robbery. I don't think there's any doubt that the cash in the box belonged to Reggie, but could Mervin have somehow got hold of a set of keys to the flat and taken the money before Brian and Birdie arrived? It's all very confusing. Why would he go to the trouble of obtaining another set of keys when there was a set in Lonnie's pocket which, if he was the killer, he could easily have taken.

Mervin is quite capable of murder. There's no doubting that. The question is, was he asked to come down from Nottingham to do the deed, or was it something he was asked to do after he had arrived? Like Bessie, he was dropping subtle hints that Reggie Tumbler may have had some involvement in Lonnie's death. I wonder if Bessie had asked him to bring Reggie's name into the conversation when he was being questioned. She must have known that Bodkin wanted to talk to him. She knew everything else about the investigation.

As things stand, Mervin is our prime suspect. He was probably the last person (as far as we know) to see Lonnie alive. His statement that he didn't see anyone at all on Station Street that night is flimsy in the extreme. Men can't usually walk fifty yards without being accosted by a prostitute up there. And then, of course, there's Seamus. He would almost certainly still be staggering his way home at the time that Mervin claims he reached the Railway Hotel.

I know Bodkin will want to check with the night staff there to see if anyone can remember seeing him. He hasn't had time to write his notes up yet, so I'll remind him it might be worthwhile having a quick word with Seamus. I know one or two of the street girls who ply their trade on Station Street from when I helped out on the Reverend Villiers' murder case. I might go up and have a word with them. They were very nice to me at the time.

My main concern about everything I've learned today is, who has been passing information about me to Bessie Dagger? Although she lives over twelve miles away and can't possibly have heard of Amy Rowlings, she seems to know everything about me, including my hobbies, my shopping habits and even where I work and live. I have to admit, I'm worried. The information can only have come from either Hetty or Erma. I really hope it isn't Erma. I like her so much. I thought she was a kindred spirit.

CHAPTER TWENTY-FOUR

After dinner that evening, Amy, wearing an extra jumper against the cold, pulled on her coat and walked up to the stop at the end of Long Lane to get the six-forty-five bus to the bottom of Middle Street. After alighting, she crossed the road towards the chip shop, which was already doing a brisk trade, and turning right, she walked down the hill until she got to the narrow lane where Bluecoat House was situated.

Bodkin had a flat on the first floor. Trixie, the secretary at the police station, lived on the ground floor and she always seemed to be the one to answer the front door, even when it wasn't her flat that was being buzzed. There was to be no confrontation this evening, however, because, as Amy looked through the plate glass at the side of the door, she could see Bodkin sitting on the bottom step, waiting for her.

'Hello you,' he said as he accepted a kiss on the cheek from Amy. She looked to her right at Trixie's door as he turned to lead her up the stairs. But if the blonde bombshell had heard Bodkin greeting her, she hadn't taken the opportunity to remark on Amy's presence.

Bodkin's flat was untidy, despite the fact that he had just

spent half an hour cleaning it. There were shirts hanging on door handles and tonight's Evening Post newspaper spread out on the floor in front of his two-bar electric fire. On the table was a small mountain of beige coloured files. He stood by the door to allow her to enter the flat, then, spotting two pairs of underpants and a vest lying on the sofa, he quickly shut the door and hurried across the room to scoop them up.

'Sorry about that... I was going to iron, but then I remembered I was supposed to be tidying up.'

'You actually iron your pants? That does surprise me,' Amy said.

'Don't you iron your kn...'

'I'm not telling you what I do with my knickers, Bodkin. A girl has to have some secrets. I was just surprised to find out that you iron your underwear when you don't seem to bother with your shirts.'

'My body is the wrong shape for my clothes,' Bodkin said, pulling a sad face.

Amy gave him a puzzled look.

'Would you like a cup of tea?' the policeman asked, quickly changing the subject. He did iron his shirts, but by the time lunchtime came around they always looked as though he'd slept in them.

'I'll be nipping to the lavvy all night if I have any more. I had two cups after dinner,' Amy said, slipping out of her coat. Bodkin took it from her and hung it on the peg on the back of his front door before walking around the sofa and picking up the newspaper from the floor.

'Have you seen the Post tonight? That idiot reporter Sandy Miles has done a piece on Lonnie's murder. He's linking it to the London mob who supposedly killed him the first time around, even though the gang doesn't exist now. What's more, there isn't a shred of evidence to suggest anyone from London was involved.' He grinned. 'I get an honourable mention again. He can't seem to leave my name out of his reports just lately.' He folded the paper in half, pointed to the last paragraph of the article, and handed it to Amy.

'Inspector Bodkin of Spinton police is hoping that the victim really is Lonnie Firth, after wasting three years investigating his murder the first time around. This reporter wonders if the inspector is a believer in reincarnation.'

'He's a fool,' Amy said, tossing the newspaper onto the chair at the side of the fireplace. She smoothed down the back of her skirt and sat on the lumpy old sofa that Bodkin had bought from Stan's Second Hand Emporium in the town centre.

'For once, the article is quite in depth and that's unusual for our Sandy, as you know,' Bodkin said. 'I'm wondering where he's getting his information from. It could be someone at the station who's given him an insight into the investigation for half a crown, but it didn't feel like it had come from a copper when I was reading it.'

'Who then?'

'I was wondering if Bessie Dagger has had an input, but then anything she gave him would have to have been before her accident today.'

'Of course... how is she, Bodkin? Ferris said she was in a bad way. Have you heard anything since then?'

'I dropped in. They wouldn't let me see her, but I spoke to a doctor, and he told me that apart from the broken arm, a couple of broken ribs and a busted leg, she'll be alright. Most of her injuries are superficial. Luckily for her, the windscreen smashed before she went through it.'

'What about Ellis? Did he die in the accident?'

'Sadly, yes.'

'What happened? Is it any clearer?'

'We have three eyewitness reports now. It seems that Bessie

and Ellis were in a hurry to get home. They were travelling at high speed along the Gillingham Road when a dark green saloon overtook them and, whilst doing so, deliberately forced them off the road. Their car ended up in a hedge. Bessie was found in a ditch after being thrown through the broken windscreen. She was lucky, Ellis was trapped inside the car. He was already dead when the ambulance arrived. The car had flipped over a couple of times before it hit a tree.'

'My goodness, how awful,' Amy replied. 'There's no doubt the collision was caused by the other vehicle then?'

'None. All three said the same thing. One was a driver who was directly behind Bessie's car. Another was in a car going in the opposite direction. He had to swerve to avoid the overtaking car. The third witness was walking her dog about a hundred yards in front. She was heading directly towards the scene. Had it happened a minute or so later, she'd have been right in the middle of the carnage.'

'Do they have a description of the car that caused it?'

'A dark green saloon. Possibly a Rover.'

'It's not much to go on, is it?'

'No, but there won't be too many Rovers owned by gang members in Gillingham. It's a good start. We just need to find a damaged one before its owner has the chance to get it repaired.'

'Someone knew Bessie was up in Spinton today, then?' Amy mused.

'I'm wondering if it's the same someone who had a chat with Sandy Miles, our erstwhile newshound.'

'Do you think it could have been Mervin?'

'I doubt it. He came up expecting to be driving his boss home again after the interview. It was my suggestion that Ellis should drive.'

'Oh, of course it was.' Amy held out her hands towards the glowing bars of the electric fire. 'It's lovely and warm in here.'

After a few seconds, she picked up her handbag and handed the report she had been working on that afternoon to the policeman. 'It's only a brief set of notes. I'll do a more in-depth one when we know more about Reggie Tumbler's involvement in the case.'

Bodkin read through the report, then folded the sheets in half and handed them back to Amy.

'Spot on, as usual. I'm glad you mentioned the spy in the camp because I was a bit reluctant to bring it up, seeing how you like Erma so much.'

'It has to be her, doesn't it, Bodkin? Unless she gave Hetty all the tiny details of my life, and I can't see why she would ever want to do that.'

Bodkin sighed. 'She's let you down, badly. When are you supposed to be seeing her again? I'd like to be there when it happens.'

'We're supposed to be going shopping this week, but I don't know if I really want to now.'

'Keep the date,' Bodkin replied. 'But stop off at the Sunshine Café. I'll meet you there. I'd like to know if she's been sharing our intimate details with anyone else.'

'I feel incredibly let down. I really thought I'd found a new friend. We seemed to have so much in common.'

'You always tend to see the good in people,' Bodkin replied, slipping an arm around her.

Amy rested her head on his shoulder, then turned her face up as he leaned in to give her a long, lingering kiss.

'Wow,' Amy said, coming up for breath. 'A Hollywood kiss couldn't match up to that.'

'There's more where that came from.' Bodkin eased Amy back onto the cushions and kissed her again. Then, after pulling away, he ran his tongue up her neck and stuck it gently into her ear. Amy shuddered as he concentrated on her neck again. His hand moved over her body and came to rest on her right breast. Squeezing it gently, he kissed her again.

Amy eased him away, then pulled off her jumper. 'I'm a bit hot,' she whispered, dropping it on the floor, then, after lying back again, she put her arms around his neck and pulled him towards her.

After more kisses, Bodkin undid the buttons on her blouse and as Amy arched her back for him, he slipped his hand behind her and attempted unsuccessfully to unhook her bra. After fiddling with the hooks for a few more seconds, he pushed his other arm around her and tried with two hands. Exasperated when he couldn't manage it, he gritted his teeth as the elastic at the back of the garment twanged and slapped against Amy's back.

'It must be easier breaking into a safe,' he complained.

Amy giggled. 'You're hopeless, Bodkin, here, I'll do it.' Easing Bodkin's fingers aside, she expertly unhooked the brassiere. 'Easy when you know how.'

Bodkin grunted his thanks, then pushing the bra up with one hand, he grabbed her breast with the other. Pulling her blouse open, he dropped his head and put his mouth over her nipple. She squirmed as she felt the spiky stubble of his beard on her skin.

Amy groaned as she felt Bodkin's fingers run over the flesh at the top of her stocking. As he moved his hand towards her knickers, she slid her own hand over her skirt and rested it on top of his.

'If I get carried away, promise you won't go too far... please, Bodkin?'

Bodkin nuzzled into her neck and slipped his fingers into her knickers. 'I promise,' he muttered.

Amy let out a long breath as Bodkin took hold of her pants and tugged them down to her thighs. His fingers explored further as Amy groaned into his ear. Somewhere in the distance, the shrill ring of a telephone could be heard.

'Oh, Bodkin,' she moaned.

Bodkin raised himself above her, kissed her passionately, and pushed his tongue inside her mouth. His hand ran over her hip, then back to her inner thigh, but before his fingers could explore further, there was a hammering on the door and Trixie's excited voice could be heard shouting.

'Inspector Bodkin. There's a telephone call for you. It's Constable Smedley, he says it's urgent.'

'Damn and blast!' Bodkin cursed as he eased his body away from Amy's. 'Perfect bloody timing, Trixie.'

Amy sighed with relief. 'Thank you, Trixie,' she whispered. 'I owe you one.'

CHAPTER TWENTY-FIVE

Amy lay on her back on the sofa and wrapped her unbuttoned blouse over her chest as Trixie insisted that Bodkin should hurry to answer the downstairs telephone. When the voices ceased and she heard the sound of the inspector's footsteps retreating across the landing, she got to her feet and began the struggle to fasten the hooks of her bra.

'Sorry about that. Did I disturb the inspector as he was inspecting you?' Amy looked up to see Trixie standing in the still open doorway. 'Would you like me to fasten that up for you?' She tittered behind her hand. 'And there's me thinking you were a goody two shoes.' She half turned away, then looked back over her shoulder 'Don't you dare criticise me in future, you're nothing but a hypocrite.'

Amy grimaced. It was embarrassing enough being caught in these circumstances, but to be caught by Trixie was on another level entirely.

After three attempts, Amy managed to fasten her bra. She had just finished buttoning up her blouse when Bodkin hurried into the flat. Noticing Amy's crestfallen face, he became concerned himself. 'What's the matter?' he asked.

'That Trixie caught me getting dressed.' A film of tears appeared in her eyes. 'It will be all over town by this time tomorrow. What if Big Nose Beryl hears about it? I'll never be able to show my face in the factory again.'

Bodkin stepped forward and took her in his arms. 'Most normal people will understand, Amy. It's not like she caught us at it.'

'That's another thing I'm concerned about, Bodkin. I lost control just then.' Her eyes dropped to her chest. 'I wanted you to carry on. I loved the way you made me feel.' She tilted her head and looked into his face. 'I was relying on you to keep your promise, but I think you'd gone too far to be able to stop.'

'I'd have stopped,' Bodkin replied. He kissed her on the forehead, then stroked the side of her face softly. 'It would have been the hardest thing I've ever done, but I would have kept my promise. I'll only ever go the whole way when you're ready.'

'That's the problem, Bodkin. That's what I'm saying. I am ready, I was ready and it could have been disastrous.' She wiped her eyes with the back of her hand and sniffed as a stream of tears ran down her cheeks. 'I don't suppose you have any of those things. Do you?'

'Things?'

'You know, the things men use... from the chemist?'

Bodkin smiled softly. 'No, I've not had cause to need them for a long time, but I can get some the next time I'm in town, if you're really sure. They sell them at the barber's too. As they brush you down after the haircut, they wink and ask if you would like something for the weekend?'

Amy's mouth gaped. 'Don't get them from the chemist in Spinton. Please don't. Everyone in there knows me. They know I'm your girlfriend, so they'll put two and two together.' She looked pleadingly at the policeman. 'I'm not sure about the

High Street barber either, Bodkin. My dad gets his hair cut in there.'

'Your dad gets his hair cut at skin 'em alive, Clive's? You're safe then. I wouldn't go in there if he was the last barber in Spinton.' He grimaced as he thought. 'I went to Clive's the first week I moved up here. Never again. There was more hair on the floor than there was on my head by the time he'd finished.' The inspector shuddered at the memory. 'I use Barnet's up near the Post Office now, but I take your point. There will be a lot of people who know we're an item in there too.' Bodkin smiled softly at her. 'If you're sure you want me to get some, I'll drive over to the chemist in Highwater... No! Better still, I'll get some when I'm in Gillingham next. No one knows you down there.'

Amy wiped her cheeks and sniffed. Then she stood on her tiptoes and kissed him on the lips. 'You're a good man, Bodkin. But thinking about it, you might as well get them locally. Everyone's going to know all about us when they hear what Trixie has to say.'

Bodkin held Amy's face in his hands and gave her a soft smile. 'You leave Trixie to me. I know a thing or two about her that she'd rather not have hit the airwaves.'

Amy sniffed again, but looked more hopeful. 'What things?'

'Let's just say there's a certain uniformed constable working at the station who came out of the evidence room with lipstick all over his mush only last Tuesday. Trixie came out straightening her blouse a minute or so later. I had a word with the constable when I saw him in the canteen. He's a married man, you see? It wouldn't go down well if head office were to hear about it.'

He pulled a grubby-looking handkerchief from his pocket and dabbed at her cheeks with it. 'I didn't say anything to Trixie at the time. I just made out I hadn't noticed.' He offered the hanky to Amy, who, after taking note of the state of it, shook her head.

Bodkin slipped the offending object back into his pocket. 'By the first thing tomorrow morning, she'll know that I had noticed.' He smiled at her encouragingly. 'Don't worry, Amy, your reputation won't be tarnished.'

When Amy had recovered her composure, Bodkin made tea and carried it through from the kitchen. She examined the drink with a careful eye before sniffing at it, causing Bodkin to choke on the mouthful he had just taken.

'It's okay,' he spluttered. 'I got a fresh pint of milk on the way home. I got bread, butter and some sliced ham too, if you fancy a sandwich?'

Relieved, Amy took a tentative sip, then leaned back on the sofa with the cup clasped in both hands, taking care not to spill tea on her bandage. 'I had dinner with Mum and Dad, thanks, but don't let me stop you from getting a sandwich. I bet you've had nothing since breakfast.'

'I had something in the canteen,' Bodkin replied. 'And I had already sampled the ham before you arrived.'

Amy blew into her mug, then took another sip. 'What was the phone call about? Was it urgent, or was Trixie just being nosy?'

'It was Constable Smedley. Bessie Dagger has woken up. As I told you, she's in a bad way, but she wants to talk to me.'

'Are you going over tonight? Can I come too? Please say yes.'

'I'm going to leave it tonight. Let her get a bit more rest. She'll need it if she's going to make any sort of recovery. I'll drive over to the Free Hospital in the morning.' He took a big gulp of tea, then his mouth dropped open and he fanned it with his hand. 'Hot,' he gasped. He pulled a face, cleared this throat, then went on. 'As for coming with me. I think that's an excellent idea. I don't want her solicitor accusing me of taking advantage of a seriously injured woman who may or may not be in control of her faculties. I'd like to have a civilian witness to corroborate what she has to say. I won't be interviewing her under caution, just in case.'

At nine-thirty, Bodkin and Amy walked down the stairs, but before they could get to the front door, Trixie stepped out of her flat with a smug look on her face. 'I see you managed to get dressed.' She put a hand in front of her mouth and giggled. 'Did you remember your drawers? It's nippy out there.'

'At least I wear them most of the time,' Amy replied. She glared at the blonde. 'Unlike some I can mention. Do you even own any?'

Trixie's eyes narrowed as she took two quick steps forward. She raised her hands, fingernails flexed, but before she could get to Amy, Bodkin intervened. 'Trixie. I'd advise you to take a deep breath... in fact, take a few deep breaths, then turn around and go back to your flat.' He turned to Amy and winked. 'Wait by the car. I'll be out in two shakes.'

Amy gave Trixie one final glare, then she let herself out of the entrance door and made her way around to the small car park at the side of Bluecoat House.

Bodkin was as good as his word, and only three minutes later, she saw him appear around the side of the building. After unlocking the car, he opened the passenger door to allow Amy to get in before closing it gently behind her and walking around to the driver's side.

'Trixie is suitably contrite,' Bodkin said before Amy could speak. He put the key into the ignition and primed the engine before turning it to start the car. 'She insists she would never have said a word to anyone about what she allegedly saw this evening. In fact, she swears that she didn't see anything other than you sitting on the sofa sipping a cup of tea.'

Amy let out a huge sigh of relief. 'Do you think we can trust her, Bodkin? You know what a gossip she is.'

'I believe we can, on this occasion at least. She'll never get another job as cushy as the one she has at the station. Honestly, Amy, she knows it's not worth the risk.'

'Would you really have put in a report?' Amy asked.

'No, although they'd both have deserved it if I had. She just can't seem to keep away from married men.'

'Or anything in trousers,' Amy said as Bodkin pulled away.

CHAPTER TWENTY-SIX

The Free Hospital was a late Victorian building that had been gifted to the town by a local philanthropist, the aptly named Sir Samuel Saviour. Staffed by trained Nightingale School nurses, the hospital initially looked after the sick and elderly overspill from the Spinton Workhouse, when its tiny, one room infirmary could no longer cope with the numbers. After a major rebuild and expansion at the turn of the century, the hospital began to train its own nurses and started to take in the working poor of the town, who, before then, had been sent to the Gillingham Royal Naval Hospital for treatment.

The Royal Naval Hospital had been built to treat sick and injured sailors, but it gradually opened up its services to the poor of the community. Although means testing was used, many extremely poor working people found that they still had to contribute to the cost of their treatment.

After first making enquiries at the reception desk in the entrance hall, Amy and Bodkin walked the fifty yard corridor to the green-painted, Oakdale ward, which had been named after the Matron who set up the nurse training facility, in the years before the Great War. However, although there were twenty beds on the all-female ward, Bessie wasn't in any of them. After getting the attention of a nurse, Bodkin was told that she had been moved to the Phillipson Ward, which was much smaller and meant for patients who could afford to pay.

The cream-painted ward had only four beds, and three of those were empty. They found Bessie in a bed by the window being tended to by a stockily built nurse.

'Who are you?' Nurse Huggett demanded to know in a broad Liverpudlian accent. 'It isn't visiting time and anyway, this patient is in no condition to receive any.' She pointed to the door of the ward as Bodkin pulled his warrant card from his pocket.

'The young lady is an important witness in a murder case,' he said, pushing the card into her face.

'I said, it's not visiting time.' The bolshy nurse wasn't impressed with Bodkin's accreditation.

'She asked to see me,' Bodkin said, with an edge to his voice. 'Her doctor has agreed to let us chat to her, providing we don't stay too long. He left on note at the reception desk.'

Nurse Huggett's demeanour didn't live up to her cosy sounding surname. Snapping an order for Bodkin and Amy to 'WAIT THERE!' she stormed out of the ward in search of the doctor, who had seemingly given permission for such a severely injured patient to be interviewed.

After watching the door swing shut behind her, Bodkin walked briskly to the corner bed, where he found Bessie propped up on three huge pillows. She had plaster casts on her right arm and left leg. There was a thick wad of dressings around her ribs and her left arm was bandaged to the elbow. Her face was covered in so many cuts and bruises it was hard to know where one stopped and another began. Amy thought she looked like the Mummy from the horror film starring Boris Karloff. She had seen it twice.

Bessie's beautiful curls had been tied off and were lying over one shoulder. Her eyes were closed as they approached, but they flickered open when she heard Bodkin's voice.

'Hello, Bessie. I got a message that you wanted to see me.' He looked up and down her broken body. 'I'm so sorry to see you in this state.'

'Where's the fruit?' Bessie muttered. She winced as she finished the short sentence.

'I don't have any fresh fruit, sorry,' Bodkin said. 'I was going to bring you some biscuits.' He looked at her swollen jaw and grimaced. 'I'm glad I didn't now.'

'Got any ciggies?' She looked towards the door. 'That cow won't give me one.'

'Neither of us smokes,' Bodkin replied. 'Sorry.'

'There's a packet of Dunhill in the drawer,' Bessie muttered through clenched teeth. 'You'll have to hold it while I suck, though.'

Bodkin opened the drawer in the wooden cabinet at the side of the bed and pulled out a packet of Dunhill along with Bessie's lighter. Putting one into his mouth, he lit it, coughed, then took a pull on it before placing the box of cigarettes and the lighter back into the drawer.

'Come on, I'm gasping,' Bessie moaned. Bodkin put the cigarette to Bessie's bruised lips and held it while she took a deep draw, sucked it deep into her lungs, then blew it out with her eyes closed. 'More,' she urged.

She had only taken another couple of drags before Nurse Huggett returned. She wasn't in the best of moods, after finding Doctor Coffman and being told that he had indeed authorised the visit. Bessie held her breath as the harridan nurse stormed into the ward. Bodkin stuffed the cigarette between his lips, his face hardly disguising the distaste he felt at having the thing in his mouth.

'Disgusting habit. I hope you haven't been feeding that muck to my patient,' Nurse Huggett snapped, picking up Bessie's chart from the bed and wafting it in front of her face.

Bodkin burst into a fit of coughing and held the cigarette away from his face. Seeing her chance, the nurse snatched the fag from Bodkin's hand, hurried across the room and dropped it into the sink, where it expired with a loud hiss.

When the nurse's back was turned, the purple faced Bessie finally exhaled. 'Christ, my lungs are on fire,' she said, her raspy voice sounding even coarser than usual.

'Get on with it then,' the nurse said as she returned to the foot of the bed. She looked at the watch on her breast. 'She'll need medicating in fifteen minutes. You won't get a meaningful sentence out of her when that kicks in.'

'I'll question my witness in private, if it's all the same with you,' Bodkin said, giving Huggett a stern look. He pointed to a chair over by the sink and waited until the muttering nurse was out of earshot before pulling up a chair at Bessie's bedside.

'I'll start again,' he said, shuffling the chair a little closer. Amy moved behind and took up a position next to the patient's cabinet. 'First, I'd like to offer my sincere condolences.'

'About what?'

'Ellis,' Bodkin replied. 'They have told you he's...'

'Dead? Yes, they told me last night.'

'I'm sorry for what happened to you, too.'

Bessie frowned. 'Why are you sorry? It wasn't you who drove us off the road.'

'Forgive me, but you don't seem very upset about your boyfriend's death.'

Bessie tried to shrug, then instantly regretted it. 'These things happen.'

'Wow,' Amy whispered, just loud enough for Bodkin to hear. 'She really doesn't have a heart, does she?'

'What was it you wanted to talk to me about?' Bodkin said, after nodding almost imperceptibly to Amy.

Bessie looked across towards the nurse, who had picked up a magazine before speaking. Swallowing hard and grimacing with pain again, she lifted her head from the three pillow pile. 'It's about Reggie's money,' she began. 'Brian Firth took it.'

'We've pretty much worked that out,' Bodkin said.

'Well, now you know for sure. What I didn't tell you when we met at the pub is that Birdie Lark came around to the shop as we opened on Wednesday morning. She was trying to get me to exchange Reggie's fivers for our Bookmaker's takings.' Bessie grimaced in pain, then let her head fall back onto the pillows.

'She's struggling to get them changed into smaller notes,' Bodkin said. 'Mervin had the same problem, and he only had a few of them. Banks are the only places you'd get them changed legally, and they'd almost certainly report it to the police if any old toerag turned up with a wallet full of them.'

Bessie tried to lift her head again but gave up after two attempts. 'She was offering to sell them to us for three quid each. I reckon she'd have dropped to two pounds ten if I'd shown any interest.'

'But you didn't?'

'Not likely. It's Reggie Tumbler's money. I'd have to pass them on myself and I'd struggle to get rid of them, too. There isn't much call for five-pound notes in my bookies' shops. We get a few pound notes, but it's mostly shillings and half crowns.'

'As a matter of interest, how do you get rid of all those coins?'

'That's for me to know and you to find out,' Bessie said. She rested back on the pillows, looked up at the ceiling and screwed her face up in pain. 'I'm ready for that morphine, the aspirin is next to useless.'

'I'd guess that you exchange at shops in the area. Twenty-five shilling's worth for a pound,' Bodkin replied. 'That's what they do up here.'

Amy leaned over Bodkin's shoulder and waited for the young woman to recover from the spasm of pain before she spoke. 'Why have you suddenly decided to tell us this, Bessie?'

'Before I asked the nurse to call the cops, I honestly thought I was going to die. The doctor's reassurance didn't really come across as genuine, and I didn't want someone who had attempted to bump me off to get away Scot free.' She coughed and winced. 'Can't you get rid of her? I could do with another fag.'

'I doubt she'll leave us alone again just yet. She wants to give you your medication.'

'You had better hurry up with the questions, then. I'll be away with the fairies ten seconds after they give me that stuff.'

Amy thought back to Bessie's previous statement. 'You didn't just want to tell us about the money, did you?'

Bessie shook her head slowly. 'No. I wanted to get a couple of things off my chest before I passed. One was the money. I thought you'd have a good idea about who took it.' She shot a glance at the nurse again before resting her eyes on Bodkin's face. 'The young man who was killed by the London mob was one of Lonnie's gang. I don't know his surname, but his nickname was Robin. I think he was called that because he always wore a red jumper. Brian Firth chose him, not Lonnie. He'd only been with the gang a few weeks, and Brian told him the meeting with the London gang was a way of earning his spurs. He knew what would happen when the poor sod turned up without the money Lonnie had stolen from them. He sent him to his death.'

'Interesting,' Bodkin said, rubbing the stubble on his chin. 'Do you know anything else about this, Robin?'

'If I did, I'd tell you. That bloody Brian Firth deserves the same fate as his brother. He might not be the sharpest knife in the drawer, but he's still a very dangerous man.'

'One last question, Bessie. Then I'll let you get your morphine. Who do you think it was that ran you off the road?'

'I thought you'd have a good idea about that, too. It was Reggie Tumbler's doing. That's what I meant about someone getting away with trying to kill me. That green Rover was one of his cars.'

CHAPTER TWENTY-SEVEN

'Are you sure about that?' Bodkin asked. 'There are a few of them about.'

'It was his. Who else would want to force us off the road?'

'Brian and Birdie? You refused to cash in their stolen fivers, remember?'

'Birdie doesn't drive... okay, Brian does, but they don't have a pot to pi... They don't own a green Rover.'

'Is there any chance at all that it might have been an accident? That the Rover got too close trying to avoid an oncoming car?'

'Ellis said it had been right behind us, and I mean *RIGHT* behind us for two miles or more. He said they got really close to our back bumper twice before they came alongside.'

'Did you get a look at the driver?' Bodkin asked.

Bessie shook her head. 'I just saw a dark shape. He was wearing a cap, not a hat, though.'

'I'll get the Gillingham police to check out Tumbler's cars this afternoon. Do you have any idea if he keeps them in one place overnight?'

'No idea. It was one of his, though. Bank on it.'

'Do you have any idea how many he has?' Amy asked. 'Are they all the same make and colour?'

'I have no idea how many he owns throughout the company. I know he has a few vans and a couple of lorries. He always uses the green Rover model 16 when he's being ferried around, though.'

Bodkin scratched his stubble as he thought. 'Do you think he's stupid enough to use his personal car to force you off the road? That doesn't make sense to me.'

'He's got more than one. When we had that meeting about Lonnie, he turned up with half a dozen of his men in three cars. All Rovers, two green model 16s, and one black Rover 10. The 10 is less powerful.'

'You know a lot about cars,' Amy said. 'I can't tell one from another.'

'They've always been Dad's passion. I got interested in them growing up. Dad was always going on about them. I keep up with all the latest models. I've got my eye on an Alvis, but it's a bit too pricey. I've had that Austin 7 for a couple of years now. There are lots of them about, so I can drive around without being picked out. The downside is, it only has a 743 cc engine and will only do fifty miles an hour downhill with the wind behind you. That Rover can do over seventy. We didn't stand a chance of outrunning it.'

Suddenly they heard the sound of nurse Huggett clearing her throat and Amy half turned to see her standing at the bottom of the bed with her white, two tier, metal trolley. 'It's time to change some of those dressings and administer her medication.'

Amy looked down at the large hypodermic needle that sat in a kidney-shaped enamel tray on the top shelf of the trolley and winced. Bodkin got to his feet and nodded towards Bessie.

'I'll come back soon. I've still got one or two things I'd like to ask you about now that you've decided to help us.'

'I just want to see that swine Tumbler get what's coming to him,' Bessie said. She groaned as a spasm of pain shot through her body. 'Bring some ciggies with you, Dunhill, if you can get them.'

Bodkin stuck up a thumb. 'I'll see what I can do.'

Bessie screwed up her face and pushed her head deep into her pillows. 'Please,' she begged. 'Hurry up with that morphine.'

Following a request from Amy, Bodkin dropped her off at the farm. Then, after performing an untidy three-point turn, he headed off back up the lane, on his way to the ironworks where he hoped to find Seamus McTaggart.

Amy walked along the track at the side of the farmhouse until she came to the wooden three barred gate at the back. Lifting the lever to release the catch, she stepped into the yard, fastening the gate behind her.

She found Alice in the yard feeding the chickens some left-over scraps from breakfast mixed in with a few handfuls of corn.

'Are we developing a telepathic link?' she asked, emptying the enamel bowl upside down to rid it of the last clinging scraps. 'I was just thinking about you.'

'I thought my ears were burning,' Amy said, giving her best friend a hug.

'That's when someone's talking about you,' Alice replied, 'and I wasn't chatting about you to the chickens.' She sighed. 'We've lost another three this week. It'll soon be time to borrow a cockerel and build up the flock again.'

'You used to have your own when we were kids. I remember

one being a right tough old bird, very aggressive. Beautiful though.'

'We had various ones over the years, but they're such noisy so-and-sos. The last one was called Captain Cluck. He used to chase young foxes. Or he did until an older one caught him. Dad loved that bird. He was a real character. After the vixen took him, Dad made a deal with Old Man Anderson. We'd get his prize cockerel for a while and he'd get half the chicks that were produced. The system worked well. I'll have to try something similar in the spring.'

'Not with Old Man Anderson, though,' Amy said. 'There are only so many compliments a woman can take. Comparing you with a heifer is one thing, but when it comes to chickens, it's all legs and breasts and you don't want him to go anywhere near those topics.'

Alice shuddered. 'You've just put me off my lunch.'

'So, what's new on the crime fighting front?' Alice said as she took baby Martha from Miriam, Alice's live-in friend and housekeeper. Martha immediately began to grizzle but Alice put her on her shoulder and started to sway while humming a melody that had worked before. Martha was fifteen months old and had been a challenge since the day she was born. Much to the consternation of Alice, it had taken a long time for the two of them to form a real bond. Even now, Martha preferred Miriam's company to her mother's.

Miriam had lived with Alice for a couple of years. She was an attractive, dark-haired, non-practicing Jewish woman in her mid-forties, who was seeing a local builder. Miriam was keen on marriage, but her man was a recent widower who didn't think the spirit of his wife would be happy if he made their relationship a permanent one so soon after her passing.

'She's getting a couple of her back teeth through and they're a bit of a pain, aren't they, Martha?' Alice kissed the top of her baby's head and continued to rock the infant as Martha made smacking noises with her lips. Alice held out her hand towards Miriam. 'Pass me her teething ring, please, dear.'

Miriam passed over the toffee coloured Bakelite ring and Alice passed it on to Martha, who immediately stuck it in her mouth and began to run her red gums over the surface. 'Is that better, my darling?' Alice said, before adding a soothing coo.

'I'll rub a little whisky on her gums when I put her down for her afternoon sleep,' Miriam said, as she pouted at the baby. 'Poor little thing.'

'You're giving her whisky?' Amy's eyes were wide.

'It works and we only give her a tiny bit diluted in water,' Alice assured her.

'I thought that was an old wives' remedy,' Amy said, pulling out a chair and sitting down at the big oak table.

'Don't knock the old ways,' Miriam said as she picked up her knitting. 'You have to give the poor lambs something.' She thought for a moment. 'My mum used to swear by Mrs Winslow's Soothing Syrup. She said it used to work like a charm.'

'Can you still buy the stuff? It sounds a lot better than whisky,' Amy said.

'It was banned in the early part of the century,' Miriam said. 'It seems it had morphine and alcohol in it.'

'Blimey!' Amy said.

'She used to collect baby teeth as they fell out. She tied them around the new baby's neck in a little leather bag like a charm,' Miriam went on. 'The neighbours used to borrow them when their babies started teething.'

Amy shook her head. 'All that superstition and folklore. I'm so pleased we've progressed as a society.'

'Oh, I wouldn't use a bag of teeth on Martha,' Miriam said. 'I haven't got any anyway. I lost our Nellie's teeth when we moved house about twenty years ago.'

'Do any of these old remedies actually work?' Amy said. 'I read somewhere that to get rid of a wart from a finger, people used to rub it with a piece of meat, then bury it... the meat, not the finger. They used to think that as the meat decayed, so would the wart.'

'Mum used to rub a potato on them if she ever got one. I don't know if it worked or not, but as for old remedies, I can think of one that definitely works, and that's the gypsy cough mixture.'

'Gypsy?'

Miriam nodded. 'It was passed down the line in our family for generations.' She put her knitting on her lap and twisted in her seat so she was facing Amy. 'What you have to do is chop up an onion into slices, then add some water and sugar, leave it overnight, then next day you strain off the water and give the child a spoonful if they had a coughing fit.' Miriam picked up her knitting again and took a quick glance at her pattern before continuing to knit and purl. 'It tastes absolutely foul, of course, but it works.'

'Really?'

Alice nodded. 'We give it to Martha if she gets a cough. You don't know what's in the bottles you buy from the chemist. Until a few years ago, they used to have opium, cocaine, or heroin in them; even now they use a lot of alcohol. I was talking to the pharmacist about it a few weeks ago. We have no idea what these companies put in their medicines. I wouldn't dream of giving any of it to Martha. The Gypsy mixture is much better for her.' She paused as she smiled down at her baby. 'We add a bit of honey to it as well, just to help it slide down.' She nodded towards the kettle. 'Do the honours, dearest. I'm parched.'

Amy got to her feet, walked across the kitchen and picked up the big, tarnished copper kettle, filled it with water from the tap at the Belfast sink, then lit the gas on the hob of the cooker in the corner. Picking up the teapot, she emptied it into the sink, then rinsed it out and placed it on the draining board as she waited for the kettle to boil.

'I remember the kettle being on all day in here,' she said wistfully. 'Your mum used to have it sitting on the hot plate on the range.'

'I've still got that kettle,' Alice replied. 'It's in the cupboard under the stairs. It leaks now, but I can't bear the thought of throwing it away. Whenever I see it, I think of Mum. She loved her tea.'

When the kettle had boiled, Amy scooped three heaped teaspoons of leaves from the ornate blue caddy into the teapot, before adding the boiling water and setting it down on the cork mat at the centre of the table. After picking up three mugs from the draining board and sniffing the milk in the jug, she carried them across the kitchen and placed them next to the teapot.

Having rocked Martha to sleep, Alice carried her carefully through to the parlour, where she laid her down softly in her downstairs cot. After pulling up the covers, she leaned in, kissed the baby on the forehead, then returned to the kitchen, pulling the door shut behind her.

'Where's that tea?' she asked, rubbing her hands together.

'Let it brew properly,' Amy chastised her. 'It'll look like Slasher's wee if you don't.'

'Her name is Jemima, as you well know,' Alice said, waving an admonishing finger. 'She's only Slasher when she's mousing.'

Alice had saved Jemima from being killed by her father when he had discovered a feral cat in the barn that had died after having her litter. Jemima had repaid her kindness many times over the years, keeping the grain sacks safe from the rats and mice in the barn. She was an outdoor cat. Alice had encouraged her to come inside into the warmth of the kitchen on many occasions over the years, but the cat preferred to live in the barn where she snuggled down with the roosting chickens when the weather turned cold.

After another two minutes, which saw Alice twice reach for the teapot, Amy finally got to her feet and, after giving the brew a good stir, she picked up the strainer and poured the steaming liquid into the mugs.

'Add your own extras,' she said, picking up the milk jug and sniffing it again.

'You always do that,' Alice said with a shake of her head. 'This isn't Bodkin's office, it's a farm, and the milk is fresh every day.' She pointed towards the newly built milking parlour through the window. 'It comes from those big bottomed heifers out there. They give it to us every morning.'

Amy stirred her tea and narrowed her eyes as she looked over the mug towards her best friend. 'And there's me thinking it grew in bottles,' she said. 'Sorry about the sniffing, dearest. It's become something of a habit. Bodkin has served up tea that looks more like chicken soup in the past.'

Alice took a sip of her tea and smacked her lips. 'Nice brew, our Amy. You're getting quite good at this.' She took another sip as Miriam crossed the room to get her drink. 'As for chicken soup, we're having that for dinner tonight.' She looked across the table at Amy. 'How's things with this new friend of yours, Emma, is it?'

'Erma,' Amy replied. 'I'm not sure what to think about her at the moment.' She spent the next few minutes telling Alice and Miriam about the interview with Bessie Dagger and where she thought her information had come from.

'Well, she won't be added to my Christmas card list this

year,' Alice said. 'It looks like she's just been using you to get information.' She paused. 'Tell me more about Bessie Dagger.. She sounds really interesting. Beautiful and dangerous. We redheads must be very similar in character because she sounds just like me.' She ran a hand through her deep auburn curls before twisting in her seat and striking what she thought might be a Hollywood type pose.

'More pout, dear,' Amy said, putting her mug on the table. She paused as she thought about how to reply.

'She is incredibly beautiful,' she said after pouring more tea. 'But she's got a black heart, that's if she has one at all. She's as tough as old boots, always gets her own way and is prepared to hurt people to make sure it stays that way.' She looked fondly at her friend. 'She isn't a patch on you, Alice. Inside or out. Her beauty is only skin deep. You are beautiful all the way through.'

Alice blew Amy a kiss. 'Ooh, you flatterer. You can come back any time you like.' She ran her hand through her hair and struck another pose.

'Better,' Amy said, 'but open your eyes a bit more when you purse your lips. You look like you're about to take someone's face off with your nails when you narrow them like that.'

'Well, that's taken me down a peg or two,' Alice said with a grin. 'Going back to Bessie. Do you think she's capable of killing?'

Amy was silent for a few moments as she thought. 'I don't think she killed Lonnie Firth herself. It's not her style and anyway, she could never have beaten him in a fight before bashing him on the head with something heavy. But she might have ordered someone else to do it for her, though she claims she had nothing to do with it.'

'Even after he turned over her top bookmaker?'

'Her two top bookmakers,' Amy replied. 'It does give her a motive, but she claims to have come to some sort of arrangement with Reggie Tumbler. He's the real power in Gillingham's crime scene.'

'Ooh, it sounds just like the Edward. G. Robinson films, doesn't it?' Miriam said, putting down her tea and picking up her knitting again. 'You be careful, Amy. You don't want to end up getting too involved with this gangster's maul.'

'Moll,' Amy said. 'They're called Molls, Miriam.'

'Ah, I thought maul sounded a bit odd.' She looked up from her pattern. 'Why do they call them Molls?'

'I don't know,' Amy replied. 'The first time I ever heard it was in the film Scarface. Alice and I saw it a couple of years ago. I asked Bodkin if he knew where the term came from and he said he thought it came from the name Molly, which is an old English slang term for a woman of ill repute, but he didn't know why the gangsters used it.'

'That's a shame,' Miriam said. 'I like the name Molly.'

The friends chatted about the local gossip for half an hour before Amy announced that she had to go. 'I promised Dad I'd swap his library books out for him,' she said.

As Amy was pulling on her coat, Alice's phone rang. Thinking there was a slight possibility that it could be Bodkin, she waited by the table as Alice walked through to the front room to answer it.

'It's okay, it's the vet. We've got a bit of mastitis in the herd.'

Amy stuck her head through the doorframe and wriggled her fingers at Alice to say goodbye. Then, after doing the same to Miriam, she walked out of the kitchen and made her way back to the lane.

Back home, she unlocked the front door and walked through to the living room, where she found her mother sitting on the sofa chatting happily to Erma Firth.

CHAPTER TWENTY-EIGHT

'Hello, Amy,' Erma said. Getting to her feet, she held out her arms, offering a hug.

Amy ignored the welcome and stepped around Erma. After looking at her father's little table at the side of his chair, she turned to her mother. 'Do you know what Dad did with his library book? I said I'd swap it out for him today.'

'It's on the table in the hall, dear. You must have missed it when you came in.'

'Do you need any books swapping out while I'm up there, Mum?'

'If you wouldn't mind, dear.' She handed Amy a copy of Walter Greenwood's novel, Love on the Dole, which was set in Salford during the early nineteen-thirties. 'It's too depressing for me. I thought it was a love story when I picked it up. Could you get me something a little lighter?'

'I loved that book,' Amy replied. 'It's just how things were up there at the time, Mum. The struggle was real for those poor people.'

'Well, I was hoping for a bit more in the way of romance,' Mrs Rowlings said.

Amy shot Erma a quick glance, then spoke to her mother again. 'Did Pablo and Rosetta get together in the end?'

Mrs Rowling's face fell. 'No, dear. Rosetta's father shot him, then he went around to Pablo's studio to get the painting as he intended to burn it, but when he got there, he found the picture wasn't a nude at all. It was Rosetta in her best dress holding a bible.'

'Oh dear,' Amy said. 'Poor Pablo.'

'It wasn't just poor Pablo. Rosetta gets hold of some hemlock and kills herself. Then her father, out of his mind with sorrow and regret, kills his wife, then himself, so they can all be together in heaven.'

Amy blew out her cheeks. 'Blimey! And you reckon Love On The Dole is depressing.' She laughed and gave her mother a peck on the cheek. 'I'll find you something nice. See you later.'

Carrying the Greenwood novel, Amy walked straight past Erma and after picking up her own book from the dining table, she walked smartly out to the hall where she grabbed her green canvas shopping bag, dropped all the books inside, then let herself out of the front door.

She had only got about fifteen yards up the lane when she heard Erma's voice calling her.

'I don't know what I've done, Amy, but I'm sorry, whatever it was. Can we talk about it?'

Amy looked to the top of the lane where her bus was just turning around at the telephone box in readiness to head back the way it had come.

'I'm going to the library, then I'm going to the Sunshine Café for a coffee and a slice of cake. We can discuss the matter in there, but I'm not going to talk about my personal life on the bus, so please, don't sit next to me.'

Amy put on a bit of a spurt and was quite out of breath as

she stepped onto the bus. Erma followed her on and sat in the seat opposite.

'I really am sorry,' she hissed.

Amy steadfastly ignored her and stared out of the window.

'Please talk to me, Amy. Even if it's just to say what a nice day it is.'

Amy turned to face her. 'What a nice day it is,' she said before turning back to look out of the window. 'Please don't follow me to the library,' she hissed. 'As I said before, I'll see you in the café if you want to explain yourself.'

At the library, Amy exchanged Love On The Dole for The African Queen by C.S. Forester and picked up a copy of South Riding by Winifred Holtby for herself. Then, spotting The Grapes Of Wrath by John Steinbeck, she snatched it from the shelf, knowing that her father would love the novel that had only been released a couple of months earlier. She hoped he would finish it quickly because she really wanted to read it herself.

After getting the library cards stamped, she dropped the books into her canvas bag and made her way down the hill to the Sunshine Café, where she saw Erma sipping tea in the window seat.

'Your usual, Amy,' Bella, the counter assistant, called as she walked into the café.

'Yes please, Bella,' Amy replied. 'But can I have a bit of fruit-cake instead of Madeira?'

Bella took the glass dome off a cake stand and cut a generous slice as Amy counted out the change to pay for her purchase. 'We don't usually see you in here on a Thursday. It's almost always Saturday mornings.'

Amy lifted her arm to show Bella her bandaged wrist. 'I sprained it at work, so I'm off for a couple of weeks. I've just been to the library to stock up on books. It would drive me mad just sitting around doing nothing all day.'

'I'd love the chance to do nothing all day,' Bella said with a dreamy look on your face. She took the money from Amy and rang it into the till. 'I'll be over in a jiffy. Just grab a table.'

The café was almost empty, with only an elderly couple sitting at a table near the entrance. Taking a deep breath, Amy walked past them and pulled out the seat opposite to Erma at the table by the window.

'Did you get what you wanted from the library?' Erma asked, putting her cup back on the saucer.

'I got a good haul,' Amy replied, then leaned back to allow Bella to put down her coffee and cake.

'Do you know, I might have a bit of that,' Erma said.

'Fill your boots,' Amy replied as she picked up her coffee.

After Erma's cake had been delivered to the table, she picked it up and took a nibble. 'Are you going to tell me what I've done to upset you?' she asked.

'You're honestly telling me you don't know?' Amy replied. 'Well, I'll give you a clue. The other day, I met Bessie Dagger, and she seemed to know everything about me, where I lived, where I worked, what I did in my spare time. My involvement with Bodkin.' She glared across the table at Erma. 'It could only have come from you... and she could only have learned it all very, very recently.'

'It might have been my—'

'Don't you dare blame Hetty,' Amy said coldly. 'She didn't know a tenth of the details Bessie mentioned. You are the only person I divulged any of that to. I thought you were a friend, but you've ended up placing me in danger. Bessie threatened me. Do you know that?'

Erma's face crumpled. She rubbed her eyes and tears appeared on her cheeks. 'I'm so sorry, Amy. I didn't know she would threaten you.' She paused as she sniffed and reached for a hanky. 'She threatened me, too. That's why I told her everything.' She reached out and put her hand on the bandage on Amy's wrist. 'Please believe me. I didn't have any choice. I was scared. She had that Mervin Challenger with her. I thought they were going to hurt me.'

Amy's face softened. 'When did this happen, Erma?'

'It was on Tuesday morning. Mum had gone out to get her cigarettes from the shop. I heard the back door burst open and before I could get off the sofa, Bessie and Mervin were in the living room. She wanted to know everything I knew about Lonnie's murder. I must have somehow mentioned your name, because she suddenly became very interested and demanded to know all about you, about Bodkin, about everything. She wanted even the tiniest details.'

'You should have warned me somehow, Erma.' She frowned. 'How did she know my name, anyway?'

'I'm guessing she got that from Birdie, but then everyone knows she has contacts inside the police force, so it could have come from them.'

'The Gillingham police wouldn't know me from Lady Astor,' Amy said, still with the puzzled look on her face.

'Who?'

'She was the first female MP,' Amy explained.

'The Gillingham police have contacts with the Spinton police and a lot of them will have known Inspector Bodkin from when he worked down there.' She wiped her eyes with her hanky, smearing back mascara all over it. 'I'm so sorry, Amy. I had to answer all her questions. You don't know what she's capable of.'

'I think I have an idea of what she's capable of,' Amy replied.

Erma sniffed again. 'I've had such a lovely day, but now it's all spoiled. I wouldn't hurt you for the world, Amy. I really wanted us to be best friends, but now...'

Amy took a deep breath, then reached out and patted Erma on the forearm. 'It's all right, we're still friends. I just felt a bit let down when Bessie told me everything she knew about me. I didn't realise you'd been threatened too.'

'She said she was going to meet up with you soon, just before she left.'

'Really?' Amy mused. 'How did she know I would be at the meeting? Bodkin and I had only decided on it the night before it took place.'

Erma hung her head. 'She might have meant she was going to call in on you at home. I told her where you lived. I'm so sorry about that, but I was so scared... it all just came out.' She dabbed her eyes with her hanky again. 'You forgive me, then? Really?'

Amy got to her feet and held out her arms. Erma stood up and almost fell into them. 'I'm so sorry,' she sobbed.

After a few moments Amy let go and Erma, still snuffling into her handkerchief, backed off towards her own chair and sat down.

'She's in no state to threaten you now, is she?' Erma said after clearing her throat. 'She got what she deserves, I reckon.'

'No one deserves that, Erma,' Amy replied softly. 'Her boyfriend died.'

'No, I suppose you're right, as usual. I wish I could forgive people as easily as you do. Maybe I should come to church with you next Sunday.'

Amy sipped her coffee, smiled and said, 'You said you were having a lovely day. What have you been up to?'

'I went to Brigdens this morning and spent the whole five pounds. I got some lovely dresses, a couple of skirts, two blouses and a scarf. Then I went to the London Connection and bought some nice underwear. It's satin. I usually buy silk, but these looked really nice. Wait until you see... oops, you won't want to see that, will you? Anyway, I went to Stead and Simpson's after that and bought two pairs of shoes. They look great with the new clothes. I went home and spent the rest of the morning trying them on.'

'Hang on,' Amy replied. 'I thought you only had five pounds to spend?'

Erma put a finger to her lips. 'I found a bit more down the back of the sofa,' she said.

'Literally, down the back of the sofa?'

Erma giggled. 'No, it's just an expression we use in our house. Let's just say I came across it.'

'Hetty isn't going to be too pleased when she finds out you've raided her stash again.'

Erma shrugged, then leaned forward with an eager look on her face. 'When are we going to go out, Amy? I can't wait to wear my Brigdens clothes. It's been ages since I got anything new.'

'Well,' Amy replied. 'We're all going to the Roxy as usual on Saturday night. Pygmalion is on. Leslie Howard and Wendy Hiller are in it, so it's bound to be good. You can tag along if you like.'

'What's it about?'

'It's about a professor who tries to teach a cockney flower seller how to speak English like a toff. I've heard it's very funny in places.'

Erma pulled a face. 'That doesn't sound too interesting. Who's going?'

'Me, Bodkin, Ferris and Bodkin's sister Sal, she's coming up for the weekend. Oh, and my best friend Alice will be there.'

'You're so lucky to have Bodkin,' Erma said. 'It must be wonderful to be in love. I've forgotten what it feels like.'

'You've been in love? That's something to keep hold of until Cupid fires his arrow again.' Amy tipped her head to the side as she looked at Erma. 'There'll be someone out there waiting.'

'I wish he'd hurry up and empty that quiver,' Erma said. 'It's been so long since he last did it.'

'What was his name? Why did it end?'

'His name was Declan. It was a whirlwind romance. Love at first sight, but after three mad passionate weeks, it was all over.'

'Oh no! What went wrong?'

Erma wiped away a tear. 'I don't really want to go into it, Amy. It's still really painful, even after all this time.'

Amy patted Erma's hand. 'I understand,' she said. 'But, honestly, Erma, you're a lovely young woman. Men will queue up to ask you out.'

'Are there any good-looking single men at the police station?'

'Smedley's a nice young man, but I believe he's working on Saturday, so it will be the usual crew again. Ferris is singing at the Milton Cocktail Bar after the pictures, so we're going to see him perform.'

'That sounds more like it,' Erma said, her eyes sparkling. 'I'll skip the Roxy, if you don't mind. I'll meet you in the Milton.'

'Can you afford to go in? You've spent all your money, haven't you?'

Erma grinned. 'I'll have another look down the back of the sofa. I'm sure I'll find something.'

CHAPTER TWENTY-NINE

Amy said goodbye to Erma at the door of the café, then made her way around the corner to the London Connection where she found the manageress, Josie, fussing around one of the mannequins.

'Hello, Amy,' Josie said, hurrying towards her. She gave Amy a hug, then looked down at her wrist. 'How's the injury coming along? We've missed you this week. Lots of our customers have been asking after you.'

Amy beamed. 'It's nice to know I'm missed.' She lifted her arm. 'The sling is off a few days earlier than I thought it might be. It's still very weak and painful, but I hope to be back at work, here at least, in a couple of weeks.'

'That's good news,' Josie replied. 'I know Georgina can't wait to get you back behind your machine at The Mill. I was speaking to her at the weekend.' She smiled a wide smile. 'It must be wonderful to be so popular.'

'You're managing all right without me, then?' Amy asked. 'I was a bit worried about that.'

'We persuaded Angela Greenaway to come in for a few hours. Her mum watches the baby for her while she's here.'

'I was going to tell you about a new friend of mine who is looking for a bit of part time work,' Amy said. 'Her name is—'

'Erma Firth,' Josie replied, cutting Amy off. 'I know, she was in here this morning, dropping your name like she was mixing with royalty.'

'Oh dear.'

Josie smiled. 'It's all right. She was a pleasant enough young woman. She didn't actually ask about the job, but she hinted at it.'

'I understand it would only be on a temporary basis, I mean, I don't want to give my job up, but if you need someone if Angela gets stuck, she might be worth considering.'

'I'll think about it,' Josie said. 'She has expensive tastes, doesn't she?'

'Does she?'

'She bought two pairs of our best silk stockings and two sets of matching satin underwear. She spent thirty shillings. She didn't look like she had that sort of money to throw away on knickers. What does she do for a living? Where does she get her money?'

'Something to do with furniture, I believe,' Amy said.

After leaving the fashion shop, Amy walked down Middle Street until she came to the police station on the corner of the Gillingham Road. Pushing open the heavy door, she stepped inside to find Constable Smedley on the front desk.

'Good afternoon, Miss. Are you looking for Inspector Bodkin, or will I do?'

Amy laughed. 'You'll do in a pinch, Arthur.'

Smedley grinned and held out his arm. 'Pinch away,' he said. 'Regarding the inspector, he's in his office. I'd let you through, but Chief Inspector Laws is in the building and I know you two aren't exactly best buddies.'

'To put it mildly,' Amy replied.

Smedley got to his feet just as Trixie, the blonde bombshell, appeared with an armful of files. 'Oh, hello,' she said, looking directly at Amy. 'Nice to see you're back on your feet.'

Amy groaned inwardly and waited with bated breath to hear what she would say next.

'She had a fall at work, you see,' she said to Smedley. Trixie counted off three of the files and handed them to the constable.

Smedley pulled a face when he saw what they contained. 'Can't you give these to someone else, Trixie?' He pointed to a pile of files on the desk. 'I've already got that lot to work through.'

'Don't get your knickers in a twist,' Trixie said, giving Amy a knowing wink. Laughing to herself, she turned around and wandered off back along the corridor.

'Can you tell Inspector Bodkin that he has a visitor?' Smedley shouted after her.

A couple of minutes later, Bodkin appeared in the corridor. Waving to Amy, and nodding to Smedley, he let himself into the foyer via the connecting door.

'What a lovely surprise,' he said as Amy kissed him on the cheek. 'Shall we sit in the car? Laws is on the prowl.'

'I heard,' Amy said, as Bodkin opened the door to the street.

'What's in the bag? Anything tasty?' Bodkin asked as he opened the door to a shiny, dark blue Morris Oxford 16 saloon.

'WOW! Is this yours?' Amy asked as she stood back to admire the car. She ran her hand over the side panel. 'It's beautiful, Bodkin. Can I have a drive? Please say yes.'

'We're testing them out... it, out... there's only one of them at the moment and Laws has his eyes on it, but Chief Super Grayson says it has to be tested in the day-to-day environment, whatever that means. I think he's saying he wants ordinary hard working detectives like me to give it a thorough going over.'

'It's beautiful,' Amy repeated, sliding onto the passenger seat and running her hand over the plush material on the driver's side. 'Ooh, this is so comfy.'

Bodkin grinned as he got into the car. 'It's got a fourth gear and a sixteen hundred engine. It can do over seventy-five miles an hour, according to the manual.' He patted the steering wheel. 'It's not brand new. It's been driven by the higher-ups in Maidstone, but they're getting some newer models, so we've got a chance of keeping this one. There might be two more if they live up to the hyperbole.'

Amy sighed happily. 'Do you think Chief Super Grayson will let me drive it, Bodkin? When it's been thoroughly tested, of course.'

'I have asked Grayson about adding you to the station's insurance policy and he wasn't averse to it. He knows how valuable you are to our investigations and he's already got you down to claim some expenses.'

'Bus fares, the odd taxi and petrol,' Amy said. 'I suppose being able to claim petrol expenses means he thinks I'll be driving.'

'I'll check with him again next time I see him,' Bodkin said. 'Chief Inspector Laws actually said we should employ you as a part-time driver the last time I mentioned it. I think he envisages you driving him around like his personal chauffeur.'

'In his dreams,' Amy said with a laugh. 'I'll stick to driving him around the bend.'

'I think the details of the crash Bessie was involved in the other day convinced Grayson that we needed some more power under the bonnet. I'd have been left well behind if I'd tried to chase that Rover in the Morris.'

'Have you got time to give me a little demonstration?' Amy asked. 'You could give me a lift home.' She pouted at him. 'My poor wrist is aching so much after carrying those heavy books.'

Bodkin snorted, then tugged at his forelock. 'Home, Madam?'

'Home, Jeeves, and don't spare the horses.'

'The steering is heavier than the Morris,' Bodkin said as he turned onto the Gillingham Road. Putting his foot down hard on the accelerator pedal, he worked through the gears until he reached fourth. 'Blimey! It's got some guts,' he said as the dial on the dashboard showed that he had hit sixty miles an hour. He dropped down to second as he took the turn at the Old Bull and eased off the accelerator to cruise gently up to Amy's cottage. Turning to face Amy, he grinned and banged both hands on the steering wheel. 'Just let Reggie Tumbler try to outrun me now.'

Amy laughed along. 'Don't forget, it's my turn soon.'

'You'll have to wait until that wrist is stronger, Amy,' Bodkin replied seriously. 'It really is a lot harder on cornering.'

Amy pulled a sad face. 'Ah well, I'll just have to enjoy the ride until then. Don't forget to ask Mr Grayson about the insurance, Bodkin.' She leaned over and gave him a soft, wet kiss. 'What have you got on for the rest of the day?'

'Writing up reports. I have to get them in by Monday and I don't want to spend the entire weekend doing them.' He grimaced. 'What about you?'

Amy patted her canvas bag. 'I've got a new book to start. It will be a relaxing night in for me.' She opened the passenger door and climbed out of the car. 'This really is beautiful,' she said. 'I can see why Bessie Dagger is interested in cars now.' She thought for a moment as she reached for the door handle. 'Did you manage to find Seamus McTaggart?'

'Yes, I found him at work. His foreman pointed him out to me. Sadly, he can't remember anything at all about that night.'

'That's a shame,' Amy said. 'Have you heard any more about Tom Piper?'

'Not a sausage,' Bodkin said.

Amy laughed a short laugh. 'He might be thinking he's got a pig in a poke.' She furrowed her brow. 'What is a poke, anyway?'

'No idea,' said Bodkin, reaching for the gear stick.

'I'll look it up in Dad's dictionary,' Amy said as she closed the car door.

Following a dinner of lamb chops, potatoes, and carrots, followed by apple crumble and thick custard, Amy sat with her parents as they listened to the news on the radio. Most of it was announcements from the government who were trying to reassure the population about the future.

After the news, Amy sat on the sofa with her mother while she started to read her new book. Mrs Rowlings still hadn't got over the sad events in her short story, so instead of reading the book that Amy had given her, she picked up her knitting and was soon clicking away with her needles. Mr Rowlings, as usual, was in his armchair with his evening paper and a double shot of whisky.

At eight-thirty, Amy put down her book after having read the same paragraph three times. She had been going over what she knew about the murder inquiry in her mind and felt that there were one or two things that needed checking. Small things that might turn out to be important in the long term. Getting to her feet, she made a show of yawning. 'I've allowed myself to become lazy since the accident. I could do with a bit of exercise.' She walked to the door and opened it. 'I think I'll go for a walk.'

'At this time of night?' Mrs Rowlings said. 'It's freezing out there.'

'I'll wrap up warm,' Amy said. 'I really need to stretch my legs. I'll only be an hour.'

'An hour?' Mr Rowlings looked up from his paper. 'Where are you walking to, Gillingham?'

Amy laughed. 'I'll just take a walk up the lane, then decide which way to go. I'll stick to the main roads, don't worry.'

Amy pulled on her coat and, after slipping her bag over her shoulder, she let herself out and set off towards the Old Bull.

She had to wait ten minutes for the bus, and she was glad she didn't have to wait much longer as she was beginning to feel the chill of the night air. It was a clear, star-strewn night, and she passed the time picking out the stars that made up the Big Dipper.

Amy got off the bus at the Market Place and made her way towards the railway station where she stopped off at the late night kiosk and bought a packet of ten Craven A cigarettes.

Coming out of the kiosk, she walked fifty yards along Station Road until she reached a small crowd of women who were standing huddled together on the pavement under a flickering streetlight that seemed unsure whether it should be working or not. The Dragon pub was almost directly opposite. They turned towards her as they heard her heels clicking on the paving slabs. Then one of them grinned and shouted out her name.

'Amy Rowlings, is that you? Have you decided to join the street girls, after all?'

CHAPTER THIRTY

Amy gave the four girls a little wave as she approached. Ruby, the leader of the group of prostitutes, took a step forward and reached out towards her. Amy stepped into her arms and immediately picked up the smell of the cheap perfume and cigarettes that were failing to hide the aroma of old sweat.

'Hello Ruby,' Amy said, taking a breath of clean night air as the street girl released her from the embrace.

Ruby was a heavily made-up woman of about thirty. Her wavy dark hair was held back from her ears with two green Bakelite clips. She wore a cheap dress under a threadbare coat that was unbuttoned from the waist down. She stepped away so that the other three women could get a look at Amy. 'You remember Fran and Jen, don't you?' She pointed to the fourth woman, who was a good fifteen years older than the others. 'This is Audrey. You won't have met her yet.'

The streetlight went out completely, then flickered back to life, only to go out again. It was the only electric powered street lamp in the area and the spot was jealously guarded by Ruby and her friends.

On the opposite side of the road, a man walked towards the

Dragon. Twisting his head to get a good look at the women, he lifted his hat, then shouted to them. 'Is work hard to come by tonight, ladies? Maybe you should all retire and leave it to the younger girls.'

Fran lifted her skirt and gave the man a good long look at her bloomers. 'There's plenty of life in this yet, Harry Knowles. More life than is in your trousers, at least.'

The girls laughed as a red faced Harry turned to go into the pub.

'Let's see what you have to say on Saturday night when you stagger out of there thinking you're the world's greatest lover.' Fran shouted. 'Be warned, it's going to cost you double this week.'

The girls laughed amongst themselves as Amy stood quietly by, trying not to attract the attention of a small group of men as they walked by.

'Who is she?' Audrey asked, looking Amy up and down as if worried about the competition. 'I haven't seen here around here before.'

'Amy is a friend of ours,' Fran said. 'She helped young Sadie and her little sister get away to safety last Easter.' Fran was a natural blonde with a large bust and wide hips.

'Ah, that's her, is it? I heard about that. Sadie and her kid sister are living with a foster family now, aren't they? She should never have been seeing men at her age. How old is she, thirteen, fourteen?'

'Fourteen,' Jen said. 'It is lovely to see you again, Amy. What brings you to this neck of the woods? You know it isn't safe for young girls like you after dark.' Jen was a tall, stringy woman with the longest legs Amy had ever seen.

'I was hoping you'd be able to help me again, actually,' she replied. She put her hand in her pocket and pulled out the packet of Craven A. 'I bought you a present.'

Ruby almost snatched the cigarettes from Amy's hand.

'Amy, you are an angel sent to us in our time of need,' she said as she tore the packet open. 'I'm gasping. I haven't had any business yet so don't have the money to buy any.' She passed the packet around, then lit her own cigarette with an England's Glory safety match. After taking a long drag, she lifted her head and blew the smoke up towards the streetlight, which had decided to come on again.

'Ooh, that's hit the spot,' she said, taking another quick pull on the Craven A. 'How can we help this time, Amy?'

Before Amy could answer, a squat man of about fifty, wearing a mac and carrying a small, battered suitcase, stopped next to them. 'How much?' he asked Amy.

'She's not for sale,' Ruby snarled, giving the man a push in the chest. 'Now clear off, you sick bastard. You know what I keep in my bag for the likes of you.'

The man stepped back immediately, then after thinking about a reply but deciding against, he dropped his eyes to the pavement and walked off towards the Railway Hotel.

'He's a dirty swine,' Fran said, spitting on the floor. 'None of the girls will go near him.' She flicked her head towards the older woman. 'Not even Audrey, and she'll take anyone on.'

Ruby watched the man as he walked away, then she turned back to Amy.

'Well, what can we do for you?'

'Were you out on the street last Thursday? The night that man was killed down there?' She pointed to the alley at the side of the pub.

'We're out every night and in all weathers,' Ruby replied. 'We were talking about that earlier on this evening, wondering if the cops had caught anyone yet.'

'They haven't,' Amy replied.

'You seem very sure. How do you know?' Audrey asked.

'I'm, erm, I'm helping Inspector Bodkin with his inquiry,' Amy said.

'Do you work for the police now, then?' Fran asked. 'We don't talk to coppers. You can't trust the buggers.'

'I don't work for them, I work *with* them,' Amy said. 'Remember when I showed you my card the last time I was here?' She pulled a pink card from her bag and showed it to Fran. 'ARIA Investigations. The police ask me to help them now and then because I can talk to people who won't answer their questions.'

'Like us, you mean?' Jen said.

'Exactly like you,' Amy said. 'Don't worry, Jen. I won't mention any names. I just want to get a few things straight in my head. There are a couple of things that a witness said that I need to check out.'

Ruby patted Amy on the shoulder, dropped the cigarette end to the floor and scraped it with the sole of her three inch heeled shoe, sending sparks across the pavement. 'After what you did for young Sadie, I'll help you any time... within reason, of course. I don't want the police knocking on my door... At least not the ones who want to ask me questions. The ones that want a bit of business can still call.'

The girls laughed again.

'I was just wondering if anyone noticed a man hanging around late last Thursday. He would have been down by the Railway Hotel about midnight.'

Ruby reached for the cigarettes again. 'This street is full of men hanging around every night of the week, Amy. Can you be a bit more specific?'

'Yes, of course. I'm sorry. This man is about five foot ten, with broad shoulders and a thick neck. He's got really close cropped hair, but he might have been wearing a hat so you maybe didn't notice that. The really standout thing about him was his accent.'

'That sounds like Donald Duck. You don't hear that accent around here very often. I nicknamed him Donald Duck because he used the word duck at least three times in the space of a minute. Here me duck, careful of that high kerb, me duck. Just wait until I get you inside, me duck. I saw him a couple of times last week down by the Railway Hotel. He was staying there.'

Amy leaned forward, eager to get more information. 'Did you see him last Thursday?'

'I did, as a matter of fact. I was working that end on Thursday night. I'd just been paid by a punter who was staying on the top floor. I saw him when I came back out onto the street again. It would have been around midnight. Maybe just before.'

'Are you sure it was him?' Amy asked.

Ruby nodded. 'You don't hear that accent around here too often.'

'And he was with someone?'

'He was with a woman. She looked youngish, but she had her back to me, so it was hard to tell.'

'You didn't recognize her then? It wasn't one of your colleagues?'

'Colleagues!' Ruby burst into laughter. 'Did you hear that, girls? We're colleagues.'

Amy waited for the laughter to abate before she continued. 'Was she a ... street girl?'

'Probably. We've had an influx of new girls recently. Since the glue factory shut down and laid its workforce off. She might've been one of those. They tend to hang around the Railway Hotel. They like to do it in the warm. They haven't got used to doing it in alleys and in the backs of cars yet.'

'Did Donald Duck go into the hotel lobby?' Amy asked.

'No, they walked around to the back. There are a couple of rooms on the ground floor that you access from there.'

'Did the woman say anything?'

'Not that I remember. She giggled a lot.'

'Is there anything else you can remember, Ruby? Anything at all?'

'They got out of a car.'

'A taxi?'

'No, it was a small black one. Austin 7 maybe. I've been in the back of a few of those.'

'Where was it parked?'

'About ten yards down the road. The driver's side wheels were on the pavement. The road narrows down there and there were cars parked on the other side so it would have been tight for traffic to get through.' She paused as she puffed on her cigarette. 'The Railway doesn't have a car park, you see.'

Amy leaned forward and planted a kiss on the woman's heavily powdered cheek. 'Thank you so much for that, Ruby. It really helps tidy up a loose end.' She took a deep breath and let it out slowly. Looking down the street towards the Railway Hotel and noticing the man with the suitcase standing outside, she thanked the girls again and, with her heart pounding, stepped away from the streetlight.

'Oi!' Ruby called after her. 'Where do you think you're going?'

Amy stopped and looked back over her shoulder. 'I'm going to ask about Donald Duck at the hotel. Maybe some of the staff remember him.'

'You're not going down there on your own,' Ruby said, tossing her cigarette into the gutter. She patted her bag. 'I've got my kitchen knife and everyone around here knows it.' She nodded towards the man outside the hotel. 'Him especially.'

Ruby took a couple of quick strides to catch up with Amy

before looking back over her shoulder. 'If Barney turns up, tell him where I am.' She wagged her finger at her friends. 'No poaching now.'

Ruby fell in with Amy's stride pattern as they began to walk towards the hotel. 'Barney's one of my regulars. He's a really nice man who has a sick wife, so she can't perform her duties for him.' She was silent as she thought. 'He's a farm worker, I think.'

Amy's mouth dropped open. She closed it quickly as she wondered if this man was Alice's farm foreman. She knew his wife was very ill and had been for a couple of years. She quickly decided to change the subject.

'Thanks so much for helping me with this, Ruby,' she said. 'I was really worried about walking down here on my own.'

'But you would still have done it, wouldn't you?' Ruby smiled at her. 'You've got guts, Amy Rowlings. You're a lot stronger than you look.'

Amy whispered her thanks, then stepped into the road as they came up to the man with the suitcase. Ruby, unafraid, stepped deliberately onto the man's foot with the heel of her left shoe. He howled in pain and dropped his case, which hit the floor and spilled open, revealing a collection of ropes, clamps and a coiled whip.

'Goodness,' Amy said and hurried towards the entrance.

'Someone needs to tell the cops about him. He'll kill someone one of these days.' She nodded towards a group of young women who were walking slowly up the road towards them. 'That's a few of the new girls. They were making glue from horses a couple of weeks ago.'

'Why haven't you reported him to the police if he's so dangerous?' Amy asked as she stopped at the front door.

'We don't talk to the cops. It's as simple as that. Honestly, Amy, they can't be trusted. They'd twist our words, then arrest us for soliciting and leave perverts like that to carry on with their evil pleasures.'

'I think I know someone who can be trusted,' Amy said.

'Just don't mention any names... apart from his, of course. His name is Oswald Shagnasty. Oops, sorry. Oswald Shaughnessy.'

Amy pushed the door open and stepped inside the hotel lobby, with Ruby following close behind. The room was almost empty, with just a two-seater sofa and a small table in front of it. The reception desk was in the corner. A narrow staircase with a dingy, threadbare carpet led up on the left-hand side. Behind the desk stood a woman wearing a dirty apron and headscarf. On the floor next to the desk was a mop and bucket.

'Excuse me,' Amy began. 'Is there a manager I can speak to?'

The woman turned around to face her. She was in her forties with greying hair and tired eyes. There was a cigarette hanging out of the corner of her mouth. She took it out and held it in her long, sore-looking fingers as she spoke. 'You can, if you're willing to get the train down to Mossmoor. Otherwise you're stuck with me.'

Amy pulled one of her pink cards from her bag and handed it to the woman.

'ARIA Investigations,' she read aloud. She handed the card back, sat down in the chair behind the desk, and stuck her cigarette back into her mouth. 'What can I do for ARIA Investigations?'

'You let a room to a man last Thursday, although he may have been here for longer. He was on the ground floor at the back.' Amy pointed vaguely towards where she thought 'the back' might be.

'Yes, Mr Smith.' She blew smoke across the desk. 'We get a lot of Mr Smiths.'

'You remember him then? Close cropped hair, a broad Nottingham accent?'

'Is that where he was from? I did wonder.'

'What can you tell me about him?'

'Not a lot.' The woman looked up at the ceiling as she thought. 'He paid up front for three nights, though he only stayed for two. We didn't see much of him. Well, I didn't and I'm here sixteen hours at a stretch. I'm in the broom cupboard at the back for the other eight.'

'The broom cupboard...Really?'

'It's about the size of one, that's why I call it that. It's my room. I get to stay in it for free, although I'm sure they dock money from my pay for it.'

'Ah,' Amy said. 'At the back, you said. Is it on the ground floor?'

The woman pointed to the door to her right. 'Through there,' she said.

'So this man wasn't around much?'

'He didn't bother us for breakfast. He went out early, came back late. There's not a lot more to say about him, really. He left his room tidy when he went. Even made the bed.'

'You don't know when he actually left, then?'

The cleaner shook her head. 'Could have been any time on Friday morning.'

'You're sure he was here all of Thursday night?'

'Oh yes,' the woman replied. 'I could hear them going at it all bloody night. The walls are like cardboard back there.'

'So he had company all night? Not just for half an hour or so?'

'No, I think he knew he was going to have company. He asked for a double room, you see. That one was the only double we had free.' She paused and took a long draw on her cigarette. Then she looked up to the ceiling, blew out a long plume of smoke and chuckled to herself. 'She was a noisy bugger. They were at it all night. I'm surprised he had the energy to pack his bag the next morning.'

'You didn't see the woman leave either, then?'

'No, but I heard her go. It would have been around five in the morning.'

Amy thanked the cleaner for her help and turned towards the door.

'What has he done?' The woman called after her. 'Was he a cheating husband? We get a lot of them in here.'

'I'm afraid I can't tell you that,' Amy said as she stopped to answer.

'I know she must have been in a hurry to get home and she'd have got a bit nippy on the way.' The cleaner chuckled to herself again. 'She left her drawers behind. They must have been kicked under the bed. Marks and Spencer, silkies and all. They're not cheap, are they?'

CHAPTER
THIRTY-ONE

As Ruby walked towards the entrance, Amy hung back.

'Do you think I could use your telephone? It's only a local call.'

'You'll have to pay tuppence for the call, like the rest of the guests,' the cleaner said, dropping her cigarette stub on the floor and leaving it to smoulder.

Amy fished out two penny coins from her purse and handed them to the woman, who dropped them into the pocket of her apron. Picking up the handset on the desk, Amy dialled the number for the police station and waited patiently for it to connect.

'Hello, Spinton police, Constable Smedley speaking.'

'Hello, it's Amy Rowlings,' Amy said. 'Is Inspector Bodkin still at work?'

'He is, Miss, I just took him a cup of tea through, as a matter of fact. He's at his desk.'

'He's quite capable of making his own tea,' Amy replied. 'He's got a kettle in there.'

'His milk's gone off, Miss. We've got a fresh bottle.'

Amy shook her head as she imagined the yellowing liquid

fermenting in the bottle on top of Bodkin's filing cabinet. 'Do you think I could have a quick word?'

'Putting you through now, Miss.'

'Bodkin.'

'Hello, it's me. I hear your milk's gone off.'

'It seems to go off very quickly in here,' the policeman replied. 'It must be all the hot air that's spouted.' He was silent as Amy laughed. 'What can I do for you?'

'I've got a bit of news about the case, but I know you're busy writing reports, so it will wait until I see you tomorrow. I'll make some notes for you.'

'That's very kind,' Bodkin replied. 'I'm intrigued, but I really have to finish these reports. It looks like being a long night.' He paused, then went on. 'If you're going to write notes, why the call?'

'Outside... or possibly inside, the Railway Hotel, you'll find a man called Oswald Shaughnessy. He's a disgusting individual, Bodkin. He's got a suitcase with ropes, clamps and a whip inside. You have to arrest him before he hurts anyone else. All the street girls are scared to death of him.'

'He's at the hotel now? ... hang on... how do you know all this?'

'I'm there myself, Bodkin, but don't get all wound up about it. I've got someone looking out for me. I just want you to get him off the streets before he hurts someone.'

Before Bodkin could reply, Ruby snatched the phone from Amy's hand and yelled into the mouthpiece. 'He's a dirty, despicable pervert who *will* kill someone before too long. If you want someone's death on your conscience, then that's up to you, but Amy has told you who he is and where he is, so if you trust her word at all, you need to get someone over here and quickly.'

Before Amy could take the handset back, Ruby slammed it

down on the phone's base. 'Sorry,' she said. 'I always get arsey when I speak to a copper.'

Amy laughed and thanked the cleaner again, then she led Ruby to the front door, where they found Oswald with his case waiting to enter.

'Get out of my sight,' Ruby snarled as she pushed past the man. Amy leaned back against the wall as he stepped into the lobby, then slipped quickly out before the door could close.

As they walked back up Station Street, Ruby lit another cigarette and looked gloomily into the almost empty packet. 'I hope I get a bit of work soon or I'll be snapping a punter's head off.'

'I'll buy you another pack before I go home,' Amy said. 'You've been so kind to me tonight.'

'You're a sweetheart, Amy. I'll pay you back when I get straight.'

'There's no need, honestly.'

'Do you think I could have one of your cards?' Ruby asked. 'I've got a friend that might need your services soon. She can afford to pay you.'

Amy fished out a pink card and handed it to Ruby. 'That's not my home phone number. I don't have one yet.' She pointed to the card. 'That's Alice's number, so she'll be the one who answers the call. She's my best friend. She owns Mollison Farm.'

Ruby slipped the card into her bag. 'Mollison, you say? That's where Barney... Oops. I shouldn't have told you that. Don't let on, you know.'

'I'll keep schtum,' Amy said. 'Barney is Alice's foreman. He's a lovely man and a good friend. I wouldn't embarrass him by letting on I know.'

'He is a nice man. We don't always do the... well, you know... Half the time he just wants to talk.'

'He comes all the way up here to pay you to talk to him?'

'Not only talk. We... Men have certain needs. Amy and his wife is too ill to give him what he wants. He's still a very fit and active man. Think of it this way. He could either come and see me or take a mistress and his life might get complicated then. I don't complicate things. I provide a service that he needs. Just think of me as being like the chemist. If he gets a cough, he goes to see them. If he wants to get other things off his chest... so to speak... he'll come to see me.'

Amy nodded and smiled at the street worker. 'I'm glad it's you he comes to, Ruby. You'll look after him.'

As the pair approached the flickering lights, a dark-coloured car came hurtling around the corner from the railway station. Amy ducked her head and looked inside as it shot past to see two uniformed policemen in the front seats.

'It looks like Oswald has had his last whip round,' Ruby said. Her lips tightened as she watched the police car scream to a halt outside the hotel. 'Thanks for doing that for us, Amy. The streets will be a little safer tonight.'

As Amy came out of the kiosk with a twenty pack of Craven A. Bodkin's new car pulled up alongside her.

'I'll just be a minute,' Amy said as she hurried back up the street towards the still flickering streetlight.

After handing over the cigarettes, Ruby gave Amy a hug and a peck on the cheek. 'Come back to see us soon, Amy.' She tapped her bag. 'I've got the card safe. My friend will call you soon.'

'Don't you go off on one about me being up here, Bodkin,' Amy said as she climbed into the passenger seat of the Morris Oxford. They both looked to the right as the police car carrying Oswald Shaughnessy passed by at speed.

'Why would I?' Bodkin said as he pulled away. 'I mean, the woman I love has just been hobnobbing with a load of prostitutes and has come close to being kidnapped by a vicious pervert. Why on earth would I go off on one?'

'I was safe. Ruby looked after me. Honestly, Bodkin, no one messes with Ruby.'

Bodkin sighed, then reached across and patted Amy's hand. 'All right. I understand. You like her, don't you?'

'She's lovely and it's not her fault she has to do what she does to make a living. She's got two kids to support and her husband left her when the second one was born. She doesn't really have a choice.'

'There's always a choice, Amy,' Bodkin replied. 'What's wrong with a bit of cleaning or factory work? She does have options.'

'Cleaning work. Pah! That doesn't pay enough to keep a family, and as for factories. She was just telling me there were a dozen new girls on the street because the glue works closed down. The war might bring women a lot of new opportunities, what with the men being away and all that, but as things are, times are still hard for a lot of women, so don't you go taking the high moral ground when it comes to people like Ruby.'

Bodkin blew out his cheeks and let the air out slowly. 'Well, that told me.' He shot her a quick glance. 'It's not up to me who you spend time with, Amy. I know you and Ruby became friends during the Reverend Villiers murder case, so I'm not having a go at you for that. I just worry when you put yourself in dangerous situations, that's all.'

'You're forgiven,' Amy said with a soft smile. 'But lay off Ruby and the girls. They're nice people and they look out for me.'

'All right, I stand corrected, but I still think you should have asked them to speak to the police if they have a problem with someone like that.'

'They'll never talk to the police, Bodkin. You know that, and you know why.'

Bodkin sighed again as he came to a halt at the junction with the Gillingham Road. 'Let's change the subject, shall we?'

Amy grinned. 'Good idea.' She thought for a moment. 'Are you going back to your desk? I'm sorry for dragging you away from your reports. I know how urgent they are.'

'I needed a breath of air and a break from them anyway, but yes, I'll be there until the early hours, I think.' He closed his eyes for a second. 'I'll have to question Oswald Shagnasty too, I suppose.'

'Ruby called him that. How come you did?'

'We've known about him for a while, Amy, but he flits around the county using the trains. He's never in one place for more than a few days and as the girls won't talk to us, we never know where he is.'

'You know where he is now, Bodkin.'

'I do, and he won't be catching a train any time soon.'

As Bodkin pulled up outside Amy's cottage, he saw Mrs Rowlings at the front window. 'Did your mum and dad know you'd gone out?'

'They did, but they thought I'd gone to stretch my legs.' She smiled at the policeman. 'She'll think I went to see you now. Don't let on, Bodkin.' She leaned across and kissed him on the lips.

'Your secret's safe with me,' he said.

CHAPTER THIRTY-TWO

On Friday morning, Amy got up at eight, had breakfast and a chat with her mother regarding her standoffish encounter with Erma the previous day. Explaining that it had been a misunderstanding.

She poured a second cup of tea and carried it through to the front room. Then, after filling her father's pen from the ink bottle in the drawer, she picked up a few sheets of paper and sat at the table to get her thoughts down on paper.

Bodkin. I know the following might not appear exactly like the reports you are used to reading, but I find it easier to get the information down as soon as the thoughts come into my head. So, apologies for mentioning you in the third person.

Following My Conversation With Erma.

I find myself feeling rather guilty after accusing Erma of passing information about me to Bessie Dagger. My heart went out to her after hearing about how Bessie and Mervin stormed into her house and made dire threats about what they'd do if she didn't provide them with the answers they sought.

She must have felt very afraid and alone. I felt afraid myself when Bessie made her threats and I had Bodkin standing close by.

I have forgiven the poor girl. I'd almost certainly have done the same in those circumstances. She was utterly distraught when I called her out in the café. I felt so mean about that.

I am rather concerned about where she's getting all the money for her new clothes from. I know she had five pounds, but she spent all that at Brigdens. She joked about finding the rest down the back of the sofa, but in reality, she would have taken it from what is left of Hetty's stash. Unless, of course, they did have access to some of Reggie Tumbler's missing fivers. I forgot to ask Josie how she paid, though I think she would have said if Erma had been trying to change a five-pound note.

She could have had the change for five pounds from Stead and Simpson though, she bought two pairs of shoes there. If they were expensive ones, she might have got away without the staff asking questions about the large denomination note.

She's meeting us in the Milton tomorrow night (Saturday). It might be wise to keep an eye on what money she uses to pay for her drinks. If she's got a purse full of pound notes or the odd fiver, Erma and her mum might well have had access to Lonnie's stash.

I wish I had a fiver to spend on clothes.

My Adventures on Station Street.

I know Bodkin hates the idea of me going out after dark alone, but I am almost twenty-two now and the days are long gone when a young woman can't leave home without a chaperon. I understand completely when he says he worries about me, but I really don't think I put myself in danger despite there being one or two hairy moments. AND (Bodkin) we ended up catching a dangerous sadist, so I'd say it was a good night's work.

Now for the juicy bits.

On the night that Lonnie was killed, Ruby had been working down near the Railway Hotel (she had actually been to a room on the top floor with a customer). When she came out, she saw Mervin Challenger going around to the back of the hotel to his room. She noticed his accent and immediately nicknamed him Donald Duck, because he used the word 'duck' incessantly. He had parked what Ruby is sure was an Austin 7 car on the kerb. MERVIN WAS WITH A WOMAN.

Ruby didn't get a good look at her, but she says she could have been one of the new street girls who have just taken up residence down there after the glue factory closed.

I went into the reception of the hotel and had a chat with the cleaning lady-cum-out-of-hours receptionist. She is on duty for sixteen hours a day and the small bedroom she is given as part of her wages is at the back, right next to the double room that Mervin had booked.

The mystery woman stayed all night. That's not usual for a prostitute, is it? I doubt she was one anyway, as she left a pair of expensive silk Marks and Spencer's knickers behind. (They somehow found their way under the bed.) The woman was (by all accounts) incredibly noisy.

According to the cleaning lady, the woman left about five o'clock. She didn't see her go, but she heard her.

My thoughts.

I've almost convinced myself that the mystery woman was Bessie Dagger. I can see her wearing silky underwear and if you remember, when she was being questioned, she hinted that she and Mervin might have had more than just a working relationship. I can remember how Ellis reacted to the bombshell.

Also, there is the matter of the car. Bessie came up here in an Austin 7. I know there are a lot of them about and Mervin might have been given one to use if he had been following Bessie's instructions to come up here and kill Lonnie. It might well have been her car he got out of at the Railway that night. Although Bessie might have been happier staying at the Milton or even the George, she might have been spotted in either of those places. She would have been confident that no one would have seen her nipping round to a room at the back of the Railway Hotel, though.

One last thing.

Mervin didn't stay for the entire time he paid for. He sneaked out on Friday morning and didn't take breakfast. So, he lied to us about that.

Final Thoughts.

I'd like to know how many cars the Daggers have in their organisation. Bessie told us that she likes to use the Austin 7 because there are so many of them on the streets, she won't be as noticeable when she's out and about. She knows all about cars, so she might have two or three Austins instead of more powerful cars that might be spotted as she's going about her business.

The only thing I can say about Mervin's night in the back room is, if he did have Bessie with him and knowing how demanding she is, it might have been him that was screaming all night.

Anyway. Here's one scenario.

Mervin is handed orders to kill Lonnie by Bessie Dagger. He is given one of the firm's Austins to drive up in so he won't stand out on the train or the bus. (His haircut would have stuck in the minds of the other passengers.) He books in for a few nights at the Railway Hotel under the name of Mr Smith and, knowing that Lonnie is in the area, he arranges to meet his old friend at the Dragon. After having a few beers, they leave and

Mervin attacks him. (We saw his bruised knuckles the day we interviewed him. He could have got those dispensing a punishment on some other unfortunate member of Bessie's gang, though.) After that, he jumps into the car, which he's left nearby, and drives up to the hotel via the back streets, which is why he didn't bump into anyone on the way.

There is the matter of the woman, though. So, either he sees her as she's standing on the corner of Station Street and Ebeneezer (we know some of the girls stand there every night), and still feeling excited about what he's done, picks her up and drives her to the hotel. OR. Bessie Dagger comes up with him and waits in the car while he does the deed, then the pair of them go back to the hotel to celebrate.

The truth is, I can't see Bessie sitting around waiting for Mervin while he gets drunk with Lonnie. And how did Mervin know that Lonnie was in town, anyway? Mind you, Bessie seems to know the movements of everyone she's interested in, so she may well have been informed of his whereabouts.

Afterword

We now know a little more than we did. The pieces of the puzzle are beginning to fall into place. I think it might be time to have another chat with Bessie Dagger.

At a quarter to one, Amy left home and walked down to The Mill to see how much Handsley's Garments had decided to pay her in wages and compensation for her injury. She walked across the shop floor waving to her friends and climbed the steps to the mezzanine. After knocking on Georgina Handsley's office door, she waited for a few seconds until she was called in.

'Hello, Amy, it's nice to see you up and about. How's the wrist?'

'Still swollen, painful and weak, but at least I've ditched the sling,' she replied.

'That's good to hear. We're looking forward to having you back at your machine. We appreciate what you do even more when your output isn't piled up in the stockroom.' She clasped her hands. 'Now, what can I do for you?'

'I thought you'd want to know how the injury is progressing, so I've come to give you a report. Sadly, I think it will be another couple of weeks yet before I return to work. Even then, it might be in the vest and underpants department.'

'We'd be happy to have you in there. We're relying on the younger machinists to work on those garments and they aren't as... how shall we say it... particular with the standard of workmanship... womanship.' She rolled her eyes to the ceiling. 'We thought we'd give them a bit of a kick up the backside by sending a skilled machinist in to work with them, but the standard hasn't improved too much. I fear that Beryl Hargreaves was a poor choice.'

'Big Nose Beryl?' Amy cleared her throat and looked at her feet as she stifled a laugh. 'I'm sorry. I meant Beryl Hargreaves, of course.' She paused and carefully considered her words, not really wanting to speak the truth about her gossipy co-worker. 'Are you going to replace her?'

'Not until you come back, sadly. She's the only one we can do without on the shop floor.' Georgina got to her feet and rubbed her hands together. 'Right, I don't know about you, but I'm ready for my lunch.' She walked to the door and opened it. 'Have you picked your pay packet up yet?'

Amy followed Mrs Handsley down the steps to the shop floor, then joined the long queue outside the foreman's office to pick up her wages. Carol, who was quite a way ahead of her in the queue, dropped out of the line and walked back to stand with Amy.

Big Nose Beryl, who was towards the end of the queue, the underwear department being further away, shouted up the line, accusing Carol of pushing in.

Carol ignored her and wrapped her arm around Amy's shoulders. 'It's so good to see you,' she said. 'It's not the same in here. We don't have half as much of a laugh.' She flicked her head towards the back of the queue. 'No one is as sharp as you at putting mouth almighty in her place.' She looked down at Amy's injured wrist. 'At least the sling's gone. When do you reckon you'll be back?'

'A fortnight, I think, but Mrs Handsley says she's going to put me in the undies' room and send Beryl back to her machine. The quality isn't good enough under her less than watchful eye, it seems.'

The queue moved forwards as Carol replied.

'She spends all her time walking around gossiping with the trainees. She's on record as saying what a doddle of a job she has now. She thinks she's in there for the duration. She's going to be furious when she finds out that you've landed her cushy little number.'

When she got to the front of the queue, Amy gave her name and clock number and received a small buff-coloured packet from the shift supervisor. 'Nice to see you, Amy. How's the wrist?' she asked.

Amy waited until she was in the canteen queue before opening her wages. Closing her eyes and offering up a quick prayer, she took out the paper pay slip and unfolded it.

'WOW!' she exclaimed, seeing that her compensation amount had been set at four pounds, ten shillings. With the half pay the company was paying her, it meant that although the compensation award would be paid over a four-week period, her actual wages were pretty much the same as they would have been had she still been at work and that included her weekly bonus.

She turned to Carol and showed her the pay slip. 'The teas are on me,' she said excitedly.

'The tea is free,' Carol reminded her. 'But thanks for the offer.'

The two women carried their drinks over to a table near the back of the canteen where the usual crowd of friends sat. Carol put down her tea and opened the canvas bag containing her packed lunch. 'Fancy one, Amy? It's only potted dog, mind you.'

'Beef or ham flavoured dog?' Amy asked.

Carol took out a sandwich and sniffed it. 'Could be either, I was running late this morning and just picked up the first jar I saw.'

'It's okay,' Amy said. 'Mum will have made something at home.'

'It's all right for some, isn't it?' Beryl's whiny voice floated across from the next table where she had just sat down with her group of serial gossips. 'Swanning around doing nothing and getting paid for it.'

Amy put her cup down and looked across at the sour-faced woman. Beryl was only in her early thirties but looked more like forty. 'I hear you've been doing exactly the same down in the undies department, Beryl.'

'Where did you hear that?' Beryl demanded to know. 'I've been working hard in there. I have to cover for the trainees as they're not up to the job.'

'It came from Mrs Handley's own lips,' Amy said.

Beryl visibly deflated.

'Someone's been pouring poison in her tea... ear... Someone's got it in for me.'

'You'll have to ask her about it, Beryl. But you know it wasn't me. I've been swanning around the town, getting paid for doing nothing. I haven't been around to pour any poison. What was it, anyway? Strychnine?'

'Oh, you think you're so clever,' Beryl whined. 'Anyway, we all know what you've been up to, making a bit of cash on the side while you've been off.'

Amy's brow creased. 'What are you talking about now?'

Beryl sniggered, then winked at her friends. 'I heard, from a very good source, that you were out and about with the totties up on Station Road last night.' She laughed a high-pitched cackle. 'How much did you make?'

Amy's face reddened, but she refused to let Beryl get the better of her.

'Who was this very good source, Beryl?'

'My hubby had nipped into the Dragon for a pint. He saw you.'

Amy saw her chance and took it. Beryl's husband was notorious in the town as being a wife beating drunk. 'Was that before or after he'd paid one of the girls to take him down the back alley, Beryl? They told me he's a regular.'

Beryl's face turned purple as the three tables around her erupted with laughter. She opened and closed her mouth, but only a gurgling sound came out. She was rescued by Winnie, one of the older ladies at the factory, and one of Beryl's staunchest allies.

'So, what if he did? It doesn't give you an excuse for being there. What were you up to?'

'I wasn't accepting her brute of an old man's money, that's for sure,' Amy replied. 'And, as for what I was doing there... that's my business.' She pushed her still full mug of tea into the centre of the table as she got to her feet. 'For your information, though. I was helping the police in a murder investigation. One of the street girls had some information that might lead to the arrest of the perpetrator.' She glared hard at Winnie, who, unable to hold her eye, looked into her cup as if studying the tea leaves. 'I'll tell you this much too,' Amy continued. 'I'd rather spend my time talking to those girls than some of the people who work here.' Amy stepped away from the table but gave Beryl one last parting shot. 'They have higher standards.'

Beryl, having recovered from the onslaught somewhat, called to Amy as she got to the door of the canteen. 'Seems I touched a nerve,' she said sulkily. 'I only asked what you were doing there.'

Amy was about to turn around when she heard Carol speak.

'Well, she told you, in no uncertain terms, Beryl. You asked for all you got.'

After lunch, Amy went up to her room and played her records for an hour before picking up her library book and turning to the page she had bookmarked. Ten minutes later, she put the book down and slipped the bookmark into the place it had been previously, having not taken in a word of the novel. Tossing the book onto her bed, she went downstairs to the kitchen, where she found her mother ironing her father's best shirt.

'Are you going out this weekend, Mum?' she asked, pointing at the shirt.

'I'm ironing it just in case, Amy. Dad did mention that it was ages since we'd been up to the Old Bull.'

'Well, I hope you have a good time if you go. You deserve it.' She gave her mother a warm smile. 'We won't be in. It's Ferris's night at the Milton, so we're going in there after the Roxy.'

'I'm so jealous,' Mrs Rowlings said. 'Your dad keeps saying he'll take me one night, but it never happens.' She picked up the shirt to examine her efforts. 'Not that I'm complaining. The Old Bull is good enough for me.'

'It's so expensive in the Milton, Mum. Dad might be saving up for it.'

Mrs Rowlings hung the freshly ironed shirt on a wooden hanger and slipped the hook over the door handle. 'I've heard it's expensive. I don't know how you afford it on your wages, our Amy.'

'I only ever buy one round every other month, Mum. Bodkin always gets one in, so does Alice and Sal when she's there, but we are given a free drink from the management as we're in

Ferris's party. It's a perk he gets. We make the drinks last, we don't have that many.'

Mrs Rowlings picked up the kettle. 'Tea?'

Amy thought about it. 'No thanks, Mum. I'm fine, but speaking of money.' She took out her wage packet and pulled out two ten shilling notes. 'Here's my board for the week.'

'Amy! We don't expect you to pay full whack while you're on half pay. Your dad's earning better money now. We can afford to let you off until you're back at work again, dear.'

'But that means you and Dad are no better off, and I'm not having that,' Amy replied, placing the money on the table. 'Anyway, I get money from the Worker's Compensation Board. It's like an insurance; they pay out if someone gets injured at work. Not all factories have signed up to it, but The Mill has.'

'Ooh, that's good,' Mrs Rowlings replied. 'You are lucky, Amy. There was nothing like that when I was working.'

'It's a new thing. It only came in last year. Anyway, it means I get four pounds, ten shillings, injury compensation. It's spread over four weeks, but it means I don't lose a penny. I'm getting pretty much my full wages all the time I'm off.' She patted the two ten shilling notes. 'So, I can afford to pay my keep.' She grinned at her mother. 'Now I think I'll get the bus and drop in on Bodkin. I've written out some thoughts for him.'

'Oh yes? Are they romantic thoughts?'

Amy laughed. 'No, Mum, I'm not turning into Jane Austen. It's just a few lines I jotted down about the case we're looking into.'

Her mother smiled softly at her. 'Don't you think the case is best left to Mr Bodkin, dear?'

'Not likely,' Amy replied. 'He'd get nowhere without me.'

Instead of getting off the bus at the police station, Amy decided to stay onboard and got off at the corner of Main Street instead. After walking around the corner onto High Street, she pushed open the door at the London Connection.

'Two days running? We are blessed,' Josie said with a smile as she got up from behind the counter.

Amy looked around the empty shop. 'You're not too busy for a Friday afternoon.'

'You just missed the rush,' Josie said.

'I've come to ask you something I should have mentioned before,' Amy began. 'It's about Erma, that young woman who kept dropping my name when she was here. Can you remember what she paid you with? It wasn't a five-pound note, was it?'

'No, Amy. We don't see too many of those. The wealthier customers pay on account, as you know. The last five-pound note I took was a fortnight ago.' She thought for a moment, then went on. 'Erma, your friend, paid with pound notes. Her bill came to thirty-five shillings for the stockings and underwear sets.'

'Thank you,' Amy said, much relieved. 'Josie,' she said after a moment. 'You don't know anyone who works at Stead and Simpson, do you?'

At Stead and Simpson's shoe shop, Amy walked along the display shelves while she waited for the assistant to take the money from a customer at the till. When she was free, she walked across the shop to ask Amy if she needed any help in choosing.

'Is Greta Turney at work today?' Amy asked.

'I'm Greta Turney.'

'Ah, good. Josie at the London Connection said she knew you and you might be able to help. I work there part time, but Josie's a good friend, too.'

'Any friend of Josie's is a friend of mine,' Greta said. 'How can I help?'

'You had a customer yesterday, a young fair-haired woman, very early twenties. She might have been carrying a Brigdens bag, possibly a London Connection one too. I believe she bought two pairs of shoes.'

'Yes, I served her. She was very particular about what she wanted.'

'If you don't mind me asking. What notes did she pay you with? Pound notes, ten shilling notes?'

'What an odd question.' Greta thought about it. 'The shoes were twelve and six and fifteen shillings. She paid with three ten shilling notes. Dirty tatty ones they were. They looked like they'd been crushed into a ball.'

Amy let out a long breath. 'Thank you, Greta. I really appreciate your help.'

She walked out of the shoe shop in a far happier mood. It seemed that Erma had indeed been fishing around down the 'back of the sofa'. So, humming a jaunty tune, she made her way to Middle Street, walked past the Roxy with its Pygmalion poster on the wall and strolled down the hill to the police station.

CHAPTER THIRTY-THREE

'Come in, come in, my dear,' Chief Superintendent Grayson said, as he got to his feet behind his desk. 'It's lovely to see you again. How's the wrist?'

'A bit better, thank you,' Amy said, giving Bodkin a nervous glance.

'Don't worry,' Bodkin mouthed. He pulled out a chair. When she was seated, the two policemen sat down.

'Bodkin here has asked me to add your name to the station's motor insurance policy.'

'That's very kind of him,' Amy replied. 'I wouldn't be driving much, just when it was needed. In case it was Bodkin who sprained his wrist, for instance, and I was available to drive... that sort of thing?'

'I think it's a capital idea,' Grayson said, beaming a smile. 'It would only be a few shillings extra on the bill and you might prove to be very handy in an emergency. We had an officer break his leg in a struggle a few weeks ago and the constable with him couldn't drive, so we had to send two more officers out, one to drive the constable back and one to pick up the stranded car.' He paused for a moment. 'I'm not saying you should be at our beck and call in case something similar happens, but it might be helpful if you're working on a case with Bodkin and he has to take to the back seat for some reason or other.' He paused and looked out of the window. 'Then there's this damnable war, of course. You're far too young to remember, my dear, but women took up all sorts of roles to help the war effort the last time around. We had our first female PC back then. Women were in the Fire Brigade too, and we've moved on since then, what with the votes and all, so I wouldn't deem it beyond the realm of possibility that we might see a woman in the CID before we finally put Adolph back in his box. We'll lose a fair few officers to the military before it's all over.'

'But aren't police officers exempt from conscription?'

'They are, my dear, but a lot of them will consider it their duty to sign up and I can see their point. It's what I'd be thinking about if I was their age.'

'But someone has to stop the criminals running amok,' Amy replied.

'That's for us over forties to sort out, along with the officers who stay on.' He smiled at Amy. 'And there might be a few ladies rallying to the cause.' Grayson took out a cigarette from a silver case and lit it with a Ronson table lighter. 'The thing is, if and when, women are asked to help out, at least one of them will find that her car insurance is already in place.'

'Thank you, sir,' Amy said. She could feel the excitement building up inside. She had to try incredibly hard to keep herself from asking if she could have a go in the new Morris Oxford soon.

'This was an extraordinary request from Bodkin, but I felt we owed you some sort of reward for all the help you've given us over the past ten months. This Shaughnessy character is the latest of your successes, I hear.'

'It wasn't all my doing, sir. I had help from a certain quarter.'

'Ah, the street girls. Yes, Bodkin was telling me. Rest assured, he didn't mention any names.' He looked at Bodkin, then back to Amy. 'I think we can ease off the patrols on Station Street for a week or two as a reward.'

'It would be even nicer if you stopped your officers going around for pleasure on their days off, then arresting the same women for soliciting the following evening,' Amy said. She grimaced when she realised who she was lecturing. 'Sorry... it's just that... well, it is a tad hypocritical.'

'You're a very opinionated young woman, Miss Rowlings,' Grayson said, getting to his feet. 'But I won't hold that against you. I wish there were more people about with your spirit. The world would be a better place.' He held out his hand. Amy got to her feet and shook it. 'Never change, my dear,' he said.

'Sorry about that, Bodkin,' Amy said as they walked along the corridor to the inspector's office. 'It just came out.'

Bodkin shook his head. 'He's all right, is Grayson. He treats you like the daughter he doesn't have.'

'I like him too. He's very forward thinking, for a man that is, and for a policeman especially.'

'Oi!' Bodkin said, feigning annoyance.

'Present company excepted,' Amy said as he waited at the office door for her to go in first.

'Tea?' Bodkin asked when she was seated.

Amy eyed the bottle on top of the filing cabinet suspiciously, then, erring on the side of caution, she shook her head. 'I only dropped in to give you my notes,' she said.

• • •

'Excellent work, but I didn't expect anything less,' Bodkin said as he dropped Amy's report onto his desk. After checking his phone number list, he picked up the phone, then dialled and waited. 'Hello, this is Inspector Bodkin from the Spinton police. I wonder if it would be possible for me to interview one of your patients again... yes... her name is Bessie Dagger. She's on the Phillipson ward... No? Why not? Right, I see. I'll be over in a couple of days, then. Goodbye.'

Amy looked at him quizzically.

'It's that blooming nurse, Hoggit. She's put her foot down, and the doctor has agreed. No more visitors until next week. She needs rest, it appears.'

'Huggett,' Amy said. 'You're suffering from a pig fixation. As for Bessie, she'll go mad if she hasn't got a supply of cigarettes. It's just like an opium addiction, isn't it?'

Bodkin nodded. 'As an ex-smoker I can sympathise with her. My Woodbines were the first thing I reached for when I got out of bed in the morning.'

'Woodbines? Why did you choose that brand?'

'They were the cheapest of the lot. Everyone used to say they were made from the sweepings up, but they were all I could afford at the time and you could buy them in packs of five if you were really short of money.'

'I think it's a horrible habit,' Amy said. 'It's not just the smoker who gets a lungful, it's everyone in the room, and the smell stays on your clothes until you wash them.'

'Maybe the government will ban them one day like they did heroin and opium.' He pulled out his pen and made a note about the next hospital visit at the end of Amy's notes. 'I wouldn't hold your breath, though.' He grinned across the desk. 'See what I did there?'

Amy groaned. 'I hope Ferris's jokes are better than that when he gets on stage on Saturday night.'

'You know the answer to that already,' Bodkin said. 'I was listening to him practice in the back office this morning.' He gave a short laugh. 'Even Trixie was wincing, and she usually laughs at all his efforts. She even laughs at my jokes.'

'She'll do anything for a bit of attention, that one,' Amy said with feeling.

Bodkin gave her a narrow-eyed look. 'My jokes, whilst not being to everyone's taste, aren't as bad as you're making out.'

Amy chuckled to herself. 'Trixie has taste?'

The conversation was interrupted when Detective Constable Ferris knocked on the door.

'Come in, Ferris, we were just discussing jokes,' Bodkin said.

'Can I join in? I've got a corker. I'm thinking of using it tomorrow.' He looked from Amy to Bodkin with an eager look on his face. 'Would you like to hear it?'

'If we must,' Bodkin said with a sigh.

'Well,' Ferris began. 'It's quite topical, really.' He cleared his throat. 'It seems that Hitler is using a common garden plant as a new fuel for the railway. He wants all the trains to run on Thyme.'

Bodkin dropped his head into his hands as Amy shook her head slowly.

'What?' Ferris said. 'Oh, I see. You don't think we should make jokes about the war. Right, how about this one, then?'

'Ferris? Forget the jokes or at least practice them elsewhere. What did you come in here for in the first place?'

'Oh, yes, I thought I'd better let you know. Sal's car broke down in Gillingham and she's had to put it into a local garage. She says it won't be ready until Monday, so she's going to be coming the rest of the way on the train. Do you want me to meet her at the station?'

'No, it's all right, Ferris, thanks for the offer but my sister will be staying with me so I'll pick her up in the new Oxford and drop her off at the flat. We can't spare you for the rest of the day and if you two get chatting, it'll be the last we'll see of you. I should be getting back to these reports, though. I really want to finish them tonight.'

'I can meet her,' Amy said. 'I can get the bus up to the station.'

'Are you sure you don't mind?' Bodkin said.

'Of course I don't mind. I've got nothing else to do. I'll be bored out of my skull just sitting around at home. It's ages since we had a chat, anyway.'

'I'd let you pick her up in my old Morris 10, but it will take a couple of days to get you on the insurance policy. I doubt you'd be able to handle the steering with your dodgy wrist anyway, so don't be too disappointed.'

Amy held her bandaged wrist up and looked at it with a sad look on her face.

'Ah well, maybe I could have a go in the new car next week if my wrist is a bit stronger.'

'We'll see,' Bodkin said. 'Now, I'd better get back to these reports.' He leaned over the desk and Amy got to her feet and kissed him on the lips. 'I'll take Sal back home with me. She can have dinner at ours. You're invited too, if you can get away. It will be home-made fish and chips tonight as it's Friday.'

'I'll get away. Count on it,' Bodkin said, licking his lips.

When Amy left Bodkin's office, she could hear Ferris talking to himself in the room opposite. Tiptoeing to the door, she stuck her head through the gap to listen.

'Why did the tomato turn red? Because it saw the salad dressing. Ba Boom!'

Amy closed her eyes as she winced. 'Please don't use that one tomorrow, Ferris,' she whispered.

. . .

Amy took a slow, steady walk up to town and stopped off at her favourite newsagent, where she was delighted to find that her regular order of Photoplay magazine had just come in. Holding it carefully, she carried on up the High Street before crossing the Market Place and taking the first right onto Station Street. After buying a bottle of lemonade at the kiosk, she sat down on a bench near the ticket office and opened up her magazine to find a story about the upcoming movie release, Gone with the Wind. She read the article twice and looked closely at the two still photographs that were taken from the film, showing Vivien Leigh and Clarke Gable performing together.

Amy was incredibly excited about the forthcoming USA December release, although she knew the film wouldn't reach her neck of the woods until the following summer at the earliest. The Roxy in Spinton had always been at the bottom of the list when it came to acquiring the latest films.

After finishing her second read of the article, Amy put her magazine on her lap and looked up as the door that led to the station's platforms swung open and a small crowd of people walked through. At the back, carrying a small suitcase, was a tall, tough looking man with his hat pulled over his eyes. Amy stared as she tried to place him. She was sure she had seen him before, and quite recently too. Then she suddenly remembered the time in Gillingham when she had hid in the car with Erma. Although she was sure he hadn't spotted her that day, she quickly picked up her magazine, flipped it open and held it up to cover her face as Vincent Jury and another hard-looking man walked across the concourse and out onto the street.

CHAPTER
THIRTY-FOUR

Amy kept her magazine in front of her face until the men had gone. As they passed her, one of them said something that Amy didn't quite catch and the other replied with a snigger. Horrified, Amy noticed that when she had made a grab for the magazine she had pulled her skirt up to her thigh, leaving a vast expanse of leg and a brown stocking top on show.

Tugging the skirt back over her knees, a blushing Amy looked out into the street to see the backs of the two men as they headed along Station Street towards the Railway Hotel.

Amy looked at her watch and, seeing that she had half an hour to spare before Sal's train arrived, she walked past the kiosk and followed the two men at a distance of about fifty yards. To her surprise, they walked past the Railway Hotel and took the next right onto Ebeneezer. When they were out of sight, Amy quickened her pace and she reached the junction just in time to see the men turn left into an alley that would lead them out half way up Victoria Street.

Not daring to follow them any further, Amy retraced her steps and arrived back at the station with ten minutes to spare. At five minutes past four, the doors to the platform opened again and Sal, along with around thirty other passengers, stepped through.

Bodkin arrived at six with Mr Rowlings, who had just got home from work. Inside, Mrs Rowlings fussed about, declaring that no one was to panic and that she had prepared plenty of food for everyone. After her father had washed his hands and face, he went into the front room and came out carrying an extra chair, which he put in place on the right-hand side of the dining table. A few moments later, when they were seated, Amy's mum brought in a plate piled high with triangle shaped slices of bread and butter. 'I'll get the dinners now,' she said, wiping her sweating brow with her apron.

Although neither was remotely religious, Bodkin and his sister bowed their heads dutifully as Mr Rowlings said grace. Immediately afterwards, as though a starting gun had been fired, Bodkin reached across the table and grabbed two triangles of bread. Piling a handful of chips between them, he bit into the sandwich like he hadn't eaten in a month.

After the meal, Bodkin helped Elizabeth Rowlings clear the table and then helped to carry in bowls of jam sponge and custard. Over the desert, Sal and Amy got into a conversation about the Milton and what Ferris might sing this week.

'He told me on the phone that he's got two new numbers to add to his repertoires,' Sal said. 'He's going to do Cheek to Cheek from Top Hat... you know, the one Fred Astaire sang? Then he's doing My Funny Valentine.'

'Oh, I love My Funny Valentine,' Amy said. 'Mitzi Green sang it in the musical Babes in Arms. I've been after the record for a few months now, but my Uncle Maurice insists that no one has recorded it yet. I find that strange as it's a beautiful song. It's very popular on the radio, though. Lots of performers do it.'

'He's got a few new jokes, too,' Sal said. She gave Bodkin an odd look as she heard him groan. 'He told me a couple over the phone... listen to this, it's hysterical.' She was silent for a few moments to let the anticipation build. 'Doctor, I keep seeing spots in front of my eyes. Have you seen an optician? No, just spots.'

'Just SPOTS!' Mrs Rowlings repeated before dissolving into a fit of laughter.

Mr Rowlings looked from his wife, who was having trouble getting her breath, to Sal, who was leaning over the table chortling away to herself. The engineer scratched his head. 'He's actually going to use that gag on stage?' He looked at Bodkin, then shook his head. 'And people pay to hear it?'

Bodkin shrugged. 'He doesn't go on until they've had a few,' he replied.

'That's probably a good thing,' Mr Rowlings said as he began to scrape his spoon around the edges of the bowl to collect the last drops of custard.

Sal, having recovered, sat up straight in her chair and wiped her eyes. 'He's going to do a Max Miller joke tomorrow night, too.'

'Ooh, I love Max Miller. He's on the radio a lot,' Mrs Rowlings said. 'Which joke is he going to do? I might have heard it.' She looked at her husband. 'James isn't too keen, are you, love?'

'He's as common as muck,' Mr Rowlings said. 'Too near the knuckle for me.'

'Go on, Sal,' Mrs Rowlings encouraged her. 'Tell us the joke. I won't be there to hear him.'

'All right,' Sal said. 'It's hilarious, honestly.' She cleared her throat, then giggled before forcing herself to keep a straight face. 'Here we go.'

All eyes were fixed on Bodkin's sister.

'Mary had a little bear,

She treated it so kind.

I've often seen her bear in front,

But never seen her bear beh–'

'That'll do!' Mr Rowlings said, getting to his feet. Walking across the room, he picked up his paper and, after giving Sal a stern look, sat down in his armchair.

Mrs Rowlings looked at Sal with an open mouth, then, a few seconds later, she dissolved into a fit of laughter which lasted a good two minutes. Eventually, sniggering and coughing, she left the table to go into the kitchen to get a much needed drink of water.

Sal looked at Bodkin through tearful eyes. 'Isn't it fantastic? So funny.'

'Hilarious,' Bodkin agreed. He turned his face to Amy, who was laughing, but more at her mother's reaction than the actual joke.

'I'll take her home,' he said.

Bodkin picked up Sal's case from the hall and once outside, opened the door of the Morris to let his still chuckling sister climb in. After putting the case in the boot, he shut the passenger door and turned to Amy, who was standing with her arms wrapped across her chest as she shivered in the cold night air.

'Apologise to your dad for me, Amy. That last joke went a bit too far. It's fine to tell it in a bar. I might even laugh myself if I'd had a few, but it's not really fit for the dinner table.'

'Oh, he'll be all right. He'll have heard a lot worse where he works.' She wrapped her arms around Bodkin's neck and gave him a kiss. 'I know what I meant to tell you. I got to the railway station far too early this afternoon and as I was sitting reading my magazine, the twenty to four train arrived from Gillingham and guess who got off it?'

Bodkin shook his head. 'Groucho Marx?'

Amy snorted. 'No, silly. It was Vincent Jury. I recognised him from Bessie's shop. Erma pointed him out to me as he walked up the road. He was with another man, a bit shorter, stockier. I didn't get a good look at his face, sorry.'

'Did he recognise you?'

'No, Erma and I ducked down in the car as he passed. He didn't see my face today either. I hid behind my magazine.'

Bodkin's brow furrowed. 'I wonder what they want in Spinton? Perhaps they came to see Bessie in hospital. They're in for a long wait, if that's the reason they're up here.'

'They didn't get a taxi to the hospital. They walked up Station Street. I thought they were going to book in at the Railway Hotel, but they didn't. They turned down Ebenezer, then took the cut through to Victoria Street, and we know who lives on there, don't we?'

'How do you know that they... oh, Christ, Amy, don't tell me you followed them.'

Amy gave Bodkin a sour look. 'I did follow them, but from a safe distance. They didn't turn around. They didn't know I was behind them.' She tipped her head back, then pulled her hand from behind his neck and wagged a finger at him. 'And stop taking our Lord's name in vain.'

'Sorry,' he said. 'But you scare me half to death when I think about what might happen to you.'

Amy wrapped her hand around his neck again and gave him another kiss. 'Well, nothing did happen. Did it?'

CHAPTER THIRTY-FIVE

The following morning, Amy got off the bus in town and walked the short distance to Brigdens Nearly New Fashion store. Inside, she found Sharon standing by the bargain rails. 'I've been guarding it for you, Amy,' she said. She moved away from the rail and nodded towards a calf length, mid-blue spotted wrap dress with a deep V back and a tie off belt that sat just in front of the hip.

Amy almost snatched it off the rail and held it in front of herself in the full-length mirror. 'Ooh, it's gorgeous.' She looked at the price tag. 'Only ten shillings... I saw a similar one in one of Mum's magazines. I'm sure it was in the spring collection this year.' She held it up and looked at it suspiciously. 'There has to be something badly wrong for it to be that cheap.'

'Look at the side seam under the wrap. It's crooked all the way down.'

Amy examined the dress, decided she could fix it, then after thanking Sharon she headed towards the till where Eileen, the manageress, was totting up some numbers.

'No!' she said immediately as she spotted Amy approaching. 'There will be no discount on that dress.'

'But the seam is crooked all the way down,' Amy protested.

'No one will know, it's all hidden,' Eileen argued back.

'I'll know,' Amy said. She held up the dress to the light. 'I'll know.'

'Well, don't buy it, Amy. I can sell that in two minutes flat. It wouldn't be on the rail now if Sharon hadn't stood over it looking like a member of the King's guard.'

'It will take me ages to fix. It will all have to be unpicked,' Amy said, giving it one last shot.

'I'm sure you'll be quite happy with the result,' Eileen said. She looked up as another customer approached the till, carrying a long, bias cut evening dress. 'So, do you want it, or is it going back on the rail?' She held out her hand and Amy laid the dress carefully on the counter before opening her purse to fish out four half crowns.

'You're such a meanie,' she said, trying to hide her delight.

'You could always try shopping somewhere else,' Eileen said, trying to hide her own smile as she carefully folded the dress and slipped it into a colourful Brigdens bag.

'You'd go bust if I did,' Amy replied. She picked up the bag and almost skipped her way to the door.

From Brigdens, Amy walked around to the Post Office where she produced her savings book and handed over two florins and a shilling to Claire behind the counter. Amy smiled to herself at being able to put the money in her savings account when she had been almost certain that she wouldn't have been able to afford to add to it for at least a month.

After leaving the Post Office she made the short walk around the corner to the Sunshine Café where she found Erma waiting for her in the same window seat she had occupied two days previously.

'Fancy seeing you here,' she called as Amy ordered coffee and cake at the counter.

'Did you find anything nice?' Erma asked as Amy carried her bag over to the table and put it down carefully on the floor at the side of her seat.

'I did, as it happens,' Amy replied. She reached into the bag and took out the dress, then, getting to her feet, she let it unfold as she held it in front of her.

'WOW! That wasn't there on Thursday,' Erma said, open-mouthed. 'I'd have grabbed it if it had been.'

Amy carefully folded the dress again and placed it back in the bag. 'I've got a spy in the camp,' she said. 'Sharon keeps her eye on the new stock for me and I tend to get first dibs.'

Erma pouted. 'That's unfair to the rest of us.'

'I've been shopping there a long time,' Amy said. 'And I do Eileen the manageress a few favours, so I get looked after.'

'I must remember to come shopping with you in future,' Erma said, looking longingly at the bag.

'Are you all set for tonight, then?' Amy asked when her coffee and cake had been delivered.

'I'm so excited, I'll have to put off getting dressed. Otherwise I'll be ready to go by two o'clock and then I'll have to sit and wait for hours, hoping I don't spill anything on my clothes.'

'Do you know what you're going to wear yet?'

'No, I haven't decided.' She looked down at the bag again. 'Are you wearing that? You'll look stunning in it.'

'No, Sadly I can't wear this one yet. It needs quite a lot of work. I doubt I'll be able to fix it until the wrist is a bit stronger so it might be December by the time I'm seen out in it.'

'That's all right then. You won't show me up tonight.'

'I never want to show anyone up, Erma.'

Erma suddenly looked crestfallen. 'Oh, I didn't mean it nastily, Amy. It just came out wrong. I'm so sorry.'

'Forget it,' Amy said, picking up her cup. 'For the record, I'm wearing my autumn leaf-patterned dress with the flared skirt tonight. I only got it a couple of weeks ago and I haven't been out in it yet.' She paused. 'Brigdens are still displaying a couple of them on mannequins near the front of the shop. They want thirty shillings for them. I only paid ten for mine. I'm just hoping that no one else buys one and decides to wear it tonight.' She took a sip of coffee. 'I, erm... I meant to ask. Have you had any visitors from Gillingham recently?'

'Not that I'm aware of, but then I've been out a lot over the last couple of days.' She picked up her teacup, then put it back down again. 'Why do you ask?'

'Oh, it's just that I saw Vincent Jury and another man coming out of the station when I was waiting for Bodkin's sister to arrive yesterday.'

'Vincent Ju... are you sure it was him?'

'I saw him with my own eyes, Erma. I followed him. He walked down Ebeneezer Steet then took the cut through onto Victoria. He would have come out right next to your place.'

'Goodness, is that the time? I'd better get off.' Erma began to gather her things together. 'I'll have to get the copper boiling if I'm going to have a bath in front of the fire before I go out.' She got to her feet as a thought came to her head. 'I don't suppose I could have a bath at your house, could I?'

Amy shook her head. 'Sorry, Erma, my dad's a bit of a miser when it comes to the bills. I'm restricted to one bath a week myself.'

'Ah well, if you don't ask, you don't get.' She bent over and planted a kiss on Amy's cheek. 'See you tonight. Don't be late. I'll be in there for about nine.'

Amy watched Erma as she left the café and walked across to the Market Place. 'I wonder what made her take off in such a hurry,' she said to herself.

Later that afternoon, Amy spent an hour playing records and half an hour reading her new library book. When she came downstairs to have her bath at four, she found her parents reading their new novels.

'What do you think of your book, Dad? Did I make the right choice?'

'This is engrossing, Amy, thank you. Steinbeck is such a talented writer.'

'What about you, Mum? Is that one a little less depressing?'

'I'm still trying to work out what it's about. When I first saw the title, I thought it was going to be a love story about a native Queen, but it isn't. It's an adventure story set at the start of the Great War... it is in Africa, mind you.'

'Are you enjoying it?'

'I'm not sure, dear. I hope Allnutt kisses Rose soon. There hasn't been a lot of romance so far to say it's supposed to be a love story.' She looked down at her book again. 'It is rather exciting, though.'

Smiling to herself, Amy walked through to the bathroom that her father had had built a couple of years before, following a windfall. She ran her bath; the water heated by the big Ascot boiler that sat on the wall above the tap end, then after washing her hair in the sink, she added a generous amount of her rose scented bath salts, made a turban out of a towel and slipped into the steaming water.

CHAPTER
THIRTY-SIX

After a half hour soak, Amy pulled on her pink floral pattern dressing gown and, still wearing the turban, went up to her room and put Al Donahue's nineteen thirty-five recording of I Live For Love on the radiogram. Humming the melody, she sat in front of her dressing table with the half-length mirror and began to rub her hair vigorously with the towel.

At five, still in the dressing gown, she went downstairs and ate the ham sandwiches that her mother had made for their tea. After chatting with her parents about the evening ahead, at a quarter to six, she went back upstairs and prepared to put on her make-up.

First, Amy plucked a few hairs from her eyebrows, then filled in the gaps and finished off the shape with an eyebrow pencil, before covering her eyelids with a thin layer of blue-coloured eye shadow. After that, she added eye-liner to her upper lash line to help define and show off her eyes. Lastly, she widened her eyes, picked up a small brush, stuck it into the mascara cake, and added some extra length and volume to her lashes.

Happy with the result, she rubbed in a little face powder

from her compact, then added a dab of rouge to the high points of her cheeks. Leaning back from the half mirror on her dresser, she judged herself critically. Then, after a brief nod, she got to her feet and opened her underwear drawer. After selecting a Rayon, ivory-coloured bra and knickers set, a matching suspender belt and a pair of silk stockings, she pulled them on and again checked herself out in the mirror before turning towards her wardrobe where she picked out the autumn leaf-patterned, button down bodice dress with the flared skirt. Finally, she pulled on her favourite black slingback shoes, and stood at the back of the room so she could see most of her body in the half mirror on her dresser.

'You look stunning, as always. Bodkin is a very lucky man.'

The voice startled Amy, and she turned to see Alice standing in the doorway. She was wearing a green slinky dress with a short black jacket and black Oxford shoes.

'You made me jump,' Amy said. 'I didn't hear you come up.'

'I'm on the scrounge again,' her best friend said. 'Do you think I could slap on a bit of your Ruby lipstick? I really do like that one. Next time you stick a mail order in from your mum's magazine, can you order me some?'

'Have that one,' Amy said. 'I can get some more for myself, though I'm not sure it works with my skin colouring.' She turned back to her wardrobe and took out a deep red jacket.

Alice pulled out her compact and put on the lipstick whilst looking in its little mirror. After applying a thick coat, she smacked her lips, grabbed one of Amy's tissues and blotted her lips before giving them one final smack, snapping the compact shut, and slipping it with the lipstick into her bag. 'You're a star,' she said.

'It really does suit you, Alice. It's perfection. It goes with your hair, your eyes, everything. It couldn't be a better colour match.'

Alice patted her handbag. 'It's in here if I need a touch up later.'

Bodkin arrived in the new car at six forty-five. Alice was impressed.

'Ooh, it looks like one of those posh cars they ferry the stars to the Oscars in,' she said, adding, 'thank you, driver,' as Bodkin opened the rear door for her.

Bodkin tugged his forelock and opened the front passenger door for Amy.

'Where's Sal?' she asked as she climbed in.

Bodkin sighed. 'She's still getting ready. She's been in my bedroom for an hour.' He lifted his arm and sniffed. 'If I smell of lavender, it's because I followed her into the bath to save on the electric bill.' He walked around the front of the car and slipped into the driver's seat. 'The water was only tepid by the time I got in. What do you women do in there? I was in and out in five minutes flat.'

'We're not giving up our most precious secrets to you, Bodkin,' Alice said from the back.

'It's all part of the process of attempting to look beautiful,' Amy said. 'We could come out with you, looking like the witches from Macbeth, if you prefer?'

Alice leaned forward and prodded Bodkin on the shoulder with a long, slender finger. 'Are you saying we look like a pair of wrinkly old hags before we utilise the black magic?'

Bodkin held up his hands in mock surrender, then he turned the key and started the engine. 'What I'm saying is... I wish I had never embarked on this conversation in the first place.' He looked over his shoulder at Alice. 'I'd rather not know what dark arts are employed to make you look so glamorous. I'm just happy to see the results.'

Sal and Ferris were waiting at the main door of the apartments as Bodkin drove up the lane and pulled into the small car park at the side. Ferris was wearing a newly pressed suit with a white shirt and a blue tie. Bodkin, who could make a suit of armour look wrinkly, deliberately walked in between Amy and Alice as they headed towards the main road so that his less than pristine look didn't stand out quite as much.

As they strolled up the hill towards the Roxy, Amy thought she saw someone bob down behind a parked car on the other side of the road as they passed by. Dismissing the thought, she smiled up at the poster advertising the night's film and made her way up the steps to the doors of the picture house.

'Here she is. Hello, Rita Haywood,' the cinema owner called across the foyer as Alice walked in.

'It's Hayworth,' Alice reminded him. Martin Le Flik had asked her to stand outside the theatre with a placard whenever they showed a movie featuring the Hollywood starlet, such was their remarkable resemblance.

After the film, Amy and Alice walked up the hill towards the town with Ferris, Sal and Bodkin just behind.

'That was so funny,' Alice said. 'I love Wendy Hiller. She was really convincing as a cockney flower seller.'

'She was hilarious at times,' Amy agreed.

Alice stopped dead and paraphrased Eliza when she had been asked if she was going to walk home, by saying in the poshest voice she could muster. 'Walk? Not bloody likely. I'm going to get the bus.'

Amy collapsed into a fit of laughter. 'Oh, Alice, that's much funnier than what she actually said about the taxi.'

'Very good,' Bodkin agreed, laughing along with the rest.

The Milton was already busy by the time they took their usual seats along the wall furthest from the stage. They still had a good view of the proceedings, but they weren't bothered by waiters nipping in and out between the tables in the centre of the room.

Ferris called one of the white-jacketed waiters over and gave him their first order, which would be free under the terms of his contract. Ferris and Bodkin had beer, Sal had a gin and tonic, Alice had a gin and Dubonnet while Amy had her favourite Pimm's with ice.

Once the drinks had been ordered, the friends sat back in their chairs to watch Nina Swingwell go through her jazz routine with the house band.

Ferris and Sal nudged their chairs closer to each other and lowered their heads to chat privately. Amy, sitting on the other side of the table, pouted as she watched them. Bodkin, having first seen Amy's pouty face, followed her gaze across the table. 'Look at them,' he said. 'Love's young dream.'

'Do you know, Bodkin, I think you are the most unromantic person I've ever met. And I include Big Nose Beryl's other half in that statement.'

'I've never met the man, so I couldn't possibly comment,' Bodkin replied.

'Do something romantic,' Amy said suddenly, causing a look of horror to cross the policeman's face. 'Go on. I dare you.'

Bodkin looked around desperately for inspiration. 'I could ask you to dance,' he said. 'Would that be romantic enough?'

Amy grinned as she got to her feet and slipped out of her jacket.

'You really are very beautiful,' Bodkin said as he stood up. 'I'm not just saying that because you wanted me to be romantic.'

'Oh, I was only joking, you silly man.' Amy took hold of Bodkin's arm and he led her to the dance floor where a few other couples were dancing close as Nina crooned Thanks For The Memory, the Bob Hope and Shirley Ross song that had been released the year before. Amy had a copy of the record at home.

Taking Amy in his arms, the pair performed a slow foxtrot, gliding across the floor as though they practiced the dance every week. Bodkin had been a nervous, clumsy dancer when Amy had first met him, but over the months, his confidence had grown and he could now perform alongside the best dancers in the club. Amy and Alice practiced together regularly, either in Amy's bedroom or Alice's huge kitchen.

When the song had ended, the audience applauded and Nina went straight into the Edythe Wright and Tommy Dorsey classic, Stardust. Amy put her head on Bodkin's shoulder as they performed a slow waltz. The first half of the ballad was an instrumental, but as Nina began to croon the lyrics, Bodkin glanced down to see Amy looking up at him through misty eyes. 'The words are so beautiful,' she whispered.

The pair were so wrapped up in the song that Bodkin and Amy continued to sway slowly for a good thirty seconds after the music had ended. They were brought to their senses by a round of applause and were stunned to find that they were the centre of attention as the other dancers stood still around the edge of the floor as they clapped. 'Wasn't that beautiful, folks?' Nina said, as she and the band joined in with the applause.

Blushing, Amy hurried away from the dance floor with Bodkin in hot pursuit. When they got to their table, they found Ferris, Sal and Alice on their feet applauding them. Alice's eyes shone as she clapped her hands, then she blew a kiss to her best friend. 'You were in another world there, dearest,' she said as Amy reached her chair.

'I just love that song. I was lost in the moment.' She looked lovingly at Bodkin as he finally reached the table, after having his back slapped numerous times on his journey across the room.

'Now that...' Amy said as he reached his seat. '...was romantic.'

She looked away from the policeman as she heard Erma's voice adding itself to the congratulations.

'That was beautiful to behold,' she said as she stepped into the space between Ferris's chair and the odd one of the six at the table. Amy's jaw dropped in horror when she noticed that Erma was wearing exactly the same autumn themed dress as her.

CHAPTER
THIRTY-SEVEN

'Erma, what have you done?' Amy said, almost dumbstruck as some of the women standing around began to point and whisper.

Erma seemed unperturbed. 'We look like sisters,' she said happily.

'I don't want to look like your sister,' Amy said, pulling her jacket from the back of the chair and slipping it on.

'I've brought my jacket with me too,' Erma said, holding up a similar garment.

'I don't believe this,' Amy said. She looked sideways towards Alice, who was glaring at Erma across the table. 'Can you believe this? It can't be a coincidence, surely?' She looked down towards the floor as Erma stepped back to allow a man to pass and saw she was wearing the same black slingbacks as her.

'You're right, Amy. This isn't a coincidence,' Alice snarled. 'She's done this deliberately.'

Amy grabbed her best friend's hand and almost dragged her to the ladies' toilets.

'It was her. I should have stopped and called her out.'

'Her? Where?' Alice asked.

'She was hiding behind the car when we were walking up Middle Street.'

'Why would she be hiding? I don't understand.'

'I think she wanted to make sure I hadn't changed my mind about what I was wearing tonight. Like a fool, I told her I'd decided on this dress when we met in the café this lunchtime. When she left the café, she must have gone straight over to Brigdens and bought one. It was on display at the front of the shop. She got the shoes from there too. They were selling almost new ones for a pound. I got my pair from the sales bin. They had a broken heel.'

'My God, why would she do that?'

'I don't know,' Amy replied, 'but I'm going to find out.' She headed towards the door, but Alice got hold of her arm.

'Hold on. Think for a moment. Don't let her know she's upset you. She's won if you do.'

Amy took a deep breath. 'You're right, of course.'

'When you go back in, keep your cool. Talk calmly. Let her be the first to lose her temper. Just be the usual even tempered Amy we all know and love.'

Amy walked across to the row of three sinks and studied her appearance in the mirror above the left-hand basin. Reaching into her bag, she pulled out her compact and dabbed her face in one or two places, then she pulled out her Vermillion lipstick and touched up her lips. Happy with the result, and now feeling much calmer, she turned to her friend. 'Okay, Alice, let's see what she has to say for herself.'

'Don't leave,' Alice whispered in her ear. 'Whatever happens, don't walk out.'

'I have no intentions of leaving,' Amy said as she walked out of the door. 'She'll be going home long before I am.'

Back at the table, Bodkin was looking on as a small crowd of women surrounded Erma. All of them making the point that as Amy had arrived first, Erma was the one who should cover up her dress, or at least keep well clear of Amy, especially if she was on the dance floor. Many of the women had seen Amy before at the Milton. One or two knew her from the London Connection shop.

'You have no class,' a blonde woman told her. 'You'd back off if you had.'

'You should apologise at the bare minimum,' a dark-haired woman said. 'Either that or leave.'

Erma wasn't at all pleased with the attention she was attracting, and when Amy arrived back at the table, she turned on her.

'I thought you were my friend, but I'm seeing you in a whole different light now.'

'Likewise,' Amy replied cooly. 'I still can't quite believe you have done this to me.'

'You mean it's not just a coincidence?' the blonde woman asked.

Amy stared into Erma's face. 'It's no coincidence. I let her look at the dresses in my wardrobe the other day and this lunchtime I told her which one I'd be wearing tonight. So she went straight up to Brigdens and bought an identical dress. I saw her earlier, on my way to the pictures; she was hiding behind a car, just waiting for me to pass so she could make sure I hadn't changed my mind. Then she went home and got ready.'

'That is scandalous,' the blonde woman said. She turned towards Erma with a scowl on her face. 'Well, what have you got to say for yourself?' The rest of the women muttered amongst themselves while giving Erma hostile looks.

'At least I paid full price for my dress. It didn't come off the pauper's rail like that one. She had to patch it up before she could wear it.'

'At least I'm capable of patching a dress up to make it wearable, Erma. All you're good for is stealing from the stash of money your gangster brother left with your mother.'

There was a series of oohs and aahs as the growing crowd stared at Erma, who was becoming redder in the face by the minute.

'She would look good in rags,' a young woman said as she smiled at Amy. She turned to give Erma a scathing look. 'You wouldn't look good if Coco Chanel's personal dresser got you ready.'

Erma finally lost it. She leaned towards Amy and hurled a torrent of abuse at her. She flicked her head towards Bodkin. 'He only wants you because you're easy.'

Amy closed her eyes. Took a deep breath, then stepped forward and slapped Erma across the face.

The room erupted with cheering.

Erma put a hand to her red cheek, then turned to Bodkin. 'You're a copper. You saw her attack me. I demand that you arrest her.'

Bodkin, who had been keeping a careful eye on proceedings, merely shrugged. 'I didn't see a thing,' he said. He looked around the chattering, smiling crowd. 'And I don't think you'll find that any of these good people saw anything, either.'

Erma stamped her foot, then spat at Bodkin's feet. Turning back to Amy, she pointed an accusing finger. 'You haven't heard the last of this.' Then, spinning on her heel, she stomped off towards the foyer and out of the Milton.

When everything had calmed down. Bodkin called the waiter over and ordered a fresh round of drinks. When he returned, the policeman was informed that the drinks had been paid for by a lady sitting on the other side of the dancefloor. As the waiter pointed her out, Bodkin raised his pint in salute, then turned to speak to Amy.

'Are you all right?' he asked.

'Perfectly all right, thank you,' she replied, taking a sip of her ice-cold Pimm's. 'I wouldn't let someone like that get to me.'

'That was a hell of a slap!' Bodkin said. 'I bet Hetty heard it all the way from Victoria Street.'

Ferris, who had just come back to the table after going backstage to change into his white tuxedo, took a long gulp of his pint, then looked around wondering why people were staring at them. 'Did I miss something?' he asked.

'Nothing important,' Amy said. She pointed to the stage. 'I think you're wanted, Ferris.'

Ferris hurried across the room and reached the stage just as the band leader stepped up to the microphone to announce him. 'Ladies and gentlemen. Please give a big Milton welcome to the one, the only ORLANDO FERRIS!'

Bodkin shook his head sadly. 'I'll never get used to that. Why on earth did he choose Orlando for a stage name?'

'Shh,' Sal said. 'He's about to start.' She looked towards the stage, then turned quickly back. 'Oh, I hope he does the Max Miller joke.'

Ferris *did* do the Max Miller joke. It went down a storm. Delighted, he followed it up with the tomato and salad dressing joke, which, sadly, didn't go down anywhere near as well. Desperate to win the audience back, he told the trains on thyme joke, but that only got a slightly better reception than the salad gag. In an attempt to help him out, Sal got to her feet and began to clap wildly, adding a whoop for good measure. After almost a full minute's silence, and after getting a nudge from the band-leader, a clearly ruffled Ferris announced his next song.

'My next song will be The Way You Look Tonight. It's a lovely slow ballad and to help me with it, I'd like to invite two of my favourite people to come onto the dancefloor. You've seen them already tonight, the lovebirds, Amy and Bodkin.'

Bodkin groaned as he heard Ferris call his name out, but Amy was on her feet almost before Ferris had finished the announcement. 'Come on, Bodkin,' she said, grabbing his hand.

The policeman reluctantly got to his feet and to a chorus of clapping and chanting, he allowed himself to be led onto the dance floor. When they reached its centre, a spotlight lit them up and Amy placed one hand on his lower back and another around his neck. Then she stepped in close as the band played the opening chords of The Way You Look Tonight, the song that Fred Astaire had made famous in the film Swing Time.

By the time Ferris had joined in with the lyrics, the dancefloor was full of couples moving slowly around the space. Alice and Sal, who had both been asked to dance, moved around with them. Amy sang along quietly as she looked up into Bodkin's eyes. Bodkin smiled softly, then lowered his head and kissed her.

At midnight, Amy, holding Bodkin's arm, stepped out of the Milton and onto Main Street. Ferris, with Sal on one arm and Alice on the other, followed them at a short distance. As Bodkin hailed a taxi, Amy looked across the street to the bus stop where Erma Firth was standing with two men, one of which she recognised as Vincent Jury. Erma lifted her arm and pointed out Amy to the two men. Then she laughed and said something to them that didn't carry across the road.

'That's Vincent Jury,' Amy said as Bodkin opened the back door of the taxi and Ferris kissed Sal goodnight. He lived above the police station and so it was only a relatively short walk home for him. He wasn't taking a taxi as he had to go back into the Milton to pick up his wages from the manager.

On hearing Amy call out. Bodkin straightened up to his full height and looked directly at the Gillingham thug. 'Wait here,' he ordered as he stepped off the pavement behind the cab. 'I'd like a word with you,' he shouted, but by the time he reached the middle of the road, the trio had turned away and were making their way towards the Market Place.

CHAPTER THIRTY-EIGHT

After the church service on Sunday, Amy and her parents said goodbye to their fellow parishioners and made their way along the ragstone slate and gravel path that led to the main gates. When they reached the pavement leading down the hill towards the area known as Bottom Acre, they stopped for a while to swap pleasantries with a couple of elderly ladies who lived just across the road from the church.

Having relived the sermon already with one of the worshipers within the church grounds, Amy excused herself and continued to walk home alone. Enjoying the cold but bright day, she took her time walking down the hill, expecting her parents to catch up, but as she passed the doctor's house that doubled up as his surgery, she looked back to find there was no sign of them. Turning at Bottom Acre, she walked by the row of large Edwardian houses and began to climb the slight incline that would take her past The Mill and up to the telephone box at the end of Long Lane. When she was opposite her workplace, a small black car pulled up alongside and before she realised what was happening, the back door was thrown open and a thickset man in his late twenties grabbed hold of her and pulled her into the back of the car.

Amy screamed, but the man placed a dirty hand over her mouth before shouting at the driver to 'GO!' The next thing she knew, the car had driven past the phone box and was heading up the Gillingham Road at speed.

CHAPTER THIRTY-NINE

Amy bit into the fleshy part of her attacker's hand, then squirmed like an eel and struggled into a sitting position as the fair-haired man tried desperately to hold her down on the back seat. Kicking out, she felt the heel of her shoe catch something soft and she heard a satisfying 'OOF' as the man doubled over.

Reaching for the handle, Amy pushed down on the catch and the driver's side rear door flew open. The car swerved as the man in front looked over his shoulder to see what was happening. Amy thought about risking a leap onto the grass verge, but before she could summon up the courage, the car veered back onto the left side of the road, leaving her looking at the tarmac.

As the man she had injured struggled to sit up, Amy half turned and clawed him down the face before screaming for help through the door that was still swinging open. The man in the back suddenly threw himself at her and pulled her into the centre of the bench seat. Amy looked out onto the road and waved her arms desperately as a dark blue Morris Oxford passed them on the other side of the carriageway.

After climbing over the top of Amy, her assailant stretched

out a long arm and, after two attempts, managed to pull the door shut. Turning back to her, he touched the scratches on his face with his fingertips and hissed. 'You'll pay for that.'

Amy squirmed and wriggled in an attempt to get from beneath the heavily built man, but he was too strong, and she eventually gave up the struggle.

'That's better,' the man said. He looked out of the back window, then shot a panicked glance towards the front. 'Put your foot down, Vince,' he said. 'That car we just passed has turned around.'

CHAPTER FORTY

Encouraged by the man's nervous shout. Amy began to struggle again and after going at him with both sets of nails and kicking out like a bucking bronco, she managed to free herself. Turning to face the back window, she began to hammer on it, whilst shouting at the top of her voice, although she knew that apart from her kidnappers, no one would hear.

As they passed the turn off for Middle Street where the police station was situated, Amy, more in hope than expectation looked out of the side window for any members of the force that might be hanging around, but the pavement outside the station was empty. Looking back along the road again, she could see the dark blue car beginning to gain on them. 'Come on, Bodkin!' she cried, as the cursing man tried to drag her away from the window. Amy dug her elbow into his face, then began to hammer on the rear window again with her fists.

'Can't you control the crazy bitch?' Vincent Jury shouted from the front. He took a look over his shoulder again. 'That bugger is gaining on us, Paul.'

'I'll chuck her out of the bloody door if she doesn't do as she's told,' Paul replied through gritted teeth. He got hold of her around the waist and tried to pull her away from the window again.

Amy began to flail with her fists and caught Paul on the nose, which bent with a loud crack.

'The cow has broken my bloody nose,' he complained, letting go of her to assess the damage with his fingers.

Amy took a quick look past him, then reached out to try to open the passenger side door. This time Paul was too quick for her, and he got his broad frame in the way, preventing her from reaching the handle. Amy cried out in frustration and took another look out of the back window. The Morris was less than a hundred yards away and closing. As they left the open countryside, and entered a built up area called Mossmoor, the traffic on the right-hand side of the road began to get heavier.

'Can't you go any faster?' Paul cursed as he saw the wet bloodstain on his shirt. 'He'll catch us before we get to the warehouse.'

'I'm doing fifty,' Vincent shouted back. 'If I press the pedal any harder, my foot will be scraping the road.'

'Do yourself a favour, stop the car and let me out,' Amy said as calmly as she could. 'That's a policeman behind you.'

'Pull the other one,' Paul said, but he took another look out of the window, anyway. The Morris was now only fifty yards away.

'What's he got under that bonnet, a bloody plane engine?' Vincent spat.

Amy waved her arms in the air, hoping that Bodkin could see them as Paul pulled her down onto the seat again. 'Honestly, Paul,' she panted. 'I'm not lying. That's Inspector Bodkin in the car behind. I wouldn't want to be in your shoes when he catches up with you.'

'Shut it!' Paul hissed. 'Come on, Vinny, you can get a bit

more out of it. I told you we should have nicked that Alvis instead of this heap.'

'We'd have stood out like a sore thumb in that,' Vincent said. He pointed up ahead towards the road sign that informed them that Gillingham was now only two miles ahead. 'If we can get into town, we'll easily lose him in the backstreets.'

'Bodkin knows Gillingham as well as you do, if not better,' Amy said, trying to keep her voice on a steady level. 'You won't shake him off your tail.'

'Christ on a sodding bike!' Vincent said, as he saw the long line of army trucks chugging along in front of him.

Paul raised his head above the back seat and looked out of the windscreen. 'Bugger,' he said. Then took a glance to his right where he saw Bodkin's Morris Oxford pull alongside.

Vincent looked desperately to the left to see if the grass verge was wide enough for him to take the trucks on the inside, but the grass strip was only a couple of feet wide and beyond that was a thick line of trees. He let out a long sigh as he was forced to pull up behind a green painted lorry. The traffic on the opposite carriageway braked as Bodkin's car screeched to a halt and skidded sideways on.

The next thing Amy knew, the door was yanked open, and Bodkin dragged her out of the car. 'Get in there,' he said, pointing to the open door of the Morris.

As Paul dived out of the rear passenger side door, the policeman pulled the driver's door open and got hold of the back of Vincent's jacket as he attempted to slide across the front seat. 'You, my son, are nicked,' Bodkin growled as the kidnapper gave up the struggle and went limp.

Bodkin hauled him out of the car and pushed him against the body of the Austin. He looked over his shoulder at Amy as the line of lorries in front began to move. 'Pull over,' he ordered, nodding towards the newly created space.

Amy slipped into the driver's seat of the blue Morris, then eased the car in front of the stolen Austin. Holding Vincent by the throat with one hand, Bodkin motioned her to stay where she was. The line of traffic on the other side of the road began to move slowly as the drivers wound down their windows to call insults at the policeman.

Bodkin ignored them and turned his attention to Vincent. Dragging him around the front of the car, he stood him up on the verge before giving him a shove in the chest. 'Do you know? I don't know whether to charge you with attempted kidnap or to punch you in the face.' He looked towards his car where Amy had got out and was standing watching them. 'I think I'll do both,' Bodkin said, and hit Vincent squarely on the nose.

Vincent sank to his knees, holding his face, but Bodkin hadn't done. After dragging him back to his feet, he hit him in the stomach. As Vincent dropped his hands to his belly, he kicked him between the legs, then hit him under the chin with a devastating right hook. Amy's would be kidnapper fell to the floor without making a sound.

'Vincent Jury,' Bodkin said, sticking his foot on the man's chest and reaching into his pocket for his handcuffs. 'I am arresting you for the attempted kidnap of Amy Rowlings. You do not have to say anything at this time, but... believe me... anything you *do* say *will* be used in evidence against you. COUNT ON IT!'

CHAPTER FORTY-ONE

'We need to find a telephone box,' Bodkin said after he had dragged Vincent back to his feet. 'This car has to be moved. It's blocking the carriageway.'

'I'll drive it into Gillingham, Bodkin,' Amy offered after retrieving her bag from the back of the Austin.

The policeman pointed to his ear, not having heard what Amy had said. 'It was stolen from Spinton so it could do with being driven back to trace the owner,' Bodkin raised his voice over the toots and beeps from the motorists struggling to get past. 'If we can find a phone kiosk, I'll get Smedley to send someone over the pick it up.'

Amy stepped closer so that Bodkin could hear her. 'But isn't this just the scenario Superintendent Grayson was talking about when he said I could go on the force's insurance?'

Bodkin rubbed his chin. 'I'm not sure the insurance will cover you in a stolen car. I'd get away with it; I've had to recover lots of cars in my time. Anyway, after what just happened, I don't think you should be driving. You'll still be in shock.'

'I'm fine, Bodkin, honestly.' Amy held out her hand towards

him. 'Look, I'm not shaking.' She smiled at him. 'It was quite exciting really but thank you so much for rescuing me.'

'I just wish I'd had Ferris with me so we could have got both of the swine. Did the other man give you a clue about his identity? Was it one of the Larks or Firths?'

'His name was Paul, so I don't think he's from either family. He seemed to be in charge. Before last night, I'd have said he was one of Bessie's henchmen, but after seeing them with Erma, they could be part of the Firth gang. He might need some medical attention before long because he's a bit scratched up and I'm sure he has a broken nose that will need setting.'

Bodkin grinned. 'I can't wait to hear the story of how he got that.' He stuck up a thumb to her. Then went on. 'The Gillingham police will know who he is. As for Bessie and that blooming Erma, I'm going to be having words with them very soon.' He turned his attention to Vincent. 'Who do you work for? Whose idea was this?'

Vincent sniffed. The blood on his nostrils was beginning to dry. 'I'm saying nothing, copper.'

'That's your prerogative at this stage, Vincent. But I think you'll change your tune when I get you back to the cells.' He leaned in close and whispered into his ear. 'There won't be any witnesses there.'

Vincent tried his best to act as though he didn't care, but Bodkin noticed a flicker of fear in his eyes.

The policeman looked up the road towards Gillingham. The line of army lorries had now disappeared and there were only the few cars that had managed to squeeze past them on the road in front. Getting hold of Vincent again, he hauled him towards the back of the Morris. 'I'll get the Austin as far up the verge as I can to let the traffic get by. Keep an eye on him for a minute.'

'I'll drive your new car home, Bodkin. Stick Vincent in the back of the Austin.'

Bodkin thought about it. 'Are you sure you're going to be all right? It's a heavy steer, remember?'

'I'll be fine. It's more or less a straight road. I'll take it easy. There might be a long queue in my wake, but they'll have to put up with it.'

Bodkin reluctantly agreed. 'All right, it does seem to be the best solution, but just remember, I'm right behind you. If you feel it's too heavy to steer or your wrist is hurting too much, just pull in to the side of the road and I'll take over.'

'How are we going to turn the cars around?' she asked.

'There's a roundabout a mile or so down the road. It's quite a big one, so you should be able to manage the turn. If you have any trouble at all. Just stick your arm out of the window to let me know you're struggling, then pull over. Even if you're only halfway around the roundabout.'

'I'll be fine, Bodkin. My wrist is a lot better now.'

As Vincent had his hands cuffed behind him, Bodkin shoved the man headfirst into the back of the Austin, then when he was lying prone across the seat, the inspector slammed the door, climbed into the driver's side and looked over his shoulder at his prisoner. 'If I hear one peep out of you, Vincent. I'll stop the car and put a gag on you, so be warned.'

Amy was standing by the boot of the Morris, waiting for Bodkin to give the go ahead. At his thumbs up signal, she climbed into the car, started the engine and, after making a hand signal to the traffic behind, pulled out onto the carriageway.

She found the roundabout on the outskirts of Gillingham more difficult to navigate around than she thought she might, and by the time she had pulled onto the road back to Spinton, her wrist was throbbing. Grinding her teeth against the pain,

Amy worked through the gears until she got into third, then she drove at a steady twenty-five miles an hour until she reached the left turn onto Middle Street where she dropped down into first gear and crawled around the corner. After stopping for a few seconds and taking several deep breaths, she put the car into gear again and turned into the police station car park. As she drove into a vacant space, she saw Bodkin pull up alongside.

When Bodkin opened the back door of the Austin, Amy climbed out of the Morris and stood by the door flexing her fingers as she held the bandaged wrist with the other hand.

Smedley, having seen Bodkin drag Jury out of the car from the window of the canteen, hurried out to see if his boss needed any assistance. After hearing a quick summary of why Vincent had been arrested, the constable looked at Amy and shook his head.

'Are you all right, Miss?'

Amy nodded and held a little tighter onto her bandaged wrist.

'You drove back after all that happened, and with that injury? Blimey, you're a lot tougher than you look, that's all I can say.'

Bodkin, who had one hand on the back of Jury's coat, turned and smiled at her. 'You don't know the half of it, Smedley.'

When Vincent was safely under lock and key, Bodkin took Amy into his office, where he offered to make her a strong cup of tea. When she gracefully declined, he held out his arms. Amy stepped into them and didn't move for the next two minutes. 'I'm so proud of you,' he whispered. 'You have such a strong character. I was a bag of nerves when I was chasing you. I just kept thinking about how terrified you must be.'

'I was terrified, but I calmed down a bit when I knew you

were behind us. I warned them that they'd be better off letting me go, but they wouldn't listen.' She looked into Bodkin's face. 'It cost them both a bloody nose.'

Bodkin shook his head as he looked at her. 'You really are full of surprises.'

'Oh, he was nothing compared to what me and Alice had to put up with at school. We'd pitch ourselves against anybody. Boys, girls. It didn't matter.' She held up her fists. 'We stood back-to-back and took on the world.'

Bodkin grinned. 'I wouldn't have been brave enough to take you on.' He put his arm around her shoulders. 'Come on,' he said. 'Let's get you home.'

'I don't really want to tell Mum and Dad what happened to me yet, Bodkin. I know how they'll react. I need to think really hard about how I'm going to explain things. Could you drop me off at the farm? Mum and Dad will assume I've gone there, anyway. I usually do on Sundays after church.'

Amy kissed Bodkin on the lips at the end of the short, rough track that led to the back of the farmhouse. After watching him perform his usual untidy three-point turn, she waved him off, and he drove to the police station to begin the questioning of Vincent Jury.

Amy walked around to the farmyard and pushed the kitchen door open to find Alice clearing away the dinner plates.

'Hello. You missed the Sunday roast. We had an early one today.'

Amy slipped her bag off her shoulder and put it on the big oak table, then with her eyes filling with tears, she held out her arms towards her lifelong best friend. 'Oh Alice,' she said. 'I've been so frightened.'

CHAPTER
FORTY-TWO

'She was never in any danger, as it turns out, Mr Rowlings, although I completely understand your concern.'

'It's a bit more than a concern, Mr Bodkin. What happened today could have ended up in a tragedy. My daughter was kidnapped by a gang of criminals.'

'But it didn't end it tragedy, Dad. If you think about it another way, your factory could be bombed or the train you go to work on might derail. The point is, it didn't. I'm here safe and well.'

'Those comparisons are ridiculous, Amy, and you know it,' Mr Rowlings said.

'All right, but listen to Bodkin, please, Dad.'

Her father pursed his lips and put his arm around his wife, who still hadn't recovered from the shock of learning what had happened to Amy. 'Go ahead, Mr Bodkin,' he said. 'But I doubt you'll change my mind regarding the matter of my daughter helping the police with their gangland inquiry.'

'It wasn't a kidnap for ransom or anything like that. The perpetrators had been instructed to release her at a warehouse location in Gillingham. Vincent Jury insists that they just wanted to frighten her.'

'They certainly did that. They frightened us half to death too,' Mr Rowlings replied.

'I'm not diminishing the severity of the offence. Vincent Jury will be charged with kidnapping and so will his accomplice, Paul Leyton, when we catch up with him.'

'You found out his identity, then? Did Vincent cough up?' Amy asked.

'No, but the Gillingham police know who's who in the criminal fraternity and there are only two men named Paul on their gang member list and the other one is in his fifties.'

'What about who sent them? Did he tell you that? Was it Bessie, Reggie Tumbler, or, as I suspect, after last night, Erma?'

'He isn't saying. I think he's even more scared of them than you were of him, Amy.'

'So what now? Do we go back to question Bessie in hospital? Or do we pull Erma in?'

'There is no *we* in this investigation, Amy,' Mr Rowlings said firmly. 'You are no longer part of it.'

Amy got to her feet and stuck her hands on her hips as she stared at her father. 'Dad. You can't tell me what I can and can't do anymore. I'm not a child.'

'You're my child.'

'I'm twenty-two next month. I'm an adult. You can't order me around anymore. I'm above the age of consent. I can vote. I have my own life to lead.'

'This is my house, Amy, and while you live in it, you follow the rules.'

Amy bit her lip, then suddenly rushed to the door in a flood of angry tears. 'Right. I'll pack a bag. I'm not going to be ordered around like I'm a five-year-old girl.' Twisting the handle, she took one final look at her father, then she stepped into the hall and slammed the door behind her.

Mrs Rowlings got quickly to her feet. 'I'll go to her,' she said and hurriedly followed Amy out of the room.

Upstairs in Amy's bedroom, Mrs Rowlings found her daughter sitting on the bed with an open, but empty, suitcase at the side of her.

'Don't take it to heart, dear. Your dad only wants what's best for you.' She moved the case towards the bottom of the bed and sat down next to her daughter. 'We were so upset when you told us what happened. I won't sleep tonight, thinking about it.'

Amy wiped away the tears, then took hold of her mother's hand. 'I wasn't hurt, Mum. I was never meant to be hurt. It was just someone playing silly games.'

'It's not a game to us, though, dear.' Mrs Rowlings' eyes began to leak. 'You have to look at this from our point of view.'

'Why, Mum? It was me it happened to. I was never in any danger. Bodkin was right behind me. He was on my trail straight away.'

'But what if he hadn't been driving by at that exact moment? I shudder to think what might have happened.'

'I keep having to remind you, Mum. Nothing happened. They were going to drop me off at a warehouse in Gillingham, so I'd have to find my own way home.' She patted her mother's hand. 'It was Gillingham, Mum. Not Glasgow. I had my purse with me. I could have caught a bus back or jumped on the train. I would have been home before you knew I was missing.'

'That's not how your father sees it, Amy. He's never been really comfortable with you working with the police. This is the straw that broke the camel's back.' She closed her eyes and shook her head slowly. 'He didn't think anything like this would happen when he agreed to let you help Bodkin.'

'That's the trouble, Mum. He still thinks of me as being his little girl and I'm a grown woman now.'

'You'll always be his little girl, dear. You know that. He'd never forgive himself if something happened to you... and today it almost did.'

'NOTHING HAPPENED TO ME! I was given a free car ride. Someone played a nasty trick on me, that's the be all and end all of it. Dad has to realise that I'm all grown up and I'll make my own decisions.' She stood up and walked towards her chest of draws. Pulling out random items of underwear, she took them back to the bed and dropped them into her suitcase.

'Please don't leave, Amy. I'll miss you so much. Just let it lie for a day or two. I'm sure it will all blow over soon.'

'I'm sorry, Mum, but I really have to live my own life.'

'I know, dear, but just think for a moment. What if you and Bodkin were married? What would you say to him if he told you that you couldn't do something that might be dangerous?'

'As it happens, we had that conversation when I was helping him with the Highwater Boat Club murder. I refused to take orders from him then and I'll do the same in the future.'

'Oh, Amy. We all just want you to be safe.'

'Without any regard for my independence or happiness?'

'I'm sure they both want you to be happy. James will be discussing what happens in the future with Mr Bodkin downstairs.'

'EXACTLY!' Amy stormed. 'Two men discussing MY FUTURE! We don't live in Jane Austen's time, Mum. I'll make my own decisions, thank you. This is nineteen thirty-nine. I'm an independent woman. I work so I can pay my way in life. I will not be dictated to.' She put her hand softly on her mother's cheek and stroked it. 'When this war really gets going, women are going to be the mainstay of this country's economy, and afterwards, we'll decide on our own futures. Men can either like it or lump it.'

Mrs Rowlings was quite taken aback by Amy's outburst. 'Ooh, our Amy. I don't know where you get this stubborn streak from. Not me, that's for sure.'

Amy laughed suddenly. 'Dad, probably.'

'You are very alike.'

'We are, and he's just going to have to learn to live with that fact.' She pulled out a couple of day dresses with a skirt and blouse from her wardrobe, folded them quickly and dropped them into the suitcase. 'Until he does, I won't stay under the same roof. I love him, Mum, but if it's a choice between living under draconian restrictions or doing what I enjoy doing more than anything else in the world, then I'm afraid it will be the latter.'

Her mother's eyes filled with tears again. 'But where will you go?'

'Alice will put me up until I can find a place of my own. I'll be safe there. You won't have to worry about me.'

She walked to her dressing table and began to pick out some of her cosmetics.

'Amy,' Bodkin's voice came from the open doorway. 'I've been talking to your father. Do you think we could have a word?'

With a determined look on her face, Amy followed Bodkin downstairs and into the living room, where she found her father sitting in his armchair cradling a glass of scotch.

'Sit down, please, Amy,' he said.

Bodkin waited for Amy and her mother to sit on the sofa before taking a chair at the dining table.

'Mr Bodkin and I have had a short discussion,' Mr Rowlings began.

'And have the mighty kings decided my fate?' Amy asked scornfully.

'Amy,' Bodkin said, but he was interrupted before he could say any more.

'You sit there, the pair of you. The two men I love most in the world and make decisions for me behind my back. Well, I won't have it, do you hear? I will not allow men to hand out orders and expect me to follow them unerringly.'

'Amy... please... listen to what your dad has to say.'

Amy gave Bodkin one of her looks. 'You'd be lost without me, Bodkin... well, not lost exactly, but... well, look how much I've helped you this year. Even Mr Grayson says I'm a big help. You can't just cast me aside now. It really isn't fair.' Feeling herself welling up again, she wiped her eyes on her bandage, then stared belligerently at her father.

'Have you finished?' he asked.

Amy sniffled and nodded.

'Good, because this could take all night if you haven't and Mr Bodkin has to get back to work.' He rolled the whisky around in his glass before he continued. 'As you are aware, I made a decision that I know you steadfastly disagreed with, but please believe me when I say I took that decision for the best of reasons. You are my... our, only daughter, our only child, and you have to understand how devastated we were when we heard what had happened to you this morning.'

Amy opened her mouth to speak, but Mr Rowlings held up his hand to silence her. 'Please let me finish before you throw up any more barriers.' He turned to Bodkin and smiled a tight smile. 'Mr Bodkin and I have had a brief conversation about the matter and we have agreed on a solution.'

'YOU HAVE AGREED!'

Mr Rowlings sighed deeply. 'We have agreed on a compromise.'

Amy looked from one man to the other. 'A compromise?'

'Mr Bodkin is not only someone I have come to see as a friend, he is almost... literally almost a member of our family and over the admittedly short time I have known him, I have come to value both his opinion and his judgement. I can honestly say that on the day you walk up the aisle together, I will be thinking that there is no one I'd rather give you away to.' He paused, noticing the look in Amy's eyes. 'I really don't like that phrase and I know you don't, but please allow me to continue.' He put his whiskey glass down. 'Amy, I am aware how much you enjoy helping the inspector with his cases and I will admit here and now that despite my reservations, I'm so proud of the way you have acted in that role. You have proven yourself to be at least the equal of any man in the force. If the police had any sense, they'd turn their ridiculous male only rule on its head and welcome you into the CID. However, I think it will be quite a few years before that happens. By the time it does, you'll probably be married, possibly with children of your own, and you might feel a little differently about wanting to join the police force. For now, though, I understand how much you enjoy being a part of things. So,' he picked his glass up again, 'I have allowed myself to be persuaded. Inspector Bodkin and I have agreed that it would be a travesty to prevent you from becoming involved in certain cases. I know how much it means to you. I always did, but I was reluctant to give my blessing.' He sighed deeply. 'As you have made it abundantly clear, you are an adult now and you can make your own decisions as to the paths you take in life. I am therefore withdrawing my previous objections, with one proviso, that in this particular case, you will not be allowed to become involved with any questioning that takes place outside of Spinton.' He took a sip from his glass and looked at her pleadingly. 'Please see reason,

Amy, these people are vicious gangsters and I don't want you to be put in harm's way.'

Amy was silent for a moment. 'So you are saying that I can continue to help the police in the investigation in Spinton? I can still help question witnesses and suspects... like Bessie Dagger, for instance?'

'If it is absolutely necessary,' Mr Rowlings said. He looked fondly at his daughter. 'What do you say?'

Amy thought for a few moments. 'It's really all down to Bodkin and Mr Grayson. If they don't want to allow me into the investigation, then I can't take part, anyway.'

Bodkin smiled. 'Amy, I can't see any circumstances in which I wouldn't want you to be part of things. I'm sure I can say the same for Chief Superintendent Grayson. That's why I did my best to persuade your father to let you continue to help us.'

'Will I still have access to the interviews you conduct in Gillingham? Can I get another crack at Bessie Dagger? What about Erma? I want to be sitting across the table with her more than anything.'

'That's all fine, Amy. We... and again, I'll add the chief super's name to this. We just don't want you to get too close to these very dangerous people on their own turf, especially as Grayson has asked the Gillingham police to run a disruption campaign on all Tumbler and Dagger's businesses. They'll be hitting their bookies as soon as they open tomorrow morning. As for Erma. You might have to wait a while. I sent a team round to Victoria Street a little earlier. It seems mother and daughter have done yet another moonlight flit.'

'Damn... Oh, heck, I mean... sorry, Dad.' She smiled weakly at her father, then concentrated hard on Bodkin. 'I will get to talk to Bessie again, won't I?'

Bodkin nodded. 'You can come with me after lunch tomorrow. It will have to be a short visit though. She's being transferred to a Gillingham hospital later in the afternoon.'

Amy gave her mother's hand a squeeze, then got to her feet and looked from Bodkin to her father. 'I accept the terms of your surrender,' she said.

Mr Rowlings burst out laughing. Then he stood and held out his arms as Amy almost ran across the room towards him. 'I'm sorry, Dad. I didn't mean everything I said. It just sort of came out.'

'You're forgiven. I'm just happy that we're friends again.' He wrapped his arms around her and hugged her tightly. 'Just promise me you won't put yourself in harm's way. I couldn't bear to lose you.'

CHAPTER
FORTY-THREE

When Amy and Bodkin walked into the Phillipson ward just after lunch on Monday, they found Bessie sitting up it bed, propped up with two pillows instead of three. Nurse Huggett was on the prowl as they made their way towards her bed. She was looking a little brighter than she had on their previous visit, the bruises on her face now looking like the dried blotches of paint on an artist's palette. Her lips seemed to be less swollen and some of the smaller cuts had begun to heal. She could also use the fingers of her left hand.

'You've got fifteen minutes, then I'm dosing her up with her medication for the journey.'

'The journey?' Bodkin said with a puzzled look. 'She's going to Gillingham, not the South of France. It's less than ten miles away from here.'

'It's a bumpy road,' Nurse Huggett replied, 'and she's got broken and bruised limbs.'

'Fifteen minutes will be plenty,' Bodkin said. 'Now, if you'd leave us alone, please?'

The nurse sniffed. 'I'll get the linen ready for the bed change after she's gone.'

When she had left the ward, Bodkin opened the drawer at the side of Bessie's bed and took out her lighter. Pulling out a pack of Dunhill from his pocket, he waved them at her. 'For the journey,' he said.

'Give me one now,' Bessie pleaded. 'I ran out last night and Nurse Crabby there wouldn't get me any.'

'Are you all right lighting it yourself? I don't really want another lungful,' Bodkin said.

Bessie eased herself up on her pillows and held out her bandaged left arm. Bodkin opened the pack, took out a cigarette and stuck it between Bessie's fingers, then he struck the lighter for her. She took in a deep draw, then burst into a short fit of coughing. 'I'm usually a forty a day girl but I've been restricted to five. My lungs are playing catch up.' She took two quick drags on the Dunhill, then blew the smoke towards Amy. 'How's Miss Prissy Pants?'

Amy wafted the smoke away with her hand. 'I'm fine, no thanks to you.'

Bessie looked puzzled. 'What have I done? I've been stuck in this bloody bed for days. They won't even let me out to use a proper lavatory.'

'Have you had any visitors lately?' Bodkin asked.

'Not since you were here last. Why?'

'Vincent Jury didn't drop by to say hello?'

'No one's been here.' Bessie took another long drag and blew the smoke across the bed. 'Ask Attila the Hun if you don't believe me. She guards that door like a sentry. I'm amazed she lets the bloody doctor in.'

'Someone attempted to kidnap Miss Rowlings late yesterday morning. They dragged her into a car and made for Gillingham.'

Bessie looked down at her plaster casts and bandages. 'Well, it wasn't me.'

'No, but you may have ordered it.'

'How? By telepathy? They haven't even let me use the blooming telephone since I've been here.'

'So you've had no contact with anyone in your organisation since you've been hospitalised?'

'I call it incarcerated, and the answer is no. I even had to get Nurse Attila to call you on my behalf, if you remember.'

'I will check,' Bodkin said.

'Check away. I have no idea what you're talking about. I haven't been in a position to issue any orders.'

'Are you honestly telling me that no one from the gang has bothered to pay you a visit or send you a get well soon card?'

'If anyone had come, I'd have a drawer full of ciggies and as you can see, I don't have any.' Bessie dropped the glowing fag end onto the floor. 'Step on that, will you, or I'll never hear the last of it. She'll accuse me of trying to burn the place down. Don't bother picking it up. It will give her something to do when she isn't haranguing me about how much of her precious time I'm taking up.'

Bodkin scraped the cigarette end with his foot, then picked up the stub and put it in the ashtray that was sitting on top of the patient's cupboard. 'You may not have made any calls yourself, but have any calls been made on your behalf?'

'One to the shop to make sure someone lets my dad know I'm all right. He'll probably have heard about the crash and he'll be worried sick.'

'Wasn't he informed when it happened? I'm pretty sure the Gillingham police would have let him know about it. They were asked to.'

Bessie shrugged, then grimaced, wishing she hadn't. 'No one tells me anything.'

'That must be hard for you when you're so used to being in control of everything,' Amy said.

'It's frustrating,' Bessie replied. 'I can't wait to get back to Gillingham and away from my jailer. If I could cross my fingers I'd be wishing for a bed in a private room where I can see as many people as I like, whenever I like.'

'Are you worried someone will slip into the boss's seat?'

'None of them would dare,' Bessie said vehemently.

'Someone has to run things while you're in hospital,' Bodkin said. 'Who will be your stand in?'

'Why are you so interested?'

'Because I want to know if whoever it is ordered the kidnapping yesterday,' he replied.

'It won't be anything to do with my crew,' Bessie said. 'Why would anyone want to kidnap her? She's not from a well off family, so she wouldn't fetch a ransom. She's nothing to us, really.' She shot Amy a glance. 'Sorry but, you really aren't important in the grand scheme of things. Not as far as we're concerned. You're obviously important to the inspector. That goes without saying.'

'If she's so unimportant, why did you ask so many questions about her when you and Mervin Challenger put the frighteners on Erma before the crash?'

Bessie's laugh turned into a coughing fit. When she had recovered, she held out her hand and croakily asked for another cigarette. When she had lit it, she continued. 'I didn't put the frighteners on Erma. I didn't need to. She telephoned me at the shop and said she had some important information that I might want to hear regarding what the police knew about her brother's murder and why they wanted to question me about it. She demanded ten pounds. She got two quid because most of what she had to say was about our do gooder friend here, and none of it was all that interesting to be honest.'

'It was important enough for you to make a threat,' Bodkin

said. 'And now we've had this incident. It's a bit of a coincidence, don't you think?'

Bessie blew out her cheeks. 'I didn't make a threat. I gave her a warning. It's two different things. Anyway, as I've said, I haven't been in touch with anyone, so I can't have ordered her to be kidnapped and no one apart from Ellis and Mervin has ever heard of her.'

'Fair enough,' Bodkin said. 'But if I find out you've lied about this, you'll be doing a longer spell in jail than your dad.'

Bessie flicked ash onto the floor and said nothing.

'I have a question before we go,' Amy said. 'When we had our chat in the Old Bull, you hinted that you and Mervin Challenger had more than just a boss and underling relationship. Was that true?'

Bessie shrugged again. 'I might have said that just to wind Ellis up.'

'Did you?'

Bessie smiled and said nothing.

'Did you spend time with him at the Railway Hotel in Spinton on the night that Lonnie Firth was murdered?'

Bessie took a drag on her cigarette, then looked at it as if she was considering throwing it away.

Bodkin sighed, exasperated with Bessie's stonewalling.

'Did you have sex with Mervin Challenger at the Railway Hotel?'

'Inspector! That's not something a gentleman asks a lady. Where are your manners?'

'Is it all right if a lady asks the question?' Amy said.

'No! My private life is just that. PRIVATE!' Bessie glared at Amy.

'Do you buy your underwear from Marks and Spencer?' Bodkin asked.

'What a question.' She winked at Bodkin. 'And there's me

thinking you were a stick in the mud. There's more to you than meets the eye, isn't there?'

'Just answer the question,' Bodkin snapped.

'Okay, yes. I buy underwear from Marks and Spencer... amongst other places.'

'Are you missing any?'

Bessie blew her cheeks out. 'All these questions about my knickers. Do you want me to send you a signed pair, Inspector?'

'How do you know I was talking about knickers?' Bodkin said.

'I saw something in your eyes,' Bessie said. She twisted her neck to look at Amy. 'I'd bet you can't afford to buy your knickers there. That's a shame. Maybe you should save up. He seems to get off on them.'

The policeman looked across the ward as the door opened and Nurse Huggett pushed a trolley piled high with bedding into the ward. 'We might come to see you in your new private room in Gillingham if we have any more questions for you,' he said. 'You'll be there for a while, I reckon.'

'I'll be counting the hours,' Bessie said.

After leaving the hospital, Bodkin drove Amy home, and then went back to the station to ring Gillingham to ask them to keep their eye out for Hetty and Erma Firth. When Amy walked into the living room, she found Alice waiting for her.

'Are you feeling better about things now?' she asked. 'Your mum's just been telling me that you've been given the okay to continue helping Bodkin.'

Amy smiled at her best friend. 'I'm over it now, thanks, dear heart. It was just the shock of it all. I didn't think I was going to be able to sleep last night, but I actually slept like a log.' She grinned. 'I woke up in the fireplace.'

'HA!' Alice exclaimed. 'Good one. You should pass it on to Ferris to use in his act. It's far better than the salad dressing.'

'Shall we go up to my room and practice our waltzing?' Amy asked.

'I don't have time, sorry,' Alice replied. 'I only popped in to see if you were all right... Oh, and to tell you that ARIA Investigations has had a phone call.'

'REALLY!'

'Yep. It was about eleven-thirty this morning. It was a man. He sounded like he was in his forties, fifties maybe. Soft-spoken, polite. He didn't go into detail about what he wanted.'

'Did he leave a number?'

'No, that was the strange thing. I did ask him for a contact number, but he just said he'd call back another time.'

'But the chances are, I won't be at the farm then either,' Amy said with a puzzled look on her face.

CHAPTER FORTY-FOUR

At one o'clock on Tuesday, Amy's mum pulled on her coat and set off for her church group meeting. The recently appointed vicar was looking for volunteers to join a proposed new choir. Mrs Rowlings loved singing and could hold a tune. The Reverend Maximus Spires was hoping to whip the choir into a good enough shape to put on a carol concert at the Town Hall during the week before Christmas.

After waving her mother off, Amy hung out the washing, then set about sweeping and dusting around the downstairs. She had just finished the front room when she heard a knock at the door. Wiping her hands on her work pinafore, she stepped into the hall and opened the front door to find a man standing on the porch. He looked to be in his mid-fifties and wore a dark hat and a brown tweed suit that was stretched over a sturdy frame. The hair at the temples was silver mixed with white. He had a broad face and hooded eyes, which had a tinge of grey in them. When he spoke, Amy picked up a soft, rural, south Kent accent.

'Good afternoon,' he said, lifting his hat.

'I'm afraid if you're selling vacuum cleaners or sets of encyclopaedias, you're out of luck,' Amy said.

The man's laugh had an almost musical element to it.

'I'm not selling anything, my dear. I just popped around for a chat.' He lifted his hat again. 'I'm Reggie Tumbler. I wonder if I could have a word with you?'

CHAPTER FORTY-FIVE

Amy's mouth fell open, and she took a step back whilst still keeping hold of the door. As she tried to close it, she found that Reggie had pushed his foot inside the gap and she was unable to shut the man out.

'Please don't be alarmed, my dear,' Reggie said.

'MUM!' Amy shouted, looking over her shoulder.

Reggie chuckled. 'If you mean an attractive lady in her mid-forties wearing a navy coat and carrying a wicker shopping bag, then she caught the bus a while ago.'

'What do you want? My boyfriend is a policeman. He'll be here for lunch. I'm waiting for him.'

'Ah, the redoubtable Inspector Bodkin. He's in Gillingham, I'm afraid.' He took in Amy's puzzled look, then continued. 'I rang the police station and asked to speak to him. They told me where he was.' Tumbler took his foot away from the doorframe. 'Shut me out if you must. I only wanted a chat. Nothing else. You have my word. I mean you no harm.'

Amy pulled the door open fully. 'How do you know who I am? How did you know I'd be at home? And why did you want to make sure that Bodkin is out of the way?' she asked.

'So many questions. I'm happy to answer them all and any others you might have.' He looked around. 'But not on your doorstep. Your next door neighbour saw me walk up the path. I'm sure she could overhear if she opened her window.'

'You're not coming inside,' Amy said.

'Fair enough. I can understand why you would be reluctant to invite me in.' Reggie smiled what seemed to Amy to be a genuinely warm smile. He half turned and pointed to the dark green Rover that was parked across the street. 'We could sit in the car while we chat.'

'I'm not getting in your car,' she said firmly.

'After what happened at the weekend, I can understand why you would be reluctant to do that too, my dear.' He held out his hands towards her, palms up. 'I'm stumped then. I presume a walk is out of the question?'

Amy was about to suggest they go down to the farm where Alice and her workforce would be able to keep her safe, but she didn't want to put her in any danger. 'We can go to the Old Bull,' she said, pointing up the lane. 'Don't go into the bar, though. I'll meet you in the snug. It will be empty at this time of day.'

'That sounds perfect,' Reggie said. 'I can promise you will be interested in what I have to say.'

'Why can't you say it in front of Inspector Bodkin?'

'Because he's a policeman and I'm a... how shall I put it...?'

'A gangster?' Amy suggested.

'Some might use that term,' Reggie replied. 'But I'm not the violent sort.' He lifted his hat again. 'Five minutes then?'

'All right,' Amy said. 'I'll just get my pinny off and grab my coat.'

. . .

Amy was sorely tempted to nip into the telephone box and make a quick call to the police station, but as she reached it, she saw that Reggie was waiting for her in the open doorway of the pub. Anyway, she was curious as to why he had come to see her. So, taking a deep breath, she crossed the road and followed him into the snug.

'What can I get you, my dear?' Reggie asked as he ordered a glass of tonic water and ice. On hearing that there was no ice available, he changed his mind and asked for a glass of ginger beer instead.

'I'll have the same, please,' Amy said. She wiggled her fingers towards Stan behind the bar.

'Hello, Amy,' he said. 'You're getting to be quite a lunchtime regular.'

Amy smiled at Stan as she took her drink, then led Reggie across the room to the stools surrounding a small round table near the unlit coal fire.

After waiting for Amy to sit, Reggie took his hat off, placed it on the table, then sat down himself. 'Chin chin,' he said, lifting his drink to toast Amy.

Amy clinked her glass against his before taking a sip. She found herself feeling much less concerned about the soft-spoken, extremely polite gangster.

'The reports I have been given about you don't do you anything like justice,' Tumbler said, treating her to a smile that reached his grey eyes.

Amy felt herself blush, and she looked down at her drink. 'You don't have to flatter me, Mr Tumbler. You have my earnest attention. Why did you come all this way to see me?'

'It's the truth, my dear. I wouldn't insult your obvious intelligence by trying to flatter you.' He took a sip of his drink, nodded his head in appreciation, then put the glass on the table. 'I've heard about how you've helped the police solve a few tricky murder cases, and I'm more than a little impressed.' Reggie smoothed his silvery white hair back with his hand. 'Firstly, I'd just like to let you know that I had absolutely nothing to do with that dreadful incident on Sunday. Nor was I involved in the atrocious episode involving Bessie Dagger.'

'She's convinced that one of your cars ran her off the road. It was a dark green Rover.'

Reggie pursed his lips. 'The car belongs to me. I'm not going to even try to deny it. The Rover was stolen from outside one of my warehouses. It was found later the same day outside a bookmaker on Percy Street in Gillingham. There was extensive damage to the bodywork. It was a pathetic attempt to point the police in my direction.'

Amy straightened up on her stool. 'Can we take a step back? You still haven't told me how you found me. Did Erma Firth sell you the information?'

'Erma? No. Why would you think that?'

'Because she sold it to Bessie Dagger. Amongst other information about her brother's murder case.'

'That sounds about right, but I didn't need to ask for her assistance. It wasn't a complicated task. I have my own sources.'

'You mean inside the police force?'

'I'm not going to go into that, Miss Rowlings.'

Amy narrowed her eyes as she looked across the small table at him. 'Did you ring my ARIA investigations number?'

'I did, but again, I'm not telling you where that information came from.'

'I still don't get how you found my house from that. There isn't an address on the card and you didn't ask Alice for it.'

'Your friend answered the phone by saying "Mollison Farm". It was easy to find on a map. I saw it was on Long Lane. That matched the other snippet of information I was given.'

'It's called Long Lane for a reason,' Amy said. 'It's long. How did you find my house? That information isn't kept with my accreditation file at the police station.' She paused. 'I'm assuming that's where you got my details.'

'I had no idea which house you lived in, but there aren't many cottages in the lane. I merely pulled up outside Holly Cottage, the house on the corner, knocked on the door and asked.' He reached for his drink. 'Mrs Albrighton was very accommodating. She didn't even ask why I wanted to know where you lived. She even pointed your mother out to me as she walked by.'

'You still haven't explained why you want to talk to me without Inspector Bodkin being present. Surely if you want to pass on some information, he'd be the person to talk to.'

'As I said. He's with the police. I can't be seen dealing with them. It's not good for my credibility and anyway, he'd more than likely want to arrest or at least question me over the Bessie Dagger incident. And if I was taken into custody and the police suddenly began to look into the people responsible for what I really came here to talk about, the fraternity I live amongst would soon put two and two together to make eighty-six.'

'All right,' Amy said. 'Can we go back to where we were? You were saying something about my abduction and Bessie Dagger's crash.'

'I think you'll find that the Firths were responsible for both incidents.'

'The Firths? They were top of our list for the kidnap attempt. Bessie Dagger denied any knowledge of it. She insisted you were involved in forcing her off the road, causing the death of Ellis Hawke, though.'

'Bessie wasn't in a position to set up something like that and she would have had no need to, anyway. You're not a threat to her or her organisation. Such as it is now.' He leaned forward and lowered his voice. 'There's a lot of infighting going on.'

'We went to see her yesterday afternoon. She was about to be moved to a hospital in Gillingham, so she's hoping to take full control again.'

'The Firths are trying to muscle in on some of her business,' Reggie said. 'But they won't get much of a foothold. Lonnie was the brains of the operation, and of course, he's not around anymore. Brian isn't half the man Lonnie was. He has neither the brains nor the strength of character.'

'You liked Lonnie at one time, didn't you?' Amy said.

'Liked? I'm not sure I actually liked the man. He was a thug, but he was useful to me and he had a lot of contacts outside of the area. Especially in London, Nottingham and Birmingham.'

'Were you sorry when he died?'

'I don't like the thought of anyone dying, my dear. It's not the way I do things.'

'So, you've never had to have anyone—'

'I've never killed anyone, despite the rumours,' Reggie said. He held up his hand as Amy began to speak, then went on. 'Things have been done by people in my organisation on several occasions but I have never given a direct order to kill someone.'

'We heard that Lonnie had stolen from you. Is that correct?'

'Do you honestly think I'd allow him to use my Spinton apartment if he'd stolen from me? Do you really think that's where he'd hide out if he knew I was looking for him?' He smiled at Amy. 'No, he didn't steal from me. He knew he'd be finished if he did. He stole from the Daggers a few times and he stole from gangs in both Nottingham and Birmingham. I had to step in to smooth the waters between the Firths and the Daggers. It cost me a bit, but on balance I figured it was worth it.'

'He had a lot of money stashed away in the flat. Was it yours?'

Reggie let out a short laugh. 'I really couldn't comment.'

'Everyone in the underworld knows it's your money, Mr Tumbler, and everyone knows the Firths have it because they're desperately trying to get the five-pound notes changed into currency they can spend.' Amy paused as she thought, then went on. 'Apart from the fact that it's hard to cash in bundles of five-pound notes anywhere, the word is that the money came from a warehouse raid in London, so the banknote serial numbers may have been logged.'

Reggie was quiet for a moment. 'Miss Rowlings. The money did not come from any warehouse raid. The money came legitimately from various businesses. Any money that may or may not have been in my Spinton flat had been issued from my bank. Those numbers can be traced too.'

'Two thousand pounds is a lot of money to leave in the hands of someone like Lonnie Firth, Mr Tumbler. It was a big risk. He handed some of it to Mervin Challenger, did you know that?'

'Lonnie was about to take a trip to Glasgow. I had an arrangement with some business associates up there. The money was part of an upcoming deal and no,' he smiled, 'I'm not going into detail about it.'

'We've been told that Challenger was handed some of that money to buy him off. The word is that you had asked Mervin to kill Lonnie.'

Reggie shook his head sadly. 'None of that is true. At least the contract killing part. Lonnie may well have handed money over for other reasons. I know he was in possession of a few hundred pounds. He stole it from the Daggers.'

'Yes, but they were smaller denomination notes. Mervin was waving fivers about on the night Lonnie was killed.'

'They could easily have come from his last raid on the Nottingham gangs. He held up one of their money changing operations. Washing dirty money, they call it. A criminal hands in currency that might be traced and is given clean money taken from a legitimate source. It's what Brian is trying to do now, but on a far larger scale. Lonnie would almost certainly have found himself with a good few five-pound notes after that raid.' Reggie emptied his glass in two gulps. 'As for me putting out a contract hit on Lonnie. That's ludicrous. The Glasgow people were expecting him at the weekend.'

A puzzled look came over Amy's face. 'I still don't understand why you wanted to speak to me instead of Bodkin. What are you getting out of this?'

'I want the police off my back. My businesses are being disrupted and I don't see why they should be when I've done nothing to deserve it. There is also the fact that I am really sorry about what happened to you and I want to see someone pay for what they've done.' Reggie picked up his glass, then, after realising it was empty, he put it down again. 'I don't hurt women, Miss Rowlings. I respect them and I won't have them used or abused. Unlike most criminal organisations, I don't run a prostitution ring and I don't deal in illegal drugs. I don't know how much you know about me, but I had a very troubled upbringing. My mother and sister were treated abominably by my father.' A flash of pain shot across Reggie's face. 'He didn't deserve the title "father". That implies someone who cares about his family. He only ever used his for financial gain no matter what the cost to them. When I was old enough and strong enough, I did something about the situation and I've looked after both of them ever since. They want for nothing and never will.'

'I have heard that you care for your mother and sister,' Amy said.

'I idolise them, my mother especially. They are my world, Miss Rowlings.' He picked up his glass and put it down again, then, nodding towards Amy's drink, he said, 'do you think you could tip a bit of that into my glass? I was really enjoying it.'

Amy reached for her bag. 'I'll buy you another if you like?'

'Thank you, but no, my dear.' He patted his stomach. 'I suffer terribly with... Well, let's not bring that up. Let's just say the fizz from the ginger beer doesn't aid my digestion, much as I love the stuff.'

Under Reggie's direction, Amy tipped a little of her soft drink into his glass. After taking a sip, he continued to speak.

'As I said before, Miss Rowlings, I have the utmost respect for women. Especially strong women, women who will fight back against the injustices of life, and there are many of them.'

'What about Bessie Dagger?'

'Bessie is a rival and a big one, but I have a lot of respect for what she does. Not many women could do what she's done given the circumstances. She's at the top of her organisation for a reason, and it's not just because she's her father's daughter. She's tough, she's intelligent, she's the equal of any man. I just wonder how she'll take it when her father gets out of prison. It isn't going to be easy for her to let go of the reins.'

'And Birdie Lark?'

'Pffft,' Reggie almost choked on his ginger beer. 'She's a foul-mouthed harridan who only thinks of Birdie Lark. Having said that, you have to give her due respect, too. The Firth organisation is pretty much finished although none of them will admit it. Brian is a waste of clean air. He's as thick as two short planks and he'd run a mile if someone popped a paper bag within earshot. She's the one running things now. She makes all the decisions. She uses Brian to pass on her commands because, unlike the Dagger gang, no one in the Firths, Brian, apart, will take orders from a woman. She's trying desperately to keep what's left of their gang together until she can get this money cashed out. Then I believe they'll try to get to America.'

'Erma will want her share of that money,' Amy said. 'Then of course there's Hetty. I can't see her standing back while Birdie hops onto a ship with a trunk full of pound notes.'

'I don't intend to let any of them have a share of the money. It's still going up to Glasgow if I have anything to say about it. As for Hetty. She's not the brightest star in the cosmos, but she's crafty and devious. I don't begrudge her an easier life. She's a mother, after all and she had it almost as tough as my own mum for a long time.'

Amy smiled. 'You do have a lot of time for women, don't you? Especially if you think Hetty is a good mother.'

'I didn't say she was a good mother, but she is a mother and that fact, on its own, deserves a lot of respect.'

Amy laughed. 'I bet you even campaigned for women to get the vote.'

Reggie shrugged. 'Of course I did.' He smiled at some old memory. 'I met Mrs Pankhurst once, you know? It was at a rally in Maidstone. I was utterly under her spell, so much so that when she spoke to me, I found myself dumbstruck.'

Reggie looked at his watch and finished the last dregs of the ginger beer. 'I really do have to be going soon. I've got a meeting this afternoon.'

'You still haven't mentioned this important thing you had to tell me.'

'Oh, yes.' Reggie tapped his head with his knuckle. 'Old age is creeping up on me.' He leaned across the table towards her and lowered his voice. 'The thing is,' he said. 'There's going to be a meeting between the Firths and the Daggers. Mervin Challenger, on behalf of Bessie, has offered to buy the money from

Brian and Birdie. At knock down rates, according to my spy in the camp. A time and date hasn't been officially agreed yet, but it will definitely happen in the next day or two.'

'But why tell me about it? I still don't understand.'

'This has to be handled delicately, my dear. If the Gillingham police got hold of it, they are so full of leaks that half the residents of the town would know about it inside an hour and the time and place would be changed at the last minute. It's the same with the Spinton police. I had to give this information to someone who would use the knowledge wisely.' He leaned forward on his stool. 'I think you are the perfect choice, Miss Rowlings. You have the ear of Inspector Bodkin and from what I've heard, he's not the sort of man to try to profit himself from the information.' He paused. 'Now we get to the crux of the matter. I would like my money back. As I mentioned before, it is money made legitimately and was issued by my own bank. The way I see it, I can attend the meeting myself, mob handed, or I can do it quietly and trust the Inspector to do the right thing. If he turns up on the day with a small, trusted group of officers, he'll not only get the killer of Ellis Hawke but the man who organised your abduction as well. Add in a thousand pounds or so of Bessie Dagger's ill-gotten gains and it could be quite a coup for him.'

'I'll certainly ask Bodkin if anything can be done,' Amy said.

'Good,' Reggie replied, 'because it could end up in a bloodbath otherwise, and no one wants that.'

CHAPTER FORTY-SIX

'Before you go, Mr Tumbler, could I ask you something?'

'Ask away.'

'It's about the young man who died when he was mistaken for Lonnie. I believe he was killed by a London gang at an abandoned warehouse in Gillingham.'

'That's right. I don't know all the details, but I know the gist of it.'

'Who was he and why was he chosen to stand in for Lonnie?'

'Ah, your Inspector Bodkin is investigating that again, is he? He made a right mess of it last time... no, that's unfair. His boss made a right mess of it. I heard that Bodkin was made the scapegoat.'

'He was,' Amy replied, 'but even if he had been running the investigation, he couldn't have made a better job of it, not with Hetty Firth identifying her son's body so emphatically.'

'That's true. She put on a hell of a performance in the morgue and in the church.' He winked at Amy. 'I paid for that funeral you know?'

'I didn't know,' Amy said. 'Did you do it to make the police and the London gang believe that Lonnie really was dead? Or did you want to make sure the young man had a decent burial? Albeit under the wrong name. Is there a grave marker with Lonnie's name on it?'

'The cops might want to exhume him now,' Reggie said. 'At least Hetty won't have to fork out for another grave. They can just stick him in the old one.'

'I don't think that's very funny, Mr Tumbler,' Amy said. 'That young man might have a mother somewhere wondering where her son is. She'll probably be unaware that he's actually dead. Who's going to turn up at his funeral when he's buried again?'

Reggie held up his hands in surrender. 'I'm sorry, that wasn't very kind, was it? I apologise profusely. You're not right about his mother, though. I heard he was orphaned at a young age.'

'So you do know something about him? What else can you tell me? They called him Robin, didn't they? Do you know why he was chosen? He was sent to his death. Lonnie must have known that was a big possibility.'

'Of course he did, but he had no say in who was chosen. That was down to Brian. Lonnie was in hiding. He was a hundred miles away at the time Robin was told to turn up at the meeting with the London mob.'

'Why pick him, though? Did he resemble Lonnie?'

'He was a fair bit younger, but about the same build and had the same coloured hair. There was also the fact that he was an outsider who had only been working for the Firths for a few weeks. They assumed no one would miss him.'

'And no one did. It's such a shame.'

'I won't argue with that sentiment.'

'How did they explain his absence?'

'I believe they told everyone he'd decided to go home. As I said, he hadn't been with them for very long. Brian put it about that he had upped sticks and done a runner overnight. He even said he'd stolen a few quid from one of the bookies, to make it sound more plausible.'

'And no one asked any questions?'

'Why would they? It's the same in my organisation. We get a few blow ins, they stay for a month, maybe two, sometimes only a couple of weeks, then they move on. It's a very transient industry. People move around from one gang to another. They're always classed as outsiders.'

'And you don't know his name? He was just Robin Redbreast, the young man in the red jumper?'

'I don't know about him always wearing a red jumper,' Reggie said with a frown. 'He might have. Every newcomer gets a nickname, sometimes a funny one, sometimes an insulting one, so that could be how he came by it. I only ever saw him a few times, mind you. I'm sure his real name was Devon... Deakin, something like that.'

'Thank you for being so candid,' Amy said, getting to her feet at the same time as Reggie. 'I'll pass on everything you've told me to Inspector Bodkin.'

'That's the only deal on the table, Miss Rowlings,' Reggie said seriously. 'If he doesn't want to take me up on it, I'll attend the parley and sort it out myself. One way or another. I will get my money back.'

'How will we know when and where the... what did you just call it... parley is going to take place?'

'I'll ring the ARIA number,' Reggie said. He smiled at her. 'You, er, you don't happen to have a business card with you? It will save me having to keep a scrap of paper in my pocket. Scraps of paper are so easily lost.'

Amy opened her bag, pulled out one of her pink business cards and handed it to him.

'Pink? How very feminine,' he said. 'Feminine, but also very professional. I really like it.'

'HE DID WHAT!' Bodkin's face was a mask of anger.

'Calm down, Bodkin,' Amy said soothingly.

'CALM DOWN! You're asking me to calm down when I've just had the news that the biggest gangster in the southeast has turned up at my girlfriend's front door. I'll swing for the man.'

'Now you know what it feels like,' Amy said with a smile.

'What feels like?'

'Getting told to calm down. Women are told to calm down all the time. It's not very nice, is it?'

Bodkin's face didn't change. 'Reggie bloody Tumbler. I'm coming for you.'

She rested her hand on his arm. They were sitting in the Morris Oxford outside Amy's house. 'At least listen to the whole story before you go chasing after him like a madman on a mission.'

The inspector took a deep breath. 'You're right, I'm sorry, it's just that—'

'I know, I know, the biggest gangster in the southeast has turned up at your girlfriend's door.' She patted his arm. 'But he didn't make any threats. He said he was sorry for what had happened to me at the weekend, although he had no part in it. He also said he had nothing to do with the Bessie Dagger incident, and to be honest, Bodkin, I believe him.'

'You can't take the word of scum like that at face value, Amy.'

'I think I can. You weren't here, Bodkin. You'd have felt the same way as I do about him if you had been. I'm sure of it.' She leaned away from him and twisted in her seat. 'He was, dare I say it, quite charming. He wasn't what I expected at all.'

'He turned up at your front door, for pity's sake.'

'He did. And I was home all alone. If he had wanted to, he could have easily forced his way in. But he didn't. When I opened the door, he put his foot inside to stop me from slamming it in his face, but when he'd finished introducing himself, he stepped back and offered to go home without telling me why he'd made the journey. Does that sound like someone who meant to do me harm?'

'He was just being careful. He didn't want to attract attention.'

'No, but then he could just have forced me inside and done whatever he wanted. I was on my own. He knew I was uncomfortable, and he went out of his way to make me feel less frightened. We ended up drinking ginger beer in the Old Bull snug, for Pete's sake.'

'All right, but I don't get why he came to see you, when he could easily have dropped into the station or phoned to arrange a meeting.'

'Where you would probably have arrested him on suspicion of murder or of some gang related crime.'

'Probably doesn't come close,' Bodkin said.

'There you go, then. He was right. This way he gets his message across without risking arrest.'

'Okay, what did he want to see you about?' the policeman said, calmer now.

'Not here,' Amy said, flicking her head towards the neighbour's cottage. 'Mrs Dormouse is taking a real interest in us. She'll start to wonder what we're up to if the windows steam up.'

Bodkin laughed; all the tension was gone. 'The Old Bull or my place?'

'Let's go to the Old Bull,' Amy said. 'Give me a minute to get my bag and coat.'

The snug was quiet, with only three other couples dotted around the room. Amy walked over to the window bench seats, took off her coat and laid it on the dark wooden seat at the side of her. Bodkin joined her a few minutes later and placed a port and lemon on the table. He took a sip from his beer and held onto it as he sat down.

'So, Reggie Tumbler, tell me about him, Amy. What's he like?'

Amy stared into space as she thought for a few moments.

'He's a soft-spoken man. If you were sitting across the table from him and you didn't know, you certainly wouldn't guess what he does for a living. As I said before, Bodkin, he's quite charming, really. When he smiles, it reaches his eyes. He has a lot of respect for women. He made that abundantly clear. He looks after his mum and sister. They want for nothing. He told me he adores them.'

'So, he's a mummy's boy. There're a lot of them about. Many of them are right nasty toerags. This particular toerag is probably the worst of the lot. He's suspected of everything from GBH to murder.'

'He assured me he's never killed anyone or given the order to kill anyone. He says he is aware of his reputation, but the vast majority of it is rumour and conjecture.'

'Hmm, he certainly cast a spell over you,' Bodkin said, then he grinned. 'I'm only joking. I'm well aware that you can read people like a book.'

Amy gave him a look, which softened as she smiled. 'He is a ladies' man, even though he doesn't have a lady of his own.' She picked up her drink. 'He met Emily Pankhurst, you know?'

'Did he work his magic on her?'

'No, he was so overawed he couldn't speak.'

'So, what sort of man is he? You're good at reading behind the face. Would you say that Reggie Tumbler has a glass half full personality?' Bodkin looked down at his pint as he smirked.

'Oh very good,' Amy said, laughing. 'Was that spur of the moment or have you been holding that one back until you found a use for it?'

'Spur of the moment. I was going to say, Tumbler's no mug, is he? But that other joke seemed better.'

Amy put the palm of her left hand on her forehead as she shook her head. 'Oh, deary me.'

Bodkin looked triumphant as he winked at her. 'Up here for thinking, down there for dancing.' He pointed a finger at his head.

'I still have no idea what that means,' Amy said. 'Now, enough of the frivolity. Do you want to hear what Reggie had to say or not?'

'I'm all ears,' Bodkin said. His earlier bad mood had evaporated, and he was eager to learn what had happened earlier in the day.

'So, what do you think?' Amy asked when she had repeated her conversation, almost word for word, to Bodkin.

'On the face of it? It's plausible. You can see why he would want us to pick them up. He'd be killing three birds with one stone. He'd be ridding himself of the competition from two rival gangs and he'd be getting his money back.' He was silent for a few moments. 'That money is earmarked. He won't want to annoy his Glasgow friends. The gangs up there make ours look like amateurs.'

'Do you believe his story about the origins of the money?'

'I think so. It can easily be checked once we have hold of it, so he knows he can't pull the wool over our eyes.'

'I agree,' Amy replied. 'He'd come out of this looking like the big winner.'

'And the alternative is what he accurately described as a bloodbath, and it wouldn't just stop at bodies on the floor of a warehouse. Something like that could drag on for years.'

'So, are you thinking of taking him up on his offer?' Amy asked.

'I'm considering it,' Bodkin said, reaching for his beer. 'I'd have to run it past Grayson first, mind you.'

'Who are we going to be dealing with here, though, Bodkin? Who set this up? That's what I'm wondering now. If we take Bessie at her word, she hasn't even spoken with her gang members while she's been in hospital, and she only got back to Gillingham yesterday. As far as I can see, this cash exchange has been mooted for a while. They've obviously been talking behind Bessie's back.'

'Good point. Birdie and Brian are on one side of the equation, that's for certain. Who they're negotiating with is the question. My money is on Challenger. He'll have access to Bessie's business profits while she's out of action. I just wonder who else is involved. He's not stupid enough to go to the parley on his own. He'll want backup... Unless, of course, that's been arranged too, to take the jeopardy out of it. Birdie and Brian on one side, Mervin and... he blew out his cheeks... and A N Other on the other side. That would be more sensible. Things like this can easily get out of hand if you have a mob on either side of the halfway line.'

'Or Reggie waits outside, then goes in when it's all done and dusted to pick up the spoils and mop up the last men or women standing.'

'That's my big concern, and he obviously knew it would be,'

Bodkin said. 'He has a blackmail threat hanging over us. He's not all sweetness and light.'

'He did let his mask slip once. He made a nasty joke about Lonnie not needing to have another grave dug as there's already a marked one waiting for him. They just have to evict the sitting tenant.'

Bodkin finished his pint and waved his glass at Amy. 'Yes, please,' she said.

When he returned with the drinks, Amy asked the question that had come to mind while he had been at the bar. 'Have you got any missing persons from three years ago with the surname Devon or Deakin?'

'The names don't ring a bell. Why do you ask?'

'It was something Reggie said when I asked him about Robin. You know, the nickname of the young man who was murdered in Lonnie's place? Reggie said he was pretty sure that one, or the other, was his real name.'

'I'll look into it tomorrow, Amy. Well done you. We're finally getting somewhere in the original murder case. I'd love to hand that one back to Chief Inspector Laws all wrapped up with a ribbon tied around it.'

'Tumbler said that Brian and Birdie put it around that he'd had enough and gone back home, wherever that was. He said that much of the casual work is done by what he called blow ins. They come and go, with new faces arriving all the time. This Devon or Deakin was only on the Firths' books for about three or four weeks. That's why he was chosen. He hadn't been there long enough for anyone to miss him.'

Bodkin rubbed the stubble on his chin as he thought. 'That all makes complete sense. We were convinced that the body in the warehouse was Lonnie, so no one looked for anyone else. A missing minion wouldn't have been brought to our attention. Especially if any new friends he might have made were convinced that he had left the area and gone home.'

'What are you thinking now you've heard it all, Bodkin? Are you likely to back Reggie's plan? You could end up catching two murderers in one net.'

Bodkin lifted his glass and Amy chinked it with hers. 'To us,' he said. 'Let's crack this case wide open.'

CHAPTER
FORTY-SEVEN

The call came sooner than anyone expected. On Wednesday morning, Alice came rushing up the lane with a piece of paper in her hand on which she had hastily scrawled the time and location of the proposed meeting between the Firths and the Daggers. Amy took the foolscap sheet from Alice, gave her a big hug, then, after grabbing her coat and bag, she set off for the phone box.

'Spinton Police, Constable Wakelin speaking.'

'PC Wakelin. It's Amy Rowlings. Is Inspector Bodkin in the building...? He is...? Wonderful. Can you tell him I'm on my way and I have big news... Yes, I'll be there in fifteen minutes.'

She found Bodkin waiting in the reception area. After taking the sheet of paper from her, he scanned it quickly, then led her through the door into the police station proper. After leading her down a long corridor, lined with sepia photographs of long dead policemen, he stopped and knocked on a door with a sign on it that read, Chief Superintendent Grayson.

Grayson got up as Amy walked into the room. 'Hello again, my dear. I hope you are well after your recent experiences.'

'I'm as good as I ever was, thank you,' Amy said, taking the proffered chair on the opposite side of the desk to the policeman.

'Amy has just given me the place and time for the proposed money exchange, sir.' Bodkin handed the note to his boss, who opened his desk drawer and pulled out a map of Gillingham.

Spreading it over the desk, he ran his finger along the edge of the River Medway until he found the road that he was looking for. 'It looks like there's more than one way in to this industrial complex. That's good news. We should be able to surprise them during the handover.' He looked up as Bodkin lowered his head over the map. 'Tumbler was as good as his word, then, Inspector?'

'It seems so, Sir, though I won't fully trust him until I have the Firth and Dagger gang members in the back of a police van.'

Grayson cleared his throat. 'Unfortunately, I've had to share our news with my equivalent rank down in Gillingham.' On seeing Bodkin's anguished face, he shook his head sadly. 'It's protocol, Bodkin. It's their patch, you know how it is. How would you like it if a team of Gillingham officers planned a job in Spinton without informing you?'

'That's not the real problem, sir. You know as well as I do that the Gillingham stations are riddled with informants. They'd sell their own grannies for half a crown.'

'I've asked Chief Superintendent Marlowe to keep this on a need-to-know basis. They'll only use officers they can trust to surround the warehouse.'

'Do you mean we aren't even going to be the ones to make the arrests?' Bodkin's eyes opened wide. 'We're handing over the operation to them?'

'Not the entire operation, Bodkin. I did my very best for you on this, but I was overruled by Maidstone.'

Bodkin sighed. 'I understand, Sir,' he said, giving Amy a

rueful look. 'Who's going to be running the operation? Do we know what they have planned?'

'They have worked out a basic plan which they've used before in what was a hostage situation. They'll need this final piece of information before they can finalise the plans, though. Oh, the supervising officer is Chief Inspector Odbone, by the way.'

'He's a good chap,' Bodkin said, with a note of relief in his voice. 'Who's assisting him?'

'Inspector Blunden.'

Bodkin's face dropped.

'Do you have a problem with Blunden, Inspector?'

'He's... oh, there's no pleasant way of saying this. He's a drunk, Sir, an alcoholic. He'd hand his best pair of boots over the bar for a double shot of Johnny Walker.'

'I'm sure he's not as bad as you paint him.'

'He's every bit as bad, sir. His nickname is Blundering Blunden. I worked under him for a time. We'd have to drag him out of the Nag's Head if we were running a raid on one of Tumbler's bookies. He'd be in no state to lead. Many an operation was called off because of him. There was one occasion when—'

'All right, Bodkin, I get the idea, but it's not up to us who they choose to lead the raid, is it?'

'No, sir.'

'No, sir, is the correct answer.' Grayson smiled across the desk towards Amy. 'I'm sorry, my dear. Things can get a little heated in here at times.'

'Don't mind me,' Amy said with a grin. 'I was enjoying it.'

'Well done, my dear. Don't let the boy's club members upset you.' Grayson turned his attention to Bodkin. 'So it's going to be down by the docks at six this evening. It seems a strange time to hold such a meeting, don't you think?'

'Not really, Sir. It makes a lot of sense. The dock workers

clock off at six. The place will be heaving with people, they'll be able to lose themselves in the crowd if they have to.'

'The plan does show a modicum of sense, I suppose. Have you finalised your team?'

'Are we still going to be involved? Won't Chief Inspector Odball... Odbone, resent us being there?'

Grayson wagged his finger at his inspector. 'Now, now, Bodkin.'

'It was a genuine slip of the tongue, sir. It was his nickname amongst the uniformed officers. He knew about it.'

'Hmm, do I have a nickname, Bodkin?'

'I haven't heard it if you have, sir.'

'Amazing,' Grayson said. 'I thought we all had a nickname amongst the ranks.'

Amy held back a laugh as the words Amazing Grayson crept into her mind. She doubted she'd be able to sing the hymn in church in the future without smiling.

'Now, where were we?' Grayson frowned as he thought. 'Ah yes, I was asking if you have finalised your team.'

'I had, sir, but I had hand-picked it for the far larger operation. I had ten men, but I'll have to downsize that if we're not going to be playing such a big part.'

'You'll be there when they are arrested, Bodkin. I believe Chief Inspector Odba...bone would like you and your team to keep an eye on the participants as they make their way to the rendezvous. Your team will follow them to make sure they aren't playing games with us. The officers waiting at the warehouse will have a transceiver in the car so they can receive a message from the central base station that will be set up at Gillingham HQ.'

Bodkin's head dropped. 'So much for this much vaunted, need to know basis. Every officer in the station will know about it. You can't hide something like that, sir.'

Grayson pulled a packet of Navy Cut cigarettes from his pocket and lit one with the Ronson table lighter on his desk. Noticing Amy wafting the air in front of her with her hand, he apologised and opened a window. Standing next to it, he blew the smoke into the aperture. 'You don't seem to have a lot of faith in the Gillingham police, Bodkin.'

'I worked there up until a year or so ago, Sir. Information about cases was passed around like a bag of Dolly Mixtures. The station was as leaky as a colander and it hasn't changed since then. If the word has got around about the base radio station being set up, then the chances are that the Firths will get to hear that something big is being planned.'

'Well, then it's down to you to drive to the rescue, Bodkin. You'll be in the chasing pack of hounds. Follow them and report in to the base station if they appear to be deviating from their original plan.'

'Sir, with respect. That means, if I notice them take a wrong turn, I'll have to stop shadowing, find a police box or telephone kiosk and call in. The officer in charge will then relay my message on to the team. What will they do with that information? All it will tell them is that the Firths and Daggers aren't coming. And how will I manage to pick up the trail again? They could be on the other side of town by the time I come out of the phone box.'

'You're seeing problems that might not arise, Bodkin,' Grayson said. He took a long draw on his cigarette. 'I do see your point, though.'

Bodkin rubbed the stubble on his chin. 'Do we even know where the main protagonists are at any given moment?'

'Now, that is something the local force have been able to find out. This Challenger character has been staying in a room above one of the Dagger bookmakers, but sadly, neither Brian

Firth nor Dora Lark have been seen since you went to Gillingham to question them last week.'

'So, we're hoping that Challenger is running things in Bessie's absence? He's only been with them for five minutes. She's back in Gillingham now, albeit in a hospital bed. She might well choose one of her trusted lieutenants to do the handover, or if she doesn't like the plan she's had no involvement in creating, she might just cancel it altogether.'

'I don't think she'll do that,' Amy said. 'Oops, sorry to butt in.'

'We're happy to listen to your thoughts, Miss Rowlings,' Grayson said, stubbing out his cigarette on the outside windowsill.

'Well, as I see it, while she's been away, her business has been disrupted. She's bound to have lost money and she won't really know when things will get back to normal, so I'm not sure she'll be able to turn down a thousand pounds in profit.'

'A thousand? That amount would tempt anyone, but how do you know that's what she's paying?' Grayson thought for a few seconds. 'She's getting a real bargain if she's buying five-pound notes for two pounds ten shillings each?'

'Reggie Tumbler mentioned it. He said we'd be able to pick up Ellis Hawke's killer, my kidnapper and a thousand pounds' worth of Bessie Dagger's money.'

'Well remembered,' Bodkin said. 'And I think you're right, Amy. Who could turn down that much profit for a five-minute handover?'

'She must have an idea where she can offload almost four hundred five-pound notes,' Amy said thoughtfully. 'Mind you, we know they aren't from the London warehouse raid and the notes are legitimately issued, so she might not find it as difficult as it might have been. Reggie has a deal awaiting the notes in Glasgow. They don't seem to have a problem with such a large number of banknotes, so Bessie might be able to find a home for them somewhere.'

'Or Mervin might have contacts. He knows all the Midland gangs and they know how to turn over large amounts of cash,' Bodkin said.

'Do you know, it's so refreshing to have a different voice in this office.' Grayson beamed a smile at Amy. 'Right, Bodkin. It appears you will require a much smaller team of officers. Give me the list as soon as you have decided who you want to take with you.'

'I've been thinking about it as we have been talking, sir. As our roles have been changed, I'd like to have two pairs of officers in two cars. The second one is only really there as a backup in case the lead car breaks down. So, I'd like Constable Ferris from my CID team and I'd like Smedley and Wakelin from uniform.'

'What about me?' Amy asked. 'You're not leaving me behind, are you?'

Grayson gave Amy a caring look. 'I'm sorry, my dear, but this is all going to happen in Gillingham, not Spinton, and we have an agreement with your father to consider.'

'The agreement states that I'm not allowed to get involved in the questioning of gang members outside of Spinton,' Amy argued. 'I wouldn't be doing that, would I? I'd be merely tootling along in a car behind one of the suspects. I wouldn't be anywhere near them physically, let alone close up and personal.' She gave Grayson her best smile.

Bodkin scratched his head and laughed out loud. 'She's right, sir... as usual.'

CHAPTER FORTY-EIGHT

The two cars set off at three-thirty with Bodkin, Amy and Ferris in the Morris Oxford and the Smedley/Wakelin team in Bodkin's old Morris 8. The two uniformed officers were wearing overcoats over their uniforms to make them less conspicuous when they were parked up on the street.

Ferris still hadn't accepted that the Spinton force had been relegated to a support role in the operation. 'Mind you,' he said, 'at least Chief Inspector Laws isn't in charge at our end. Imagine him and Blundering Blunden running things. It would be utter chaos.'

'Now, now, Ferris,' Bodkin admonished him. 'You're on duty, so keep your personal opinions regarding our esteemed, much loved senior officer, to yourself.' He pulled out onto the opposite carriageway to overtake an army supply truck, then pulled back onto the left-hand side of the road and eased off the accelerator until Smedley had caught up. Then he gave Amy a sideways glance and winked. 'For your information, Ferris, the chief super has a similar view of his capabilities. The operation would have been all about him and the furtherance of his career, so he was sent down to Maidstone HQ to deliver a report of the utmost importance regarding future staffing levels. Paying particular regard to the recruitment of men over forty who will, in all probability, miss the call up.'

Bodkin put his foot harder on the pedal and made ground on another military vehicle. 'I think Grayson believes we can persuade men with previous experience to return to the force, thereby saving money on the cost of training schemes.'

'Good luck with that,' Ferris replied. 'They won't take a pay cut to rejoin the force. They can earn more driving a train these days.'

'True,' Bodkin replied. 'But I have a feeling the officers that remain after the call up will be paid a bit more than they are now. The government will have to keep the force's pay competitive with industry.'

'Hey, they might even let women join the CID,' Amy said.

'I wouldn't hold your breath, Amy,' Bodkin replied as he pointed out the sign revealing that Gillingham was a mere two miles away. 'They won't pay the same rates anyway, no matter how good they turn out to be at the job. There will still be that old-fashioned attitude of 'a woman's place is in the home,' and 'women working for pin money,' amongst the males in the force.'

'I know where I'd like to stick those pins,' Amy said, getting a laugh from both Bodkin and Ferris.

Bodkin pulled into a parking space behind a delivery van with the name Bran Bunsen Baker emblazoned on the side. From his vantage point, he could see the house where Challenger had been staying. A small, but steady stream of men, some in work clothes, others in suits, stepped in and out of the shabby front door to place their bets on the afternoon steeplechase race cards at Hexham and Pontefract. Smedley parked the Morris 8 a good ten yards further back, where he could keep an eye on the inspector's car.

Bodkin watched as two men wearing long, white aprons carried sacks of flour from the van to the baker's shop on the other side of the road. When they had emptied the vehicle, they closed the door of the shop, flicked the sign hanging on the door from closed to open, then disappeared from view. When he returned his eyes to the illegal bookmakers fifteen yards in front, he felt Amy tap him on the shoulder. As he twisted in his seat to face her, he saw her point out of the passenger side window and mouth the word 'chemist'.

At first puzzled, Bodkin eventually got the message and stuck up a thumb to Amy. Turning to look into the back seat, he gave Ferris his orders. 'Keep your eye on that grey Baby Austin, Ferris. Amy can't see it from her seat, and I need to get some aspirin. I can feel a headache coming on.' He opened the driver's door and checked the street before climbing out. When he reached the pavement, he looked back towards Amy, grinned and again stuck up his thumb. A few seconds later, he disappeared through the half glass front door of K. Phizwell Chemist.

Amy watched through the window as Bodkin perused the various posters and notices on the walls of the chemist while a woman at the counter served a lady holding a wriggling infant. When the customer stepped away from the counter and made her way to the door, Bodkin opened it for her, then walked slowly towards the front of the shop. Amy held a hand in front of her mouth to stifle a giggle at Bodkin's obvious embarrassment. After a quick conversation, the woman turned away and headed into the back of the shop. A man in his fifties, with wispy white hair sticking out at all angles, replaced her.

'He's out!' Ferris suddenly shouted. 'He's climbing into the car.'

Amy reached to press the horn but quickly withdrew her hand, thinking the sound might alert Challenger to their presence. Ferris slid across the rear seat and reached for the handle on the rear door, but Amy had opened the front door before he could reach it. 'See which way he goes at the junction, Ferris.'

She remained in her seat facing the shop so that Mervin couldn't get a good look at her as the Austin moved slowly past them. A few seconds later, Amy got out of the car, stepped quickly across the pavement, pushed open the door of the chemist's shop, and stepped inside. Bodkin was just slipping a brown paper bag into his inside jacket pocket.

'Hurry, Bodkin! We have to go now. We can't wait,' she shouted.

As Bodkin hurried towards the door, Kenneth Phizwell grinned and held up both thumbs. 'Blimey,' he said. 'She's keen.'

Just as Bodkin reached the pavement, the baker's van in front pulled away, giving the policeman an unrestricted view of the bottom on the street. There was no sign of the Austin. 'Which way, Ferris?' he asked as he leapt into the driver's seat.

'Smedley's on him, sir,' Ferris replied. 'They turned left at the T junction.'

Bodkin started the engine and pulled away from the kerb. Trying to call up a mental map of the area, he drove to the bottom of the street and turned left onto Parr Avenue, which ran for half a mile in a straight line through the town. Looking ahead, he could see Smedley's Morris about a hundred yards in front. As he followed, the car turned left onto Rosebery Road, which would take them towards the docks area.

'They're on course,' Bodkin muttered to himself. 'I hope Blundering Blundell doesn't mess this up.'

Part way along Rosebery Road, a frustrated Bodkin saw the Morris 8 veer to the side of the road. As he pulled alongside, Amy wound down her window and Bodkin leaned across to shout to Smedley.

'What happened?'

'We lost them, sir. They overtook a bus. They must've turned off without us seeing which way they went.'

Cursing, Bodkin pulled away. Then, after braking hard, he performed a quick, but ugly three-point turn, causing the cars behind him to brake heavily. Pushing the accelerator pedal hard with the wheels squealing, he straightened up and drove back the way he had come until he reached a right-hand turn leading him onto Lincoln Road where he pulled up quickly as he spotted the back of Challenger's Austin parked on the corner of Hamilton Road. Easing past the car, he turned his head to look inside, then pulled up to the kerb another twenty yards further on. Twisting in his seat, he looked back along Hamilton to see Challenger walking down the narrow path from the house on the corner, with both Hetty and Erma Firth following behind.

After they had climbed into the Austin, Mervin reversed onto Lincoln Road, then took the left-hand turn to go back onto Rosebery. Bodkin waited until he had turned off Hamilton before driving the Morris across the road and up onto the verge opposite. From that position he turned hard on the wheel, then pulling back onto the road he shot out across Lincoln and, with his back wheels spinning, turned onto Rosebery, where he saw Mervin's Austin about fifty yards ahead.

'He's heading away from the dock area,' Bodkin said. 'Either we've got this completely wrong and Merve the Swerve is taking the ladies for a day out, or they know the plan has been compromised and they've changed the venue.' He hit the dashboard hard with the palm of his hand as an army truck pulled out of a side road in front of him only a few yards before a main junction. When they reached the crossroads, the lorry driver stalled the engine, and it took him a full minute to get it going again. Bodkin pulled hard right on the steering wheel, but there was too much traffic coming the other way for him to be able to overtake the static vehicle. Eventually, the lorry turned right and Bodkin eased forwards looking around frantically, but there was no sign of Challenger.

'Damn and blast it!' Bodkin cursed. 'What the hell do we do now?'

'We need to think about this,' Amy said, as Bodkin crossed the junction and pulled up at the side of the road some thirty yards on. 'Who else but Mervin would be representing Bessie at this meeting? If he isn't, why would he be taking Hetty and Erma for a day trip… shopping trip, whatever?' She paused for a few moments. 'We have to look at this from a different angle. If Brian, Birdie and co are sticking to the plan and meeting Bessie's representatives at the original location, then the Gillingham police will pretty much have them by now and it will be a waste of time tootling off up there. We might as well drive across to the main police station to see how it all went. We really can't influence proceedings.' She wafted away a stray strand of hair from her face. 'However, if Mervin has been asked to step in, we need to find him quickly. I still think he is the man we should be chasing. I'm not sure what he's doing with Hetty and Erma, but knowing those two, they could have struck a deal with Challenger. They know Brian and Birdie better than anyone. Perhaps they're all in this together and taking the opportunity to steal Bessie's money. One way or another, they'll have to meet up with Brian and Birdie somewhere and it won't be in a public place.'

'There's a lot of sense in that, Amy. We really don't have a choice now. Our only option is Challenger. We just have to hope he'll lead us to Brian, Bridie and hopefully the man who abducted you.' The inspector threw up his arms in frustration. 'But where do we look?'

'I think I know,' Amy said.

CHAPTER FORTY-NINE

'What are you thinking?' Bodkin asked eagerly.

'When I was being abducted, Paul mentioned a place he called 'the warehouse' as though it was a location well known to them and a place they were very familiar with.' She furrowed her brow as she concentrated. 'Bodkin, was the abandoned warehouse where you found what you thought was Lonnie Firth's body, over by the docks?'

'No, it's in an industrial area down by the railway stat... BRICKFIELDS!' he yelled and pulled out away from the kerb, causing a passing car to swerve violently onto the other side of the road. 'Of course it will be Brickfields... Amy, you are a genius.'

Driving well above the thirty miles per hour speed limit that covered the built-up areas in towns and cities, Bodkin made his way through the backstreets until he came to New Road, then, after swinging right onto Brickyard Lane, he slowed and pulled up at the entrance to a brickworks. Peering through the windscreen towards the abandoned warehouse next door, and spotting the Austin sitting alongside a black Ford, he clenched his fist and muttered, 'Got you.'

'Well done, Bodkin,' Amy said excitedly. 'What do we do now? Do we wait until they come out? That seems easiest.'

'Not likely,' Bodkin replied. 'I want to catch them in the act. We've got a chance of clearing this up ourselves. Gillingham will get all the credit if we just sit here and wait for them to turn up.'

He grinned, but his face was set hard as flint.

'Ferris. You're with me. Amy,' he took a quick look at her before throwing the door open. 'Stay here.'

'But...' Amy sighed as the policemen quietly closed the car doors and, in crouched positions, made their way across the rubble strewn frontage towards a broken door which allowed a flickering light to pass through.

Her patience lasted a full three minutes from the moment Bodkin and Ferris's shadows disappeared into the building. Climbing out of the car, she tilted her head towards the warehouse, but being unable to pick up any sounds, she slowly followed in Bodkin's tracks and walked carefully in the rapidly deepening twilight towards the one-storey wreck of a building.

The warehouse looked like it hadn't been in use for years. Part of the roof had collapsed and the six pane casement windows on the left-hand side were all broken or cracked. When she saw a long shadow appear in the broken doorframe, she hurried along the side of the building, almost tripping over a mangled half sheet of corrugated iron that had fallen from the roof. Gritting her teeth to hold in an ouch, Amy crouched and crept to the first in the row of broken windows. The light flickered from inside as she raised her head to peer into the building.

She gasped as she saw the backs of the heads of Mervin Challenger and Hetty Firth only a few feet in front of her. She craned her neck to look to the side, but there was no sign of Erma. Lighting up the corner of the warehouse were six kerosene fuelled metal box style hurricane lamps, the light pouring through their port hole glass windows. Standing opposite Mervin and Hetty were Birdie Lark and a man who Amy assumed to be Brian Firth. There was a battered-looking suitcase on the floor in front of him. To his right, kneeling amongst the broken bricks and pools of filthy water, were Bodkin and Ferris. Standing behind them was a man Amy recognised instantly as Paul Leyton. He was holding a gun.

Trying desperately to think of a way she could help the policemen, Amy wracked her brains trying to remember if they had passed a telephone kiosk on the way along Brickyard Lane but she had been far too engrossed in the chase to notice if there had been. Looking on the floor for anything she could use as a weapon, she picked up a six-inch length of lead pipe and weighed it in her hand.

'Mine's bigger than yours,' a woman's voice came out of the gloom. 'And what's more, I've used this one before.'

Amy spun around to see the figure of Erma Firth standing only four feet away from her. She held a foot long piece of metal tubing in her right hand as she slapped it into the palm of her left. 'It's packed with sand,' she said. 'So, I wouldn't try anything.'

Amy dropped the lump of lead and held up her hands like she had seen outlaws do in the movies when confronted by a gun toting sheriff.

Erma took two steps back and flicked her head towards the warehouse. 'After you,' she said.

'If you harm a hair on her head, you'll pay for it ten times over,'

Bodkin snapped as Erma pushed Amy into the dilapidated warehouse.

Paul snorted. 'I don't think you're in any position to make threats, copper.'

'Over there.' Erma gave Amy another shove and pushed her towards the small crowd of money changers.

'On your knees with the cops,' Paul ordered.

'You can't make her do that. She'll ruin that lovely dress,' Erma said in a childish voice.

'Down.'

Amy duly obliged and winced as she knelt on a lump of broken brick.

'You won't get away with this,' Bodkin said after mouthing, 'we'll be fine,' to Amy.

'I think you'll find we've already got away with this,' Challenger said with a sarcastic laugh. 'Half the Gillingham police are at this moment surrounding an empty building up at the docks. The rest are either off duty or sitting in the canteen waiting for their hero mates to bring us in.'

'Enough of the banter. Let's get on with the trade,' Brian said, kicking the suitcase holding Reggie Tumbler's money.

Mervin looked down at the canvas bag sitting at his feet. 'There's a grand in pound notes in there, me duck, courtesy of Bessie Dagger.' He laughed again. 'Not that she knows anything about it.' He looked suspiciously at Brian. 'How much is in there... the full two thousand?'

'We managed to offload forty-five quid's worth, so there's one thousand nine hundred and fifty-five pounds of Reggie's hard earned fivers in the case. I counted it before I came out, just to make sure the missus hadn't used any to top up her whisky stash.' He looked at Birdie and grinned. Birdie gave him a sour look in return.

'Hetty, count it,' Challenger said, giving her a push.

Hetty took a few steps forward and reached for the case, giving Brian a wink as she bent down. Flicking open the catches, she lifted the lid, then began to rummage about in it. After only thirty seconds, she looked back at Mervin. 'It's all there, done up in one hundred pound bundles.'

'Count it out onto the floor, where we can all see it,' Mervin commanded.

Hetty shot Brian a quick glance. Brian closed his eyes for a second as he sighed. 'Paul,' he said, 'put the gun on Robin Hood over there. Mum, grab that bag.'

Paul swung up his arm and pointed the pistol at Mervin. 'Sorry, me duck,' he said.

Hetty took four quick strides, grabbed hold of Mervin's canvass bag and carried it back to where Birdie was standing with her hand out.

'Give it to me,' she said.

Hetty passed over the bag, and Birdie tipped the contents onto the floor. She crouched down and, after a quick count; she stuffed the money back into the sack. 'It's all there,' she said. 'Now, Paul. Do what you're here to do.' She picked up the canvas bag, then reached to grab the handle of the suitcase.

'Hey! What's this?' Erma cried, taking a step towards Birdie. 'I thought we had a deal?'

'You know what thought did,' Birdie said, picking up the case. 'Come on, Brian, you never could stand the sight of blood.'

When Erma growled, it sounded like an animal who had just cornered its prey after a day-long hunt. She launched herself at Birdie and swung the home made cudgel at her head. Birdie held up the case to ward off the blow, but the blackjack slid across the handle and caught her on the wrist.

'Bitch,' she screamed as she dropped the case onto a small pile of rubble.

'Birdie!' Brian reached towards her as Erma lifted the club again.

Paul lowered his arm as he looked from Challenger to Erma. By the time he looked back, Mervin had his own gun pointed at him. 'Drop it,' he ordered.

Paul dropped the gun.

'Now, kick it over here,' Mervin said.

Paul kicked it towards the Nottingham man.

'Well done, me duck. Now on your knees with the cops.'

Erma and Birdie meanwhile were struggling together, Erma trying to keep hold of the cudgel and Birdie, fighting like a Dervish, trying to take it from her.

'Ladies,' Mervin said, 'is that any way to behave in public?' Erma suddenly stopped struggling and twisted around to face him. Birdie, seeing she had the advantage, clawed Erma across the neck and grabbed hold of the club.

'DROP IT!' Mervin yelled as Birdie lifted the cudgel above her head, ready to strike. He fired the gun into the air, the bullet flying harmlessly through the gap in the roof.

Birdie glared at him like a cornered rat, but did as she was told.

'That's better,' Mervin said. 'Now, let's all calm down. I'd add and have a nice cup of tea, but my flask is in the car.'

'What are you going to do now?' Brian asked nervously as he stood with his hands in the air.

'Do? To you?' Challenger shrugged. 'Nothing, I'm going to walk out of here with all this lovely money. I can have these fivers turned into pound notes at the drop of a hat back home. I might buy a house with it, maybe move abroad, get away from the bloody country before it asks me to fight for it.' He looked towards Erma. 'Did you remember the garden twine?'

Erma patted her pocket.

'Righto, get their hands tied.' He waved the gun towards Birdie. 'Start with her.'

Birdie flatly refused to turn around to have her hands tied. 'You'll just shoot us like a tethered cow in an abattoir,' she snarled.

'I might be many things but I'm not a murderer,' Mervin replied calmly. 'Now, turn around like a good girl and let Erma tie your hands.'

Erma produced a ball of twine and a penknife from her pocket.

'Why should we believe you? You say you're not a murderer, but you killed my brother,' Brian said, stuttering over the words.

'I repeat, I am not a killer. I did not kill your brother. I may have beaten him to within an inch of his life, but I didn't kill him.'

'Then who did?'

Mervin shrugged.

As Erma once again tried to tie Birdie's hands, she backed off and pointed at Mervin. 'You won't get away with this, Challenger. You'll get the same as the last stinking Nottingham scumbag who thought he could weasel his way into the family business.' She laughed manically. 'You just wait, me duck, you'll get what's coming.'

Challenger lowered his arm as he stared open mouthed at Birdie. 'What do you mean by that? Are you talking about Declan?'

'Of course,' Amy whispered to herself. 'Amy, you fool, it's been staring you in the face all the time.'

Bodkin looked sideways at her. 'What?' he asked.

'Declan didn't go home, did he Birdie?' Amy said aloud. 'Brian sent him to his death when he ordered him to meet the

London gang that night. He was murdered in this very building.'

Erma dropped the ball of twine and spun around to face Amy. 'What...? How do you... are you sure...?' She turned towards her brother. 'Is this true, Brian? Did you kill my Declan?'

'I didn't kill anyone... Look, Erma, someone had to go to that meeting and Lonnie wasn't here to make the decision so it was down to me. I figured, last in, first out. He did resemble Lonnie in some ways. We had to get the London mob off our backs.'

'You BASTARD!' Erma screamed and threw herself at Brian.

Challenger, meanwhile, had got his wits about him again. He lifted the gun and pointed it at Brian. 'Declan was my brother,' he said quietly. 'You killed him, so now you'll get what you deserve.'

'You all deserve a slow death... well, most of you at least,' said a voice from near the door. All heads looked across the room to see Reggie Tumbler and four other men, all pointing guns in different directions. 'I think you'd better put that thing down before you get hurt yourself, son.' He lifted his arm and pointed his gun at Mervin. 'Come on, I haven't got all night. Carefully now, we don't want it going off by accident.'

Mervin reached down and placed his pistol on the floor, then straightened and lifted his hands into the air.

'Right, Jimmy, grab the case. No, don't worry about the bag. Inspector Bodkin here can have that.' He made a *get up* motion towards Bodkin with his gun. Then he walked across to Amy and held out a hand, still pointing the gun at Challenger with the other.

Amy took it and he helped ease her up from the floor. As she got to her feet, she rubbed at her sore knees, then smoothed down her dress. 'I hope that stain comes out,' she said.

Reggie smiled fondly at her. 'If I were thirty years younger, I might think twice about staying a bachelor.' Turning his face away, he looked at Bodkin. 'Young Amy here assured me that you can be trusted, so I'm taking her word on that.' He nodded towards the guns lying at Mervin's feet. 'Pick those up, will you? You might find you need them after we've gone.'

Bodkin nodded towards Tumbler, then reached down and picked up both of the guns. Passing one to Ferris, he turned his own on Mervin. 'It's your turn, Mervin. On your knees.'

Ferris pointed his gun at Brian and ordered him to do likewise but before he could give the same command to Erma, she threw herself towards Birdie and picking up the cudgel lying at her feet; she swung it with all her might, bringing it crashing down on her rival's head. Birdie let out a slow groan and fell to the floor as Erma stood over her with angry tears rolling down her cheeks. 'You gave that order,' she hissed. 'Brian would have just gone along with it.'

'Young girls today,' Reggie tutted. He smiled at Amy as he backed off towards the door. 'Present company excepted, of course.' Turning towards Bodkin, he pushed his gun into the pocket of his coat. 'There's a phone box just down the road. I'll give the cavalry a ring, shall I?'

CHAPTER FIFTY

In the interview room at Spinton police station, Amy and Bodkin sat opposite Mervin Challenger and Erma Firth. Erma had just been charged with the attempted murder of Birdie Lark.

'Are we sitting comfortably?' Bodkin asked. When neither of the two replied, he went on. 'Good, then I'll begin. There are a few points I'd like to clear up before we complete the list of charges against you.' He held out his hand towards Amy. 'Miss Rowlings has a few things she'd like to add, too.'

Erma glared across the table. 'She can—'

Bodkin sighed. 'You're no longer in a position to make threats against Miss Rowlings.'

Erma's eyes swivelled towards Bodkin.

'Paul gave you up, Erma. He sang like a canary. He's admitted abducting Miss Rowlings, and he told us who ordered him to snatch her off the street.' He looked hard at the scowling woman. 'That would be you. He also admitted that along with Vincent Jury, they stole a Rover car belonging to Reggie Tumbler and forced another vehicle off the road, resulting in the death of Mr Ellis Hawke and causing serious injury to Miss Bessie Dagger.'

Erma spat on the floor and said nothing.

'You can clean that up before you go,' Bodkin said with a look of distaste on his face. He turned his attention to Mervin. 'Have you got anything to say before I charge you with the murder of Lonnie Firth?'

'Only that I didn't do it. He was alive when I finished hitting him.'

'On that subject. What did you hit him with? There were more than just fists involved to leave him in a state like that. His head looked like it had been run over by a steamroller.'

'It was mainly fists and the odd kick, but I hit him with my blackjack to subdue him initially.'

'The blackjack that Erma used on Birdie tonight?'

Mervin nodded. 'I had the gun. She asked me for the cudgel.'

'How did you know where Lonnie would be that night? Had you arranged to meet him at the Dragon?'

Mervin shrugged again and said nothing.

'Did you go there intending to kill Mr Firth?' Bodkin asked.

'I didn't kill anyone.' He sighed. 'Look, Inspector. Bessie Dagger had a few issues with Lonnie and she wanted him to be taught a lesson, so she asked me to hand it out.' He scratched his spikey scalp before continuing. 'I refused. While I didn't class Lonnie as a good friend, we had worked together a few times and I had plans to work with him again, so I wasn't about to give him a going over without a damn good reason.'

'And Bessie gave you that good reason, didn't she, Mervin?' Amy said. 'She told you that Lonnie had sent your brother to his death.' She gave Bodkin a quick glance. He nodded for her to carry on. 'The rest of the Firths knew that young man as Robin. Bessie told us it was because he always wore red jumpers, but it wasn't because of that. The reason they gave him that nickname was because of his Nottingham accent. Robin was short for Robin Hood.'

'He wore red jumpers too. He was a Nottingham Forest supporter,' Erma said.

'It didn't click at first,' Amy said, 'but when we were in the warehouse, all the pieces fell into place as I remembered the interviews with Bessie and Mervin, plus what Reggie Tumbler told me. You see, Bessie called Mervin Robin Hood because of his accent. Mervin has a lighter with the initials DC engraved on it. The initials stand for Declan Challenger. He said it was a gift, but it wasn't a gift to you, was it Mervin? It was a gift for your brother, *from* you.'

Mervin nodded slowly. 'I bought it for his birthday, but I never got the chance to give it to him as he left Nottingham in a hurry. I kept it myself because he never came home. When I heard he had disappeared, I got the Thompsons to ask where he'd gone. The Firth's told them he'd run off to London as he'd met a girl from there.'

'They told me he'd gone home to Nottingham, and he'd stolen money from the family so he couldn't come back,' Erma said bitterly. 'I believed them like a fool.'

Amy shook her head sadly. 'What a family.'

'You can't choose them. You're born and then you're lumbered with them,' Bodkin said with feeling. He gave Amy a short smile. 'Carry on, please.'

'Reggie Tumbler told me he thought the lad's name was Devon, or Deakin and I assumed that one of those would be his surname, but of course it was actually his Christian name, Declan. It all made complete sense the moment I heard Mervin say his name.'

Bodkin beamed at Amy as he patted her on the wrist. 'Well done,' he said. After turning back to Mervin, the smile left his face. 'Are you still claiming that you didn't kill Lonnie Firth?'

'I told you, I'm not a killer,' he replied. 'I could have killed any one of you, maybe all of you, earlier this evening. I had a loaded gun, remember? I could have shot the lot of you and walked out of there with Erma and the money to start a new life, but I didn't. I didn't shoot you all because I am *not* a killer.'

'You're not the only gangster I've heard say that recently, and I don't believe either of you,' Bodkin said. He drummed his fingers on the table. 'Mr Challenger. You have admitted viciously beating Lonnie Firth. I think you did kill him, or at least left him for dead after breaking his skull with that length of lead pipe. You're already going to be charged under the Offences Against The Person's Act of eighteen sixty-one. Threatening or making someone believe they are about to be killed is covered in that act. I am now about to charge you with murder. Do you have anything to say before that charge is brought?'

'I don't think it was him that delivered the final blow,' Amy said.

Bodkin's mouth gaped open.

'I've just remembered something that was said to me at the warehouse, Bodkin.' She turned her head to look directly at Mervin. 'You will hang if you don't tell us the truth about that night, Mr Challenger. You're already looking at a long term of imprisonment, but you're still a young man. You could get out with plenty of time to enjoy what's left of your life.' She turned away from him and looked towards Erma. 'She delivered the fatal blow, didn't she?'

Erma began to protest, but Mervin buried his head in his hands. 'I'm sorry, Erma,' he said. 'I don't want to hang.'

'Let me tell you what I think happened,' Amy said. 'You just fill in any gaps or correct me if I get something slightly wrong.'

She was silent for a moment as she gathered her thoughts. 'I think it went something like this.' She held up a finger. 'Bessie asked you to give Lonnie a beating, but you refused. Then she told you that Lonnie was responsible for the death of another young man from Nottingham and wondered if you knew him. When she gave the description of the red jumper and the nickname Robin, you knew immediately that you had been lied to and that your brother hadn't run off to London, Lonnie Firth had sent him to his death. So, you ask around and find out that Lonnie is hiding away in Spinton. When you ask a few questions about Robin, you find out that he was in a relationship with Erma and the pair were besotted and that Erma was devastated when Declan left her. So, you do a bit more digging and find out from Brian or Birdie... it would have to have to have been one of that pair... where Erma was living. When you realised she was up here too, you knew that you would almost certainly be able to track Lonnie down through her. So, you borrow Bessie's spare Austin 7 and drive up to Victoria Street, where you tell her all about Lonnie's treachery. Erma is incandescent with rage. She absolutely adored your brother, so told you how you could get in touch with Lonnie via the phone at Reggie's flat. When you call to arrange a night in the pub to talk about a job you have coming up, she insists on coming with you to confront Lonnie herself.'

She paused for a moment, then went on.

'Erma waits in the car while you go to meet Lonnie in the Dragon. You can't really set on him inside the pub. There are too many witnesses, and you know that Lonnie is a bit of a hard nut himself, so you decide he'd be an easier target when drunk. So, you make out you're having the best of times with an old mate and you make sure he's pretty much legless by the time you leave. When you get outside, you're about to start work on him, but two other drunks come out of the pub and you have to stand in the shadows while Lonnie urinates up the wall. You must have let him finish that because he wasn't soaked in the stuff when he was found.'

Amy shuddered at the thought, then continued. 'This is a bit of conjecture, but I think you'd parked the car down the lane, just before it narrows, and you went back to it to pick up your trusty lead pipe. You either invite Erma to join you as you walk the few yards back to the pub or she follows you. It doesn't matter, the important thing is, she was with you when you set about her brother. How am I doing so far?'

'It's mostly all correct,' Mervin said. 'Erma insisted she join me the minute I grabbed the blackjack from the glove box of the car. She'd worked herself up into a right state while I'd been in the pub with Lonnie. She said she'd had to fight the urge to come in and confront him in the bar.'

'So, what happened next? We know you gave him a beating. Did he have the chance to defend himself?'

'No, he'd just finished pissing up the wall when I called him out, he turned around, and I hit him across the face with the blackjack, then I dropped it and set about him with my fists, telling him all the time that this was payment for what he did to my brother.'

'Did he deny sending Declan to his death?'

'I didn't give him the chance. Bessie had already told me he was the one responsible.'

'What happened at the end, Mervin? When Lonnie was lying on the floor, begging for mercy?'

'He wasn't. He was a tough old bird. I'll give him that. Even after I'd worn myself out punching and kicking him, he managed to drag himself up to his knees.' Mervin's chin dropped to his chest. 'That's when Erma picked up the cudgel and smacked him over the back of the head with it. He went down again. I think he was dead before he hit the floor, but Erma made sure by giving him one last whack with the club.'

Amy nodded slowly. 'She boasted to me that she'd used it before when she found me outside the warehouse this evening and there was no doubting that, the way she set about Birdie.'

Erma looked belligerently at her, but said nothing. So, Amy continued.

'The pair of you hurry back to the car and you drive up to the Railway Hotel to celebrate. We know that, Mervin, because you were seen going around the back of the hotel with a woman. We know she stayed all night because we have a witness who was in the next room. She heard the noi... she heard what was happening. Then she found a pair of silk M and S knickers under the bed. She assumed you'd forgotten them.' Amy half smiled at Erma. 'You told me you'd had silk knickers before, but never satin ones, when you bought your new undies from the London Connection. It wasn't much of a clue and it's very circumstantial, but it was you who forgot to pull on your drawers before you went home, wasn't it?'

'I left them as a souvenir,' Erma said. She gave Mervin a soft smile. 'I just wanted to reward him.'

Bodkin stood up and asked both Mervin and Erma to get to their feet. 'Mervin Challenger, I am charging you with the offence of accessory to murder under the Accessories and Abetters Act of eighteen sixty-one. You do not have to say anything but... well, you know the rest Mervin, you've heard it plenty of times before.'

Bodkin then turned to Erma, who looked at him stony faced. 'Erma Firth, I am charging you with the murder of Lonnie Firth, you do not have to say anything....'

CHAPTER FIFTY-ONE

Bodkin dropped Amy off at home at ten o'clock, then returned to the station to get his reports done for the following morning. Along with the charge sheets for Mervin, Erma and Paul Leyton, Bodkin had to prepare a report for the Gillingham police who had charged Brian Firth and Birdie Lark with being accessories in the murder of Declan Challenger and also accessories in the murder of Ellis Hawke. Vincent Jury and Paul Leyton would also be charged with the murder of Ellis. There would be many more charges, ranging from larceny to embezzlement, theft, and robbery to follow. Bodkin was in for a busy few weeks.

Amy's father was already in bed when she walked into the cottage, but her mother was waiting up for her, sitting on the sofa reading her library book and sipping a hot mug of Ovaltine.

'Hello, dear. Have you had a nice evening?' she asked.

'I've had a lovely time,' Amy said. She kissed her mother on the cheek, then yawned a huge yawn. 'But it has left me quite exhausted.'

. . .

The next morning, Amy got up half an hour later than usual. Her father had gone to work, but her mum was sitting at the table with the morning newspaper, The Gillingham and District Times.

'It's all been happening in Gillingham, our Amy. It seems that there was a shootout between the police and two rival gangs in a disused warehouse. There were lots of arrests and some of the gang members have been charged with murder.' Her eyes widened and her mouth formed a huge oval shape. 'What is the world coming to? It's Gillingham, not the East End of London.' She got to her feet, put her hands on either side of Amy's face, looked her lovingly in the eyes, then gave her a kiss on the forehead. 'You see, your father was right. Aren't you pleased you weren't involved in any of that nonsense?'

That evening, Amy lay on Bodkin's sofa with her blouse unbuttoned as he once again struggled to get her bra unfastened.

'Let me do it, Bodkin, or we'll be here all night,' she said.

After unhooking the offending garment, Amy lay back and put her arms around Bodkin's neck as he nuzzled into hers.

'Where did you put your things?' she whispered as his hand ran up her thigh.

'In the pocket of my suit jacket,' he said.

'Don't you think you ought to get one?' she said. 'Before things warm up any further.'

'I put the suit into the dry cleaners this morning,' he said, not looking at her face.

'Oh, Bodkin, you're hopeless,' she replied.

Suddenly she heard him chuckling away to himself, his face buried in her shoulder. 'I took them out first,' he said.

'You pig,' Amy said, slapping him on the back.

Bodkin turned sideways on and smiled at her. 'Speaking of pigs, you'll be delighted to know that Tom Piper has been found, along with the prize porker who, by the way, is still very much alive.'

'Blimey!' Amy said. 'Where was he?'

'He lives in a hut on the outskirts of Mossmoor. The pig was found chomping away at his veg patch in this garden. It seems he fell in love with the thing and couldn't bear to have it killed.'

'Well done, Tom Piper!' Amy exclaimed. 'Oh, I found out what a poke is, by the way. It's a bag or a sack. Hence, a pig in a poke means you don't know what you're getting because you can't see it.'

'You learn something new every day,' Bodkin said, as he ran his hand over Amy's thigh. 'I'm glad I can see what I'm getting.' He reached into his trouser pocket and pulled out a paper packet with the word Durex printed across it. Bodkin put the pack on the arm of the sofa and pulled Amy towards him again. After unfastening his belt, he unbuttoned his trousers with one hand while he tugged at Amy's pants with the other.

Somewhere in the distance, the shrill ring of a telephone could be heard.

The End

Acknowledgments

Huge thanks to Maureen Vincent-Northam, who has been with me from the start in 2009. I wouldn't dream of publishing as much as a short story or even the back of the book blurb without utilising her expert skills.

Many thanks to my eagle eyed proofreader, Paul Lautman. I extend my heartfelt gratitude to Paul for his meticulous attention to detail and his invaluable contribution in refining this work and getting it fit for publication.

I'd also like to add my thanks to SpellBound books, Nikki East for her final edit and yet another wonderful cover.

Finally, thanks to Sumaira Wilson from SpellBound books for everything she does for her authors.

You are all very much appreciated and this book wouldn't have seen the light of day without you.

ALSO BY T. A. BELSHAW

AMY ROWLINFGS MYSTERIES IN ORDER

Murder At The Mill

Death At The LychGate

The Murder Awards

Murder on The Medway

Ten Years After

Printed in Dunstable, United Kingdom

64699463R00231